FI
YOU

Carrie Elks lives near London and writes contemporary
romance with a dash of intrigue. She loves to travel and
has lived in the USA and Switzerland as well as the UK.
An avid social networker, she tries to limit her Facebook
and Twitter time to stolen moments between writing
chapters. When she isn't reading or writing, she can usually
be found baking, drinking wine or working out how to
combine the two. www.carrieelks.com @CarrieElks

FIX YOU

Carrie Elks

CORVUS

First published in e-book in Great Britain in 2014 by Corvus,
an imprint of Atlantic Books Ltd.

This paperback edition published by Corvus, an imprint of
Atlantic Books Ltd, in 2016.

10 9 8 7 6 5 4 3 2 1

A CIP catalogue record for this book is available from
the British Library.

E-book ISBN: 978 1 78239 712 0
Paperback ISBN: 978 1 78239 824 0

Printed in Great Britain

Corvus
An imprint of Atlantic Books Ltd
Ormond House
26–27 Boswell Street
London
WC1N 3JZ

www.corvus-books.co.uk

FIX
YOU

Prologue

12th May 2012

RICHARD HAD FILLED out nicely since she had last seen him. The thin cotton of his shirt clung to his biceps, skimming his taut abdomen as it tucked into his dress pants. His hips were still lean and tight, and she closed her eyes as she tried not to remember how they had felt between her thighs, as he had moved inside her, breathing softly in her ear, as she had moaned and whimpered and—

She shook her head. She wasn't standing in his large, oak-panelled office just to take a trip down memory lane, as pleasant as that might be. She had flown here, over three thousand miles, to tell him what he deserved to know.

Inappropriate laughter bubbled up in her throat as she considered the ridiculous melodrama of the situation. Her seventeen-year-old self would be rolling her eyes, wondering how this twenty-nine-year-old woman had managed to turn a seemingly promising life into a soap opera.

She glanced up at his face, looking at his lips, which had turned down into a deep scowl. His eyes had narrowed beneath his brows, and his straight, patrician nose was slightly crinkled in response to her presence.

The contempt he felt toward her was radiating from him.

1

Hanna tried to keep her breathing steady, reminding herself that although she was in *his* office, on the penthouse floor of *his* building, this was *her* show.

She was in control.

If he viewed her with contempt now, God only knew how he would feel once he'd heard what she had to say. He had been an integral part of her life for so long – as a friend, a confidant, even a lover – but never before did he have the power to break her.

"As nice as it is to see you," he drawled, the tone of his voice making it patently clear that her being in his office was anything but nice, "I have a meeting in five minutes. Exactly what is it that you want?"

He had no idea, but this was it. Time to open her mouth and tell him what he needed to hear. Her arms suddenly felt heavy, and her fingers trembled, a physical manifestation of her nervousness. Her laughter was replaced by something more unsettling as she tried to take in a deep breath and form the words that she had travelled all this way to say.

Her tongue darted out to moisten her lips. She watched his gaze move down to her mouth, staring at it with dark eyes, as her teeth drew in her bottom lip.

"Richard." Her voice was surprisingly strong. She could do this. She could tell him the truth, and then get the hell out of here.

Back on a plane.

Back home.

Back to *him*.

"Richard, we have a baby."

One

31st December 1999

ER SUITCASE SHOULD have appeared by now. She watched the rubber belt move past, carrying luggage of every description. Perhaps her battered, brown case was embarrassed to be seen amongst the Louis Vuittons and the Henks.

Hanna knew the feeling.

She was biting her nails again. They were already torn down to the quick, and the black polish she had applied only a couple of days before was peeling off in chunks. Her stepmother couldn't understand why Hanna didn't opt for the '*much classier*' French manicure, and why she failed to keep regular appointments at the beautician's. Finally spotting her case making its way down the baggage reclaim belt, Hanna tried to push past the harassed mother of two in front of her. In one arm the woman held a toddler. The other was rhythmically moving a stroller back and forth, as she tried to rock a tiny baby to sleep.

"Excuse me," Hanna muttered, leaning forward far enough to grab the handle of her case. She pulled her body back as she swung it onto the grey, tiled floor. It was heavy, full of winter skiwear and warm clothing. She'd barely had time to wear any of it.

Hanna wasn't even supposed to be travelling today. She was still meant to be at her father's chalet in Val D'Isère, along with her stepmother and her eleven-year-old half-sisters. But he'd been disappointed in her from the start. The first time he'd taken a good look at her, his nose had wrinkled in dismay.

"Have you done something different with your hair?" His stare was full of angry disapproval.

Hanna had attempted to swallow a grin in response to his understatement. In the year since she had last seen him, she had become a Goth. She'd dyed her hair a dark reddish-black and changed her make-up. Now she had pale skin and dark, dark lips. She completed the look with a black flowing skirt and a tight black corset.

The memory of Philip's furious expression as he took in her new style made Hanna's lips curl up in amusement. She swung her suitcase onto a luggage trolley, its bulk making her movements awkward.

Philip had been almost apoplectic at her new style, and Olivia had decreed Hanna was to remain in the confines of the chalet at all times, fearing one of their friends might spot her. Hanna was to be their dirty little secret for the week. After two days of reading and filling her face with chocolate, she was bored.

She had found out that Philip, Olivia, and her sisters were planning to spend New Year's at their friend's chateau about fifty miles from Val D'Isère, and Hanna wasn't invited. There had followed an almighty row, which resulted in Hanna being banned from the chalet and placed on the next flight to London, at no little expense to Philip's bank balance.

She swore to herself, now that she was nearly eighteen, that she would never again subject herself to the torture of another Alpine holiday. If her dad wanted to spend time with his old-

4

est daughter – and in Hanna's mind this was not necessarily a given – then he would have to travel to London to see her.

Hanna and her mum were London-poor. In any other part of the country they could have lived comfortably, in a decent-sized house with a garden and a garage. As it was, Diana's income from her party-planning business afforded them a tiny, two-bedroom flat near Putney. From the moment she had run away from her marriage to Philip Vincent, and from Manhattan society, Diana had refused to take any money from him. She didn't mind him buying things for Hanna, but she refused to take a single dime for herself.

When Hanna arrived home in the late afternoon, it was already dark outside. The road was bathed with the soft orange glow of the street lamps. It was lined with Victorian terraced houses, red bricked and ornate, with peeling stucco and decaying walls. Hanna loved the genteel facade of the once-grand terraces, with their painted white porticos and their black and white tiled paths. They contrasted starkly with the noise and modernity of London life.

She fished in her bag for her keys, knowing that Diana had been out all day working, organizing the Larsen family's annual party. Though Hanna had never met them, she knew the Larsens were one of her mum's best customers. New Year's Eve was always Diana's busiest night of the year. The fact it was the eve of a new millennium just took things to a higher level.

Hanna had only been in the flat for two minutes when the phone started to ring. A glance at the display told her there were already three voicemail messages. Somebody was obviously in a hurry to speak with her or Diana. She sincerely hoped it wasn't her father.

"Hello?"

"Hanna? Thank God you're home. Are you okay? Was the flight good?" Diana hardly paused to breathe. "Honey, I've had three girls go down with that damn winter vomiting bug. I need you to put on a uniform and come over and help me. This party is going to be a bloody disaster." She lowered her voice into a whisper for the last sentence, leading Hanna to wonder who else was in the room with her.

"Okay, just give me the address." Hanna wedged the phone between her ear and her shoulder as she reached for a piece of paper.

"It's number five, Cheyne Walk. In Chelsea. Get a cab and I'll pay you back. Oh and Hanna..." Diana's voice dropped down an octave.

"... Can you tone down the look?" Hanna chanted, knowing exactly what her mum was going to say.

A shower, nail polish removal, and a make-up tone-down later, Hanna managed to find an empty black cab. Her red-black hair was pulled back into a neat bun, and the cosmetics on her face were soft and barely there. She was wearing a typical waitress get-up. Short, black skirt with a plain white blouse.

When she got to the house, she rapped the large, brass knocker on the smartly painted black door a couple of times. A uniformed man opened the front door to her. She didn't recognize him, so he couldn't have been one of Diana's employees. The Larsens were rich enough to employ full-time staff.

Walking into the entrance hall, her breath was taken away by the splendour. The room was open to all three floors of the house, with a marble staircase sweeping up in a curve to the second floor. Right in the middle of the ornately tiled floor stood the biggest Christmas tree she had ever seen. Understated white lights twinkled all the way up to the star on top. It had to be at least twenty feet tall.

"See something you like?" Hanna's hackles rose at the sound of the smooth, American drawl. She whipped her head around to see a young man standing at the bottom of the staircase. His loose, dark-washed jeans hung almost obscenely off his lean hips. His T-shirt was tight and black, with 'Columbia' emblazoned across the front in blue writing.

His face, *Lord* his face. It was all jaw and plump lips, straight nose and mossy green eyes. His smooth forehead was framed by an artfully styled mop of light-brown hair. He looked like every clean-cut Manhattan boy she'd ever had the misfortune to come into contact with.

She took in a short breath, looking Prep Boy straight in the eyes. "Not really. I was just wondering if Charlie Brown was missing his Christmas tree."

She spun around and flounced toward the kitchen, barely hearing his bark of laughter as she walked away. She bit back the smile that was threatening to creep across her lips.

Tonight had just got interesting.

Her mother was standing in the middle of the kitchen with a spoon in one hand and a battery-powered walkie-talkie in the other. The kitchen wasn't the usual well-heeled, oak and granite affair. Instead it was all stainless steel with professional grade ovens – the sort of kitchen any chef would kill for. It was hard to picture anybody using the ten-burner hob just to boil an egg.

"Hanna, sweetheart, it's so good to see you." Diana ran around the central island, and threw her arms around her daughter. She relaxed into her mother's arms, screwing her eyes tightly shut as she felt the misery and stress of the past few days seeping away.

She'd missed her mum.

"It's good to see you, too."

7

"I've half a mind to call your father and tell him what I think of him. I can't believe he treated you like that, the stuck up, holier than thou bast—"

"Mum, it's fine." Hanna flashed her mother a rueful smile. "I think my tirade was probably enough for the both of us. I just want to forget about it now."

"Diana, darling, is there anything you need help with?" A soft voice came from the kitchen door. Hanna turned around to see a petite woman smiling at the two of them. Her heart-shaped face was framed with soft, auburn curls.

"I think we have it all under control," Diana replied. Hanna could see her fingers crossed behind her back as she spoke. "Claire Larsen, I'd like you to meet my daughter, Hanna Vincent."

Claire walked forward, her arms open as she greeted Hanna, pulling her in for an air kiss. "Hanna, how lovely to meet you. I've heard so much about you from your mother. Of course, I also know your father and his wife."

Hanna grimaced at the mention of Philip and Olivia before quickly rearranging her features. "It's a pleasure to meet you." She smiled at the lady in front of her. She was at least half a head shorter, and that was in expensively made heels.

"What a beautiful accent you have. And I love your hair. The colour is so interesting."

Usually, when someone said that something about Hanna was 'interesting' it turned out to be a thinly veiled insult. Olivia seemed to use the word a lot whenever Hanna was around. But the kind tone of Claire's voice led Hanna to believe she genuinely meant what she said.

"Thank you."

"I must introduce you to my family later. My husband, Steven, would find you fascinating. I think he's a closet Marilyn

Manson fan. And Ruby and Richard would just love you." Claire was gushing. Hanna stepped back from her American host. She wasn't used to being treated with such friendliness.

"Richard and Ruby?" she questioned.

"Ruby is my daughter. She's ten years old. She's at school at St. Nicholas's."

Hanna nodded. It figured; St. Nicholas's was an expensive London prep school. She suspected that Ruby Larsen would turn out to be as annoyingly spoiled as Hanna's own half-sisters.

"And Richard is my husband's son from his first marriage. He's in his final year at Columbia. I'll miss him when he goes back to New York." Claire's smile faltered as she continued. "My own boy, Nathan, is somewhere in the Andes trying to 'find himself.'"

"How utterly careless to lose himself somewhere so remote," Hanna replied, causing Claire to laugh in response.

"So like your mom." Claire cupped her hands around Hanna's cheeks in a surprisingly intimate move before drawing back. "Make sure you come and talk to me tonight. It will make for such a refreshing change from all those stuffed shirts."

"I'll bring you a sausage roll." Hanna winked at Claire, and then turned to her own mother to ask where she was needed.

Between the friendly mother, the handsome, preppy son, and the Marilyn Manson-loving father, Hanna thought she might come to rather like this family.

RICHARD LARSEN ACCEPTED another glass of champagne from a waiter, as he weaved his way through the party crowd. It was cold to the touch, and icy beads of water ran down his fingers where he held it. Taking a sip, he quickly scanned the room for someone – anyone – interesting to talk to.

He was wearing his usual tux, with a fitted white dress shirt and black tie. The suit fit him like a glove, and the jacket clung smoothly to his wide shoulders. His pants were perfectly sized for his narrow waist. He had the physique of someone who played a lot of sport.

Since he'd come to London, he'd been able to act like a twenty-year-old man for the first time in a long while. He had worn jeans, T-shirts, and hooded sweaters without so much as an eyebrow being raised. He had visited pubs, consumed pints of beer, and flirted with pretty girls. Most of whom his mother would have deemed to be far below his social standing.

Unfortunately, this sort of party was reminding him a little too much of home, and of his mother and her society friends.

Seeing his father and Claire standing in the corner of the drawing room, he pushed his way past the throng of people to get to them. As he walked, he heard snippets of conversation.

"Of course, John is on-call for when the millennium bug strikes..."

"I'm so excited about the river of fire. Bob Geldof is like a modern day Gandalf..."

He didn't understand any of this talk. He found it hard to even decipher the accent, let alone comprehend exactly what it was these English people were trying to say.

"Richard." Claire spotted him when he was about a yard away. Richard stepped forward and kissed his stepmother on the cheek. She smelled of lavender and roses. She reached out and touched his lapel. "You always look so handsome in a tux. And so much older."

"And you look spectacular as always, Claire," he replied. She smoothed down her dress and gave him a huge grin.

"You charmer. You're getting more and more like your father every day."

In his peripheral vision, he spotted someone approaching their little group. Whoever it was, they were dressed in black and white. He assumed it was one of the waiting staff.

"Can I offer you a Cumberland chipolata, blanketed in choux pastry, with a honey and mustard dip?" Richard recognized the girl. He'd seen her standing in the hall earlier. Her dark hair and pale skin were hard to miss.

"It looks like a sausage roll to me." Claire smiled at the girl. They seemed way too familiar with each other for a waitress and her employer. "Hanna Vincent, please let me introduce you to my husband, Steven Larsen, and my stepson, Richard."

"I've heard so much about you, Hanna." His father spoke first. "Claire seems to think that I should make you a mix tape."

Richard's eyebrows drew together in confusion. How the heck did they know this girl? She didn't look like the sort of girl that hung around at parties like this. She was like a bundle of unkempt energy, seemingly without a vocal filter.

"Maybe I'll make *you* one." Hanna grinned.

"I'd like that. I don't think I've ever been given a mix tape by such a beautiful young lady before." Steven was full of smiles and natural charm. His innocent flirting made Hanna blush. Richard watched with fascination as the warm blood filled her cheeks, making her skin glow.

Hanna turned to Claire. "Just how much champagne has he been drinking?"

She had the English affliction of excessive modesty, too. Richard wanted to see her flustered again. "Hanna Vincent, it's delightful to meet you." He took her hand and raised it to his lips, expecting a shiver, a sigh. Anything.

Nothing. She just stared back at him, eyes dancing with amusement, as he released her hand.

11

"You too, Prep Boy. I almost didn't recognize you in black tie. It ages you."

Prep boy? His tux aged him? How did his father get the coy looks and blushes, while he got biting ripostes?

"Well, Goth Girl, I apologize for bewildering you with my attire." He drawled his words on purpose, knowing sarcasm was the lowest form of wit.

Hanna turned to give him a grin. "It was a pleasure to meet you all. I really must go and ply the rest of your guests with pig innards stuffed in pastry." With that she was gone, moving toward the group in the other corner of the room. Richard watched as she walked away, admiring the way her tight, black skirt clung to her round behind.

Steven had one eyebrow raised. A speculative expression covered his handsome face as he stared back at his son. Richard said nothing, just shook his head and grinned.

After midnight arrived and they'd sung 'Auld Lang Syne', Richard wandered out into the entrance hall and was thinking about going to bed. He spotted Hanna sitting at the top of the stairs, next to a tiny form that bore a striking resemblance to his sister.

He and Ruby were close, despite living in separate countries. He found himself worrying about her constantly. She wasn't a typical pink-loving, shopaholic ten-year-old. She was quirky and funny, read books like there was no tomorrow, and loved to draw whatever she laid her eyes on. She was different, and that made her a target. He knew she hated school, and being looked down on by the other girls. Even here, in London, she was treated like a pariah.

Tiptoeing up the stairs, he decided to eavesdrop on their conversation, before alerting them to his presence. From what he could hear, Ruby was doing most of the talking. It was unusual.

"... no, I kinda liked the Spice Girls. I hate Britney Spears, though, and Christina Aguilera sucks big ones. I mean, they were Mouseketeers for God's sake."

"What's a Mouseketeer?" Hanna's voice was gentle and amused. Only a few steps farther and he would be able to see her face.

"From the *Mickey Mouse Show*. They do stupid dances and sketches and stuff. It's so dumb." Ruby's voice was low, as if she knew that she shouldn't be out of bed talking to a stranger at the top of the marble staircase.

"Sounds like hell on earth. Thank God you got out of America while you could."

Ruby giggled. "I prefer Nine Inch Nails. Trent Reznor is the man."

This time, Hanna joined in the laughter. "I can't believe a ten-year-old likes Nine Inch Nails. I blame your father. Claire tells me he's a huge Marilyn Manson fan."

"Oh. My. God. No, no, no. He keeps getting confused between Marilyn Manson and Marilyn Monroe. He's a fan of the blonde bimbo, not the singer. He's such an embarrassment."

Richard barked out a laugh in response to Ruby's words. Steven was always trying to keep up with the latest trends, and usually made a complete ass of himself in the process. Not that he ever minded; the ability to laugh at himself was one of his father's best attributes.

"Is that you, Richard? Are you sneaking around again?" Ruby's voice rang out clearly. He climbed up the last few steps, seeing his sister sitting next to Hanna, leaning on her as they talked. Hanna's legs were propped up, her knees hugged to her chest. He was finding it hard not to stare at her calves.

Hanna glanced up at him. "You caught us. Now are you going to be a good Prep Boy and keep our secret, or do we have to gag you?"

Richard felt the urge to respond with a dirty comment. He bit back his retort, reminding himself that his sister was sitting nearby.

"What are you doing up here, Squirt? I thought you didn't want to come to the party?" He smiled at Ruby indulgently. If he'd known she wanted to join in, he would have happily escorted her.

"I wanted to watch the midnight celebrations. I'd hate for anybody to ask me what I was doing when the new millennium arrived, only to hear that I was hiding in my bed like a social misfit."

Richard winced. Sometimes she was so grown up, and over-perceptive. He hated that she felt like a freak.

"I'm sleepy now, though," Ruby continued. "Hanna, would you take me to bed?" She held up her arms and looked like a child again.

"Let me help you, Hanna," he breathed, suddenly liking how her name felt on his tongue. Turning to Ruby, he scooped her up. "Your carriage awaits, milady."

Ruby giggled as he carried her along the hallway, putting her hand up to muffle the sound so the guests below wouldn't notice her presence. Hanna followed closely behind them, making Richard hyper-aware of her close presence.

Feeling docile, Ruby nuzzled her head into her big brother's tuxedoed shoulder.

"Thanks Richard. You make a great big brother."

"Better than Nathan?" Richard carried Ruby into her bedroom, twisting slightly so that he could angle her legs through the doorway.

"Nathan isn't a brother, he's an animal. Every time I see him, he throws me up in the air. I'm always scared he isn't going to catch me." Ruby's voice was slurred with sleep. Laying her down on the bed, he pulled the covers back over her. Hanna was standing at the door, watching them. Smiling at her, he could feel the flesh at the corners of his eyes crinkling. When she returned his smile, her plump lips curling up at the corners, he felt something in his stomach drop.

"Well, Squirt, I can promise I'll always be there to catch you," Richard whispered, kissing his sister's forehead. Ruby was already asleep, her short, soft breaths coming out in a gentle rhythm.

"Your sister is very sweet," Hanna said, as he met her at the door. "She's the opposite of my evil sisters. You're very lucky."

"You have sisters?"

"Half sisters," she replied. "I like to remind myself we are only half-related. They're the devil in the guise of eleven-year-old twins. They already think I'm their social inferior."

"They sound delightful." He drawled his words again. Something flickered in Hanna's eyes.

"They're a real treat. We can swap, if you like." That made him smile. Her sisters sounded like just the sort of kids who would treat Ruby like crap.

"What are you doing up here, anyway? Aren't you supposed to be stuffing canapés down unsuspecting guests' throats?" It was funny how light-hearted he felt, upstairs with Hanna, away from the party and the crowds.

"I'm on a break. I have..." Hanna glanced at her watch. "Fifteen minutes left."

"Wow, all the things you could do with those fifteen minutes. Endless possibilities." He grinned, his body brushing against hers as he walked through the door on the way to the hall. "Would you like to come to my room?"

"Bloody hell! You don't waste any time do you?" Hanna exclaimed, making Richard re-examine exactly what it was he'd said.

"Oh shit, I didn't mean it like that." He twisted his hands nervously. "Seriously, it wasn't a proposition – not that you aren't cute or anything. What I meant was... I have a new PlayStation, a Tony Hawke game, and two controllers with our names on them. Would you like to join me?" He was flustered now, taken aback by his own obtuseness and her vocal response.

"In that case, how could I say no? I have to warn you, though, I'm absolutely useless at computer games."

While Richard set up the PlayStation in his bedroom, Hanna stood next to his shelves, looking at the CDs, like she was trying to gauge what sort of music he was into. He smiled when he saw her perplexed frown. His taste was eclectic; it was hard to categorize him when his CDs ranged from Puccini to the Prodigy.

"You have some good music. I hate to think how much your collection is worth." She ran her fingers over the plastic spines of the CDs. Richard suppressed a smile, deciding that it would be foolish to tell her that this was just a small part of his collection, that he had thousands more CDs back in Manhattan.

"Do you want to have the first go?" His eyes met hers. He sat down on the carpet, leaning back against the edge of his bed with his legs bent in front of him. Hanna walked over and sat down beside him, refusing the proffered controller with a small shake of her head.

"You go first; I'll watch and learn."

Three aerials, two flips and a grind later, his 'special meter' was up and running. He was able to execute more special moves, showing off a little for Hanna's benefit.

"You make it look so easy," she complained.

"Everything is easy when you know how. And I don't sleep well, so I've had a lot of practice. It's your turn."

Hanna took the controller and looked with grim determination at the TV screen. The skater moved slowly along the rail before bailing off the edge. Taking another try, her face screwed up in frustration as exactly the same thing happened again.

"I'm so shit at this." Her voice was thin and whiny as she stared at the screen.

"Come here, let me help you." Richard gestured to the floor, indicating where Hanna should sit. He was almost shocked when she crawled straight over to him, shimmying herself between his legs and leaning her back on his chest. Circling her with his arms, he put his fingers on top of hers as she held the controller and showed her which buttons to press in order to execute an aerial flip.

The sensation of her back rubbing against his chest, and her behind wriggling against his crotch, made him instantly hard. His erection was pressing into her spine. With only two thin pieces of material between his skin and hers, he knew for sure that she could feel it.

Hanna turned around and amusement danced across her face. She raised her brow quizzically. "Wow, you must really like this game."

"Don't take it personally. I get hard-ons just from watching the National Geographic channel."

She burst out laughing, shaking her head. His hands were still on top of hers, and he showed her how to combine an aerial and a grind.

"Jesus! I've got special points. I'm da man. I. Am. Da. Man." Hanna squirmed in happiness at having scored something other than a bail. As she moved, her body ground against his erection, making him wince at the painful pleasure her movement caused.

Glancing at his watch, Richard was almost relieved to see that her break was over.

Two

19th July 2000

HANNA PULLED AT her thin vest, the material momentarily sticking to her skin before giving way, allowing the cool air to circulate around her damp flesh. Even for July the weather was unusually hot; the heavy Goth clothing she had packed in her suitcase remained neatly folded and forgotten, like a maiden aunt at a stag party.

Ruby Larsen lay on a hammock next to her. They were reading aloud to each other from *Harry Potter and the Goblet of Fire*, having bought the new book from the small shop in town the previous day.

"Do you think Hermione would like me if we met?" Ruby asked, passing the book over to Hanna.

"She'd bloody love you. What's not to love? You're clever, you're funny, and you'd beat the hell out of the boys in potions class."

They had been at the Larsen's country cottage in the west of England for a week. Claire Larsen had asked Hanna to take on the job of being Ruby's paid companion for the summer while she travelled back to the States to look after her sick mother. Hanna had agreed readily. It beat working at Safeway.

"Sometimes I wish I could go to Hogwarts. It sounds so much nicer than St. Nicholas's." Ruby picked at the small silver sequins attached to her T-shirt.

"There are mean people everywhere, Ruby. Just remember what an asshole Draco Malfoy was to Harry," Hanna replied wistfully. "Anyway, it's the school holidays. We're not supposed to be thinking about lessons, or uniform, or homework. We should be having F.U.N."

"You don't ever have to think about school again," Ruby complained. "You're so lucky."

Hanna dropped her head back on to the hammock, remembering her last day of school. After a long spring of exams, coursework, and nightmares about *Jude the Obscure*, it was nice to finally breathe without wondering when on earth she was going to fit in her next assignment.

She'd been Ruby's regular babysitter since they met at New Year. It didn't really feel like work – although she was always grateful for the money – because the two of them always managed to have fun. Hanna enjoyed spending time with Claire and Steven as well; only seven months after their initial meeting, the Larsens already felt like her second family.

"School days are supposed to be the best days of your life."

"I think we both know that that's a lie." Ruby kicked at Hanna's hammock, sending her swinging wildly.

In the distance, they heard the French doors slam. Hanna looked up to see a tall man with light-blond hair walking toward them. Shielding her eyes with her hand, she could see it was Tom McLean, waving a piece of paper in his large, tan hand.

"Hi Tom," Ruby shouted, falling out of her hammock and running to give him a high five. He was the grandson of

Mary, their cleaner. He had been in and out of the cottage all week doing small jobs. Hanna suspected Ruby had formed a tiny crush on the blond teenager.

"Hey, little Rube. How're you doing?" He winked at the small girl, then looked up at Hanna, his lips unfurling into a slow, lazy grin. "You look a little too comfortable right now."

With that, he reached out and grabbed Hanna's arm, catching her easily as she tumbled off the hammock. Her book crashed into the dirt below.

"Tom!" she shouted crossly. "Put me down. And if you've ruined my book, you will pay with your life." She swatted at his arm, hand meeting flesh with a resounding 'thwack'.

"Hey! Mind my guitar-playing arm. I haven't insured it yet." He looked at her with a mock-injured expression. "I only came over to invite the prettiest ladies in town to our gig tonight."

Hanna snatched the flyer from his hands. "It's at a pub, Tom. I can't take Ruby to a pub. Her parents would kill me."

At the same moment, Ruby piped up. "Please can we go? I've never seen a band play before."

"There'll be loads of kids there. At least five of my nieces and nephews are coming. Come on, I'll even treat you to a Coke." Tom put on his best puppy-dog expression.

"With an offer like that, how can we refuse?" Hanna replied dryly, and an expression of delight formed on Ruby's face.

At least she'd managed to keep somebody happy.

THE CROWDED PUB echoed to the sound of clashing chords and deep vocals. On the stage, Tom glanced up through his eyelashes and smiled directly at Hanna. She found herself biting her lip in an effort not to smile back. She wasn't sure how she felt about the attention he was giving her. From the moment they met, Tom had flirted with her outrageously. He told her how much he loved her style; Hanna rolled her eyes in response. When he asked her out for a drink, she used Ruby as an excuse to refuse his offer. Now, surrounded by local groupies and a couple of A&R men from record labels, it seemed he only had eyes for her.

"Do you want another Coke?" Hanna asked.

"Yes please. Can I have a straw, too?" Ruby's mid-Atlantic accent sounded strangely out of place in an English country pub.

"Of course, milady." Hanna gave a mock curtsey, made her way up to the bar, and placed her order. When she came back, the band had moved on to a cover of Coldplay's 'Yellow'. Tom began to strum the soft introductory chords on his electric guitar, and leaned toward the microphone, his bright, blue eyes firmly fixed on Hanna's.

His voice was deep and gravelly, perfect for the song. She watched as his sandy hair fell into his eyes, and his lips curled into a smile. A few heads in the room turned to follow his intense stare, some of them looking surprised when they saw him gazing at the petite girl sitting in the corner with her young friend.

Ruby, oblivious to his blatant staring, continued to sip at her Coke.

"This is our final song. I'd like to dedicate it to the beautiful girl with the perfect smile. This one's for Hanna."

She felt her face heat up as blood flooded her cheeks. Tom flashed her a brief smile, and then winked when he noticed her blush.

"Do you and Ruby spend a lot of time in the pub?" Hanna's attention was drawn to the deep voice to her left. Spitting out her mouthful of cider in surprise, she looked up with horror as Richard Larsen walked toward her.

"Richard." Ruby jumped off the bench, nearly spilling the remnants of her Coke bottle in her haste to greet him.

As he held his sister tightly to him, Richard's eyes met Hanna's.

She stood up straight, placing her hands on her hips, and looked him over for the first time since New Year's Eve. He was smartly dressed in tailored black pants, the sleeves of his pale blue shirt rolled up to his elbows. She tried not to look too closely at his muscled forearms: skin stretched over tight tendons, and covered with a dusting of dark brown hair.

He looked out of place in the pub, among the jeans, the cargo shorts and the band T-shirts. Like a Renoir hanging on a wall of lurid graffiti.

"I couldn't find you at the cottage, so I called Mary McLean. She told me that her grandson had invited you out on a date." Richard's nose turned up as he finished his sentence.

"I didn't know you were coming to England." She decided to ignore the date jibe.

"I've been in Europe for a few days. I'm working for my stepfather over the summer. He's got a few things going down in Paris." Richard smiled at her for the first time. His lopsided grin reminded her how much she'd liked him at New Year.

"You should have called us. What if we hadn't been here?"

"It's only a couple of hours by train, Hanna."

The way he said her name made her feel warm inside. She glanced over at the stage in the corner of the pub, noticing Tom looking over at them, his forehead wrinkled with curiosity.

"Did you bring me a present?" Ruby was almost jumping up and down with excitement. Her enthusiasm made Hanna smile.

"At least she's not materialistic," Richard whispered to her, in a mock-aside. "I'd hate to think she only loves me for my money."

Ruby grinned and hung on to her brother's shirt with her grubby fingers. "You know I love you. So what did you bring me?"

"I'll show you when we get back to the cottage, Squirt," he replied, then turned to look at Hanna. "Are you ready to go?"

"I'll let Tom know we're leaving." Ignoring Richard's frown, Hanna left him standing with his sister. She walked over to Tom, ready to take her leave. His face lit up with a smile.

"What did you think?" He pulled her toward him, putting his hand on her waist in a proprietary gesture. His familiarity unsettled her, especially when she could feel a pair of narrowed eyes watching her every move.

"You were great. Ruby and I loved the songs." She pulled away. "We have to go home now, though."

"You're leaving so soon? Who is that guy, anyway?"

"Ruby's brother."

"Oh." Tom's face fell.

"He's come to see Ruby," she blurted out.

Tom's smile returned almost instantaneously. "Does that mean you have a babysitter available?"

"*I'm* the babysitter, remember?" Hanna replied dryly.

"That's a shame. I guess I'll just have to take up residence under your window and serenade you with love songs." He winked at her.

"Feel free, I wear ear plugs. I'm sure the local cats will enjoy it, though."

"Are you ready, Hanna?" Richard and Ruby went to join them.

Hanna could feel the heat flood her cheeks again. "Richard, this is Tom McLean. He's with the band." And she was a loser. Jesus, could she sound any lamer?

"Pleased to meet you." Richard shook Tom's hand firmly. For two guys of a similar age, their differences couldn't be more apparent. Next to the unkempt, slightly dishevelled singer, Richard looked older and much more sophisticated. And totally out of her league.

"Can we go?" Ruby tugged at her arm, desperate to get home and open her promised gift.

"Okay, okay, we're leaving." Hanna tried to swallow a laugh at Ruby's desperation. She wasn't successful.

Tom leaned forward to kiss her cheek, just as Hanna turned her head to look at him. She was still mid-laugh, and her open mouth clashed against his. She felt him gasp as they touched. The blood rushed to her lips, and she felt his mouth start to move slowly against hers, the tip of his tongue running a wet line along her plump skin.

She quickly pulled away, her face heating in humiliation as she saw Richard raise his eyebrow at her, his lips pulled back into a thin, straight line.

The night just kept getting better and better.

*F*OR FIVE DAYS, Richard joined in their routine: reading aloud with them as they finished Harry Potter, and choosing his favourite character as they acted out scenes from the book. Without the suit and tie on, it seemed like Richard Larsen was a different person.

In the evenings, after putting Ruby to bed, they sat together and watched TV. A new programme had started on one of the channels, some sort of reality-based experiment. Ten people were forced to live together in a closed house. Hanna found it fascinating.

"It's not really like *1984* though is it?" Richard mused, offering her another chocolate cookie from the packet they were sharing. "I mean, Big Brother would make them stand to attention and swear loyalty to him. Not let them laze around in the yard, talking to chickens."

When the adverts came on, Hanna made her way to the kitchen. Opening the fridge, she took out two bottles of Becks, prising the lids off with a bottle opener as she walked back to the living room. Looking over at Richard, she noticed his eyes darken almost imperceptibly as he stared directly at her bare legs. The intensity of his gaze made her breath hitch.

With Ruby's bedtime routine, a favourite TV programme, and their sharing of beer and cookies, they were turning into a parody of an old, married couple…

Minus the sex.

ON RICHARD'S FINAL night at the cottage, they decided to walk into the village to buy their dinner from the chip shop. The evening air was warm and fragrant as they sat on the village green, eating their last supper of fish and chips straight out of the paper. Ruby perched on the concrete steps of the war memorial, throwing chips at pigeons as they swooped down trying to steal her food from her fingers. They watched the sun go down, their fingers coated with vinegar, salt, and grease.

A smudge of ketchup clung to the corner of Hanna's mouth. Richard stretched out his hand to rub it away with his thumb. He felt the strangest urge to move his thumb slightly leftward, to plunge it inside her soft mouth, just to see how it felt. Instead, he put it to his own lips and licked the sauce off. Hanna stared at him with her rosebud mouth slightly parted, and he could see a small hint of tongue just behind her lips.

"Are you growing out your hair colour?"

"I'm trying to reinvent myself for university. I'm going for more of a rock-chick look. Goth is so last century."

Richard laughed at her idealistic enthusiasm, her belief that you could simply reinvent yourself with a change of hair colour. If only it were that easy.

"Rock chick?" He looked at her skeptically.

"Yep, I'm getting bored of only wearing black. Even I need to wear colour occasionally."

"Well, I look forward to meeting the newly reinvented Hanna Vincent. Maybe you can send me a photo."

"Maybe you can bite me, perv," she replied, bumping him with her shoulder. Richard bumped her back and she fell from the wooden bench, landing on the hard, dry grass with a thump. Her outraged expression made him laugh long and hard.

The next morning, Richard left the cottage early to catch the first flight to JFK. The plane was crowded, but the Maxwell family always travelled first class. Even if Richard was a Larsen, his stepfather wouldn't let him travel any other way.

A black Lincoln was waiting for him at the arrivals gate. The driver took his luggage, and Richard followed him to the parking lot. He sat in the back as the driver steeled himself to go up against the New York traffic. It was more than an hour before they pulled up outside the brownstone townhouse.

He was home, though it was a strange word to describe this place. The interior of the house was too pristine, too stark. Too much like his mother. Yet if anywhere, this was the one place that should be home to him. He'd spent the best part of fifteen years here.

Once inside the door, he walked toward the kitchen where he could hear Consuela singing as she cleaned the floor. She had worked for the Maxwells for a long time and was living at the townhouse long before Richard and his mother moved in.

"Ricardo." A smile lit up her face. "You're home. Come here and give me a kiss."

He lifted her up and swung her around as she swatted at his arms, trying to get him to release her.

"Where is everybody?" he asked, letting her back down.

"Your momma is in the Hamptons. And Daniel had to go to work with his father. He wasn't very happy about it, either."

Daniel was Richard's seventeen-year-old stepbrother, the only son and heir of Leon Maxwell. With a multi-billion dollar empire encompassing everything from real estate to financial advisory services, Leon Maxwell had a vast range of investments spread across the globe.

Richard leaned around Consuela and took a still-warm roll from the cooling rack. She reached out and slapped his hand.

"Are we entertaining tonight?" He bit into the roll.

"Mr Maxwell has invited the Brookes to join you for dinner."

"At eight?"

"Yes, sir." When she spoke to him, the 'sir' was always accompanied by a teasing smile. It was different than when she said it to Leon or Daniel.

"Well, in that case, I'll be in my room, sleeping off the jetlag." Richard winked and left the kitchen.

When he got upstairs, he wasn't surprised to find that his room was cleaner and more fragrant than when he had left it over a week ago. Consuela had attacked it with gusto during his absence. Throwing his suitcase in the corner and kicking off his shoes, he lay down on top of the comforter, closing his eyes as soon as his head hit the pillow.

Three

5th October 2000

"So, HANNA VINCENT, what is your USP?" Josh Chambers, editor of the student magazine, leaned back in his threadbare swivel chair, removing the pencil that he had put behind his ear some moments before. He tapped it against his teeth, as he stared at her.

Hanna frowned. What the hell was a USP? She wondered if it was some sort of journalistic term she should be aware of. She didn't want to look stupid and admit she knew virtually nothing about writing for a newspaper.

She'd applied for the position of unpaid staff writer on the university magazine as soon as she'd arrived in Nottingham the previous week. Now, she was being interviewed by the highly intelligent editor and already making a fool of herself.

"What I mean, Hanna, is what is your Unique Selling Point? What makes you special? What do you have that all the other applicants don't?"

He had obviously taken pity on her. It seemed the 'deer in the headlights' look got her somewhere in life after all. It was a shame she couldn't use it on her family as easily.

"Well, Josh Chambers." She allowed herself a small grin at using his full name in the same way he had said hers. "I have many Unique Selling Points. I'm hardworking, I'm determined, and I never take no for an answer."

"You and everybody else I've spoken to today. That doesn't make you unique. That just makes you desperate." Josh shook his head, smirking at her response. He was on the right side of attractive, with his mop of dark-blond hair, strong jaw and day-old stubble. He had perfected the 'geek-chic' look, with his black-rimmed glasses that kept sliding down his nose. Though he was in the final year of his journalism degree, to Hanna he seemed so much more than two years her senior.

Out of the corner of her eye, she spotted a large poster on the wall advertising a gig taking place the following week. She turned her head to look, smiling as she recognized the man posing on the front of the poster. He was wearing a tight black shirt, his wild hair flying everywhere as he strummed his guitar.

"I know Tom McLean from Fatal Limits." She gestured over to the picture on the wall advertising the band as the headline act. "I could score an interview with them."

Josh leaned forward, his curiosity sparked for the first time that morning. "Are you shitting me?"

"No!" Hanna laughed at his expression. "Seriously, I met him in the summer. They've just been signed by an independent label. I can call him right now if you like."

Josh was still regarding her with interest, his pencil firmly wedged in between his teeth. "Okay. Let's agree that if you score an interview with Fatal Limits, *and* if you write a good enough article, then I'll put you on a three-month trial." His smile was genuine.

"Thank you!" Hanna was incredulous, finding it hard to believe that out of nearly a hundred applicants, she had been given a trial. She felt like doing a little celebration dance.

"I'll warn you now, I'm a pretty hard taskmaster. I've been known to make grown men cry with my editing. I don't take any bullshit, and if you're after an easy ride, then this isn't the job for you."

"I'm not after any kind of ride, thank you very much," Hanna replied pithily, returning his stare with a piercing one of her own. "And a lot bigger men than you have tried, and failed, to make me cry."

"I'll take that as a challenge, then."

"Please do."

Josh put out his hand and grabbed hold of Hanna's. He shook it a couple of times, as if to seal the deal.

"I look forward to working with you, Hanna Vincent."

"Please call me Hanna. Vincent is my surname. It sounds weird when you say it like that."

"Okay then, I look forward to working with you, Hanna." He paused. "No Vincent."

"You just couldn't resist it could you?" She shook her head at him.

"You think you're irresistible?" His brow rose up.

"Not as much as you do."

Josh removed his glasses, placing them on the desk to his right. Running his hand through his hair, he leaned forward until his face was only inches from Hanna's.

"Are you hitting on me, Hanna Vincent?" She could feel his soft breath against her skin. He was that close.

"If you have to ask, then the answer's no. If I was hitting on you, you'd know it."

"Then I look forward to knowing it."

"Don't hold your breath." She pushed herself up from the chair, picking up her résumé and portfolio. "Thank you for the job offer. I look forward to you publishing my first piece."

Sounding more confident than she felt, she gave Josh a quick nod and walked out into the main newspaper office. Closing the door behind her, she breathed a sigh of relief. She wasn't sure if she was attracted to Josh Chambers… or if she wanted to kill him.

WHEN SHE GOT back to her room, there was a small brown parcel wedged into the postbox by her door. Pulling it out, she saw it had come from New York. The customs form affixed to the back had been smudged in the rain, the writing illegible.

She wondered what on earth her father was doing sending her books. Part of her couldn't wait to see what sort of inappropriate present he had sent this time. She supposed at the very least, she should give him kudos for remembering her.

Once inside her room, she picked up the package and began to unwrap it. As soon as she tore the brown paper apart, her mouth dropped open with surprise. The book inside wasn't pristine and new. It had that unique, dusty odour that only old books possessed. A hardcover with a bottle-green dust jacket. It was extremely well preserved for its age. The large white script across the front cover left her in no doubt that the gift was not from Philip Vincent.

It was *1984* by George Orwell.

As Hanna opened the front cover, she saw the words 'first edition' written in pencil on the title page.

An envelope fell out from its hiding place between the pages landing softly on her white, embroidered bedcover. She could feel her heart start to beat faster as she picked it up, putting her finger into the gap at the edge of the flap and moving it along the edge in order to tear it open. Pulling out the expensive cream notepaper, she unfolded it and began to read.

Dear Hanna,

The beginning of your university career is something worth celebrating, but as Thomas Carlyle said, "The greatest university of all is the collection of books." As soon as I saw this, I couldn't help but think of you. Thank you, not only for your kindness to Ruby over the summer, but for also entertaining her lonely, and occasionally annoying, Big Brother.

If the newly invented Hanna Vincent is anywhere near as interesting as the old one, I look forward to seeing you again soon.

Yours,

Richard

She stared at the letter for a while. It was so short – just a note, really – but she couldn't help but find herself getting a little overcome at the gesture. He'd bought her a book – a first edition, no less. It wasn't the sort of thing you could pick up at a charity shop or a thrift store.

Plus, he'd called her interesting. For some unknown reason, she liked that. She *really* liked that. The way the Larsens were lavishing that word on her was making her change her mind about it. For the first time, it felt good to be interesting, to be different.

After spending ten minutes wondering how to thank him, she decided to go down to the computer suite in the basement of the halls of residence and send him an email.

FROM: HMVincent@Nottingham.ac.uk
TO: RSLarsen@Columbia.edu
SUBJECT: Big Brother

Dear Richard,

Wow, thank you so much for your impressive gift. I've never owned a first edition of anything before, so I'm very excited to start this new collection. I probably have some way to go before I can have anything approaching Thomas Carlyle's 'university of books' but a girl has to start somewhere, right?

I'm slightly concerned, however, that you sent me a book which basically tells me that Big Brother is watching me. Should I be worried?

Hanna

PS: I have been assigned room 101 as my bedroom.

She clicked on the 'send' icon, and sat back, deciding to Ask Jeeves exactly how much a first edition of *1984* was worth.

Within moments she wished she hadn't. There was no way she could keep that thing in her bedroom. It was worth more than the rest of her possessions added together. And then some.

Just as she started to consider returning the gift, her email alert pinged.

FROM: RSLarsen@Columbia.edu
TO: HMVincent@Nottingham.ac.uk
SUBJECT: Watching You?

Hanna,

You are most welcome. And as to your question, it very much depends on what you've been doing.

Richard

PS: Does room 101 contain your worst fear?

She smiled as she read his words, feeling inordinately happy that he had replied so quickly. She glanced at her watch. It was 4:00 p.m. in the UK, which meant it was around 11:00 a.m. in New York. She assumed he was either in the library or at home at his desk, working on his laptop. After chewing on a fingernail for a while, she decided to respond.

FROM: HMVincent@Nottingham.ac.uk
TO: RSLarsen@Columbia.edu
SUBJECT: My Worst Nightmare

Richard,

Since you've read Harry Potter, I suspect you already know what my worst nightmare is. But since I cannot say the name, I'll tell you instead that I'm sharing a bedroom with a six-foot-tall, chain smoking, French-speaking Amazonian. I have no doubt that anybody with a name beginning with V would be scared shitless by her. I know I am.

Hanna

FROM: RSLarsen@Columbia.edu
TO: HMVincent@Nottingham.ac.uk
SUBJECT: Embarrassing…

Hanna,

I'm trying to keep some street cred and not let on I've been reading children's books during my summer vacation. Can we keep this between you and me?

When does the next book come out, anyway? Can I borrow it from you?

Richard

FROM: HMVincent@Nottingham.ac.uk
TO: RSLarsen@Columbia.edu
SUBJECT: Embarrassed… you?

Richard,

It's always a shame when a rich Manhattan boy like yourself can't afford to buy a book. I'll ponder on that while I'm eating the refectory's latest dinner offering. I believe we're in for a treat tonight – tuna casserole with a side of over-boiled spinach. I'll think of you while I'm masticating.

Hanna

PS: There's these strange things called libraries…

FROM: RSLarsen@Columbia.edu
TO: HMVincent@Nottingham.ac.uk
SUBJECT: I'd rather read yours

Seriously.

Richard x

Hanna smiled at the kiss on the last email as she logged off. All in all, today was turning out to be a good day… a really, really good day.

HE FOLLOWING FRIDAY, Hanna found herself in the back-stage area of the university's concert hall, pushing her way through the packed corridors. They were teeming with rock bands, comedians, and variety acts, all vying for dressing space.

As the headliners, Fatal Limits had been given their own room, set apart from the rest of the performers. Hanna pushed her way inside and she could see that at least one of the band was already taking advantage of having a groupie following.

A whisper in her ear sent a shiver down her spine. "Ever since we got signed, the rest of the band seem to have become animals."

She turned around to see Tom McLean standing right behind her. He gave her a lopsided grin, and then pulled her into his arms, his hands locking around her waist as he hugged her.

In the two months since they last met, Tom's life had taken a 180-degree turn for the better. Fatal Limits had been signed by a small, independent label who were working hard to build up the band's reputation. Step one of that plan was sending them on a tour of British universities, aiming to develop a strong student following for the band, enabling them to release their album to a pre-existing fan base.

"Look at you, Tom." Hanna pulled at his hair, noticing how it had been expensively trimmed, his sandy locks still falling slightly onto his forehead, but somehow looking more groomed. "You've gone all Chris Martin on me."

Tom hugged her tighter. His face was touching hers, and he murmured into her ear. "If you compare us to Coldplay in your article, I'll stuff the magazine down your beautiful neck."

"If you insist on playing 'Yellow', I'll have no other option."

"If I insist on playing 'Yellow', you'll melt at my feet, just like you did last time."

Hanna pulled back from Tom, turning to look up at him with her brows raised.

"Seriously? You think I was impressed by a Coldplay cover?"

"I don't think it's my singing that impresses you. I suspect it's my body."

Hanna started laughing and hit him on the arm.

"Mind the guitar arm!"

"Haven't you got it insured yet?" Hanna put out her hand and rubbed at his bicep, surprised by how hard it was. The boy had clearly been working out.

"I'm working on it. Apparently, Keith Richards insured his arm for $3 million."

"Well, Keith Richards is an idiot. And probably has a small cock, too."

"You'll be pleased to know that I don't have that problem. Maybe I can show you later?"

"Maybe you can keep it zipped in your pants, or find a willing groupie." Hanna pushed him away, taking her note-pad out. "We're on the record now, so if you want to continue being a sleaze-ball, feel free." She winked at him to let him know she was only kidding. His flirting was automatic: he couldn't help but do it to every girl he spoke with. It was part of his natural charm.

"Okay, Lester Bangs, we can do the sex thing later. What's your first question?" Tom gave her a slow, easy grin. He looked like he was enjoying himself.

Hanna rolled her eyes, pulling her pen out of her pocket as she turned over the page of her notebook.

"My first question, Tom Mclean, lead singer of the up-and-coming rock band Fatal Limits, is 'when did you become such a dick?'"

Four

AFTER EVERYTHING THAT had happened last year, Hanna couldn't believe she had agreed to visit with her father in New York. He'd called her in November, suggesting a change to their usual routine. Neither of them was keen to meet in Val D'Isère for Christmas. Within a couple of hours he arranged for his secretary to book Hanna on a flight to JFK. This whirlwind of activity had taken Hanna by surprise. She was too gobsmacked to think of an excuse. She did allow herself a small smile when she thought about her stepmother's reaction to the news of her visit.

She was hoping to see some bands play while she was in New York – that thought made the trip seem more bearable. The New York music scene was scorching. She was looking forward to feeling a bit of the heat. Since joining the university magazine in October, Hanna was the paper's regular rock reporter. In between her writing, she managed to fit in lectures, tutorials, and assignments. It had been a busy few months.

Just like that, Hanna had discovered her first love: music journalism.

Not that she felt like a journalist right then – sitting in the back of the car her father sent to pick her up. She felt like a scared little girl being dragged to see the principal because she'd done something wrong.

"We're here, Miss Vincent." The driver's voice brought Hanna back to the present. He pulled up outside her father's office near Wall Street. Her forehead wrinkled in surprise. It was a long time since she had been to New York to visit her father, five years at least. Only once had he taken her to see his office.

"My father wants me to be dropped off here?" She could hear the confusion in her own voice. God only knew what the driver thought.

"Yes, I'm to take your luggage back to the townhouse. Give your name at the security desk, and they'll let him know you're here."

Hanna nodded, shuffling over to the door and pulling at the handle. She wasn't going to wait for the driver to get out and open it.

"Well, thanks for picking me up."

"No problem, Miss Vincent. Welcome to New York."

Welcome indeed. As soon as the car door opened, Hanna's ears were assaulted with the noise of the streets. Humming engines punctuated the air along with the staccato pumping of horns. The drumming of a road compactor a couple of blocks down accompanied the constant drone of voices as she was suddenly surrounded by people milling about the sidewalk. The sights and sounds of London seemed like mere whispers compared to this. The height of the buildings, and the closed-in feeling that they gave her as she walked along, took her breath away.

To her left, the twin towers of the World Trade Center loomed over the financial district, like two sentinels standing guard over New York harbour. Hanna couldn't help but be impressed by their stature. She decided then and there that she'd definitely make a trip up to see the observation deck at some point during her visit. The view over the Atlantic Ocean on one side and Manhattan on the other had to be impressive from there.

Tearing her eyes away, she walked the five yards to the office building, which housed the company her father co-owned. When she got to the security desk, she gave the guard her name and waited for somebody to come and collect her. The foyer reeked of money; the marble floor was pristine, as if it were being constantly buffed by an invisible army, and all of the furniture was high end.

"Hanna?" She was shocked to see her father was the one who had come to meet her. She was so sure it was going to be one of his minions, maybe an intern or something.

"Hi Dad." She allowed herself to be hugged by him. His dark grey hair was perfectly arranged as usual, his suit well cut and fitted.

"How was your flight? Did you get here all right?" They walked through the security turnstile and over to the elevator bank. When the elevator arrived, Philip pushed the button to take them to the fourth floor. Vincent-Jones took up the entire floor, with the best offices reserved for her father and his partner.

"The flight was fine. It was nice to travel in first class. Thank you for paying."

"You're welcome. I just need to make a couple of phone calls, and then we can go and get something to eat." They'd reached his secretary's desk. The blonde sat there looked up at Hanna with interest.

Hanna assumed she was probably trying to work out how this dishevelled eighteen-year-old, wearing ripped jeans, a band tee, and a wrinkled black jacket, could possibly be related to Philip Vincent.

It was something Hanna often wondered herself.

"Can I get you anything, Miss Vincent? A coffee? Something to eat perhaps?"

"I'm fine. I'll just sit here and wait."

Ten minutes later, her father walked out of his office, pulling a smart, black, woollen coat around his shoulders.

"I won't be coming back today, Grace," he said to his secretary as he passed by her desk. "If anything urgent comes up, call me on the cell phone. Otherwise I'll check my emails tonight."

"Of course, Mr Vincent, have a good evening. Good night, Miss Vincent." Grace gave her a small nod as Hanna stood to join her father.

This was all getting a bit surreal. First of all, he had invited her over to his home in New York, something he hadn't done for a number of years. Then he had taken off early from work, just to spend some time with her. She could guarantee this was something he had never done before.

Anyone would have thought he was feeling guilty.

"I thought we could get an early dinner, then I'll take you home and you can catch up with Olivia and your sisters."

Oh joy.

"Sounds good." Hanna smiled at her father for the first time in two years. "But I'm not really dressed for dinner."

"We'll hit a diner."

"In that case, *you're* not really dressed for dinner." Perhaps this *entente cordiale* could last for longer than five minutes. Hanna was still sceptical.

"Don't sweat it. Half of Wall Street will be eating there."

"Okay." She bit back her original retort, where she had

43

been about to ask him who he was and what he had done with her father. She didn't want to do anything to spoil the moment.

When they were seated, Philip ordered a Reuben and Hanna opted for a burger. As they sipped at their drinks, she searched vainly around in her brain to find something neutral to talk about. Luckily her father got there first.

"This place is my guilty secret. Olivia would kill me if she could see me now. She thinks 'diner' is short for 'cholesterol dining'." Philip swallowed a mouthful of sandwich, picking up his glass of root beer to chase it down.

"I guess you'll have to bribe me for my silence, then." She still felt weird, sitting with her father, having a grown-up conversation. Her mouth was almost aching with the need to ask him why he was doing this.

"I'll give you my Saks Fifth Avenue charge card. It seems to work with all the rest of the women in my life."

"S'okay. I don't expect Saks will stock my taste in clothes, anyway," she mumbled, starting to rip at the napkin she had placed in her lap.

Philip's eyes softened, as he saw her sad expression.

"I never got to tell you how sorry I was about last year. I know that Olivia and I didn't treat you as well as we should have, and I know that I neglect you sometimes. I'm not going to go into all the reasons why it's hard for me, and I'm certainly not going to talk about how difficult things have been between your mother and me. But I'm going to try, okay? I'm going to do my best to be a better father."

Hanna couldn't meet his eyes. "Okay."

She looked down at her burger, picking it up and taking a huge bite, glad to have a diversion. No matter what her father said, or did, or tried to do, there was always a little part of her that would doubt him. Hanna wasn't sure she'd ever be able to change that.

O N HER SECOND DAY in New York, she took a trip to Columbia University to meet Richard Larsen for coffee. Since October, she had been exchanging emails with him regularly. When she told him she was coming to Manhattan, he suggested a meet-up.

It was a clear, bitterly cold day, and Hanna decided to take a hike up to the academic acropolis of Morningside Heights. When she got there, she spotted Richard standing on the steps, his blue woollen pea coat buttoned up to the top, a striped scarf hooked around his neck. Hanna stopped for a moment, feeling suddenly shy. Should she go and hug him, or would he be expecting a pretentious air kiss? Maybe a handshake would suffice.

Then he saw her, and his face erupted into a huge smile. All thoughts of embarrassment left her mind, and she ran over to him, throwing her arms around him. "Oh my God, it's so good to see you."

Richard hugged her tightly. "It's great to see you, too."

"Thank you so much for meeting me. I'm so happy to see a friendly face."

"I was going to suggest we hang out on the Low Steps, but it's way too cold. Let's go get a coffee in the diner instead." Throwing an arm around her shoulder, he pulled her to his side as they started to walk. "There's a coffee shop in the library, but I thought you might like Tom's restaurant better."

"Why's that?" Hanna asked.

"You'll see." Richard started humming under his breath as they walked down the street, so quietly that Hanna couldn't quite hear the tune.

As soon as they turned the corner onto Broadway, she realized what he was singing.

"Hey! That's 'Tom's Diner' from that Suzanne Vega video." The corners of Hanna's mouth turned up as she looked at the stone and glass facade. "I love that song."

Richard took her hand and pulled her through the open door. The warmth of the diner contrasted sharply with the freezing outside air.

"You know, this is the second time in two days I've been in a diner."

"Welcome to New York."

"Can I get you a drink?" The waitress asked, putting napkins down on the table.

Richard glanced up. "I'll take a coffee."

"Could you make that two, please?" Hanna added, watching the waitress as she walked over to the filter machine.

"So, how's the visit going?" Richard asked.

"Okay, I guess. We're both trying our hardest not to antagonize each other. It's easier said than done sometimes."

"In what way?"

Hanna sat back and took a sip of coffee, the hot liquid warming her mouth. She scrunched her face up in concentration. "I suppose we're walking on eggshells. We're not really being ourselves, in case we upset each other. And then, when I do say something that reveals the real me, it's like he reverts back to type. Last night I was telling him that I want to go to see a band on Thursday night, just so I can write about it for the paper, and he started to go off on one. He was shouting that I was underage, that I couldn't be seen in a drinking establishment, and that I didn't have an escort, so I'm not allowed to go."

"But you're going anyway?"

"Damn right I am." Hanna caught his eye. "There's an unsigned band I really want to see. They're a regular at the Mercury Lounge. Could be the next big thing."

"I kind of understand where your dad is coming from. It probably isn't safe for an eighteen-year-old to be wandering around Manhattan late at night."

"I wander around late at night all the time at home." Hanna shrugged.

"It's not the same." Richard looked at her over his coffee mug, the steam rising up to obscure his view. "A quaint town in England isn't exactly Gotham City."

"Well, Bruce Wayne, I think I'll take my chances." The tone of her voice echoed the finality of her words.

"What if I came with you?"

"You'd do that?" She put her empty coffee cup down at the table and scrutinized him. Everything about him screamed money – from his buttoned-down blue Oxford shirt, open at the neck, revealing a hint of chest hair, to his navy pants. She wondered if he knew how out of place he would look at the Mercury Lounge.

She shrugged inwardly. It was a risk she was willing to take if it meant she could go to the gig, and keep her father happy.

"Sure. I don't think I've ever been there before." He spoke as if his offer wasn't a big deal.

"So what should I do for you in return?" Hanna's cheeks flamed as soon as the words escaped her lips. She hadn't meant to sound quite so provocative.

Richard nearly spat his coffee out of his mouth.

She looked at him with narrowing eyes. "I was offering you, as a friend, the opportunity to have something in return. I don't see what's funny about that."

He took the opportunity to muse. "In that case, let me take

you out to dinner before you leave. You show me your world and I'll show you mine."

"Okay, Henry Higgins, dinner it is. Do your worst."

RICHARD WATCHED HANNA charming her way into the Mercury Lounge, despite having no valid ID and being underage. He couldn't help but be impressed by the way she played the security staff with her engaging banter, sweet smiles, and tales of being an English journalist.

"Are you coming?" She turned around to Richard, her cheeks flushed with cold, her eyes sparkling under the lights of the entrance.

"Right behind you."

Following Hanna into the main music area, all of his senses were attacked by the atmosphere – the cacophony of the crowd, the smoky smell of the air, the feeling of the floor sticking to the soles of his shoes. He could even taste the excitement in the room as the throng of people milled about waiting for the band to come on stage. There had to be at least three hundred people all squashed in together.

"What's the band called again?" Richard asked. Hanna grabbed his hand to pull him farther forward.

"The Strokes. They're a five-piece garage band. Lots of buzz going on around them."

Three members of the band walked onto the stage to a loud roar of applause from the audience. Richard could tell his ears were going to be ringing by the end of the evening. His T-shirt was already starting to feel moist. The wet heat of the room was even making Hanna's hair frizz a little. It looked good on her.

Glancing up at the stage, his eyebrows rose in surprise and he leaned in to whisper in Hanna's ear.

"You know, I recognize at least two of the band members."

Hanna's head whipped around to look at him, and he gave her a shit-eating smirk.

"Really?" She looked at him sceptically.

"Seriously, I recognize them from Dwight. Definitely prep-school boys."

"Just goes to show that even prep boys can be reformed. So when do I get to see you in a band?"

Richard chuckled, taking a sip from his beer bottle. Hanna looked on enviously. Without an ID, she was stuck with soda.

"If you heard my singing voice, you wouldn't have to ask."

As they talked, the band was still wandering about the stage, doing last minute checks.

"So what are you planning to do after graduation?" Hanna asked.

"A couple of us are planning to move out to California. A friend and I have some plans for an internet start-up."

Another member of the band walked onto the stage to rapturous applause. Richard waited for the clapping and cheering to die down before he continued. Instead, any noise he made was obliterated by the opening chords of the first song. The crowd started moving, forcing them toward the stage. There was no resisting the surge pushing them forward, and Richard glanced at Hanna in alarm, worried she would be trampled in the rush.

Looking back at him, she grinned widely. "Isn't this fantastic?"

Her cheeks were flushed, and her lips plump and glossy. She wasn't wearing much make-up – a contrast to the Hanna he had met nearly a year ago – but she still looked stunning. He noticed a few guys looking at her as she pushed her way past them. It was hard to keep the smug smile off his face when he saw their disappointment, realizing she was with him.

He had to admit the band was good. As they launched into their next track, it was like they were casting a spell over the audience, bewitching them as they sang along and danced madly to the music.

The people behind them were still moving forward, forcing Richard and Hanna apart from each other as the wave crashed toward the edge of the room. He grabbed hold of her hand, pulling her back toward him, circling his arms around her so he could keep her safe.

He couldn't decide where to put his hands. Her waist seemed too familiar, too sexual. If he held on to her hips and felt her ass against him, he was pretty sure he would lose his mind. He settled on the relative safety of her upper arms, trying to keep the fabric of her T-shirt between his hands and her skin. But she was moving too much, grinding her body to the beat of the music. He took a half step backwards, removing his crotch from the danger zone. He didn't want to be accused of liking the band *that* much.

Hanna turned her head and tried to shout something to him. The noise of the band, and the calls of the crowd, drowned her words out.

"What?" Two small lines formed between his eyebrows as he tried to concentrate on her mouth.

"I said this is my favourite song."

"What's it called?" They were still mouthing words at each other. To try to actually vocalize would have been futile.

"'Last Night'." She whipped her head around as the guitarists played the instrumental bridge, the discordant sound of the bassist's chords jarring against the melodic notes of the lead guitar. The lead singer opened his mouth, his voice a deep echo as his lips moved closely against the microphone, his eyes closed as he sang the words.

The crowd was going absolutely wild, the fast tempo of the track leading them to jump up and down as one. Those unfortunate enough not to join in were starting to panic, feeling themselves being dragged under. Richard moved his arms until they were tightly clutching Hanna's waist. He didn't care about his reaction to her body, he just wanted to keep her safe.

Leaning back into him, her hands clutched his arms as they moved together, submitting themselves to the will of the crowd.

It was electrifying.

After the show, Hanna tried to grab a few minutes with the band. It was clear they were on the cusp of something big, and the other journalists there also wanted to get their pound of flesh.

"Are you ready to go?" Richard glanced at his watch. It was nearly midnight. When he picked Hanna up earlier, he'd promised her father he wouldn't keep her out too late.

"Yes, I think so." She was still giddy, on a high from the stimulating atmosphere of the gig. He could feel her trembling next to him.

"I guess I don't have to ask if you liked them."

"I absolutely loved them. I can't wait to write about it. I just hope my article isn't too sycophantic," she said. They walked side by side out of the hot, sweaty bar, and into the cold night.

Coming to an abrupt halt, they both noticed the change as soon as their feet hit the sidewalk.

While they were watching the band, New York had transformed itself into a winter wonderland.

The streets and cars were blanketed with a soft, fluffy layer of bright white snow. The only blemish on the pale landscape was the black footprints of the revelers who had left the concert.

"It's snowing!" Hanna's face was bright, her smile wide as she looked up to the sky and saw the oversized flakes slowly floating their way down to the ground. "Oh my God, Richard, look!"

She reminded him of Ruby with her child-like excitement. She twirled around, her head still raised to the sky. He watched as she opened her mouth, poking her pink tongue out, trying to capture a snowflake on its surface.

"I noticed," he deadpanned. A lifetime of New York winters had somewhat inured him to the pleasures of a wintry storm.

"Aren't you excited? We can make snowmen and snow angels. You might even get a snow day. Doesn't everything sound so much better if you put 'snow' in front of it?"

"Like snowbound, or snow-blind?"

Hanna rolled her eyes. "It's like being in the most beautiful city in the world with Ebenezer Scrooge. Where's your enthusiasm?" She pulled away from him, running her hands through the snow that had fallen on the wall adjacent to the club.

"I'm sorry to disappoint you. Perhaps the Ghost of Christmas Past will help me mend my ways."

"Or maybe a snowball will help?" Her aim was magnificent. The cold ball hit him right in the chin, breaking on impact, the icy snow dust falling down onto his neck.

He ran toward her, scooping some snow up with his hand from the wall as he approached.

"No!" she squealed, trying to run away from him as he approached her menacingly, but only managing to slip and slide on the frozen slabs. "Please don't!"

"I thought you said everything was better with snow in front of it?" He was pulling at the neck of her T-shirt now, trying to shove his handful of snow down it as she wriggled, protested, and begged.

"I didn't mean it, please don't!" Her voice was a mixture of panic and giggles. She grabbed hold of his wrist, moving it away from her chest and trying to make his hand release the snow.

Suddenly, they were standing close. Too close. He realized that most of his body was in contact with hers. She was looking up at him, her face flushed with cold, her lips bright pink and slightly open. Her eyes captured his. He wondered what she would do if he leaned forward and pressed his mouth against hers.

Then he shook his head, realizing how stupid it was. She was younger than him, lived thousands of miles away. Thinking of her as anything other than a friend was more than foolish.

"Let's get you home." He flashed her a quick smile, stepping away to put some distance between them.

She looked confused for a moment, then straightened herself, shaking the snow from her hair. "Okay."

AFTER DROPPING HANNA at her father's apartment, Richard decided to sleep at the townhouse, rather than make the journey uptown to his dorm. The lights were still blazing in the Maxwell household; both Leon and Caroline were night owls, and rarely retired to bed before the early hours of the morning. His mother had the luxury of being able to lie in bed until late, while Leon just needed very little sleep.

"Richard, darling. What a lovely surprise." His mother placed her wine glass on a side table. Rising up from her chair, she walked over to him. She offered him her cheek, and he inclined his head to kiss her. "I wasn't expecting you."

"I was in the area. I thought I'd sleep here tonight."

As she pulled back from their embrace, Caroline did a double take. "What on earth are you wearing, darling? Where have you been?"

"I was watching a band play in a bar, over on the Lower East Side."

"Why? Who were you with?"

"Hanna Vincent."

"Do I know her parents?" Always the same question.

"She's Philip Vincent's daughter."

Caroline stared up at him, her forehead wrinkled in confusion. "But his daughters are only nine or ten, darling."

Richard laughed out loud at the thought of taking Hanna's sisters to the Mercury Lounge. "His other daughter, from his first marriage." Richard walked over to the drinks cabinet and poured himself a tumbler of whisky. He had a feeling that this was going to be a long night.

"Now there was a woman who didn't know how to conduct herself. My God, poor Philip, she was such an embarrassment to him." The tone of Caroline's voice was derisory as she made her feelings toward Hanna's mother abundantly clear.

"You knew her well?" Richard asked sceptically. His mother seemed to 'know' everybody.

"We sat on some of the same committees. She was forever turning up late, or not at all. And the clothes she wore, oh my goodness, they were so inappropriate."

Richard took another sip of whisky, not really sure what to say to his mother. She was on a roll, and he let himself fall back onto the sofa, deciding that if he had to listen to her tirade, he may as well do it in comfort.

"So, what is her daughter like? Does she take after Philip or Diana?" she asked.

There was nothing left but to swallow the lot. Richard tipped his head back and let the amber fluid slide down his throat, burning as it went down. "I'm not sure she's like either of them. She's an original." He was wracking his brain to think of a suitable way to divert his mother. He wasn't sure he liked where this conversation was headed. "Where's Leon tonight?"

"He and Daniel went out for dinner. Leon wanted to do the father–son thing. Daniel has been in trouble at school."

"Trouble?" Richard seized upon his mother's tangent.

"He's been cutting lessons. His GPA is reaching rock bottom. It's going to take a lot of funding to get him into Columbia."

Funding meant bribery. Leon Maxwell usually got what he wanted, even if he had to grease the wheels a little first. Richard was relieved his own acceptance to Columbia had required no such help from his stepfather.

Not that he was surprised to hear about Daniel's troubles; the kid was a walking disaster. He was a boy with a sizeable drug habit, and an even bigger bank balance. With such unlimited access to funds, the only intervention Richard could see working would be to cut him off without a dime.

"We've been invited to Henry Jones's wedding in October. Are you going to be around?"

Richard sighed. They'd had this conversation so many times, but every time he tried to explain to Caroline she cut him off, telling him she didn't want to hear it.

"I'm planning to have moved out to San Francisco by then."

The tightness of her lips as she glanced over at him made him want to roll his eyes.

"Leon really wants you to join him at Maxwell Enterprises. You've a guaranteed job there, and maybe one day you could take the helm." Her voice was clipped, her tone disapproving.

"Maxwell Enterprises is all Daniel's. You know I have no interest in working there." Richard fought the urge to shake some sense into her. "John and I have set everything up. We're moving out west in September."

Five

*I*T HAD BEEN a hideous week. Instead of sitting out in the beautiful spring weather, Hanna had been buried beneath books in the library trying to cram for her end-of-term exams. The previous day, she'd had a phone call from Ruby – who had been asked to her school disco by a boy, only to discover that he had done it for a bet. Hanna had been unable to soothe her young friend, eventually resorting to calling Richard to ask him for advice.

To top it all off, Josh-bloody-Chambers had cut her article to shreds, and put it at the back of the magazine. She wanted to rip his throat out and feed it to the ducks swimming in the university pond.

She ignored the curious stares from her fellow students, pushing past them, as she made her way to the magazine office. She was a girl on a mission. A Josh-bloody-Chambers gutting mission.

Ignoring the greetings of her friends, she stalked straight across the floor to the closed door of the editor's office. Curling her hand around the stainless steel handle, she twisted it sharply, pulling the door toward her in a jerking movement. It banged against the wall, making everyone turn to look at her.

Josh was sitting on the corner of his desk, talking to the pictures editor, while going through her portfolio of photographs.

"Hanna, I wasn't expecting you. Can this wait?" It wasn't really a question, more a command. She chose to ignore it.

"It can't wait. Would you excuse us, Ciara?" It was all she could do to keep her tone civil, even with the pictures editor, who had never done anything to inflame Hanna's ire. "I need to talk to you now, Josh." Her copy of the magazine was rolled up in her hands. She shook it at him.

"Can you give us a minute please, Ciara?"

"Sure, no problem." Ciara gathered all her photographs up at top speed. She looked eager to get out of the room, away from the toxic atmosphere.

Josh remained silent as Ciara left, closing the door behind her. He was staring at Hanna through narrowed eyes.

"Perhaps you'd like to tell me why the hell I should listen to anything you have to say after that performance?"

Anger curled in her belly. "I don't expect anything from you. You don't even have the guts to tell me you've edited my articles to shreds. I thought you had more class than that." She threw the magazine on his desk, narrowly missing his thigh.

"Your article was crap. There were typos, grammatical errors, and – worst of all – it bored me."

It was like a punch to the stomach. Her reaction was to fight back.

"It was a good article. You just don't know how to edit."

"Don't push me." He leaned toward Hanna, his height dominating hers. She fought off the temptation to cower away.

"Then don't cut my words." Her heart was beating fast, fuelled by adrenaline and indignation. "And I'll push you if I

58

want to." As if to demonstrate it, she poked her index finger into the middle of his chest.

Josh grabbed her wrist and pulled her toward him. "You're sailing close to the line. Stop acting like a child."

"Stop treating me like one."

His lips came crashing down on hers, his hand pulling at the hair on the back of her head, his whole body shaking violently. He was standing right in front of her, pulling her closer until her legs were wrapped around his waist. She could feel he was hard already. She wondered whether he had been like that for a while – if he had been turned on by her extreme anger. Then he opened his mouth and slid his tongue against hers. Hanna curled her hand around the back of his head, trying to pull him closer. She wanted to lose herself in him.

"Am I treating you like a child now?" Josh moaned into her mouth, causing her legs to tremble as she tried to grind herself against him even harder. Inappropriate wasn't strong enough to describe the levels they had stooped to.

Breathless, Hanna moved her head back, gasping for air as Josh stared down at her.

"Shit."

"Fuck."

Her heart thumped harder. She wanted to reach out and rearrange his hair, move it out of his eyes so she could see their piercing blueness. His light-grey T-shirt was lopsided on his body, exposing the right-hand side of his shoulder. She felt the sudden urge to touch it.

"This is all a bit *Woman of the Year* isn't it?" She tried to bring levity to their situation.

"A bit what?" His brows dipped in confusion.

"It's a film starring Spencer Tracy and Katharine Hepburn. They're feuding journalists who eventually get marri—"

Hanna stopped suddenly, embarrassment flooding her cheeks. She looked down at the floor avoiding his gaze and mumbled, "It doesn't matter."

Josh let out a short laugh, his cheeks puffing up in amusement. "How can you annoy the shit out of me in one moment, then make me laugh like an idiot the next?"

"Pure talent." She managed to look up from her feet and give him a small smile. "It's one of my many amazing attributes."

"It seems that way. For the record, I think you're a hugely talented journalist, and I have no doubt you'll go far. But you need to be able to listen to constructive criticism without being a bitch."

"I know." It was her turn to rake her fingers through her own hair in aggravation. "When I looked at the magazine I saw red. I wanted to rip your balls off."

"I left you a note on your desk last week to tell you I'd edited it down. Didn't you see it?"

"It must have slipped off my desk. Maybe next time you could tell me face to face?"

"If I promise, will you let me kiss you again?"

"If I let you kiss me again, will you give me the front page?"

"No."

"Ah, sod it. It was worth a try, though." She grinned impishly at him. He leaned toward her, pressing his mouth against hers. She closed her eyes and felt their lips move together. He ran the tip of his tongue along her lips until she parted them, inviting him in.

His hand moved to her neck, stroking down to her shoulders, then running his index finger down her spine making her body shiver at his touch. She let out a soft moan against his mouth, causing him to increase the pressure of his lips and his tongue until she couldn't think straight any more.

Six

3rd September 2001

SHE COULD TELL it was early from the quality of the light streaming through the thin curtains covering the windows. She squeezed her eyes shut, her mind chasing sleep until Josh's insistent fingers began to brush firmly against her breasts, causing her body to awaken, even if her brain was left behind.

"Mmm." Hanna refused to open her eyes fully. His lips wrapped around her nipple, his tongue bathing and teeth grazing as it hardened in response to his touch.

"Did I wake you?"

"Still asleep." She smiled as she answered him, knowing she had given herself away.

"Pretend this is just a dream then, a really nice dream." His lips were moving downward, and she found herself fisting the bed sheets, her body responding to his touch.

Nice as it was, this was definitely no dream.

They had spent the whole summer together, travelling around England to attend different gigs and music festivals. In late August they returned to London where Josh had got a job working at the *Guardian* as a trainee journalist.

"I have to get up, baby. I need to be in the office by eight." Josh leaned down and kissed her neck. "I'm shadowing a guy who is travelling around some farms, trying to write an article on foot-and-mouth disease."

"Are you wearing wellington boots? Can I call you Farmer Brown?" Hanna smiled at the thought of Josh having to wallow through mud and interview farmers about their foot-and-mouth experiences. The disease had ravaged farms all across the country, culminating in a mass cull of animals. Even Hanna had cried when she saw the images of carcasses stacked in huge piles and being burned. She'd found it hard to get out of her mind for a long time.

"No and no. But you can get down and dirty with me when I get home tonight. What have you got planned today?"

"It's Ruby's first day of school. I promised I'd walk her there with Richard."

As soon as she said the name, the corner of Josh's lips turned down with a scowl. When she introduced the two of them last Saturday, they'd seemed to take an instant dislike to each other. It made everything feel very awkward.

"What are you going to do for the rest of the day?"

Hanna read his subtext. He was asking if she was going to spend the rest of the day with Richard. She swallowed hard, knowing just how much she wanted to spend time with her friend. Ever since he'd arrived in England he'd been so much fun. Smiling and laughing, and constantly winding her up purposely, hoping to provoke her snarky responses.

"I'm not sure yet. I've been sent a reading list for next year, so I should go and pick up some books. And I said I'd pop to Mum's for tea."

"What time will you be home?" His words were staccato, and his frown even more pronounced.

Hanna loved that he was jealous, and she loved even more that he was describing his pokey little one-bedroom flat as her home. Feeling amorous, she flung the sheet away from her and ran over to him, throwing her arms around him as she felt her naked body crush against his, the droplets from his skin moistening her flesh.

"Whenever you want me."

He grabbed hold of her and crushed her against him. She could feel the telltale movement of his towel as he reacted to her touch. "I want you all the time, that's the problem. But some of us have to work for a living, so I'll be home by eight."

"Okay, darling, I'll have your ironing done, your dinner in the oven, and the children will be in bed. Would you like your pipe and slippers, too?"

"Fuck the pipe and slippers."

"I'd rather you fucked me."

"Don't worry, I will."

WHEN HANNA ENTERED the Larsen house, she could hear Ruby squealing all the way up in her bedroom.

"Hanna, you made it. Ruby will be so pleased." Claire Larsen walked into the hall from the kitchen, her hands at her ear as she fastened a small pearl earring to her lobe. "As you can hear, there's been no shortage of screaming going on this morning."

"Is she excited?" Hanna asked.

"So very excited, especially since both her brothers are here to accompany her to school. And her favourite friend, of course." Claire winked at Hanna.

"Nathan is here?" Hanna had never met Nathan Larsen, Claire's son, although she had heard tales of his giant stature, his laid back nature, and his ability to throw Ruby high up to the ceiling.

"Yes, he arrived back last night. I'm afraid he hasn't had a chance to shave yet, so he looks like the Wildman of the Andes."

"Hanna!" Ruby spotted her, and was running down the marble staircase.

"Hey, Ruby." Hanna caught her at the bottom and squeezed her tightly, evincing yet another squeal from the tiny girl. "Let me look at you." Pushing Ruby back, Hanna took in the plaid skirt and white blouse, the tie perfectly knotted at her neck. "You look fabulous. You're going to wow them all with that outfit."

Ruby laughed. "Everyone will be wearing the same uniform. I don't think I'll impress them much."

"So this is the famous Hanna."

She heard a loud voice behind her. She hadn't noticed anybody walking down the stairs. Hanna turned around.

Nathan was even bigger than she had expected. It wasn't really his height – although he did tower over her – as much as the sheer size of him. He was bulky all over, and his hair and beard made him look older than his twenty-four years.

"Hi." She gave a closed-mouthed smile, feeling shy under his scrutiny.

"Hey, you're as cute as Richard said you were." Nathan leaned forward and hugged her, his bristly beard chafing her skin. He quickly kissed the side of her mouth. "In fact, you're cuter."

"I'll tell your girlfriend," Ruby sang. Hanna's cheeks flushed in response to both his words, and Ruby's threats to tell his girlfriend. She didn't know where to look.

Glancing up, she caught Richard standing on the stairs staring at her bare legs.

"Hi."

Richard smiled, then grabbed at Ruby and swung her

around. Ruby started to scream again, the noise bouncing off the walls. "Let me go!"

"Shall I give you to Nathan?"

"No, no, Hanna, save me."

Hanna ran over and tried to pull Ruby from his grasp. "Let her go, you bully."

The four of them took the tube to Ruby's school. They were a motley crew, with Nathan resembling some sort of vagrant, Ruby all brightly scrubbed and in her new uniform and Richard looking preppy and delicious in his jeans and T-shirt. Glancing down at herself, Hanna realized that her short-shorts and tight vest top did nothing but make their group look even odder. She noticed a few commuters glaring over at them as they stood talking and laughing.

"When are you flying to San Francisco?" Hanna asked Richard. The train stopped suddenly in a tunnel. The flickering lights and the intermittent darkness made Ruby gasp.

"Next Tuesday. I fly out of London this Friday. That gives me three days to pack."

"Are you excited?" The train juddered before pulling away and picking up speed. The force of the movement caused Hanna to lose her footing, and she went barreling into Richard's chest. Almost immediately his arms went around her. Hanna found herself locked in an embrace with Richard.

"Are you okay? You hit me pretty hard."

She took a deep breath, trying to gain control of her racing heart. "I'm fine." She nodded, to emphasize the point.

The train came to a stop at the platform. As always, it was an effort to get off, the four of them pushing their way through a large crowd of commuters who were trying to get on the train at the same time. There was no such thing as politeness during rush hour. It was every man for himself.

Nathan was standing directly behind Ruby, shielding her with his body as they shuffled forward and stepped on to the platform. Richard was just in front of Hanna, and he kept glancing back at her to make sure she was okay. After a moment or two he reached back and took her hand, pulling her along with him in an attempt to keep them together.

Even his hands were perfect. His palm was warm and soft, and his long, sculpted fingers curled around hers perfectly. His nails were cut short, with a small crescent of white at the tips. Her own nails were still ragged and bitten. She'd long since given up trying to keep any polish on them.

When they reached the top of the escalator, they fed their tickets into the machine, walking through the metal barriers and out into the waiting world. Ruby had been silent ever since they left the platform, and Hanna started to worry. She was radiating nervousness; her face had turned pale, her lips pulled together into a thin line.

"Are you okay?" Hanna leaned down to whisper in Ruby's ear, trying not to let Richard or Nathan hear. "It's fine to feel nervous, you know. We've all been there, and I can promise your brothers were every bit as worried as you are when they started high school."

"Not Nathan," Ruby whispered back. "He beat a teacher up on his second day there. By the end of the week he was on suspension."

Hanna bit back a laugh. The Nathan she had seen so far today was like a gentle giant. She couldn't imagine him beating anybody up, let alone a teacher.

"Why did he do it?"

"The teacher was shouting at a girl he liked. He told me he just saw red."

"I hope she was worth it."

"Nathan seems to think so. It was his girlfriend."

Hanna had never met Lucy, although Ruby had shown her some photos, and Hanna had found herself feeling dull and dowdy in comparison to the tall, blonde beauty.

"We're here, Squirt."

Ruby stopped suddenly, looking up at the large brick and white stucco school building bordered on all sides by walls and a thick green hedge. Her knees were shaking, and Hanna found herself reaching out to grab Ruby's hand.

Dropping down to a crouching position, Hanna's face reached the same level as Ruby's. Still holding her hand, she reached the other out to stroke Ruby's cheek.

"Ruby, it's going to be okay. You can do this. When you come out tonight, I bet there'll be a smile on your lips."

Ruby's face crumpled, and tears welled in her eyes. "I don't think I can." Her voice was very small. Hanna wished for all she was worth that she could go in to the school in place of the tiny girl.

"You're stronger than you think. Remember how scared Harry Potter was on his first day at Hogwarts?"

"And then he met Malfoy and Snape," Ruby replied.

"But he met Ron and Hermione, too. And Neville Longbottom, don't forget him."

"How could I forget somebody with such a silly name?"

Hanna watched as Ruby slowly walked through the main gate, never once turning back to look at them. When she looked over, Richard's face was pulled down into a frown. Even Nathan looked glassy-eyed.

"Do you fancy a coffee?" Hanna suggested, trying to find a way to cheer them all up.

"I'm meeting a couple of friends this morning, but you go ahead." Nathan leaned forward and gave Hanna a gentle squeeze. "It was a real pleasure to meet you, Hanna. The way you look after Ruby is awesome."

"She's an easy kid to love."

"Somebody should tell her that." Nathan agreed, and then gave Richard a slap on the back before walking up the street, back toward the tube station.

Hanna turned her gaze back to Richard. "Coffee?" she asked again with a gentle voice.

Richard turned to look at her. "That sounds good." As he stared down at her, she could see the good humor returning to his face, his lips curling into a crooked smile.

She reminded herself that it was just a coffee. They would sit opposite each other and discuss inanities while sipping lukewarm – rather mediocre – coffee, from a chipped, over-used mug. It meant nothing; it was just two friends sharing some time together. She wouldn't be looking at him and wondering if he liked her. She wouldn't be thinking about that snowy night in New York City, when for one electrifying moment she thought he might be about to kiss her.

She wouldn't be doing a lot of things.

Telling Josh about this coffee date was one of them.

THEY WERE RESTING near the statue of Peter Pan in Kensington Gardens, blanketed by the warm late summer air. Richard lay back, his head propped on his rolled-up jacket. Hanna lay curled up beside him, her cheek resting on his chest. An empty bottle of expensive wine lay on its side next to them. They were both feeling a little drunk.

"Ruby will be home soon," he murmured, his hand tangling in her hair, playing with her loose tendrils.

"Mmm." Hanna's eyes remained closed. He could feel a slight moistening of his T-shirt where her mouth was.

"Are you dribbling on me?" He lifted his head to get a better look.

"I don't dribble." She was suddenly awake, whipping her head around to catch his eye, surreptitiously wiping her lips with the back of her hand. Richard laughed at her telltale gesture.

"Come on, admit it, I make you salivate."

"Your modesty is scaring me." Staring up at him, she bit her lip to restrain a smile before poking her tongue out and licking his T-shirt. "But if you're going to accuse me of something I haven't done, then I'm going to do it, anyway."

Clocking the expression on his face, she jumped up and grabbed her bag, running over the open grass. She passed the statue in the middle of the lawn, heading toward the wooded area surrounding them. Grabbing his coat, Richard ran after her, his long, fast strides allowing him to catch her before she even reached the first oak.

"You've got no chance," he laughed. Hooking his arms around her waist, he pulled her body back to his. He could feel the softness of her stomach rising and falling in line with her short, sharp breaths.

Hanna tried to wriggle against him, tugging at his arms, trying to escape. He held firm, keeping her body contained within his embrace, fighting off her attempts to get free. Her breathing slowed. He could feel his own heartbeat starting to calm after the unexpected burst of activity.

They went back to pick up their rubbish, disposing of it in a nearby bin, and began their long walk back through the park. It was nearly 3:00 p.m., and though Nathan was picking Ruby up from school, Richard had promised to be waiting for her at home as soon as they arrived.

"So, how are things with Josh?" he asked. They reached

the Long Pond, following the path around until it became the Serpentine.

Watching as a smile crossed Hanna's face, his stomach clenched in response to her happiness. He tried to work out why her obvious attachment to her boyfriend caused such a reaction in him. They were just friends. So why was he feeling jealous?

"He's good. We're good. It's going to be strange not having him with me at university this year."

The pain in his stomach lessened. "Why won't he be there?"

"He graduated in July. He has a trainee journalist position here at the *Guardian*. He's moved into a little flat in Earls Court."

"Are you guys going to stay together?"

"Yeah, of course. We're only a couple of hundred miles apart. We can see each other at weekends and holidays."

The large oak trees shaded the wide, paved walkway that ran alongside the Serpentine. They found themselves stepping to one side to avoid a rollerblader who was hammering down the middle of the concrete, intent on picking up as much speed as possible. On the edge of the water, dappled-brown ducks and elegantly pale swans lay waiting for the legions of London children who came to feed them daily.

Richard pulled Hanna toward him, putting his arm around her shoulders in a friendly gesture. She curled her arm around his waist.

"I'm going to miss you when you move to California. Will you be coming over here for Christmas?" Her voice was soft.

"I don't know when I'll be back in London, or even New York, come to that. If Chris and I want to get this business off the ground, then I think we'll be working too hard to leave San Francisco for any length of time."

"Tell me again what you're planning to do?"

"Okay, have you heard of Friends Reunited?" He decided to try to start at the basics, to help her understand the concepts.

"Yeah, my mum has made contact with some of her old school friends through that."

"Well, Chris and I want to use that sort of concept, but make it wider, and more modern. Not just catching up with old friends, but keeping in touch with your current ones, chatting, letting them know how you are doing. Maybe even playing games against each other, that sort of thing."

"Why would you do that when you can just pick up the phone and call them?"

"Because this way you can keep in contact with hundreds of friends at once. With a click of a button, you can let everybody in your life know what's going on with you. Say, for instance, you want to tell them that you've graduated. You either have to phone or email them, send them a letter, or rely on word-of-mouth. With our site, you'd be able to write a line to say you've graduated, and all of your friends will read it at once. You've spent less than a minute updating them, and can spend the rest of your day reading Jane Austen, or whatever the hell it is you want to do."

"Hmm. I can't really see why I'd ever want to do that."

"Did you ever think that you'd want to have a cell phone?"

"A what?"

"Surely you know what a cell phone is?" Richard felt incredulous, pulling his Nokia 8250 out of his pocket and showing it to her.

"Oh! You mean a mobile phone?" Hanna took the phone from him, looking at the chromatic display. "Ooh, this one is nice."

Richard shook his head. "As I was saying, although you may not have thought about needing a mobile phone," he drawled the last two words, "now everybody has either got one, or wants one, and it's changing the way we communicate. It will be the same with websites like ours. We're fulfilling a need people didn't even know they had. That's the way to innovate."

"Well, I'll let you know if I ever feel the need to tell hundreds of acquaintances that I've just bought a loaf of bread. Until then, I'll reserve judgement." Hanna smiled, as if she was enjoying winding him up, and Richard realized he was enjoying it, too.

"I'll expect a very public, web-based apology. Perhaps some grovelling, too."

"I can do dribbling, if that helps?"

"I noticed."

They had reached Hyde Park Corner. Hanna jammed her hands in the pockets of her shorts. "You'd better get back. Ruby won't be happy if you're not there when she gets home. It was so nice to see you again."

"And you. I'll miss you."

"It doesn't sound like you'll have time to miss me."

"I'll make time."

"Then make sure you email me. Or invite me to join your website. I'm still all about the grovelling."

Richard laughed, running his hand through his hair. He looked down at her smiling face. "I can't wait for the grovelling."

"Seriously, good luck with it all. Don't be a stranger." Hanna pulled her hands out of her pockets and threw her arms around him, pulling him closely for a brief hug before she released him and stepped back.

He leaned down and brushed his lips against the soft skin of her cheek, taking a moment to breathe her in. Hanna turned and walked down the steps, into the depths of the underground station. Standing at the top of the steps, Richard watched her retreating body until she had reached the bottom and he could see her no more. Touching his lips briefly with his fingers, he turned and walked along the sidewalk in the direction of Chelsea.

Seven

11th September 2001

$\mathscr{T}$HE SHRILL SOUND of the telephone, ringing in the kitchen, cut straight through the silence of the apartment, and it took some moments for Hanna to drag her mind from her book and back into present-day London. Looking around desperately for something to use as a bookmark, she finally pulled her hairband out, placing it in between the pages as her hair cascaded down her back.

Running through the living room, she made it to the kitchen just as the phone rang off. It wasn't the first time this had happened to her, but the frustration still tightened her jaw as she realized that her mad dash had been for nothing. Feeling her stomach growl with hunger, she decided to make a sandwich.

As she walked over toward the refrigerator, she was interrupted once again by the sharp tones of the telephone. She lifted the handset, speaking a loud 'hello' into the mouthpiece.

"Hanna? It's Josh."

"Did you just try to call me?" She bit her lip in confusion. He wasn't supposed to be calling her until tomorrow.

"No, I've just escaped from a meeting. Are you okay?"

"Why wouldn't I be?"

"Are you watching the news?" There was murmuring in

the background, and she wondered just how many people were at this meeting.

"No, I was in my room, reading. What's going on?"

"There's been a plane crash in New York. Two planes, actually. They've smashed into the World Trade Center."

"Oh my God, Josh. That's right next to my dad's building." Her hand was shaking as she held on tightly to the telephone, as if it were a lifeline to her father.

"It's fucking mayhem over there, nobody knows anything. I've been called back to the office in London to man the phones for the night, so I'm leaving now. I'll try to call you when I get there."

Hanna's heart dropped. All she wanted was for her boyfriend to come home to her, to hold her, to tell her it was going to be okay. She placed the phone back in its cradle, her legs walking as if on automatic toward the living room, her arm reaching out robotically to press the 'on' switch.

She couldn't bring herself to sit down as she watched the coverage, though her stomach was churning in response to the visual disaster playing out on the screen. Her whole body was shaking, and a sob escaped from her throat as she watched the panicked responses of both the public and the journalists. They were already describing the attacks as 'an act of war'.

It wasn't just her father and his family she was worried about; there was Richard and the Maxwells, and all those other unknown members of the public who were being hit by tragedy before her very eyes.

Still trembling, she walked back into the kitchen and tugged open the drawer that contained their telephone books. Pulling out the tattered, black leather journal and flicking to the page with her dad's numbers, she systematically dialed each one only to get the same response.

A busy tone.

Trying again, and again, she could feel the tears starting to tumble down her cheeks as she hit the buttons in frustration, knowing before even pressing the final number she would just hear a dead, monotonous response. Yet she still did it.

Pulling at the skin around her thumb with her teeth, she hunted through the book until she came to the *L*s. Running her finger down the page, she found the number she was looking for and dialled it quickly, her heart lifting slightly at the familiar sound of a ringing tone vibrating down the earpiece.

"Hello?"

"Claire? It's Hanna." As soon as she heard Claire's soft voice, the tears started to run thick and fast. Another strangled sob escaped from her mouth, and she heard Claire's soft gasp in response.

"Sweetheart, have you heard anything from your father?"

"No. I can't get through. Have you heard from Richard?" Her heart hammered against her ribcage. She wasn't sure she was ready to hear Claire's response.

"No, we've heard nothing. Steven is locked up in his room trying to get some information. He's pulling in all the contacts he has," she said, referring to Richard's father.

"When was he supposed to be flying to San Francisco?"

"He's meant to be flying this morning, Hanna." Claire was audibly crying now, emotion punctuating every word as she spoke. "We don't know what time, or which airline."

Hanna started to rock forward and backward on the balls of her feet, setting up a rhythm that was somehow comforting to her.

"Is Diana with you?"

"She's organizing a party in Hertfordshire. She won't be back until later tonight." Hanna sniffed at the thought of her mum.

"You're alone? Oh, Hanna." Claire sounded aghast at this revelation. "I'm going to send a car over for you. You can't be on your own at a time like this."

As SOON AS she arrived at Cheyne Walk, she was swept inside the house by Claire and Nathan, the two of them almost carrying her until she was placed gently down on a slouchy sofa. Their eyes were rimmed with red, wetness shining off their skin as they mourned the passing of life as they knew it. They tried not to vocalize the fear they had for Richard.

"Steven is putting feelers out for your father," Claire said as they sat and watched the muted TV. "He has contacts in the embassy and the state office. They're doing everything they can, but it is a mess over there. Nobody can contact anyone: all of the communications networks are down. It's going to take a long time before we find out anything."

Hanna could feel a numbness wash over her skin as she continued to watch the news coverage. She didn't flinch when footage of a third plane crash into the Pentagon was broadcast, nor did she comment when a fourth plane crashed into a field in rural Pennsylvania. She just sat, her eyes wide open, her mouth still breathing, her heart still beating. She didn't want to see the recordings of the plane crashes being played on a continuous loop, but she could not tear her eyes away. It was like being hypnotized against her will.

They sat, and they watched, and they remained mute, until a loud bang came from Steven's office. It sounded like something being thrown against a wall. There was a noisy, splintering sound, followed by the frantic wail of a grown man.

Claire stood up and ran over to the office door. Hanna and Nathan stared at her body as she moved, their faces frozen with fear.

77

As Claire reached the door, it was flung open to reveal Steven standing there. His normal suave facade had disappeared, replaced by that of a desperate man. His shirt was askew, his hair falling all over the place. What really pierced Hanna through the heart was the expression on his face. As long as she lived, she would never forget that look. It was a mixture of fear and misery, frustration and inaction. It was a father fighting for his son.

"The fourth plane was heading for San Francisco," he whispered.

Hanna's shaking returned. She hugged her arms around her stomach in an attempt to stop herself, but instead found herself rocking forward and backward again.

"Where did it take off?" Claire asked.

"Newark."

"Steven." Claire's voice was a wail. She flung herself into her husband's arms, her sobbing increasing as he held her tightly.

Hanna started to shake her head, as if she was trying to deny what was happening. She looked over at Nathan, to see him sitting with his hands covering his mouth. His blue eyes stared straight back at her.

"Was he definitely flying from Newark?" she whispered to Nathan, grabbing for any flicker of hope, like a drowning man searching for a life jacket.

"I don't know. I don't think Dad knows which flight he was getting. But he's flown from Newark before."

Glancing at the television screen, Hanna could see from the clock in the right-hand corner it was almost 2:30 p.m.

"Ruby," she whispered, trying not to watch Steven and Claire's desperate embrace. "If I leave now I can get to school in time to pick her up." Hanna needed the fresh air, and the purpose that such a trip would give her. Distance and time were what she craved.

"I'll go with you. I don't want her to hear about this from anybody else," Nathan whispered.

"Do we tell them we're leaving?" Hanna looked over at Claire. It was like she and Steven were in their own bubble. Nathan's gaze followed her stare, and his face crumpled again as he watched their misery unfolding before him.

"You go and grab your coat, I'll tell them we're picking her up."

IS MOTHER WAS awake when Richard walked in, curled up on the silk-covered sofa in the drawing room. He was pleased to see her hand wasn't wrapped around the stem of a crystal wineglass, although they were pale and shaking, just like the rest of her. Her hair fell around her face in pale strands, and her lips were red and dry from the constant scraping of her teeth.

"I'm going to shower and then come right back," he told her. She looked up at him with glassy, blue eyes.

"Hurry, darling. I don't like being alone."

The shower was necessary. His hair was covered with dust, and his skin was itching from the effect of the wind and detritus in the air. More than anything, he wanted to wash away the memories of today, and watch them follow the grey sludgy water down the drain. Unfortunately, dirt was more easily dealt with than thoughts.

He went back downstairs with his hair still wet. His mother hadn't moved; she was still staring at the same spot on the wall, looking at the pictures of their family and friends. Photographs of happier times, when life was predictably good, and evil was just a concept in an old book.

"Was it terrible out there?" Even Caroline's voice seemed to have deadened. She spoke through thin, dry lips.

"It wasn't pleasant. I gave blood then went to see the—" He couldn't bring himself to say the words, although he suspected at some point he would need to do so.

"Is there any hope?"

He knew she was asking if there were more survivors being rescued. He shook his head.

"Please don't leave me, Richard." A single tear emerged from the corner of her eye. It ran down her cheek, dripping from her chin to make a stain on the silk sofa. "I know I said I didn't want you to move to California before, but I mean it. I don't think I can do this on my own."

"I'm not going anywhere." He moved to sit with her, took her hand in his own and squeezed it gently.

"They're saying they'll issue death certificates soon, even if no bodies are found. I've tried calling our family lawyers, but there's never any answer. I don't know what I'm supposed to be doing."

"We'll work it out. I'll try calling them again tomorrow." He scratched his head as his eyes wandered over to the drinks cabinet. The whisky bottle was calling him like a siren. He tried to ignore the craving; he didn't want to encourage his mother to start drinking again. Not when she was sober for the first time in four days.

Still holding her hand tightly, he asked, "Has Daniel come down yet?"

"Consuela took him up some lunch, and she said he was quieter, but he still doesn't want to see anybody."

"I'll check on him in a minute. He shouldn't be alone."

"He told me he doesn't want his inheritance, that he doesn't want anything of Leon's." Her voice broke as she said her dead husband's name.

"He's mourning his father. He doesn't know what he's saying." Richard closed his eyes for a moment, trying to imagine how he would feel if it was Steven who had died in the attack. The thought tore a hole in his heart. God only knew how Daniel was feeling.

"He's going to own the majority of Maxwell Enterprises, so many people are going to be relying on him. I just know he's going to crumble." Caroline took her son's face in her hands, pulling him closer so she could stare straight at him. "You know Leon bequeathed a share of the company to us, as well. You need to go in there and protect our interests. Leon would have wanted you to be in control, at least until Daniel is ready."

"I've already spoken with the chief financial officer; we've decided to rent some office space uptown for now. We're meeting tomorrow to discuss interim arrangements." He didn't tell her he'd contacted his friend and tendered his resignation from a company he had yet to set up. Such details seemed unimportant at a time like this.

EARLY THE NEXT morning, before leaving to meet with the board of Maxwell Enterprises, Richard sat in his deceased stepfather's oak-panelled study and used his state-of-the-art computer to check his emails. It was the first time he had done so since 10th September, and he was surprised to see so many unread notes there. Scanning his eyes down the list of senders, he saw the majority of them were friends, possibly concerned for his safety, seeking reassurances that he was okay.

Near the bottom of the page, he saw the words 'Hanna Vincent'. Just seeing the lines of her name kick-started something inside of him, like a small pilot light was being lit in the boiler of his soul.

FROM: HMVincent@yahoo.co.uk
TO: RSLarsen@aol.com
SUBJECT: You

Richard,

I hate that I have to write this email. I hate that I can't be there for you, and that I can't even contact you by phone. Everything about this situation is horrific, and I'm going crazy trying to imagine how you must be feeling right now.

I spent the day of September 11th with your family, and I was amazed not only by their fervent love and worry for you, but also for the support they showed me at a time when we were all at our lowest ebb. They adore you so much, and the relief we felt when we heard that both you and my father were safe was indescribable.

And yet, it was tinged with sadness as soon as we heard that your stepfather had died in the tragedy. I am sorrier than you can ever know. If you need a friend to talk to, or a shoulder to cry on, I am here, day or night, just call.

You know that, right?

I love you, my friend. I wish I could be there to hug you right now, and as soon as I meet you next, please expect for the breath to be squeezed out of you by my puny arms. I'll be that happy to see your ugly face.

Don't worry about replying. I'm sure you have hundreds of emails like this from your female admirers.

Hanna x

FROM: RSLarsen@aol.com
TO: HMVincent@yahoo.co.uk
SUBJECT: You

Hanna,

Thank you for your words. At a time like this, what I crave is levity. There is so much going on here right now, not just in New York, but also in my own life, and knowing that normality still exists in the rest of the world, is somehow reassuring.

My father told me how much you did on that day, the way you looked after Ruby, and supported Nathan, despite your own fears. So I can categorically say that when you squeeze me, I shall be clasping you back much harder. May I suggest you practice your breathing techniques in the meantime?

I have to leave for a meeting now, but I'll try to write again soon.

Love,

Richard

An hour later, Richard made it to the makeshift conference room at the top of Maxwell Industry's newly rented office building. The remaining members of the advisory board were standing around in clusters, talking rapidly, their eyes wide as they exchanged stories of the day their lives changed irrevocably. The majority of them hadn't been in the office on the morning of the crash, but the shock of their near miss remained etched on their faces as they chattered, their eyes sliding over to Richard as he entered the room. They were sizing him up as a potential replacement for Leon Maxwell.

Taking a deep breath, Richard squared his shoulders and walked to the head of the conference table, keeping his pace even and measured. He pulled the chair out, deliberately scraping it loudly across the floor, making all eyes turn his way.

"Ladies and Gentlemen, I suggest we start. We have a business to run." As they all sat down, Richard remained standing, moving his eyes around the room. He looked at each board member in turn. Some of them appeared sceptical, others hopeful. The cannier amongst them kept their expressions blank as they glanced back at him, making it hard for him to read their features.

"As you all know, Leon Maxwell, the owner of this company, is missing, presumed dead. In his absence, I am here representing the new owners: my stepbrother, my mother, and myself.

"I can see there are some among you who remain unconvinced that I can step into his shoes and turn the fortunes of this company around. To those people, I say: either you are with me, or you are against me. If you don't want to work here, I'm very happy to accept your resignation right now."

Richard paused, his eyes scanning the room again to see if any of them would take him up on his offer.

They all remained silent.

"I'm glad we've got that settled. Just like my stepfather, I expect you to work hard, and I demand your loyalty. Our business has suffered a huge body-blow in the past week, as has America. But the camaraderie and the determination I have seen out there on the streets has been absolutely amazing. If we can channel that same grit right here into this company, then I truly believe that we can rebuild this company brick by brick, and make it an enterprise that Leon Maxwell would justifiably be proud of."

Richard noticed a few heads nodding at his words. He remained stoic, not allowing himself to sigh or even show a flicker of emotion as he spoke to them. He didn't dare demonstrate any weakness.

"Now, I'd like you all to go out there and motivate your people. I'll be meeting with you individually, and we'll be making plans for the future. In the meantime, I look forward to working with each and every one of you."

Thanking them for their time, Richard finally allowed himself to sit down, trying to hide the trembling in his legs. They all started to clap, standing up to give him a heartfelt ovation.

The first person to actually approach him was Joe Garfield, the chief financial officer. A close confidant of Leon's, Joe's face was drawn down in grief as he shook Richard's hand, muttering the usual trite condolences as he looked him straight in the eye.

"Thank you, sir," Richard replied, wondering how, in the space of a few days, he had turned into a man that everybody was looking to, someone who was supposed to know how to run a multi-billion dollar business.

Joe must have clocked the nervousness in Richard's face, or perhaps it was the shaking of his hands as they clasped his own. Either way, the older man took pity on him.

"If any of these fuck-ups give you trouble, come and see me. I'll give you every bit of support I can."

"I'm grateful for your backing. Thank you."

Glancing down at the sheet of paper in front of him, Richard could see his temporary assistant had already set up individual meetings with board members. His entire day was filled, right up until 8:00 p.m. that evening. It was clear his life was no longer his own.

To fail at this, would be to let down thousands of people, employees and customers and shareholders that were relying on him to make this company a success.

That was not an option.

Eight

29th June 2002

"WHAT'S THIS?" JOSH picked up the package from her bed as Hanna continued to pack her backpack, stuffing things in as tightly as possible.

Hanna glanced over as she watched him pull the T-shirt out of the packaging. It fell open in front of him revealing the vintage 1973 New York Dolls band tee Richard had sent her.

"It's a present from Richard."

"I don't like the way he keeps sending you things." Josh let it fall back onto her bed, flicking his fingers as if he was trying to remove any traces of the gift from them. "It's weird."

Hanna stopped packing, leaning over to brush his cheek with her hand. "He's just a friend, Josh."

"Friends don't send friends gifts worth hundreds of pounds, Hanna. He clearly fancies you. Christ, the guy can hardly take his eyes off you."

Hanna choked back a laugh. "Josh, you know there's nothing going on there. He lives thousands of miles away, and I'm with you. Have a little faith, okay?" Leaning forward, she touched her lips against his. "I'm going to be away until Sunday, let's not leave things like this."

"I still don't like it."

Despite her entreaties, his bad mood continued all the way to Paddington Station where he dropped her off. She gave him a quick kiss before exiting the car, feeling his irritation as he responded with a quick peck. She had barely pushed the door closed before he sped off, and she watched the car as it disappeared into the London traffic, her worry for her relationship with Josh reflected in the anxious nausea gripping her stomach.

As soon as she was on the train, Hanna breathed a sigh of relief, deciding she would worry about their argument when she was back in London. She touched her pocket to check that Richard's letter was still there, and pulled it out to read one more time.

20th June 2002

Dear Hanna,

Thank you for the present. After all these years, to finally receive the promised mix tape made me grin madly. When I read the track listing I laughed out loud. Starting with 'The Wall Street Shuffle' may have seemed rather obvious, but to follow it with 'Money for Nothing' by Dire Straits was an inspired touch. Your final song, Puff Daddy's 'It's All About the Benjamins' is actually one of my favourites.

Anyway, to thank you for your gift, you'll be pleased to see that I spent a few Benjamins on a T-shirt for you. I'm not sure if you are a New York Dolls fan or not, but just seeing it made me think of you, and the night we saw The Strokes.

Let's do it again soon, okay?

Richard

Sitting in the backstage bar of the Glastonbury music festival, Hanna watched as Tom McLean crossed the room and placed five ice-cold bottles of Stella Artois on the sticky plastic table in front of them. She picked one up and leaned back on the flimsy folding chair, necking a huge gulp of beer, much to the amusement of the rest of the band.

"So, what did you think?" Tom asked, trying to appear nonchalant as he pulled up another chair, placing it right alongside Hanna so their thighs were almost touching.

"On the record or off?" Hanna teased. She fingered the backstage journalist pass that hung around her neck.

Tom stared at her for a moment, his eyes narrowing as he considered her words. "Whichever I'm going to like the best."

"I'm kidding, you goof." She was smiling broadly. "You were absolutely fantastic. I loved the new set. It was brilliant. You had the crowd hanging on every note."

"Were we better than Coldplay?" Robert, the bass guitarist, leaned forward, his chin placed on top of his palms. He looked at Hanna with clear, wide eyes.

She couldn't believe how interested they were in her opinion, although the little ego-boost their anticipation gave her was quite welcome. It wasn't the first time since she'd been at the festival that a band had genuinely seemed engrossed in what she thought about them. Somehow her judgement had become sought after. She assumed it had something to do with the fact that she was interning for *Music Train*, and had their logo hanging from her neck everywhere she went. All the bands wanted a good write-up from the nation's most popular music magazine.

"Coldplay was excellent, everybody was singing along to them." Tom physically blanched at her words, and she hurried to continue, "But you guys were something else. People weren't just singing, they were worshipping. They were throwing themselves down as sacrifices to the gods of rock."

A broad grin spread across Tom's face. He stood up, walked over to her, and pulled her into a tight embrace, his lips swooping down on hers with a loud smack. "Hanna Vincent, I fucking love you. Now make sure you call me a rock god in your review."

"You know that *Music Train* has proper writers here, right? I'm going to be lucky if they even print an indefinite article without sending it through five editors." She wriggled in a feigned attempt to escape his grasp. Not that she minded him being overly demonstrative – she was used to it by now. He was like an overenthusiastic five-year-old, throwing himself at everybody, not just her.

"I spoke with your boss earlier and I promised them an exclusive interview, but only if you wrote it." He winked as he pulled away from her, moving to sit back down.

"Oh my God!" she squealed at him, trying to restrain herself from starting the whole hugging fest again. People were starting to look.

"Oh my *Rock* God, if you please."

They stared at each other, matching smiles on their faces. It was hard to believe that only two years previously she'd been watching him play in a small pub and had no inkling he was going to become internationally famous. How things had changed.

"Tom, sweetie!" A thin, highly pitched voice came from across the room. Hanna watched in amusement as a tiny blonde ran over, throwing herself into Tom's arms, wrapping her legs around his waist as she placed her lips firmly on his.

"Is that Pinkie Jones?" Hanna asked Robert in a whispered aside.

"Oh yeah, she's been the bane of our existence all summer. Whenever you turn around, she's there. She's been hovering around us like a fly over a pile of shit."

"Nice simile. Especially when you compare yourselves to manure," she replied dryly, watching as Tom sat back down on his chair, pulling Pinkie onto his lap. Hanna bit her bottom lip in an attempt to stop from giggling, causing Tom to raise his eyebrows in response.

"Are you not singing today?" Robert drawled over at the blonde. Pinkie giggled and shook her head before burying it in the side of Tom's head, nuzzling at his throat. Hanna noticed a flash of something just underneath the surface of his eyes. And all of a sudden she realized that Tom McLean was smitten with a Z-list celebrity and runner-up in that year's *Rock Star* reality show.

Hanna tried to restrain the wide smirk that was trying to unzip its way across her lips because she knew that Tom would think she was mocking him, even though she wasn't. In fact, a little corner of her heart was heating up fast at the sight of her friend being bowled over by a woman.

"Pinkie, this is Hanna Vincent, one of my oldest friends." Tom looked up and winked at Hanna.

"You don't look that old." Pinkie replied, her face frowning in confusion. Hanna heard Robert start to guffaw next to her.

"No, sweetie, she's not an old friend, as in years, she's old as in I've known her for years."

"I'm twenty." Hanna decided this would be easier if she just came out with it.

Pinkie repaid Hanna's frank reply with a dazzling smile, and Hanna could see exactly what Tom saw in her. Her face was open and guileless, and even if she didn't appear to have too much going on between her ears, whatever was there seemed kind and friendly.

"Have you two known each other long?" Hanna asked, very interested in the reply. She had a feeling she was going to be able to live off this story for the next few months.

"We met at the *Rock Star* wrap party. Tommy came up and told me that he'd voted for me a hundred times every week."

The need to laugh washed over Hanna again. With his street cred and her tabloid appeal, Tom and Pinkie were going to be paparazzi fodder of the highest order.

HANNA ARRIVED BACK at Josh's flat earlier than planned that Sunday. Riffling through her handbag, she found the front door key and let herself in, trying not to breathe in the rancid, damp air that lingered in the hallway. She swung her backpack onto her shoulder, her sandalled feet stepping onto the threadbare carpet of the stairs. She slowly walked up to the second floor, her muscles feeling leaden in reaction to the sudden exertion. Her body ached. She wanted nothing more than to jump in Josh's admittedly tiny shower, then crawl under the covers with him for a couple of hours.

The apartment was silent as she let herself in, and she realized that her first supposition – that he hadn't even bothered getting up – was the correct one. His wallet and keys were still on the counter of his tiny kitchen. Pushing his bedroom door open, her eyes adjusted slowly to the gloom of the curtained room. She placed her rucksack down beside the door and walked over to his bed.

Her legs reacted before her mind did, as if they sensed the wrongness of the moment. Hanna stopped suddenly, seeing the two of them sleeping, their naked bodies entwined beneath the draping covers of the thin white sheet. Josh's arm was flung across the woman's waist, his head buried in her neck as he gently breathed – his slumbering face a picture of innocence.

Numbness enveloped her body. She recognized the woman. They'd met a few times when Hanna joined Josh and his workmates in the pub on a Friday night. He had introduced her as his boss, and the two of them had barely interacted during all the times she had seen them together. Now the connection was way too close for comfort, and Hanna closed her mouth in an attempt to quiet the cry that was trying to escape her throat.

Fight or flight? She bit her thumbnail, her face screwed up with misery, as she tried to decide the best thing to do. Should she confront them before they had time to make up a story to cover up their indiscretions? Or should she run and leave the room with a small modicum of her dignity intact?

Her mind was made up for her, when Josh moved languorously, lifting his arm from the woman's waist and stretching it over his head, his eyes opening slowly and blinkingly, as they reacted to the dim light. Raising his head from the pillow, he looked over at Hanna and smiled, opening his mouth to say something before he looked down and saw the naked woman lying beside him.

The look of horror that crossed his face was almost comical.

"What the fuck?"

"I think that's supposed to be my line." Hanna's voice sounded surprisingly controlled to her as she surveyed the mess that was her relationship.

"What are you doing here? I thought you were in Glastonbury." He pulled the sheet up to cover their naked bodies. A bark of laughter wound its way up her larynx as she realized that he was trying to put the fault straight back onto her. And then the laughter was replaced by a sob, and she knew she had to get out of there right now.

Reason had kicked into her brain, punching its way through the numbness, and she turned around to pick up her backpack before walking out through his bedroom door. She could hear him shouting at her, but didn't reply, increasing her pace until she crossed the few feet to his front door.

It was like her whole body had been hit hard. Her muscles felt tight and edgy as she ran down the stairs, barely noticing the weight of her backpack as she moved. Her heartbeat sped in response to the shock of seeing them there. She had no idea how she made it outside without falling over.

Hanna wanted to slap the palm of her hand right across Josh Chambers' face until she heard the satisfying thwack of his teeth hitting his inner cheek. She wanted to climb up into her mum's lap like she was five years old again, and a simple cuddle would erase all of the hurt.

Most of all, she needed to go home and crawl into her little single bed, pull the duvet over her head and bawl her eyes out.

Nine

$\mathcal{R}$ICHARD WALKED OVER to the wall of glass that stretched across the entire south side of his office. Being on the fifteenth floor, it afforded him an impressive outlook of Lower Manhattan, and he could see all the way out to the port. The view of the office buildings, contrasting with the natural beauty of the waterway, was breathtaking. It was the vista that sold the office space to him in the first place.

Since taking control of Maxwell Enterprises, his life had turned into one endless Groundhog Day of waking at five, running in Central Park, then showering and being driven to work before seven. He'd be in meetings, conferences, lunches, and presentations until the evening when he would respond to emails, write reports, and catch up on correspondence until late, barely getting home before midnight.

Yet, despite the hard work, and the lack of sleep, there was a part of Richard Larsen that loved his new life – the excitement of the chase and the jubilation when a deal was struck. This, coupled with the knowledge that he was rebuilding Maxwell Enterprises, got him through the endless days and restless nights.

His telephone buzzed, and he walked back to his desk and pushed the button.

"Yes, Lisa?"

"I have your mother on the phone. Would you like to talk to her?"

Richard grimaced slightly before responding. "Sure, put her on."

A couple of clicks later, and Caroline's smooth tones came down the wire and out of the speaker.

"Richard, how are you?"

"I'm good, busy as always. How are things with you?"

"I just got back from seeing Daniel. He seems so much better. Whatever they're doing with him at the new clinic seems to have calmed him down. He asked for you a couple of times, and I told him you might be able to get there at the weekend."

"I've saved some time on Sunday, I should be able to get down then."

"Are you free for dinner tonight? One of my old friends from Radcliffe is joining us. Her daughter is in her third year at Columbia."

He couldn't help but sigh. All year, his mother had been trying to get him to come to dinner with various girls. They were always daughters of her friends, and always extremely eligible. But he didn't have the time or the inclination to make small talk with yet another society girl.

"Not tonight, I'm afraid. I have to work late."

"You're always working late, darling. Why not give yourself a break?"

"I can't, we're working on a big deal. Maybe next week. I'll ask Lisa to check the diary."

Hanging up the phone, his intercom buzzed again. He pushed the button, wondering if a few uninterrupted minutes were too much to wish for.

"Yes?"

"Richard, I have a young lady out here who claims to be your sister."

He frowned, wondering what the hell Ruby was doing in New York. Then he scowled as he remembered that it was Claire's mother's ninetieth birthday that weekend, and that the whole family had travelled over to celebrate with her. How could he have forgotten that?

"Send her in."

His door opened and Ruby walked in, a huge grin plastering her face. She'd grown again since he'd last seen her, and he shook his head at the sudden realization that his baby sister was a teenager. Jesus Christ, where had the time gone?

"Richard!" She launched herself at him, throwing her arms around his waist and nuzzling into his chest. "I can't believe how long it's been since I've seen you. You've been neglecting me." All these words were said with a straight face, but he couldn't help but curl his mouth up in response.

"Hey, Squirt." He paused, his eyes searching out the expression on her face. "Am I even allowed to call you that anymore?"

"Not in public." Her face had turned a brighter shade of pink, and her voice turned into a whisper. "But I don't mind you saying it in private. In fact, I still kind of like it. Anyway, I have been sent up here on a very important mission." Ruby's tone turned serious. "I'm here to ask you to join us for lunch, and then I need to put a pouty expression on my face until you say yes because Mum tells me when I beg I'm irresistible."

"Where are they all, anyway?" Now that he knew they were here, in his hometown, he was suddenly desperate to see his family.

"Dad has a meeting at the bank and will be joining us at the restaurant, and Mum and Hanna are shopping."

"Hanna's here?"

"Yeah, Mum gave her the flight here as a Christmas present. She has to go back to University next week, so this is her final bit of fun."

"How is she?" They'd exchanged some emails, but ever since her break-up with Josh, he'd found it hard to find the right tone with her.

"She seems much better now. She spent most of last summer crying, and even I noticed that she had lost weight, and I never pay attention to anything like that. But since she's been home for Christmas, she seems much happier."

For some reason, that made him smile.

WHEN THEY ARRIVED at La Trattoria, the rest of the family were already seated around the large, circular table. His eyes immediately sought out Hanna. As soon as he looked at her face, he caught her staring back at him, the strangest expression moulding her features.

"Hey Son, it's been too long." Steven stood up and threw his arms around Richard, hugging him tightly in an embrace. He patted his back in a move perfected by fathers the world over. They'd seen each other a couple of times over the past year, and Richard still found it hard to remember their emotional reunion when Steven flew to New York as soon as he could after 9/11. To see his father cry openly in the middle of the very public airport had made Richard feel uncomfortable, although at that time, everybody was showing their emotions and wearing their hearts on their sleeves.

Claire stood up and joined in the hug, leaving only Hanna still seated, staring at them with a small smile covering her lips. Richard walked over to her, putting his hand out and pulling her toward him.

"Hey you," he whispered into her hair as he held her tightly against his chest. Her hands circled his waist, fisting the fabric of his jacket.

"Hi," she whispered back softly.

"How are you doing?"

"Good, thank you. How are you? Claire tells me you've become a workaholic."

"I don't really get a choice."

"Well, maybe I can try to cure you over the next few days."

"That sounds intriguing. I'm free tonight." He surprised himself with this invitation; there was no way he was going to get the presentation finished today. He really needed tonight to add the final touches.

"I have to go to my father's for dinner at seven. Maybe I could meet you afterward?" The hopeful tone of her voice made Richard smile.

"Why don't you come and meet me at the office? It'll give me a chance to finish up some stuff. We can get a drink or something?"

Later that evening, Richard was just shutting down his computer when Hanna arrived. He glanced up, taking in the black dress, natural make-up and long brown hair. "How long ago did you leave the Goth look behind?"

Hanna laughed. "I haven't been a Goth since I went to university. I still prefer dressing down, but I didn't want to give my father too much of a heart attack."

"The dress suits you." It clung to her curves in all the right places, the hem falling at mid-thigh to expose her long legs.

"You seem to have changed your style, too." She walked over, a small smile dancing across her face as she came to a stop in front of him. Lifting up his tie, her fingers played with the soft silk. "I don't think your suit came from Marks and Sparks."

"Marks and Sparks?" Richard shook his head in confusion.

"Marks and Spencer. I'm pretty sure they don't stock Gucci."

"You recognized the designer?"

She laughed out loud, still holding his tie, slowly pulling him forward until their faces were almost touching. Putting her mouth next to his ear, she slowly breathed. "Nathan told me you won't wear anything else."

Shit, he was getting a hard-on from feeling her exhalations on his skin. He didn't know whether to just surrender to it, or pull away. Hanna made the decision for him, moving back to sit on the chair next to his desk.

"How is corporate life treating you? You're looking good in it." She stared at his suit again.

Richard closed his laptop and swivelled around to face her. "You know, I actually love it. I'm learning quickly, people listen to me when I talk, and I make things happen. In three years' time, I might actually know what I'm doing."

"So, you don't regret not going to San Francisco?" She was leaned toward him, her elbows propped on the desk, her chin resting in her hands.

"I try not to think about it. I'm all about looking ahead. Speaking of which, what do you have planned after graduation?"

Hanna smiled broadly, her eyes dancing as she thought about her own future. "I've been offered a job on *Music Train*, where I interned last summer."

"Wow, that's excellent news. We should celebrate."

"Yes we should," she agreed.

Standing up, he took her hand. They walked to the elevator, keen to get out of the office and finally spend some time together.

A few drinks later and he'd managed to get her to open up about Josh. Richard wasn't sure why he was so keen to hear about their split – whether it was out of genuine concern for her, or if he just wanted confirmation that everything was really over. Either way, he sat in the booth with Hanna, his arm loosely around her shoulders, and she leaned against him, her face screwed up as she tried to explain her emotions.

"… He kept trying to say that he only slept with her because he was afraid of his feelings for me. That he thought I wasn't committed to the relationship, and he wanted to show me that he didn't give a fuck. Then he'd change his mind, and tell me it was a complete mistake, and that he was out of his mind with alcohol. He wouldn't even tell me if it was a one-off or if the relationship had been going on for some time."

Richard grimaced, knowing from Josh's lack of candour, it had to be the latter.

Hanna turned to look Richard straight in the eye. Her face was only a few inches from his, and he could see the intensity of her emotions swirling beneath the chocolate brown of her eyes. Opening his mouth to reply, he found himself struck dumb by the intimacy developing between them. His expression softened as he gazed back at her, watching her skin react to their closeness, a flush staining the apples of her cheeks.

Some moments passed as they stared, and he could feel the familiar yearning start to tug at his stomach. Slowly, hesitantly, he reached out a hand, and lightly brushed his fingertips across her cheek. She continued to look straight at him, her eyes unblinking.

"I think we need to leave." Her voice was choked. Her neck bobbed visibly as she tried to swallow.

His heart dropped. "I'll take you home."

"I want to go home with *you*." She looked surprised at her own words, her eyebrows rising up, and the flush in her cheeks deepening.

"Hanna…" He wanted to kick himself for hesitating, but he refused to be anybody's rebound. "I'm not sure this is a good idea."

"Richard, this is a fabulous idea." She cupped her hand around the back of his head, pulling his face toward hers. She hesitated when her lips were millimetres away from his. He could feel his breath hitch at her close proximity, the familiar tightness starting to stir.

The warmth of her breath bathed his skin, and he closed his eyes, trying to remember the last time his body felt as alive as it did right now. Her fingers continued to play with the hair at the base of his neck, sending shivers down his spine and making resistance almost impossible.

"Let's go."

*T*HEY WALKED INTO his apartment, and Richard threw his coat over a chair in the hallway, reaching out to take Hanna's from her shoulders. "Can I get you a drink?"

"A glass of water would be nice."

He didn't move, just stood a couple of feet away from her, half smiling, as his soft green eyes stared right into her own.

"You really want some water?"

"I would *really* like a glass of water, Richard. In fact, I've been looking forward to a nice drink of H_2O all day."

"Not wine, not beer, not a cocktail. You want water." His voice was deadpan, although the crinkling of the corner of his eyes gave his amusement away.

"If you're going to be an asshole about it, what I really

want is a cup of tea. But you're American, so I decided to go easy on you."

"I have tea."

"I don't believe you." She placed her hands on her hips, a small smile flashing across her face as his eyebrows raised. Her expression screamed "Bring it on."

"I have teabags, I have milk, and I even have a teapot somewhere. My stepmother is an Anglophile, Hanna. So, would you like a cup of tea?"

Instead of moving toward the kitchen, he took a step forward, that crooked half-grin still plastered across his face. He reached out to touch her on her upper arm. His finger traced a line of fire from her shoulder to her elbow, the softness of his touch sending a shiver all the way down to the base of her spine.

"I think I'll have a cup of tea later."

"Really?" He closed the gap between them, his body just inches from hers. His hand moved around to the small of her back, and he placed it flat against her, the warmth of his palm seeping through the thin material of her dress. For a moment they both stood there, unmoving, and Hanna could feel her body start to hum in reaction to his proximity. Lifting her head up, she looked straight into his eyes, unsure whether she was challenging him or begging him.

"Yes." She wasn't sure whether she was replying to his question, or just urging him on.

Everything felt different, and everything felt the same. He was her old friend; someone she had laughed with, and played with. But the Richard standing in front of her was all man. And that suit, oh God that suit; when she first set eyes on him as he walked into the restaurant earlier that day, it was like her whole body had been lit on fire. She was stuck somewhere between familiarity and discomposure, feeling strangely anxious and yet knowing that no matter what happened, she wouldn't regret this.

"Are you sure?" His hand pulled her toward him, closing the gap, until her chest was just touching his abdomen, the rest of her body barely skimming his. She couldn't see his face, her eyes reaching only up to the dip in the base of his neck, slightly exposed by the unbuttoned crisp collar of his white shirt.

"Absolutely."

She wanted to bury herself in his skin, inhale his scent. She softly pressed her lips to the exposed part of his chest. She kissed him harder, sucking gently at his skin, letting her tongue drag its way along the soft dip under his collar.

"Hanna." His voice cracked, and he placed his thumb under her chin, pulling her face up as he bent down, until they met in the middle. She placed her hands on his shoulders, her fingers splaying across the white of his shirt, using him as leverage to bridge the final gap between his lips and hers.

When there was only a millimetre between them, she felt him sigh against her. He crushed his mouth to hers, any gentleness forgotten in the need to touch, to taste, to consume. His hand pressed hard against the back of her head, pulling her closer until their teeth were almost scraping together, her mouth opening as soon as she felt the tip of his tongue running along her lip.

She brushed her hand against his cheek, touching the soft emerging stubble peppering his skin. Her mind was feverish as she pushed her body against his, wanting to feel his reaction, hoping that he was as aroused as she was.

"Jesus." He pulled his lips away from hers, leaning back so he had a clear line of sight to her face. His hand was still cupping her head as he stared down at her, the intensity in his eyes making her feel breathless. "Hanna, this is just..." He shook his head, unable to articulate his thoughts.

She felt the need to justify herself. "I know we shouldn't do this. And I know that you probably think I'm on some kind of rebound from Josh. But I've been thinking about this all day, and he was just a rebound from you—"

"Would you shut up about Josh when I'm trying to seduce you?"

"Sorry." Hanna inwardly kicked herself, wondering what the hell she was thinking even mentioning his name. If Richard had mentioned an ex in this situation, she'd be hopping mad.

"Come back here." He moved his hands around and grabbed both of hers, walking backward toward the couch as he pulled her, the smile still playing around his lips. Hanna padded softly across the bare wooden floor, and then came to a stop as he lay down on the couch, pulling her on top of him.

She had to hitch her dress up to be able to place her legs on either side of his hips, and suddenly she realized that she was in control. Richard was lying beneath, staring up at her, waiting for her to make her move. She loved that he was ready to let her set the pace, to cede the decision to her.

Sitting back, she undid his buttons one by one – each time pulling at his shirt until his whole chest was revealed. Sliding her hand down his abdomen, she could feel the hard muscles, then the ribbing of his stomach as he tensed beneath her touch. He was breathing rapidly, his body moving up and down under her hand as she dragged her finger down until she reached the buckle of his belt.

"May I?" She glanced up at him, catching his eyes as he looked up at her. He reached out and grabbed her wrist, his fingers curling around it as he halted her progression.

"Wait." He pushed himself up until he was sitting, his face close to hers. "I want to see you first." He pulled at the hem of her dress, and she lifted herself up as he dragged it up her stomach, and over her arms, until she was left straddling him, clad only in her bra and panties.

A strangled moan escaped from his lips. He moved his arms around her, unclasping her bra. Shrugging his shirt off, he threw it to the floor along with her dress. He took her hands and pulled her up against him until their bare chests were touching. Flesh against flesh, the sensation of his body on hers caused her nipples to harden. He moved his lips to her breasts, sucking at each in turn, flicking his tongue over them until she began to sigh.

She was fumbling at his buckle again, this time managing to get it undone before she grasped at the button on his fly, her fingers shaking as she tried to undo it. She could feel him smile against her skin as his hands moved down to help her, easily unfastening his trousers and shucking them off his legs.

Moving back on top, he aligned his body with hers, and she could feel the prominent ridge of his erection through the fabric of their underwear as he rocked against her. At that moment all she could think of was the need to feel him inside of her.

"Richard, please..."

She was rotating her hips against him, and he bent down to kiss her again. His right hand moved underneath her behind to cup it, to grind against her some more. "I need to—"

"Soon."

He moved his lips down to a place on her neck, just beneath her jaw. It was so sensitive that she nearly squealed in delight. "Let me take care of you."

Sitting back on his knees, he dragged his hands along the side of her body until he reached her panties, hooking his thumbs through them and pulling them down. As soon as they were off, he grasped her legs and pulled her toward him, his lips brushing against her inner thighs as he moved them up, until he could start to kiss and lick at her, making Hanna squirm at his touch. Letting her head fall back, she moved her hand down, her fingers tangling in his soft, thick hair as she felt him hum against her, the pleasure of the vibrations shooting through her core.

Just as he was bringing her to the edge, he pulled his mouth away, and through her half shut eyes she watched him lean down to grab a condom from the pocket of his discarded trousers, and roll it on. Moving back to her, he aligned their bodies until he entered her with one smooth thrust of his hips, the sudden feeling of fullness causing her to tip over, her whole body stiffening in response to her orgasm. Her back arched against him as he held her close, kissing her madly as she gasped into his mouth.

"Fuuucckk." That was Richard, because Hanna's mind was so full she was finding it hard to remember her own name, let alone articulate any words.

"Sweetheart, are you ready?" he asked.

She nodded, unable to speak. Letting her fall back on the couch, he grasped her hips, his fingers digging into the soft skin as he started to move inside her, his lips never leaving hers, each move punctuated by a soft pant that made Hanna's heart thud.

She moved her arms around him, hands clasping his ass, feeling the muscles flexing as he moved. She begged him to move faster, harder, as she pulled him against her. He was getting breathless, pulling his mouth away from her, to gasp for air. She got a good look at his expression, his green eyes dark with lust, his face betraying the pleasure he was feeling. Her body was still tingling, little bursts of ecstasy shooting down to her feet, making her toes curl in reaction.

"God, Hanna, I'm going to—"

"I want to feel you come." Her words were just a whisper, but she wanted him to have it all, to feel as good as he'd made her feel. His movements became erratic and harsh, until he suddenly stopped, a deep moan releasing from his mouth. Crashing his weight down on hers, he kissed her hard as he thrust a couple more times.

Hanna held him tightly, unwilling to let him go, to let him withdraw from her when she was feeling so raw. As if he understood her vulnerability, he began to move his lips against her face, her neck, whispering sweet words as they slowly came back to reality. She ran her fingertips up and down his spine, loving the feeling of his body on hers, not caring that he was crushing her. She felt him slowly pull out of her, his lips still on her skin, his hand moving down to protect the condom.

"I need to take care of this." He stood up, moving over to a door on the other side of the apartment that she could only assume led to the bathroom. Alone on his couch, she was aware of her nakedness, but couldn't bring herself to put on her underwear and dress. She was unwilling to admit the evening was over. Instead she plucked his shirt from the pile of discarded clothes, slipping her arms into it and doing up a couple of buttons to maintain some semblance of modesty. The bathroom door clicked, and she looked up to see Richard approaching, a small white towel wrapped around his hips, a smile playing on his lips as his eyes darkened in response to her clothing.

"Nice shirt."

"Thank you. Nice towel."

"Thanks." He was in front of her, pulling her up until she was firmly in his arms, his body cradling hers as he hugged her. He buried his face in her hair, and he mumbled, "I'll go get you that cup of tea now."

Ten

2nd February 2004

"WE SEEM TO have all of our most romantic moments at airports." Hanna buried her face in Richard's shirt, her wet eyes mixing with her mascara until there was an inky stain on the white cotton.

"Not quite all," he drawled, bringing his lips to hers. He brushed them softly, as he wiped away the moistness around her eyes. "I seem to remember that last night was pretty romantic."

Hanna laughed. "You seem to be getting mixed up between romance and sex. The two aren't mutually inclusive."

"For us, they are."

He kissed her again, this time without restraint, and her knees started to shake at the onslaught. The fact they were making a scene in the middle of Heathrow Airport didn't matter. Every few weeks they had to go through this parting, and it hadn't become any easier. As time passed, she was finding it hard to remember exactly why she was so opposed to moving to New York.

Then something would happen to bring her back to reality. Like the time he formally introduced her to his mother, and she received a very pointed cold shoulder. At those moments, she realized she really wasn't cut out for life in Manhattan. The only part of New York she wanted to have anywhere near her was Richard.

His kisses were getting more demanding, and she felt him drop his bag and move his hands to her waist. His fingers dug in to her soft skin as he squeezed her through her black T-shirt, trailing his lips from her mouth to her neck. Her head dropped back, allowing him access to the sensitive flesh of her throat.

"If we're not careful I'm going to end up doing a Justin on you," he murmured. The previous night they had watched the Super Bowl and had both been in fits of giggles when Justin Timberlake had pulled Janet Jackson's top down to reveal her nipple.

"If you don't stop kissing me there, I'm going to let you."

"You know, I've never watched football in the middle of the night before, but it had its advantages." The sensation of his smile against her flesh told her he was remembering the way they made their own half-time entertainment. And it didn't involve nipple piercings.

"You're going to be late." Her voice was still breathy.

"I know." His hands were moving down her hips, back to cup her behind as she felt him responding to their embrace. It took every ounce of willpower she had to put her hands up and push him away.

"It's going to take you forever to get through security." She gestured over at the long queue of travellers, snaking around the airport. "Even American Airlines won't wait for you if you're late."

Richard smirked and she narrowed her eyes at him, moving her hands in a shooing motion.

"I'll call you from the lounge, okay?" He placed a kiss on her nose.

"And from the runway, then from JFK, your car, and your apartment..." she teased.

He leaned down and kissed her one last time. "I'll see you in a month, okay?"

"I'm counting the hours."

"You don't have to count anything. Come with me now." He said it every single time.

"I can't."

"There's no such thing as can't, baby. Just won't."

"Then move to London." She was smiling through the tears, the familiarity of their interchange somehow grounding her.

"I want to—"

"But you can't." She finished his sentence for him and kissed his cheek one last time. "We'll work it out somehow."

"We'll have to because this is killing me." He bent down to pick up his bag, noticing the black mascara stain on his shirt for the first time. His eyebrows rose as he looked at her pointedly.

"What?" She tried to look innocent, but the smile couldn't help bursting through. "I was sad, so sue me."

"Remind me to buy you some tissues next time." His expression was soft as he looked at her.

"I'm leaving now." She started to back away from him, waving briefly, her eyes never straying from his.

"Without a goodbye kiss?"

"What the hell do you think we've been doing for the last half hour?" Her eyebrows knitted together in a mock-frown, as she moved a couple steps farther back.

"That was just a warm up. Now I want the final goodbye kiss."

*

THE FOLLOWING EVENING, Hanna rushed out of the *Music Train* offices on Wardour Street and into the humid Soho air. Being so close to the West End of London, the road was always thronging with people, and she followed them up toward Oxford Street, diving into the tube station along with the rest of the weekday commuters. As she stepped onto the stairwell, she felt her phone vibrate, and pulled it out of the pocket of her jeans to read the text.

Have I told you I miss you today?

She hurriedly tapped out a reply.

I've got five hours on you Larsen! I win in the missing stakes.

Taking the tube, she emerged from the station at Putney Bridge and into the cold night air. Her breath caused vapour clouds to appear in front of her as she hurried along the streets to her mum's apartment. It felt like they hadn't seen each other for a lifetime; either Hanna was away at a concert, or Diana was busy organizing an event. They'd agreed to meet that evening to catch up.

Her mother was waiting at the door when she walked up to the apartment, a big grin covering her face. She pulled Hanna to her in a huge embrace.

"Oh sweetie, it's so good to see you."

"You too. I can't believe how long it's been. We live in the same city, for God's sake."

"You've been busy, with work and Richard." Diana winked, pulling her inside by the hand and closing the door behind them. As soon as Hanna stepped into the flat, she felt a calm, familiar feeling sweep over her. Everything about this place made her feel at home.

"I ordered beef in black bean sauce for you," Diana called out as she walked into the small kitchen. "Do you want any prawn toasts?"

"Is the Pope a Catholic?" Hanna shouted back, standing up and following her mum so that she could offer to help. Diana glared at her, moving her hands in a shooing motion until Hanna got the hint, and walked back to the living room.

"How has work been?" Diana asked, her voice echoing slightly against the tiled floor of the kitchen.

"Great, I spent the day in the studio with a band recording their second album. They've gone all concept and spent most of the day playing me each track in order so I can understand their narrative."

"I don't think I understood a word of that." Diana's face was a mask of confusion.

"They're trying to tell a story with each song. They rap about this guy losing a thousand pounds, and everything that happens, and then, in the final song, he finds it down the back of his TV."

"Sounds riveting. When do I get to hear it?"

Hanna laughed out loud. Diana was a classicist, if by classics you meant Abba, Elton John, and Cliff Richard.

"It's out in April. I'll buy you a copy."

"I can't wait," Diana said dryly, carrying two lap trays into the room, handing one to Hanna along with some chopsticks.

"Aren't you hungry?" Hanna stared pointedly at Diana's plate. Only a small helping of rice and an even smaller spoonful of chicken had been placed on the white china. Glancing up at her mum, Hanna saw her hollowed cheeks. "Bloody hell, Mum, how much weight have you lost?"

She couldn't believe she hadn't noticed it as soon as she'd walked in through the door, but Diana had always looked the same to her – petite, perfectly proportioned, though maybe slightly heavier on the hips than on the chest. Whenever Hanna thought of her, she usually pictured her mother as being around

35 years old, still wearing the fashions of the mid-nineties, her unlined face smiling in delight at Hanna's latest escapades.

Looking at her now, she could see that her face was lined, the skin drawn back across the bones. The shadows under her eyes were darker and more pronounced than usual.

Diana looked down at her plate, drawing her bottom lip in between her teeth in a move that seemed familiar. Hanna watched as a single tear dropped out of Diana's left eye, falling onto the plate, bouncing slightly as it met the china surface.

"Mum, what's wrong? You're really worrying me now." Hanna put her plate down on the side table and moved over, doing the same for Diana's lap tray. Kneeling on the floor next to her mum's legs, she took both of Diana's hands in her own, squeezing them as she urged her mum to look at her.

"I've been at the hospital today. I don't want you to panic, and I know it's going to come as a shock, but I've found a lump in my breast, and they've taken it for a biopsy."

The ground shot out from under Hanna's feet, leaving her reeling and dizzy, her head trying and failing to make sense of the words. She shook it, the side-to-side movement not helping her sudden feeling of nausea.

"I said don't panic, not yet." Diana leaned forward and enveloped her in a warm embrace. "They're pretty sure it's cancer, but there are all sorts of tests and things they need to do before they can give me a prognosis."

"Why the hell didn't you tell me this before?" A surge of anger rose up through Hanna's chest. She wasn't sure what she was mad about – whether it was her mother's lack of sharing, the fact that cancer had invaded her mother's body, or the whole world in general. She grabbed hold of the emotion and stayed with it, preferring it to the sensation of hopelessness she had felt only a moment before.

"I didn't want to worry you until I knew for certain there was something wrong. It would have been awful to have you all twitchy and nervous like this, and for the lump to turn out to be a boil, or even worse, a figment of my imagination."

"Have they told you what they think they can do – what treatment you can have? I wish I'd gone with you to the hospital today." Spending the day listening to a guy rapping about losing his money seemed to be a poor substitute for supporting her mum in her hour of need.

"Sweetie, I have another appointment on Thursday, I'm hoping they'll be able to tell me more then." Diana squeezed her one last time. "Now go and eat your food before it gets cold."

Eleven

30th November 2004

OE GARFIELD SAT back in the leather captain's chair, folding his arms across his suited chest. His chocolate-brown eyes surveyed Richard with interest. The lines around them deepened into furrows as he spoke. "You did well to make the decision so quickly, Richard. If you find a cancer growing, you have to cut it out before it has time to take hold."

Richard winced at the mention of the disease. It seemed to be at the centre of his and Hanna's life. Not that the cancer Joe was referring to was of the medical kind. It was the discovery that the head of the real estate division had been taking backhanders from a number of construction companies. Even so, hearing the word was enough to send Richard's mind across the Atlantic.

Things hadn't been so easy on this side of the pond, either. Firing half of the executive team in the real estate division hadn't been his favourite job, and searching for their replacements was proving even more difficult. He had called the meeting with Joe to discuss their short-term plans.

"We need to build the division back up quickly." Richard stood up and walked over to the large picture window that overlooked the financial district. "I'm going to appoint an interim head while we let the executive search team do their job."

"It sounds like a good plan to me." Joe nodded his head as he looked at the organization chart that Richard had left on his desk. "We can't afford to take our eye off the ball when it's such a growth market."

They'd had this conversation a number of times. They were both amazed at how real estate prices were increasing exponentially, and the over-inflation of land values had made them wary. Maxwell Enterprises had agreed on a strategy of investing in the short-term while keeping their eye on the market, ready to withdraw at short notice should a downturn threaten.

Richard's biggest fear was by the time the crash arrived, it would be too late. He was trying to diversify the company's interests as much as possible, but he wasn't foolish enough to withdraw from such a lucrative part of his business.

That was why finding the right person to lead the division was so important.

"Have you heard from Daniel at all?" Joe glanced at the photograph of the Maxwell family that Richard kept on his desk, picking it up and rubbing his thumbs over the gilt frame.

"I managed to track him down to a resort near Miami. He's adamant that he won't go back into rehab, and there's little we can do to make him." Richard rubbed his head wearily. It had been a hell of a month, and it wasn't looking like things were going to get much better.

"He's becoming a big liability to this company," Joe remarked, putting the frame back on Richard's oak desk. "We're going to need a strategy for cutting him loose; we don't want to be at his mercy forever." Joe laced his fingers together, leaning forward until his elbows were on Richard's desk. "He's an addict, Richard, and you and I both know that he's never going to change. I'd hate for us to be here in a few months' time having an emergency meeting because he's sold his share of the company for drugs."

"The lawyers drew up a first refusal document, so he can't sell it without giving me the option to buy." Richard sighed, his fingers rubbing harder than ever at his temples. "I can arrange the finance easily enough if he does want to sell."

"Maybe you need to make him an offer he can't refuse."

Richard laughed. "You're making me sound like the Godfather. This is Daniel we're talking about, not Sonny Corleone."

"We just need to be prepared for the worst. There's no room for sentimentality in business. Now, I'm going to go home, kiss my wife, and get ready for this damned gala."

"You sound as excited about it as I am."

"Oh believe me, Richard, I'm probably the only person in New York who is less excited about it than you."

"Well, old man, I'll see you at the Astoria at eight. I'll be the one in the monkey suit."

"And I'll be the one with the most beautiful woman in the world on my arm, particularly since you couldn't persuade Hanna to come with you tonight." Joe gave him a small smile, knowing that the past months had placed a huge strain on Richard's relationship with Hanna. "I'm only sorry that I won't get to dance with her. Make sure you pass on mine and Emily's regards."

"I will." Richard walked across the office with Joe, opening up the large oak door to let him out, closing it softly behind him. Pulling his cell phone out of his pocket as he walked back to his desk, he checked his watch before pressing the speed dial.

"Hey." Hanna's soft voice coming down the earpiece made him smile. He sat down in his leather chair, pushing it back on its wheels until he could put his feet up on his desk.

"Hi, sweetheart. How's Diana?"

"She's having a good day, she managed to eat some soup. We even went for a short walk in the garden." Hanna sounded wistful, and his fist clenched in an effort not to throw down the phone and run to the nearest airport. Christ, he missed her.

"That sounds hopeful. I'm hoping to fly over in the next couple of weeks, once we've managed to sort out the new head of real estate." Not wanting to burden her with his troubles, he quickly changed the subject. "Joe asked me to give you his regards. He's devastated you won't be dancing with him at the gala this evening."

"Oh God, I forgot that was happening tonight, I'm so sorry." Her tone turned tearful, and Richard bit his lip in response. "I'm really upset that I can't be there with you."

"Hey, we agreed you wouldn't feel guilty about this," he chided. "You'd only be bored, anyway. I plan to run in, make my speech, and then hot tail it home."

"Richard, you know you can't do that. The only reason the tables sell for so much is all the women want to get their hands on you for a dance."

"There's only one woman I want to be dancing with tonight, sweetheart. Since you won't be there, I'll just sit this one out."

"I love you."

He could almost hear her smile.

"I love you, too. Now try to get some rest."

RICHARD'S CAR PULLED up outside the Waldorf Astoria. As he strode under the gilt-edged canopy and entered the lobby, he saw his PA waiting for him, wearing a silver ankle-length gown, her auburn hair swept up and back from her face to reveal her smiling features.

"You're late."

"I know." He held his hands up in surrender. "I only left the office an hour ago. Have I missed much?"

"Your mother was very disappointed that you weren't on her table for dinner, and I've had to give your apologies to about a thousand frustrated ladies who are desperate to mark your dance card."

"Do dance cards still exist?" He gave her a wry smile. They began walking toward the Grand Ballroom. Lisa fussed over his bowtie and jacket, smoothing them down until he was perfectly turned out.

"If they do, then along with the rest of your cards, I've marked them," she replied dryly. "Your speech is cued up on the screen of the lectern, and Jon Stewart has done a wonderful job of warming up the crowd. You just need to get in there and do your thing."

"You make it sound so easy." He grinned, batting her hands away as she tried to smooth down his hair. "And leave me alone, I'm trying to perfect the hobo look."

"You're doing a damn fine job," Lisa muttered. "And don't worry about the speech, nobody will be listening; they'll have either drunk themselves into a stupor at dinner, or they'll be planning who they're going to schmooze with next. Think of yourself as the gala equivalent of a B-movie."

121

Later that evening, he found himself standing at the bar, a glass of whisky in hand, surrounded by people that he only had a passing acquaintance with. The 3rd Annual Leon J Maxwell Memorial Foundation Dinner was being held to raise money for the families of victims of 9/11. It was only the fact that it was such a good cause that kept Richard anywhere near the Astoria that evening. With just under a thousand guests present, the foundation hoped to raise upwards of $3 million during the gala.

"Darling, there you are, I've been looking for you all over. Please don't tell me you came alone tonight." Richard looked up to see his mother approaching, looking resplendent in an emerald-green evening dress, her hair lying softly against her shoulders.

"Mother." He leaned forward and kissed her, his lips softly brushing her cheek. "And yes, I came alone, you know Hanna can't leave England right now."

"You really should find yourself a partner for times like these," she chided, ignoring Richard's reddening face. "It doesn't look right when you turn up without anybody on your arm."

"It doesn't bother me." He drained his whisky, putting the empty glass on the bar.

"How long is this going to go on, darling? I can't stand to see you turn up at these occasions on your own. You really need the support of a woman. You're far too busy to be concerning yourself with the small things." Caroline brushed a piece of lint from his sleeve. "People are starting to notice."

"I couldn't give a damn what people are saying." Richard was angry, his voice louder than he intended. "Diana is dying. What do you expect Hanna to do, fly out and leave her on her own?"

"I expect her to stand by her man, just like the rest of us would."

"Because appearances always come first," he said bitterly.

"No, because when you are in love with somebody, you want to be with them. When was the last time you saw Hanna?"

"I spoke with her this evening." His words were firm and flat, and invited no response. Caroline continued, ignoring his warning.

"Well, just think about it. If Hanna can't accompany you to important occasions such as this, having a friend to stand in would be a better option." Like his own, her words were short. She took another glass of champagne from a passing waiter before squeezing Richard's hands. "I don't mean to nag you, darling, but I worry about you. When you're not working you're either on a plane or visiting Hanna. A man like you needs somebody to look after him."

Her words hit a tender spot. Without Hanna, he felt incomplete, and to attend functions without her on his arm was difficult. It wasn't the fact that single women of a certain age seemed to make a beeline for him, because he was easily able to swat them off. It was more that he felt her absence profoundly.

They had been together – as a normal couple – for such a short time before Diana had found the lump in her breast. In the nine months since, she had gone through the ups and downs of treatment: hope, fear, and finally despair. It was understandable that Hanna didn't want to leave her for any amount of time because the doctors had given her months, not years, to live. He wasn't going to be the selfish bastard who took her away from her dying mother.

Richard felt the sickening feeling of guilt when he wished that she would fly over and see him, or that they could spend some time alone in London, without having to be with Diana all the time. An even darker part of him – one he would never admit to knowing existed – missed their physical contact, the romance, the love, and especially the sex. If you discounted his hand, he hadn't had a fulfilling assignation for quite some time.

"Have you talked about what you are going to do afterward?" Caroline asked.

"After Diana dies? I don't think that Hanna can even conceive of a world without her mother, let alone how she's going to feel, or where she's going to want to live."

"Will she ever want to move to Manhattan?"

"I don't know." Richard shook his head slowly, not wanting to follow the direction that this conversation was heading. "There are too many what-ifs and buts to even start to think about the future. I just need to concentrate on the now, and look after my girl."

Twelve

9th February 2005

*T*HE LIGHT CREAM walls were illuminated by the afternoon sun, dappled by the branches of the tree outside, as it shone through the window into Diana's room. Hanna sat on the easy chair next to her mother's bed, watching Diana's thin body as her chest rose and fell with rhythmic sleep. Her dry lips emitted wheezing sounds as she exhaled every ten seconds or so.

The past year had been a slow, downhill ride; sometimes the gradient had been so low Hanna had thought they were actually making progress. The diagnosis of stage 4 breast cancer hadn't fazed her at first. Then treatment was complicated by metastasis, and the cancer spreading led to words like *pain management, months, perhaps weeks*, and finally, *dignity*. Any hope Hanna had was completely deflated, like a birthday balloon left out in the cold.

They'd agreed to move Diana to the hospice last week, when it was clear it was only a matter of waiting. Neither Hanna nor Diana had wanted those final days to be spent in a sterile hospital environment, and St Luke's Hospice – an elegant Georgian mansion set in its own grounds – had offered a different kind of death. One where Hanna could stay with Diana as much as she wanted to, where they could walk in the grounds and see the first shoots of spring bulbs emerging from the grass. One where Diana could die without fanfare or the constant noise of hospital monitors.

"Is she asleep?" Hanna glanced up to see Claire Larsen standing at the door. Her gentle eyes crinkled into a smile, taking in Hanna's dishevelled state.

"She's been down for a while, she may wake up soon." Hanna stood up, realizing her legs had gone numb from the way she had been sitting on the chair. Her back ached, too. She stretched to try to wake up her body.

"How is she?" Claire walked into the room, carrying a Hermès bag in one hand, and a Dictaphone in the other. It was a strange combination.

"She's been out of it for most of today, but yesterday, she was lucid for the longest time; we had a great talk. Hey, what's that?" Hanna pointed at the small recording machine in Claire's hand.

"Nothing." Claire hid her hand behind her back.

Hanna looked at Claire curiously. "What are you two up to?"

Claire laughed – a quiet, tinkling sound that seemed to echo off the walls. Diana didn't as much as stir in response to the noise.

"You make us sound like teenage hooligans, Hanna. It's a secret. I promised not to tell."

"You can tell me. I won't let on."

"If I told you, I'd have to kill you, darling. Stop asking questions."

"It's okay, she's been sharing her words of wisdom with me, too. Yesterday she spent hours telling me about her life, and how she has very few regrets." Hanna frowned as she remembered their conversation.

They'd been sitting in the heated conservatory that over-looked the lawn.

"You were the best thing that ever happened to me, my darling." Diana's voice was thin, and each word was punctuated by short, sharp breaths. "I was so lucky to have you in my life. I'm thankful to be leaving you in this world. You're my masterpiece."

Hanna smiled, embarrassed at her mum's hyperbole. "You may be over-exaggerating a bit, but I'll take it." Looking up, she saw a nurse bring in a tray of tea and water. She placed it on the coffee table in front of them.

Her mother continued, already caught up in her memories. "When I married Philip, I was so in love I could hardly think straight." She gestured over to her cup of water, and Hanna held it to her mouth, allowing her to sip from the plastic straw. "I was so certain love could conquer all."

Diana closed her eyes as if she was remembering her days back in New York. Hanna, desperate for more information, prompted, "But it couldn't?"

"No it couldn't. I should never have married him, sweetheart. I knew I didn't want to live in New York, and I knew I'd hate being a banker's wife. I really thought love would be enough."

Hanna blinked, feeling the sting of tears just under her eyelids. Diana never talked about her relationship with Hanna's father; in fact she rarely spoke of Philip at all. Hanna wasn't sure whether her mother had been trying to spare her feelings, or whether it simply hurt too much to articulate. She was beginning to suspect the latter was true.

Diana managed to get her breathing back under control. "I wish I'd been able to make it work for your sake. Because I have never, for one single moment, regretted having you. I know your relationship with your father has never been easy. I have to take the blame for that."

"You don't!" Hanna protested, taking Diana's hand in her own. Her skin was cold and papery. "It would have been so much worse if I'd lived there, and suffered everything you did."

She looked over at her mother. She was staring out of the window, watching the birds perching in the bare branches of the tree to the left of the conservatory. They swooped down, landing in twos before flying off again to a higher branch. Their tiny wings fluttered as they moved.

"I broke your father's heart. I turned him into a bitter, cynical man, and it was all my fault. I should have loved him enough to let him go before things went too far." A tear ran down Diana's cheek, leaving a shiny trail along her translucent skin. Hanna simply sat and held her hand, willing her own tears to dry up.

Wiping at her nose with a tissue, Hanna tried to get her feelings under control. There was so much they needed to say to each other over the next few days. They had so little time. Each second passing was a reminder she would soon be alone, and Diana would be just a memory. She decided to hide her mother's words away for now, and reflect on them when she was ready. To think about them now would unplug the dam. She wasn't ready for that.

SLEEP WAS AN elusive commodity for her those days; she spent most of the night chasing it, and most of the following day craving it. That night, she managed to fall off sometime after 4:00 a.m. A few hours later, she was woken by the dipping of the mattress. She was so groggy it took some moments for her to realize Richard was lying next to her, still wearing his suit and his tie, his head resting on the pillow as he gazed at her.

"Hi." His voice was a whisper as her eyes opened and stared at him.

"I'm so sorry I didn't meet you at the airport—"

"Hush, you needed to get some sleep." He placed a gentle finger over her mouth. She kissed it, watching his face as he stared back at her, unable to mask his concern as he took in her thin frame and drawn expression. "My father picked me up; we even managed to grab a spot of breakfast before he dropped me off."

"That's nice."

"He sends his love. They want us to join them for dinner tomorrow night, if you're up for it."

"I don't know; I may have to be with Mum."

He pulled her toward him, until her body lay over his. Her leg hooked around his thigh, and her arm stretched out across his chest. She closed her eyes and nuzzled into the fabric of his suit, smelling the aroma of the wool mixed with the sandalwood of his cologne.

"We'll just play it by ear, okay?" His words were soothing, and she closed her eyes and submitted to their soft cadence. "We'll do what we need to do, and I'll let them know one way or another. It doesn't matter, none of this does."

She could feel his breathing – his chest gently rising and falling, making her head move up and down. Without thinking, she undid the buttons of his jacket and laid her ear against the thin fabric of his shirt until she could hear his heartbeat hammering against his chest. The heat of his body seeped through the cotton, warming her cheek, awakening feelings she'd been suppressing for weeks.

Lifting her head up, she shuffled until her face was next to his, their eyes so close it was impossible to stare into them

129

without everything going blurry. Her chest was pressed against him. The need to feel more shot through her body like a cannonball.

Suddenly she couldn't get enough.

Her kiss wasn't gentle. It was hard and fierce, and took him by surprise. She could feel his eyelids flutter against her face as he opened them and stared at her, trying to work out what she was doing. For the last few months, whenever they had been together, she had found herself unable to do more than hold him, and give him gentle kisses and soft embraces. Sex had been out of the question.

But now, she could feel her whole body tingling as she pushed her tongue against his lips, dancing along the skin until he parted them and touched it with his own. He kissed her back until they were both finding it hard to breathe. She didn't pull away. Instead she put her hand around his head and pulled him closer until she could feel her lungs start to burn.

It was Richard who broke the kiss, unable to speak through his harsh breaths. A flush of embarrassment covered his cheekbones when he glanced down and saw his erection was digging in to her hip.

"I'm sorry." He could barely meet her eyes as he spoke, instead gazing over her shoulder at the blue wallpaper.

Hanna silently placed her hand under his chin, adjusting his face until his gaze met hers. She watched as a look of confusion washed over his features. When she was sure he was looking at her, she leaned in again, brushing her lips gently against his, increasing the pressure until he could feel the desperation seeping through her every pore.

Her hands tugged at his shirt, pulling it from his trousers. She reached inside and touched the skin of his stomach. The sensation of her gentle hands against his abdomen did nothing to calm his reaction to her, making him almost painfully hard.

She unbuttoned his shirt, pulling at his trousers, peeling her own pyjamas off with shaking hands. Her heart raced as she felt her flesh against his, her response to his naked body visceral and intense.

"Are you sure? I feel like I'm forcing myself on you," Richard whispered.

Hanna pulled him on top of her, her hands reaching for him, circling around him as she tried to line him up with her body. "You've got that the wrong way round." Her eyes closed as she felt him enter her, gliding through her until he was all the way in. "I need this, Richard. I need you, please don't stop."

Thirteen

3rd July 2005

*H*ANNA WORE HER despair like an iron blanket pressing down on her body; it comforted and caused pain in equal measure, yet was somehow reassuring in its relentless misery. Like the sun rising, she could rely on it being her constant companion during daylight hours. And at night, while she lay curled up on her childhood bed, she let the hurt consume her as strangled cries fought their way out of her mouth, her hands curled up into fists as if she could somehow fight the anguish off.

It was a battle she couldn't win.

For the first month after Diana's death, it seemed right and proper that she should mourn her mother, and she didn't give a second thought to the way she felt. Richard had returned to New York a week after the funeral, begging her to join him, but the memories of Diana and the need to settle her estate anchored Hanna to London. During their separation, she felt increasingly alone, unable to answer his calls or return his emails without breaking down, finding excuses to prevent him visiting her. She wanted to conquer her depression on her own without him ever finding out just how low she felt.

But as time went on, and the flowering bulbs of spring gave way to early summer heat, her misery continued unabated.

She only left the flat for the most pressing of reasons, and even then she found herself rushing back home as soon as she could.

By June, things had reached an all-time low. She turned down any social invitations, and made every excuse not to meet with the Larsens or speak with Richard. Being with them reminded her of everything she had lost, and the jealousy she felt whenever she saw their tight, family unit consumed her. She hated herself for it.

At work, she was given a warning for lateness and absenteeism. With every word that her editor said, she had found herself nodding and agreeing with him; she was lackadaisical, uncaring, and unprofessional, and his poor opinion of her only confirmed that she was right in having an equally low opinion of herself.

Now it was 11:00 a.m. on a Sunday morning, and she was still half asleep, her hair dull and greasy. Her ten-day-old pyjamas were in desperate need of a wash. The knocking on her door was an accompanying sound to her misery, like the backbeat of a drum, and she didn't even have enough energy to drag herself out of bed to answer it.

Then the shouting started.

"I know you're in there, Hanna, open up!" The voice carried across the hallway and into Hanna's room and she closed her eyes in the hope that whoever it was would go away. Just as she snuggled back into her soft, feather pillow, she heard a key turn in the lock, then the bang of the door as it hit the wall.

Clearly she had company.

She could hear the footsteps as her visitor walked across the hall, each click becoming louder as they approached her bedroom. A sense of resignation washed over her as she realized that she would have to face whoever it was, and try to get them out of her apartment as quickly as possible. Didn't they know she wanted to be left alone?

"Jesus, it stinks in here." Ruby wrinkled her nose up as she walked into the bedroom, immediately glancing over at Hanna and seeing her curled up under three-week-old sheets.

"Go away, Ruby." Even to her own ears, Hanna's voice sounded monotonous and dull.

"I'm not going anywhere. I've finished my last exam; I've got all the time in the world to devote to making you get in the shower." Ruby wandered over to the window and yanked open the curtains, a soft shower of dust falling from the fabric to the floor below.

Hanna blinked a couple of times, trying to adjust her eyes to the morning light. A scowl covered Ruby's face and her usually calm demeanour was somehow agitated and nervy, increasing Hanna's anxiety.

"I just need to go back to sleep. I'm so tired." Hanna closed her eyes.

"Hanna, we're so worried about you. You never call Richard. You won't come and see Mum and Dad. You haven't texted me once to see how my exams are going. It's completely unlike you."

Hanna refrained from responding, because she wanted to tell Ruby that she couldn't care less how the Larsens were feeling, or how they never heard from her. She was like a cuckoo in the nest, poisoning their happy unit with her misery and jealousy, and they were better off without her.

She was so angry that she didn't have a mother to hold or love her anymore.

"I'm fine, Ruby. A bit tired, and a bit emotional, but nothing I can't handle." Hanna pulled the sheets further up her

134

body, until they were covering her face. Ruby was right; the stench in her bedroom *was* foul.

"You're not fine." Ruby's eyes were getting watery, and her voice reflected her mood. "You're anything but fine. Please let me help you."

"I just need to close my eyes. I'll be better tomorrow."

"Have you at least gone to see a therapist?"

"There's no point. I know what's wrong with me; I just can't bring myself to care."

"Why won't you call Richard? He's going out of his mind." Ruby's face started to crumple; she sucked her lips inside her mouth, biting down on them with her teeth.

"I don't know what to say," Hanna whispered. Each night, she fell asleep with his name on her lips, and awoke in the early hours of the morning with the thought of him squeezing her heart like a vice.

"He loves you, Hanna. He's going out of his mind."

"He's better off without me. I'll just bring him down, too." She let her head fall back to the pillow and closed her eyes.

"Let him come over and see you, he's desperate."

"I can't." The tears that came so easily nowadays were bubbling over from Hanna's eyes. She kept her lids tightly shut as if she could somehow cage them in.

In five months of sleepless nights, she had spent so much time thinking about her relationship with him, and still couldn't see a way forward. They had spent some time together – always when he flew over to see her for a stolen weekend – but it wasn't enough to solve any of her dilemmas. She was never going to fit into his life in New York, no matter how much she tried to change and adapt.

They were at an impasse; there was nowhere for them to go but downhill. She wouldn't live in New York, and he was unable to live in London. One of them was going to have to break the cycle.

She wasn't sure if she was strong enough.

$\mathcal{T}$WO WEEKS LATER, she was taping up the final box when the buzzer signalled the arrival of the removal company. Hanna was pleasantly surprised to see they were fifteen minutes early, and she pulled the door open wide to let them in.

Her heart dropped as soon as she saw Richard leaning on the doorjamb, his hand raking through his hair. His suit was so dishevelled, it looked like he'd spent the night in it.

She supposed he had.

"What are you doing here?"

Richard barged through the door, taking in the piles of boxes stacked in the hall. "What the fuck is this?" he asked, holding up an envelope. His tone was soft but his words were harsh, and she winced upon hearing them. "You tried to break off with me in a letter?"

"I didn't know how to tell you…"

"How about the phone. Or even wait for me to visit you. A fucking letter?" His face was bright red. He lifted the paper up and started to tear it into strips. "What the hell were you thinking…?" His voice trailed off as he looked around the room, taking in the boxes for the first time. "Are you moving?"

Hanna slowly shook her head.

Coming to a stop in front of her, Richard reached out to touch her face, and she found herself stepping backward.

"Then what's happening?" His voice was too quiet.

"I'm leaving London, I'm planning to travel."

"Why didn't you tell me? Were you just going to disappear?"

"I've written you a letter." She felt nauseous, and tried to will her body to calm down. She couldn't show him that she was falling apart.

"Another fucking letter?" His voice cracked. "Don't do this, baby, please."

Oh God, she was going to cry, or throw up, maybe both. She ran to the bathroom, slamming the door shut and turning the lock behind her. For the longest time she knelt on the cold tiled floor, her head bent over the bowl of the toilet, her body heaving. Her hands were shaking as she braced herself against the basin.

When she emerged, he was standing outside, his cell phone in his hand, shouting orders down the mouthpiece. He must have let the removal company in – there were men everywhere, dressed in overalls and carrying boxes and furniture out to the van they had parked in the middle of the street.

Hanna watched as they manoeuvred her bed and mattress out of the front door. More than anything she wanted to climb back inside and bury herself under her duvet, and put herself in storage alongside her belongings.

Richard was following her every move as he stood in the middle of the room unsmiling, his green eyes staring directly at her. It was unnerving.

"I catch a flight from Heathrow tomorrow," she blurted out, just to shatter his silence.

"Where are you going?"

"I'm flying into Sydney."

"I'll come and visit you."

"No!" Her reply was firm. "I need to do this alone."

"I can't agree to that." Any sense of anger had left his voice. Hanna realized that, despite being in the pit of despair, she was the one who was going to have to be strong.

"I'm not worth it."

His voice was little more than a whisper. "You're more than worth it, this will never be over."

Walking over to him, she wrapped her thin arms around his waist, pressing the side of her face into his chest, unsure which of them was shaking more. Tilting her chin to look at his face, she watched the tears streaking his cheeks, mirroring her own, and she stood on her tiptoes to brush her lips to his mouth.

Falling back on her heels, she walked over and picked up her bag, pulling the strap over her shoulder as she made her way to the front door.

She couldn't look at him again, knowing that to see his expression would change her mind. Instead, she closed her eyes, keeping her hand on the door handle as she swung it open, waiting for the creaking sound to stop to make sure he could hear her.

"I'm so sorry, Richard."

Fourteen

4th March 2006

"ARE YOU SURE you want to do this?" Richard looked his stepbrother straight in the eye, searching for any sign he was wavering. Daniel lifted a glass to his mouth with shaking hands, his lips twitching as he swallowed. Over the past year, his nervous tics had increased; now Richard wasn't sure what movements were intended and what weren't.

"I don't want to be part of it anymore; I can't even walk into the building. Heck, I can't even be in Manhattan without having a panic attack." Daniel's batophobia had started suddenly, after he had left rehab and attempted to stay clean. The first time he had tried to walk into the Maxwell Enterprises lobby, he'd collapsed on the ground and been taken away by ambulance.

It was almost impossible to live in Manhattan when you had a gripping fear of tall buildings.

"What are you going to do with all that money?" Richard asked.

"I'm going to find somewhere with low buildings and constant sun." Daniel gave the merest hint of a smile.

"That narrows it down," Richard had to remind himself that his stepbrother was nearly twenty-three. They had agreed to meet at the Stone Creek Inn on East Quogue, not far from the house Daniel had inherited from his father in the Hamptons. He stayed there intermittently, preferring it to the terrifying trips to Manhattan, although now he had also put this residence up for sale, along with his part of the company.

The rest of the time, Daniel flitted from place to place, staying with friends and acquaintances long enough to wear out his welcome. His drug taking seemed to be irregular although he had already had one stint in rehab this year.

"I want to travel for a while first, see what's out there. I'm not even sure I want to live in America anymore."

"What does your girlfriend think of that?" Richard couldn't remember her name. They tended to change on a monthly basis and were pretty interchangeable: blonde, statuesque, and happy to accept the gifts Daniel lavished on them.

"Marie and I split up. She started talking about engagement rings and buying a house together." Daniel shuddered visibly. "I suddenly saw my whole life flash before my eyes."

Richard remained silent, trying not to think that as a result of Daniel's decision, the one who was going to end up like Leon Maxwell was Richard himself.

The avocado salad was well dressed, and they both cleared their plates pretty quickly. Daniel grabbed a roll and smeared it with butter before stuffing it in his mouth.

"Talking of ex-girlfriends, have you heard from Hanna?"

This time it was Richard who took a huge mouthful of wine before placing his glass back down on the crisp, white tablecloth. "Ruby tells me she's still travelling."

It wasn't a lie, but it wasn't the full truth, either.

"Does she ever contact you?"

"Not really."

"Maybe I'll bump into her while I'm travelling, too." Daniel looked up as the waitress served their main courses, his eyes lighting up at the sight of his steak. "That would be neat."

Richard coughed, nearly spitting his wine out in the process. He wasn't sure if the tears it brought to his eyes were from the choking or irritation.

"It's a big world, Daniel. I'm pretty sure it would be like finding a needle in a haystack." He couldn't keep the sarcasm out of his voice.

"It would be fun, though. I miss her. She was one of the few people I looked forward to seeing when I was stuck in rehab."

"She visited you twice, three times max. I was there every week." The corner of Richard's mouth turned up a little.

"She was memorable. And she used to send me emails."

The lobster risotto turned to ashes in Richard's mouth. He remembered the emails, and the texts, and the letters, and the presents. Not to mention their physical reunions.

"I'm pretty sure she's not hanging out in a drug den in Marrakesh."

"Did I hit a sore point?" Daniel dropped his knife onto the floor with a clatter as his arm twitched wildly. He sat back in his chair and took a deep breath as a waitress brought him over a clean one. He gestured to her to pour the last of the red wine into his now empty glass.

Richard shrugged and finished his risotto, carefully placing the cutlery on his empty plate. "It's not a big deal. Anyway, we're here to talk about your plans. I need to know where you want the money transferred. As soon as your lawyer gives us the signed papers on Monday, we'll need to sort out the wire."

"Just put it in my bank account."

"I don't think that's a good idea. Do you know how much money you're getting?"

"I'm not an idiot, Richard. I do have a financial advisor."

This time, it was Richard's turn to give a wry smile. Maybe Daniel would be okay after all.

Fifteen

20th January 2007

THE PORCH HAD been decorated with balloons and streamers, like a lurid, slightly off-kilter rainbow. Ruby's name was arched over the door in glittery pink letters. Hanna stood at the bottom of the steps, her nerves getting the better of her, clutching a purple, patterned gift bag. A low throb of music was escaping the house, and flashing disco lights shone through the window, indicating the festivities were in full swing.

She wasn't sure if she could do this.

Tom had promised he'd be there all night and wouldn't leave her side for a moment. He had already arrived, having agreed to play a song for Ruby, and needing to set up his equipment. Hanna knew she would only be alone in there for a matter of minutes before she was under his protection.

But minutes were all it would take. She hadn't seen Claire or Steven since she arrived back in London last November. She was so afraid of what they might say.

"Are you coming in or what?" Ruby impatiently pulled open the front door. "You've been standing there for hours."

Hanna smiled, and ran lightly up the stairs. "Happy birthday, darling." Throwing her arms around Ruby, she squeezed her tightly.

"I'm so glad you could come. I was worried you wouldn't."

"And miss Tom's performance? I can't wait to watch you fan girl all over him." Hanna watched as Ruby's cheeks flushed.

"I don't fan girl, I just think he's a really good singer."

"You keep telling yourself that." Hanna winked and handed Ruby her present. "Don't show this to Claire or Steven. I wanted to get you something pretty to wear in bed."

"Is it sexy?"

"No!" It was Hanna's turn to blush. "But it is pretty and sophisticated, as befits a young lady. I'm not sure your parents would understand."

As she stepped inside the hallway, a feeling of familiarity washed over her, like walking into a half-remembered dream. Everything still looked the same.

"Tom told me to bring you straight to him. He's set up in the den." Ruby grabbed hold of Hanna's hand and pulled her over to the stairs leading down to the basement. "He's going to start his set in about half an hour."

"Has he told you what he's going to play yet?" Hanna asked, wondering if she would be able to blog about it later.

"No, he wants it to be a surprise."

They reached the bottom of the stairs, and Hanna could hear Tom plucking at the strings of his Les Paul guitar. As soon as they walked into the room, Tom looked up through his thick golden lashes and gave her a big grin.

"Hey you."

"Hi." She felt like a child who had just found her comfort blanket. Suddenly she could breathe again.

"Have you told her?" He had turned to Ruby, a slight frown marring his brow.

"Not yet, I thought we'd better do it down here."

"Told me what?" Hanna asked, a feeling of apprehension washing over her.

"Mum and Dad want to see you." Ruby blurted, her eyes darting over to Tom as she realized she had let the cat out of the bag.

"Right now?" Somehow she thought she'd have time before seeing them. She was so unprepared for their reactions to her reappearance in Ruby's life.

Tom rose from his chair and carefully placed his guitar in the stand. Walking over to the two of them, he put his arms around both girls.

"It's going to be okay. You had to see them again sometime."

"But I'm not ready. I don't know what to say." Somehow 'sorry' didn't seem to cover it.

"It's the perfect place to see them again. It's a party, and you can't even hear yourself think."

Hanna stepped backwards and sank down into the overstuffed plaid sofa, her heart racing at the thought of having to explain to Claire why she disappeared from all their lives. From her therapy, she knew it was a necessary step to rebuild her relationships and reopen the dialogue. Now she was baulking, wanting to delay the inevitable. She wasn't sure she could stand the rejection, or the look of derision she was bound to see in their eyes.

"Do they know I'm here yet?" It had been months since her last panic attack, but she recognized the signals immediately. She needed to get control of her breathing and work on getting the negative thoughts out of her mind. God, why wasn't she taking the medication anymore?

"I told them you'd be here pretty soon. They've already seen Tom—"

"They're delighted you're coming, you have nothing to worry about," Tom added.

"You weren't the one who left their son." Hanna pointed out. "Of course they'll be pleased to see you."

"We all know you weren't well, Hanna." Ruby stroked her hair. When did their roles get so switched? "You weren't yourself, but you're better now. Richard doesn't hold a grudge, and neither do my parents."

Closing her eyes, she reminded herself nothing was going to hurt her; she was going to be okay. She repeated the mantra her therapist had taught her: *my heart is still beating, I am still breathing, I can do this*. She inhaled through her nose, then exhaled through her mouth, gradually slowing her intake of air until her heart rate had calmed into a slow, rhythmic pattern.

"I'm okay." She attempted a reassuring smile. "I haven't had one of those for a while."

Ruby looked frightened, worrying her lip with her teeth as she continued to stare at her with wide eyes. "I'll just tell them to stay away, Hanna. You don't have to see them."

Hanna turned in her chair to look at Ruby face on. "I'll be fine." Her voice was stronger, and she hoped, reassuring. "I need to see them sometime. After all, we're almost family."

She had barely spoken before Ruby threw her arms around Hanna, nuzzling into her neck. "I'm so pleased you're back for good. I missed you so much."

"I missed you, too." Hanna found her eyes watering as she hugged her back. "I really did."

CLAIRE WAS STANDING in the kitchen when Hanna finally found the courage to go and find her. It was like the clock had turned back seven years, and Hanna was seventeen again:

146

unsure of herself and her place in life, feeling inferior compared to the rich Larsen family and their social confidence.

The absence of Richard was like a knife to the gut. Everywhere she looked there were reminders of what she'd had, and what she'd lost. A love so foolishly discarded. More than ever, she wanted to turn the clock back, to be that girl again, the one who joked with the Larsens, and helped her mum out at parties

"Hi."

Claire turned around, her blank expression transforming into a bright smile as she put her hand on her heart. "Oh, Hanna, I can't believe you're here." Dropping the napkin she held in her hand, she ran around the counter and over to the door, pulling Hanna into an all-encompassing embrace.

Hanna froze at first, surprised at the enthusiasm of Claire's welcome. A moment later, she hugged her back, burying her head in Claire's shoulders as she felt the first hot tears emerge from her eyes. She couldn't remember the last time she'd been held, not like this, and it reminded her so starkly of what she'd lost. Not just Diana – although her mother's death had been devastating enough – but Richard, too.

A moment passed before she lifted her head from Claire's shoulder, wiping the tears from her cheeks as she did. Claire moved her hands to Hanna's bare upper arms and stepped backward, looking at her with a sad smile tugging at her lips.

"I've missed you so much. Don't you ever run off again."

Her reprimand made Hanna smile through the tears. Claire pulled her into the kitchen, pushing the door behind them to give them privacy, and some protection from the loud bass pumping out from the music system.

"I'm so sorry, Claire." Hanna swallowed hard in an attempt to prevent herself from breaking down. "I don't know what I was thinking. Or maybe I wasn't thinking."

"You were in mourning for your mother, it wasn't your fault. I know you needed space, but I prayed every day you'd come home to us."

"Like a prodigal daughter?" Hanna tried to joke, though the sobs were a giveaway.

"Like a much loved family member, Hanna, and you are loved so very much. I hope you know that."

"I was so frightened you'd hate me for running away."

"I could never hate you." Claire was crying now, too. Inky, grey tears streaked her cheeks, winding down her face. They were both going to need a touch-up before they could be seen in public again. "I couldn't blame you anyway, you were so sad and depressed, and reaching out for something you couldn't find. I hoped you'd manage to discover a level of peace in Australia."

Hanna closed her eyes and thought of her time in Sydney. At first she had been lost, realizing the misery she was running away from had followed her across the world. It had been a stark wake-up call, and one which hit her hard. But, bit by bit, she managed to climb her way out of the pit of despair. It hadn't been easy or quick, and she had fallen more times than she cared to remember, but eventually she made it out into the bright light of day.

"I'm working on the finding peace part," she admitted wryly, "although it's easier said than done."

"Why don't you tell me about this new job you've got? Ruby says it's something to do with blogging, whatever a blog is?"

For the first time a genuine grin crossed Hanna's face, lighting up her eyes as she began to speak. "An old colleague has set up a website for music reviews, although she wants to expand it to include other stuff, too. I'm the music editor, which is fantastic, and although at the moment it's just me, I'm recruiting some freelancers to help out."

Claire stood watching her, a smile pulling up at the corner of her lips. "You look so animated when you talk about work, it's beautiful to see."

"It was the only thing keeping me sane," Hanna admitted. "When everything else was going to hell, it was something I could rely on."

"You could have relied on us, too." Claire's voice was low. "I want you to remember that, if you ever feel so low again."

The nerves returned as Hanna realized just how much her rejection must have hurt. If Claire was feeling this bad, then what the hell had she done to Richard?

"I will." Her legs were shaking, and she leaned on the kitchen counter to stop herself from falling. "Thank you for being so kind—"

She was interrupted by the sudden opening of the door and the swell of music it created. They both turned their heads to see Steven standing there, dressed in a pair of grey trousers and a blue sweater, his blond hair falling over his forehead.

"There you are. I think Ruby is ready for us to join them in the den." Steven smiled at Claire before realizing there was someone else there. "Oh, I'm sorry, I didn't mean to interru—"

He stopped talking the moment his eyes fell on Hanna. His mouth dropped open.

"Oh, Steven, Hanna came to the party, just like she promised Ruby she would."

Hanna looked at Steven and saw a man torn by his emotions. It was like part of him wanted to celebrate her return, and the other part was angry she left in the first place. She wasn't sure which side would win.

"Hello, Steven."

"Hanna." His response was terse.

From the corner of her eye, she could see Claire gesturing at him, although she couldn't make out what she was trying to signal. Steven raised his eyebrows and gave a slight nod. "How are you?"

"I'm good, thanks." She sounded so stilted and false, no wonder he was staring at her.

"You had us all worried for a while, especially Richard."

"Steven!" Claire's voice was a warning.

"It's okay, Claire, I know he's right. How *is* Richard doing?"

Steven walked forward and stopped in front of Hanna, his height making her feel dwarfed in comparison. He reminded her so much of Richard, from the way he stood, to the way he talked, and it both hurt and comforted her.

"I'm not going to lie to you, Hanna. He took it very hard." His words were controlled, like he was acting as a check on himself. "For a while he was as depressed as you were, but he's doing much better now. He seems to have moved on with his life, and accepted you're not coming back."

His words clattered around her mind like a can being kicked down an alleyway. It was too late. In her effort to save herself, she had killed their relationship and any respect he must have for her. Feeling a fresh sting of tears against her eyelids, she squeezed them shut again, reminding herself this was supposed to be a happy occasion; it was her best friend's birthday, and she was going to do her damnedest to celebrate.

Sixteen

12th March 2008

HANNA WAS DELIBERATELY running late, driving Tom mad with her procrastinating as she went back into the apartment. First, she had to check she'd turned the heating off. Then she wanted to make sure she had unplugged her hair straighteners. Finally, she went back in to make sure she had switched the burglar alarm back on, having turned it off the previous two times.

She knew she was putting off the inevitable, but it really didn't make her feel any better.

"Are you sure you want to go through with this?" Tom reached out and took her hand, keeping his other palm steady on the steering wheel as his car idled outside her building.

"Not really." Hanna swallowed down the feeling of nausea. She reminded herself she had gone through much worse than this before.

"We don't have to stay for too long. Let's watch the ceremony, drink the free alcohol, then drive back to town and have a party for two."

Hanna smirked. Their parties for two nowadays had toned down to a cup of tea in front of the evening news. Some days she felt much older than her twenty-five years.

"I'm not going to let the Larsens down, Tom. I promised them a real-life celebrity at the wedding, and by God they're going to get one."

Her words caused Tom to glance in the rear-view mirror. The usual black utility vehicle was following behind them, driven by his security advisor. It had amused Hanna when she first met Damon, and she found herself constantly quoting from *The Bodyguard*. She had no greater wish than to see Damon carry Tom away from a perceived threat. It would have made her day.

"They want me to take the heat off them," Tom muttered. The prevalence of cell phone cameras were making his life a misery. He was constantly complaining he "couldn't even take a slash without it being on Perez Hilton the next day".

"You're going to stay with me at all times, right?" she asked, leaning forward to switch on the radio, wincing when the drum and bass came out at full volume. "Jesus, how can you stand to listen to this shit?"

"Would you rather I was playing a Fatal Limits album?" Tom looked amused. "Because I might have a few in the glove box."

Hanna turned and stared at him, her eyes narrowing. "The new one?"

"Do you mean the recently recorded, unedited, unreleased version?" Tom was still drumming his fingers against the steering wheel in time to the cacophony emanating from the car stereo.

"No," Hanna deadpanned. "I only like hearing your old songs."

Slapping at her thigh, he reached across her and pulled open the glove box. All the CDs he had pushed inside came tumbling out onto Hanna's legs, some falling around her feet, making her scramble around to pick them up.

Ignoring her remonstrations, Tom picked up a blank CD and pushed it into the stereo, the soft sounds of a piano soothing Hanna's ears.

He lasted a couple of minutes into the first song before he asked her what she thought.

By this time, she had stuffed the glove compartment full again and snapped it closed, making a mental note to never let it be opened in her presence. It was an accident waiting to happen.

"It's a change from the last album," she ventured, her brow dipping as she concentrated on the music, noting the guitar-based band was going heavy on the electronics. A discordant bass seemed to thread its way through all the tracks.

"We wanted to try something new." Tom attempted a nonchalant shrug then, noticing Hanna's concentration, he shut up and let her listen.

They remained silent throughout their hour-long journey. Hanna was so intent on listening to the music, she barely noticed when Tom pulled the car into the driveway and came to a halt. It was only when she looked up that she realized they were at the venue, ready to see the eldest Larsen son be married off to his fiancée of a year.

She let out a puff of air, staring straight ahead at the dashboard as she reminded herself she gave up the right to feel this way three years ago.

Richard had every reason to move on. She had all but begged him to. She had told him there was no hope for them, and she didn't want him to follow her.

So why the hell did she feel so low?

"You ready?" Tom pulled the key from the ignition and leaned toward the rear-view mirror, pulling his lips over his teeth and rubbing them with his finger, as if he was checking for bits in between them.

"Yes." Hanna pulled the door open and slid her legs around, smoothing the tight blue dress over her thighs. The heels of her stilettos buried themselves into the gravel, and she found herself having to work extra hard to walk across the driveway.

"Wipe that smirk off your face, McLean," she growled, as Tom watched her efforts with amusement. "Otherwise you're gonna have to carry me."

"I'd love to, but I've got a world tour coming up. I don't want to do myself an injury."

They were ushered into the main ballroom, which had been set up for the wedding ceremony. Hanna and Tom sat in the back row of chairs, both of them hoping to dip somewhere under the radar – albeit for different reasons.

The few minutes before the ceremony was due to begin allowed Hanna the chance to look around without being watched, and she luxuriated in her anonymity. She could see Claire and Steven, seated in the front row, along with Ruby and Claire's mother, Lillian, who was still going strong at ninety-three.

Then Hanna's heart began to race.

In front of them, Richard and Nathan stood to the right of the room. Neither could stand still, and she watched as Nathan jabbed Richard in the side, swiftly followed by a return slap on the arm from Richard. Claire leaned forward and said something to them and, whatever it was, it made them both crack up with laughter. Hanna gasped as she saw Richard's profile as he turned, the sunlight through the front window creating a halo effect behind his head.

He was still as beautiful as she remembered. She traced the line of Richard's straight nose, past his lips and to his razor-sharp jaw. She couldn't tell from here if he was clean shaven

– although she assumed he was – but somewhere in her mind the memory of breakfasts in bed, stubbled jaws and clothes strewn around the room came to the surface, causing a prick of tears to her eyes.

Richard leaned down and whispered something to the woman seated beside Lillian, and the girl reached out and smoothed down his jacket. Hanna held her breath as Richard looked at the girl, his smile gentle and crooked. Ruby had already told Hanna about Meredith, Richard's fiancée.

Before Hanna could find an appropriate reaction to the scene playing out before her, the 'Wedding March' started, and everyone turned to see Nathan's fiancée, Lucy, walking down the aisle on her father's arm, followed by an assortment of bridesmaids. Turning to watch the bridal procession also alerted the guests to Tom's presence. Hanna watched in angry astonishment as more than a few people started to take pictures with their camera phones, ignoring the bride altogether.

She began to wonder if bringing a famous singer to a Larsen wedding was such a good idea.

"Looks like the cat's out of the bag," she whispered. Tom tried to act nonchalant and ignore the flashes. "I'm so sorry."

"It happens all the time," Tom replied, glancing over his shoulder to see a security guard trying to remain invisible at the back of the room. "Don't sweat it, Hanna. I'm here for you."

They had debated back and forth for days whether she should even attend the wedding. At first she thought it had been a cursory invitation, only issued in the hope she would refuse it. But both Claire and Nathan had called and urged her to attend, and promised her there would be no weirdness between Richard and her. Claire had even gone as far as suggesting Tom be her 'plus one', no doubt urged on by Ruby, who maintained an impressive devotion for the singer.

After the ceremony, they moved into the dining room for the customary wedding breakfast. She and Tom were sat at a round table full of twenty-somethings in the middle of the room. Hanna couldn't stop herself from sneaking glances at the top table, her eyes seeking out Richard, her gaze lingering on his face.

"You need to stop looking over there," Tom whispered to her, after a particularly long stare. "Eventually he's going to notice."

Hanna blushed and dragged her eyes away yet again. Glancing at her watch she wondered how the hell she was going to get through the rest of the day. She wasn't sure if she could go for another eight hours without making a fool out of herself.

"Keep reminding me," she replied, before turning to the guy called 'Mosh' who sat on her left. He was trying to regale her with a particularly lurid anecdote involving Nathan, a forgotten toothbrush and a toilet scraper. Hanna was pleased she'd finished her food before he started his story.

The toasts followed dinner, and when Richard rose to give the best man's speech, she felt Tom put his arm around her shoulders once again. Hanna leaned into him, grateful he was there to support her. To hear Richard talk about true love was like a knife to the heart, no matter how light hearted and funny he made his speech. His lips moved softly as he spoke, and occasionally his eyebrows rose up to accentuate a joke, at which point the guests all joined in the laughter. Her favourite part was when he made the toast to the happy couple. She watched as he picked up his champagne to take a sip, and his pronounced Adam's apple bobbed below the taut skin of his neck.

As afternoon darkened into evening, the guests returned to the ballroom for the entertainment. A band had set up in the corner, playing modern, middle-of-the-road music, which both Hanna and Tom found amusing. Slowly, people trickled onto the dance floor, fuelled up with alcohol and food and ready to bust a move.

Tom wandered to the bathroom, promising Hanna he would return as quickly as he could. She found herself at the bar, ordering a beer in the hope it would lend her some of that Dutch courage people always talked about.

"Hi."

Hanna turned to see Richard standing alongside her. Meredith was next to him, her petite frame somehow accentuating his broad chest. Hanna's mind momentarily blanked, and she could feel her panic starting to rise as she tried to think of something to say.

"Hi." It wasn't much, but it helped her avoid looking like an idiot.

"Hanna, I'd like you to meet Meredith Devries. Meredith, this is Hanna Vincent." Hanna automatically shook the girl's hand, surprised at her soft skin and limp wrist.

"It's a pleasure to meet you, Meredith." Hanna was surprising herself with her social graces. They were like a reflex action. So ingrained, that saying the words was automatic.

"You too. Are you a friend of Lucy's?"

Richard had never told Meredith who she was? Hanna found this interesting, and for the first time turned to look at him. He stared right at her, focused on her face, but not her eyes. It was like he was gazing at her lips, and for some reason she found herself moistening them with the tip of her tongue.

"No, I'm Ruby's friend." It was as good an explanation as any.

"Hey, what have I missed?" Tom's voice was like cold lemonade on a hot day, and Hanna reached out to take his hand.

"Richard was introducing me to Meredith." Hanna replied.

"Oh my goodness, you're that singer aren't you? My sister loves your music." Meredith's smile lit up her face, and Hanna found herself cataloguing all the reasons she hated beautiful American women.

"Ah, thanks. Are you a music fan?"

Meredith leaned forward and whispered, conspiratorially, "I don't really listen to music at all."

Hanna's eyebrows shot up as if they were trying to merge with her hairline. She was trying not to look amused, but clearly failing. Her eyes automatically moved to look at Richard. As soon as he looked back at her, a grin broke out and Hanna found herself returning it.

God, it felt good.

Despite the band's mediocrity, Hanna and Tom made an ironic attempt to dance. She collapsed in a fit of giggles when he started throwing himself all over the place in a parody of John Travolta, causing more than a few cell phone cameras to be turned to 'video'. She couldn't help but feel grateful to him, for supporting her at the wedding, for throwing himself under a bus to make her smile. He was a true friend.

Ruby joined them after a while. Wanting to give her at least something to talk about when she returned to university, Hanna gestured to them she was going to the bathroom, leaving Tom and Ruby performing an interesting rendition of the Macarena.

It was getting late, and the guests had thinned out. The bathroom was empty when Hanna walked in. It was elegantly decorated with guest towels and Molton Brown soap – no hand dryer and blue soap for guests at Chalkley Manor.

Rubbing hand lotion into her palms, she opened the door to walk outside, only to see Richard standing right there, his face serious, his lips thin. His brows were knitted together into a frown.

"Can I ask you something?" He gently pushed her back into the bathroom, and Hanna felt her heart beat faster at the sensation of his hand as it circled her wrist. They'd both been drinking all night, and she wondered if it was him, or the drink, talking.

"Yes." It was the only reply that sprung to mind, and she breathed it out like her life depended on it.

"Are you and Tom fucking?"

Hearing him say it made her eyes fly wide open and her mouth drop. For a moment she felt angry, for his intrusion and his coarse language. But her face softened as she started to wonder his reasons for asking.

"No, we're just friends." She watched as relief washed over his face, and suddenly she felt angry again, knowing he had somebody new and she was all alone.

Even if it was her own fault.

"In fact, Richard, since you asked so nicely, I haven't fucked anybody in three years." The implication was there; he was the last man she had slept with.

He moved closer, so their bodies were inches apart, and she felt herself stiffen in reaction to his proximity. A tiny step forward and their chests would be touching. All she'd have to do would be to tip her head up and allow him to dip his down, until their lips met in an explosive kiss.

And she could guarantee it would be amazing. The way they were both breathing heavily, they were seconds away from acting on it.

"Why not?" His voice was strained, and she could see his hands curl into fists, as if he was trying to stop himself touching her.

Hanna hesitated. The answer was dancing on her lips, playing on her tongue, but to say it would be to let him know exactly how she felt about him. Was she ready for that?

She found herself leaning toward him, and though they were both fully clothed, she felt raw and exposed. His eyes searched hers, and she felt the need for honesty, to throw herself before him and admit what she'd done.

"Because it's only ever been you."

A flush crept up his face, and his expression changed from confusion to complete and utter rage. Hanna stepped back, fearing his response. He let out a furious growl before turning and slamming his fist into the mirror attached to the bathroom wall, making it shatter into jagged shards and fall over the basin and onto the tiled floor.

The seconds that passed seemed like hours as they were both glued to the spot, unable to move in the face of her revelation and his reaction. Richard was cradling his wrist, and Hanna moved to touch it, seeing blood beading at his knuckles, wanting to do something to take the pain away.

The physical pain, at least.

"You can't do this." Richard's face was still feral. He unclasped his hand and moved it up to lift her chin. "You can't come waltzing back into my life and tell me you only ever wanted me. Admit it's a lie."

Hanna shook her head, unwilling to answer his demand.

"Fuck it, Hanna. Sitting out in the ballroom is the girl I've asked to marry me, and she doesn't have a goddamned clue what's going on. Do you expect me to break her heart, the way you broke mine?"

"No." The tears were flowing now, and she could feel them running down her cheeks. "I'm so sorry."

She meant it. About everything.

Richard reached out his injured hand and shakily drew it down her cheek, wiping away her tears, until he reached her mouth. His thumb lingered at her lips, touching them so lightly she could barely feel it. Knowing he was close to the edge, she stood very still, unable to move for fear of what he could do.

"I'm going to go now, and I'm going to try to forget every word you said to me." Richard leaned toward her, and brushed his lips against her wet cheek. It took every ounce of strength Hanna had not to turn into the kiss and press her mouth against his. "Please don't follow me, or try to talk to me, I don't think I'd be able to restrain myself."

"Okay." Hanna's voice was still a whisper, and she stood still as a statue among the debris of glass scattered over the floor.

Richard backed away from her, never once averting his gaze until he reached the door. After pulling it open, he turned to look at her one last time.

"I've never seen you looking as beautiful as you do right now."

Seventeen

19th February 2009

RICHARD SCANNED HIS eyes down the list of new rentals, barely listening as the head of the real estate division took the board through the quarterly business review. Since the subprime disaster the previous year, the division had been haemorrhaging dollars, and he had to keep a much closer eye on what used to be regular transactions.

New rules had been created, including more severe credit checks, increased deposits and a deep dive into their renters' accounts, ensuring they were renting to companies that had a future.

"What's this one?" Seth Brown pointed to a small transaction at the bottom of the first page. "Buzz Media sounds like a bit of a risky choice."

"They're an internet media company based in London." Nick Martin, the head of real estate, pushed his lanky dark hair out of his eyes. "They've passed all our checks, and our realtor has met with their representative, and has given me a full rundown."

"How long have they been in business?" Richard asked, turning the pages in front of him until he found the more detailed transaction.

"Nearly three years; they're not a start-up. One of the partners has flown out to set up their New York office; she's the one our realtor has been dealing with."

Maxwell Enterprises owned real estate across the country, and rarely dealt directly with their renters. Instead they employed a third-party to manage the rentals for them, and only recently had Richard even had to play a role in making sure the leases were signed with companies that weren't about to fold.

It was a sign of the times.

As he reached the bottom of the page, he saw her name, and did a double take. The last person he ever expected to see renting a property in Manhattan was Hanna Vincent.

"Are you sure they're in it for the long term?" He stared at her name again. His mouth felt dry as he tried to take in the news.

"Absolutely, they're in the process of recruiting a director to be based over here. Their representative from London assures me it is a long-term deal."

Richard leaned back and steepled his fingers, allowing the rest of the board to continue asking questions as he pondered the fact she was back in New York. After all she'd said about this town, and all the times she'd refused to move here when they were together. Now she was living here, and he hadn't even known it.

He chuckled quietly, berating himself for even thinking about her. The last time he'd seen her – at Nathan's wedding – he'd made it clear he didn't want her to contact him again. So why would he expect her to tell him, after he had been so adamant that night? But the knowledge she was living only a few miles away from him came like a bolt from the blue.

The bigger question was why his father hadn't let him know, and Richard was pretty sure he knew the answer to that. Steven had seen the state he had been in after she'd left him, and had even noticed their meeting at Nathan's wedding. He'd left Richard in no doubt how he felt about him following her into the bathroom.

The door of the conference room opened, and Lisa poked her head around the door, pointing to the phone she held in her hand. Richard got the message and pushed himself up to standing, wandering over to the door and whispering to his assistant.

"Who is it?"

"It's Meredith, she says it's urgent. She has your mother with her."

Richard pulled the door closed behind him and walked into the corridor, lifting the handset to his ear.

"Meredith?" He didn't mean to sound quite so severe, but they'd already discussed the frequency of her calls, and what was urgent to her didn't always mean he should be disturbed during a meeting.

"Richard, we're at the Westchester Country Club." In the background, Richard could hear his mother's voice as she whispered something to Meredith. "It looks amazing, their wedding services are fabulous. And they've recommended the most fantastic planner. She's not cheap, but she's the best and we really need to give her a call."

"Couldn't this wait until tonight?"

"But I'm going away tomorrow, and I want to call and make us an appointment. If we don't get in soon, they're going to be fully booked. They're already full until summer 2011." Her voice was breathless with excitement, and Richard closed his eyes momentarily, wondering why he had to get involved with the organizing at all.

"Give them a call, then, and set something up. You'll have to tie up with Lisa about timings."

Meredith squealed into the phone, causing Richard to pull the earpiece away from his face. A small smile tugged at his lips.

"So summer 2011 is the plan, right?" He wondered if he could cope with these phone calls for the next two years.

"Of course, it's going to take that long to plan everything."

$\mathcal{I}$T HAD TAKEN a few phone calls, but he'd managed to glean some more information about Buzz Media, and their New York office. The company had been prospering despite the recession, mostly due to their ability to create an interesting website with a limited budget. The expansion in the US was generally seen as a good move for them.

This was the sort of crap Richard never got involved in. The transactional value was way too low for him to show more than a cursory interest, and all indications showed the company was sound. Which was why he was almost shocked to find himself sitting in the back of the car, on the way to Tower 6, to see why Hanna Vincent was working in Manhattan.

Jack pulled the car up outside the office block in midtown, and Richard asked him to wait, not planning for this meeting to take very long. He wanted a few answers – felt he deserved them – before he could go back to his work, his fiancée, and his plans for the future.

His best laid plans.

The unit let to Buzz Media was on the third floor and had an uninspiring view. It was one of their cheaper offices, and Richard wasn't surprised by the low-budget fittings and cheerful colours that greeted him as he stepped out of the elevator.

Buzz's newly hired receptionist took her job seriously, and took a long look at Richard's security pass before she allowed him through the door. "Miss Vincent is through the second door on the left. I'll give her a call and let her know you're here." She let go of his pass and he placed it back in his pocket.

"No need, I'm an old friend. I want to surprise her, Amanda." His voice was low and confident. He always found using the receptionist's name got him what he wanted.

Richard walked around the corner and pushed open the door, smiling as he heard music pumping through an iPod dock. Hanna was standing with her back toward him, leaning over a catalogue, her hair cascading over her shoulders.

His fingers twitched with the tactile memory of those silky locks between them. Trying to ignore his own reaction, he cleared his throat, causing Hanna's head to shoot up, and her body to whip around.

For a moment, she stood and stared, and he waited for her to respond. He wasn't sure whether he was expecting a warm welcome or an angry tirade, but he was taken aback when a huge grin slowly spread across her lips.

"You shocked me." Hanna's eyes glistened as she placed a hand on her chest, as if to calm her racing heart.

"I didn't mean to." His voice was lower than he'd expected, and he cleared his throat again. "I can come back later—"

"Goodness, no." She walked around her desk and over to him, stopping when she was a few feet away. "It's lovely to see you."

"You, too." He marvelled at the way she still looked the same, her soft creamy skin highlighted by her flushed cheek-bones, her dark brown eyes looking so alive. She was the girl he had first met all those years ago. He tore his eyes away from her face and tried to remind himself he was angry with her. It was difficult when she was looking so damned enchanted to see him.

"So what brings you here? Did Claire tell you I was in New York?"

"No, you happen to be renting office space owned by Maxwell Enterprises. I decided to come and check you out." He suppressed a grin at the meaning of his words. "You, as in Buzz Media, not you as in Hanna Vincent."

Hanna laughed, tucking her hair behind her ear, and sat down on the front corner of her desk. "Are we going to pass muster?"

"I don't know yet. Why don't you tell me why you're here?" His tone was nonchalant, but he was beyond interested to hear more. He pulled out a chair and sat down, leaning forward, keen to hear her response.

"I was conned," she admitted, shrugging her shoulders. "My boss cajoled me until I agreed to come out and set up the New York office. Nobody else was available, they're all having babies or completely loved up, and I was the only one with dual nationality. Before I'd even had time to think, I was walking through the baggage reclaim area, wondering how the hell I got here."

Richard smothered a grin at the thought of Hanna standing in the middle of JFK, realizing somehow she had moved to New York despite her best efforts to never do so. The irony wasn't lost on him.

"Where are you living?"

Hanna started to swing her leg, drawing his eyes to her short skirt, leading to the long, smooth skin of her thighs. "I'm squatting at Steven and Claire's apartment. I think I might be bringing down the tone of the neighbourhood."

"Too many drugs and parties?" Richard joked, trying to look anywhere but her legs.

"Not enough manicures and haircuts." They both glanced at Hanna's torn nails before she moved her hands behind her, trying to hide them from his scrutiny. "And apparently sneakers aren't the appropriate footwear for a lady over the age of twenty."

"Have you been talking to Olivia?" he asked, remembering the way Hanna's stepmother used to criticize everything about her. She shook her head with a grin.

"Oh, how rude of me, I forgot to ask after Meredith. How is she?"

"She's good, going crazy planning the wedding. I'm hoping she won't turn into a bridezilla." He looked closely at her face to gauge her reaction, but she remained placid and open, her lips curled as she returned his gaze.

"It's the moment every girl dreams about, I'm sure she's allowed to be a prima donna about it." Hanna's voice was quieter now, and he began to wonder if she was putting on a facade. Or was he kidding himself?

"Do you dream about it?" As soon as the words escaped his mouth, he wanted to take them back. He watched Hanna's face fall and her brows dip.

"I don't allow myself to dream, Richard. I'm trying to stay in the here and now."

The urge to gather her in his arms and pull her against him was gut-wrenchingly strong. She was such a mix of the girl he knew before, and the one he had glimpsed after her mother's death. Her sudden vulnerability made him feel almost angry, and like a caveman, he wanted to drag her away and hide her from the world.

"How long are you planning to stay?" He tried to keep his voice light.

"At least five more months. There's so much to set up,

and I still haven't recruited the right person to run the place yet."

"Give my head of HR a call. She might be able to talk you through some strategies." Richard pulled his cell from his pocket and scribbled down a number on a piece of paper, holding it out for Hanna to take. She smiled at him before hesitantly reaching her hand out and placing her fingers on his.

The instant their skin touched, she pulled back as if she was burned, leaving a corner of torn paper in his out-stretched fingers.

"I'm sorry." She looked down at the ground. "I'm a little jittery."

"It's okay. I guess I'd better go anyway. It was great to see you again."

"You, too. Thanks for dropping by."

"Would you like to join me for dinner next week?" It was like the words came from nowhere, but he couldn't regret saying them; his whole body tingled at the thought of seeing her again. "It would be great to catch up."

"That sounds nice."

"I'll let you choose the restaurant." He needed to get out of there now, before he did something he was going to regret. He scribbled his cell number on another piece of paper, wondering if she still remembered it, as he'd kept the same one all these years. Passing it to her, he kept his fingers well away from hers, knowing neither of them could take the shock of contact again.

Leaving her with a goodbye, he strode back through the corridor, feeling grateful the elevator took only a few moments to arrive. As he walked inside, he leaned his fevered head against the cool mirror, trying not to look himself in the eye as he wondered exactly what the hell he was doing.

Because to all intents and purposes, it felt like he was about to fuck up his life.

Again.

T HE CHERRY BLOSSOM Café was only a few blocks from her apartment. Hanna had chosen it because she knew the owners, and loved the laid-back atmosphere they created in the evening. In the basement they held performances each night. Sometimes, a band would play. Other nights there would be poetry recitals, or even small one-off plays. You never knew what you were going to get, you just turned up, ordered your food, and hoped for the best.

The fact they would have something to distract them from the need to make small talk played a big part in her choice. She was afraid of the intimacy of a sophisticated dinner-for-two, but was equally wary about the heated adrenaline of a gig. The café was the best of both worlds; there would be a table between them, but they wouldn't feel alone.

Hanna had loved this place since the first time she'd stepped inside a few months before. Alone, and slightly nervous, she'd aimlessly wandered the streets near her apartment, and as soon as she pushed the door open, it had felt like home. The dark-blue matte-painted walls, and the battered wooden floor, offered a level of unpretentiousness she'd valued, and the warm welcome of Alonso and his wife, Elaine, had only added to her comfort.

Walking in, she waved at Elaine who was taking orders from a large group in the corner, her black hair piled high on her head, and her sixties-style geometric print dress comple-menting her curvy figure. Elaine pointed over at a table at the back, a few feet away from the performance stage, and Hanna tried not to laugh when she realized they'd have the prime position for watching poetry. She hoped Richard was ready for it.

The table was empty, and the thought she'd arrived before him buoyed her up, so she wasn't feeling nervous anymore. They were two old friends, meeting for dinner and a chat, and she was totally up for that.

And then she saw him.

Blood like acid shot through her veins, her heart hammering against the cage of her chest, making want and need pierce her body like sharp icicles. She stared in appreciation as he leaned on the bar, his face in profile to her. Her eyes traced his jawline from his ear to chin, appreciating the sharpness of his bone structure, and the way his dark stubble defined it. He was leaning in, talking to Alonso, who was handing him a bottle of beer. Even from this distance she could see he was smiling, the pull of the skin surrounding his eyes telling her it was genuine.

As he picked his beer up, Richard turned toward her, wearing dark trousers, with a white shirt tucked in. She thought maybe he had come straight from the office, deciding to remove his tie and roll up his sleeves as a concession to the casualness of the evening. He'd undone two or three buttons on his shirt, exposing a few inches of chest, and she saw a fine dusting of hair curling against his skin.

"Are you ready to be seated, Hanna?" Elaine's voice shocked her back to the present.

She swallowed down the memories and turned with a smile. "Yeah, looks like my guest has arrived." She motioned in the direction of the bar. "I'd better go say 'hi.'"

"Go get seated and I'll bring you a drink. Sancerre?"

"Sounds great."

As she approached the bar, Richard noticed her, pushing himself up from the stool to stand. The sleeves of his shirt were slightly crumpled, and she couldn't help but look at the way his forearms emerged from the rolled-up cuffs, all warm skin and golden hair, the lines of his tendons firm and clear.

Memories of rough hands and soft lips assaulted her mind as she inhaled deeply. Just one step further and her face would be against his chest. She had to scrape her scant nails against her palms to stop herself from doing it.

"Can I get you a drink?" Richard asked, bending down to kiss her on the cheek. It was barely a second of contact, but it was enough to make her feel like she was on fire.

This was such a bad idea.

Why had she ever thought she could handle this? Hanna had seen this as a chance to redeem herself, a way to apologize to him for her disappearing act. She wanted to wish him well for his future with Meredith, but instead she was transported back in time, to those golden months when their lust had exploded, before her mother's illness had ripped her heart in two.

"Elaine's bringing me one over. Shall we sit down?" She managed to keep her voice nice and even. Perhaps if she played the part of a friend, her mind would eventually catch up.

They walked to the table, Hanna leading the way, and without him in her eyeline she managed to regain a little equilibrium. It lasted for all of two seconds, until they were seated at the small bistro table, the warm glow of the candle reflecting off their faces.

"I don't think I've ever been here before," Richard said, lifting the paper menu from the table and glancing at it. "It seems a nice place, though."

"I thought you must know it, since it's only a few blocks from your dad's apartment."

He shrugged, taking a sip of his beer before glancing up from the menu. "I guess we must have missed this one. Do they do breakfast?"

"I think so. I don't really eat before lunch, so I've never asked."

"I remember." He grinned wryly, and she thought her heart was going to stop.

"I never really got to apologize to you," she babbled, trying to find a way to fill their empty conversation. "About the letter. And me leaving."

His smile dropped. He placed the menu carefully back down on the table, smoothing the wrinkles with his palm. Looking back up at her, his face was a picture of calm. "You want to talk about that?"

She nodded. Even if they never saw each other again – and with her stupidity and faux pas it was a distinct possibility – she wanted to offer him the one thing she had left. Her regret.

"I want you to know I appreciate everything you did for me. When mum was so ill, you were the only one who kept me going. I know they say you hurt the ones who love you most, but it's no excuse for me upping and leaving." She ran her fingers nervously around her wine glass, smoothing out the beads of condensation. "If it's any consolation, and I'm sure it isn't, I pretty much want to kick my own ass for what I did."

His responding laugh was light. "I'm not sure I come out of this with a gold medal. For what it's worth, I'm sorry for the way I treated you at Nathan's wedding. I don't usually get violent in bathrooms."

A brief vision of a tiled floor covered with glass. "I pretty much deserved that, too."

"You're being hard on yourself; I've come to terms with it all. What's done is done, and hopefully we've both come out of it a little wiser."

His magnanimity cut her to the quick. Either he was truly over it, in which case she should be happy he'd moved on, or he was a damn fine actor.

"Tell me about Australia."

She smiled at his attempt to change the subject, deciding to take the proffered olive branch. "It seems such a strange time, like remembering a Christmas when you were a small child. When I look back, it's like I'm seeing someone else, a different me, who took over my life for a while." She shrugged. "I don't know, maybe I have multiple personality disorder or something."

"Did you keep in touch with anybody?" His words were light, but she glanced up to see if his eyes were giving anything away. They weren't.

"Ruby, of course, and I had to keep in contact with Jamie and Natalie for work reasons. I met up with Tom and the band once, when they played in Sydney, but that was a clusterfuck. I ended up getting drunk and crying all night, and they were too scared to let me go home. They thought I might do something stupid."

Something flashed in Richard's eyes, and she tried to define it, wondering if it was a trick of the candlelight. Taking a sip of the wine Elaine had given her, she continued. "It took me a while to realize you can't outrun depression, and eventually I knew I needed to go home. I was putting off the inevitable. There's a certain comfort in being with the ones you love."

She glanced at him nervously, embarrassed at her own

words. He must have been thinking them through as much as she was. He held her stare for a moment too long.

Sensing his discomfort, she changed the subject. "So, tell me about Meredith, she seems like a lovely girl."

"She is," he agreed, the tenseness of his facial muscles belying his unease. "We met at an art exhibition."

"I bet Caroline loves her," Hanna drawled, trying to coax a smile from him.

He nodded amiably. "They appear to share the same taste in wedding venues at least."

"Have you set a date?"

He shrugged, his face turning serious again. She wondered why the smile had disappeared. "We're looking at 2011, just need to firm up the plans."

As Elaine brought over their main courses, he changed the subject again, explaining how the recent economic downturn had impacted Maxwell Enterprises, and their attempts to shore up their income stream. She asked him about Daniel, and tried not to let him see the tears forming in her eyes when he explained about the buyout, and Daniel's recent difficulties.

Whether it was the impact of the alcohol, or the relief of unburdening their regrets, the atmosphere between them had loosened by the time the poetry performance started. Elaine had cleared the table, leaving their drinks, and Richard moved his chair around to sit beside Hanna, so he could get a better view of the stage. The fabric of his shirt brushed her bare arm, and she didn't know whether to stay put, or pull away.

His closeness unnerved her.

"If they try to pull me up and recite poetry, I expect you to save me, okay?" he whispered in her ear, making her lips pull up in amusement.

"I'm so going to volunteer you." She grinned at him wickedly. "I can't wait to hear your poem about the economic downturn."

"I imagine it would be something like… oh hedge fund of mine, you led to the subprime, we thought derivatives were it, but landed us in the…"

"Hush." She hit him lightly on the arm, pulling her hand back in embarrassment. "I swear I'm going to bring you to open mike night if you don't behave."

"You started it." His voice turned to a whisper as a woman swept up onto the stage, her dark flowing skirt creating a dramatic entrance as it flared out behind her.

They were silent as she began her recitation; her dramatic words accompanied by an over-enthusiastic steel drummer. She showed no stage fright or discomfiture at all, and though Hanna had little interest in poetry – despite having a degree in literature – she couldn't help but be impressed by the way the poet threw herself into it. Even Richard managed to keep fairly still, only having to hide his amusement with a cough a couple of times. Hanna swallowed the impulse to poke him in the ribs.

He was sitting so close to her; it felt unnatural to hold herself so stiffly. As if they were still together, her body wanted to lean to the right, put her head on his shoulder and her palm in his. His thigh was barely an inch away from her own, and she kept glancing at the hand he had resting lightly against it, willing it to move until he was touching her skin.

Was he feeling the pull as strongly as she was?

Hanna wanted to slap herself for even thinking it. He was engaged to somebody else, and he wasn't hers to lean against.

It didn't stop her body from wanting, though. Her back started to ache with the effort it took to maintain her rigid pose. In her mind she could picture exactly how her cheek would feel, leaning against his chest, soaking up the warmth of his body through his shirt. She burned to feel the rhythmic movement of his ribcage as he exhaled, the reassuring sound of his heart beating against her ear. She was thankful when the performance was over.

Eighteen

28th August 2009

IT WAS NEARLY evening by the time he pulled into the gravelled parking lot. Richard found he had to pause a moment to rearrange his features, reminding himself that it was all going smoothly.

Out of all the charitable efforts the Maxwell Memorial Foundation supported, Camp Leon was the one that touched Richard's heart. It wasn't about glitzy clothes, or seeing and being seen. It was about the children, the offspring of those who had died, and those who had barely survived. For six years, he'd watched them grow, some of them turning from young children into angry teenagers who couldn't understand their place in the world. Others were maturing into amazing men and women who returned as counsellors. They all had a special place in his heart.

The foundation bought the abandoned campground in 2002. In the first year they rebuilt the cabins, making the area safe by clearing out the long-abandoned lake. By 2003, they were able to hold their first series of camps, offering them to the children of 9/11 free of charge. For some of the kids it was their only chance to escape the introverted air of the city; for others it was their one opportunity to act their age. The only difference between Camp Leon and other, less specific camps was that they employed a number of therapists to help the children open up and discuss their bereavement in a safe environment.

"Richard, you made it!" Ruby ran over and hugged him tightly, a beaming smile plastered across her face. "Can you hear the music? The kids are all raving about it."

The concert was a new addition this year. Back in March, during a visit to *The Buzz*'s New York office, he'd confided in Hanna that some of the teenagers were sick of the usual camp fare. They'd been through six years of canoeing, climbing, and swimming, and Richard wanted to offer them something different. He couldn't for the life of him think what that would be.

She'd surprised him by suggesting a teen-only music camp, offering to organize the activities and participants herself. Five months later, she'd managed to call in enough favours to put on a full-scale concert on the final day, as well as various workshops throughout the week. She'd taken a week's leave from work to be able to run the camp. His only regret was that work had kept him in the city until today.

"It sounds great." Richard hugged his sister, trying not to chide her for her short mini-skirt and tank combination. It was over eighty degrees, after all. He had to remind himself she was twenty years old.

"Is Meredith not coming?" Ruby asked, unaware she was hitting a sore point. Richard rolled his eyes, remembering their heated discussion before she left for the Hamptons.

"She's away." His reply was curt, but he offered Ruby a smile to soften the blow.

Ruby smiled back, but her eyes didn't join in. "That's a shame; she's going to miss a great show."

He tried not to laugh. He loved Ruby dearly, and was amazed by the way she always saw the best in people. "I'll make sure to show her some pictures."

"Have you had a good time?" he asked. Ruby's face lit up as she remembered the past few days. It was the first year she'd attended as a counsellor, and she positively glowed at the trust he'd put in her. He was pleased he'd listened to Hanna when she suggested he give Ruby a call.

"It's been amazing. The kids are fantastic, and Hanna's let me be involved in all the organization. She hasn't stopped running around, and when she's not sorting out the bands she's been sitting with the kids, or playing softball with them."

He wasn't sure how he knew she was near. Maybe he saw something from the corner of his eye, or perhaps the hair on his skin stood on end at her closeness. Either way, when he heard the familiar cadence of her laughter, he swung around.

Hanna was chatting animatedly with a counsellor, flinging her arms around and grinning wildly. Every movement was exaggerated, and her vibrancy made him want to run over and sweep her up in his arms. Like Ruby, she was dressed for the steaming hot weather. Short denim cut-offs curved over her behind, and she'd knotted a sleeveless black band T-shirt over her navel, revealing a sliver of tanned skin. Even from here he could see she'd caught the sun.

Richard walked over to the two of them, noting with pleasure that when Hanna lifted her head up to see him, an unguarded smile spread across her lips.

"You're here!" The evening sun reflected off her tanned skin. "What do you think?"

"You've done a fantastic job. The director keeps calling me up and asking if you can do the same thing next year."

Hanna laughed. A throaty, sexy chuckle, which made his body ache. "You know, I'd love to. I'm so amazed by the kids, they're all so brave."

"I don't know how to thank you for what you've done." He burned with the need to hug her. But since their reconciliation they'd kept each other at arm's length, as if they were both aware that to step into the murky waters of physical contact would break down the delicate dam they'd created.

"I couldn't have done it without Ruby." Hanna hugged his sister against her side, and for a moment he felt a pang of jealousy. "She's been like my right-hand man. I'm thinking of offering her the job of manager in our New York office." Her tone was light and teasing.

The fortunate side effect of her failure to recruit a suitable candidate to run the office was that she had stayed in Manhattan longer than she had originally planned. He wasn't sure how much effort she was putting into the search any more, but if he had his way she'd be cancelling the contracts with the agency and agreeing to stay out here full time.

He liked having her around. She was easy to talk to and bounce ideas off. She was the first person he wanted to call when he was having a bad day – or a good one, come to that. She was his friend – probably his best friend – and it made him happy to have her near.

"I've got to go and sort out the next band." She smiled at him, and he could feel a little flutter in his heart. "I'll catch up with you later, okay?"

"Sure." He agreed easily, knowing he needed to circulate and catch up with the kids. "I'll try to grab you before the fireworks."

Hanna was talking to a group of donors when the final band finished, looking incongruous in her festival clothing amongst the linen dresses and smart suits. It didn't seem to faze her as she answered questions and accepted their compliments.

Richard stood and watched for a while, liking that she didn't know he was staring. Meredith had once described her as "zany", which was as good a description as any, though it probably had the opposite effect to the one Meredith was hoping to create. Hanna's quirkiness endeared her to him.

Maybe he was just jittery about the wedding. Even with more than a year to go, Meredith was ramping things up, spending weekends with the organizer, trying to coax him out to try different caterers and bakeries

"There's absolutely no way I'm making a speech." Hanna's voice rang clearly through the night air now the music had stopped. His lips twitched at the thought of her standing up, her tiny body dwarfed by the main stage, and stuttering her way through a long list of people to thank.

"You deserve the accolades," Mimi Flynn, a wealthy donor and 9/11 widow, was saying. "My son tells me you managed to get so many great bands organized."

Hanna coughed out a laugh. "I think Sean may be a little biased." Richard didn't have to look to know she was blushing. "But thank you, anyway."

Tired of being a spectator, he walked toward the group, his presence drawing their eyes away from Hanna. Keeping half an eye on her, he spoke with the donors, smiling and thanking them for their help. He knew most of them well – from their links with the foundation, as well as bumping into them at other events – and it was hard to keep their exchanges to pleasantries. They were his friends.

Hanna finished talking with Mimi, then glanced over at the rest of the donors. "I think the fireworks are about to start. I've arranged for some drinks to be served just outside the donors' tent."

Her words were greeted with pleasant murmurs of agreement. Within moments, the lure of champagne and canapés had cleared the group, and he watched them walk toward the white canvas tent.

And then there were two.

"Hey." Hanna was rubbing at her arms, and he could see the goosebumps lifting at her skin. The evening air was still warm, but her clothes weren't appropriate for sundown.

He wished he was wearing his jacket, just so he could drape it over her shoulders, but he'd left it on the backseat of his car, along with his tie. "You look cold."

"It's the absence of body heat," she joked. "I've been okay as long as I've been in a group of people. I'm like the poor kid stealing next door's milk from the stoop."

She started to shiver. Not teeth clattering, full-on shudders, but her body was shaking enough to make him want to do something about it. He stood for a moment, reasoning with himself that if it was any other female friend, he wouldn't hesitate to pull them closer and wrap his arms around them. Maybe run the palms of his hands over their skin until the shaking stopped.

She didn't seem like any other female friend, though. Standing there in front of him, her face was illuminated by the floodlights dotting the lawn. She looked like the Hanna he used to know, the one who dribbled on him in parks, and flirted with him at parties. She looked like *his* Hanna.

"Come here." It was a demand, not a request. He didn't wait for her answer. One step forward and he had his arms around her, breathing in the fragrance of her shampoo as he gathered her body against his.

Jesus, she was cold. Her skin felt like ice to the touch, and he was kicking himself for not doing this earlier. It wasn't a sexual embrace at all. It was the gesture of one human to another, offering warmth and comfort.

That was his line, and he was sticking to it.

Hanna opened her mouth to say something, but her voice was drowned out by the noise of the first of the fireworks exploding overhead. Purples and greens cascaded through the air, drawing a collective gasp from the crowds.

She was holding herself awkwardly in his arms. Like she was afraid to move, or put her arms around him, and it made him hold her closer still. She felt like a wild animal, curious enough to allow itself to be picked up, but nervous once in his arms. He willed Hanna to let herself relax, let him warm her up, because right now she felt like a frozen icicle, all rigid and inflexible.

When the second firework exploded, Hanna lifted her head to watch, her features fixed in an expression of wonder. Maybe that was why he found her so much more fascinating to watch than the display of pyrotechnics overhead.

"Did you arrange these, as well?"

Hanna suppressed a smile. "When you mention kids and 9/11, it's amazing how generous people can be."

She caught his eye for a moment, and it was enough to make him twitch. As her body warmed up, his need to protect her was being replaced by something stronger and more primal. This was a dangerous line he was treading. He'd forgotten what it was like to be involved in a maelstrom of emotions, his heart beating faster and his blood racing. Was it preferable to the calm, reassuring certainty offered to him by Meredith?

He wasn't sure.

"It's amazing how generous you've been." He cupped her cheek with his hand, causing a shock of surprise to flash across her face. "You've spent the last few months sorting this out, and I know you've given up so much of your free time, not to mention your vacation."

She was so still in his arms, he thought she might be in shock. He wondered if she was afraid, like he was, of breaking down the walls they'd so carefully constructed. They'd both made separate deals with the devil, promising not to step over the invisible line if it allowed them to be in each other's lives. They'd made the mistake once before of trying to be lovers, and look how that turned out.

"I like being able to help..." Her voice was just a murmur, her words trailing off when the next round of fireworks started up. This time she didn't watch, just stared at him as her face reflected the colours of the explosions in the sky. She went from orange, to green, to red, and he licked his dry lips, trying to decide on his next move.

Letting go wasn't an option he considered.

"Hanna," he murmured, so quietly she couldn't hear him. He wasn't sure he wanted her to. He dropped his forehead to touch hers, her eyes widening when she saw the expression on his face. He thought of his wild animal analogy again. She was never going to be his, but it was enough to see her, watch her from afar, to ensure she was safe and happy.

Nineteen

9th February 2010

HANNA WASN'T SURE how she'd ended up sitting in the corner of a dingy bar, pouring the dregs out of a bottle of wine. Her wine glass was well used, marred by lipstick and finger marks, red droplets clinging to the rim. She nodded at the barman to order another, figuring she may as well end this day the way she had begun it.

In a complete state.

She hadn't even realized the significance of the date until she was on the subway train, rocking on her tiptoes so her fingers could grasp the rail to prevent her flying into a fellow commuter. The man next to her was reading the *New York Times*, folding it up into quarters so he didn't disturb anybody else, and it was then that her eyes had flicked over the numbers on the corner of the page.

It had been years since she'd last had a panic attack, but Hanna recognized the symptoms straight away. Her heart raced, her breath became harsh and she felt as if she was about to fall down and convulse on the dusty train floor. It seemed like the worst place in the world to have a seizure. It was all she could do to hang on to a thread of sanity before the train came to its next stop.

She didn't bother to look to see where she was, just ran out through the sliding doors and up the platform, panicking again when her card didn't open the barrier the first time. Her hands were shaking hard, the feeling of nausea bubbling away at the pit of her stomach, and she only cleared the exit by a couple of feet before she doubled over and pebbled the floor with the remnants of her breakfast.

The morning rush hour had carried on around her. People walking into the station entrance gave her a wide berth, assuming she was either inebriated from the night before, or was some sort of mad woman, muttering to herself as she leaned against the dirty brick wall of the subway station. She was a small inconvenience – probably forgotten by the time they'd stepped onto their train a tiny speck in the myriad of eccentrics that populated the great city.

It was times like this that Hanna wished she was still in London. She would have called up Natalie, or Tom, or maybe caught a cab to Claire's to throw herself into her arms. She would have been plied with sweet tea and hugs until she cried herself out and braced herself to face the day.

Instead, she was alienated in Manhattan, with a cell phone filled with numbers of work colleagues and acquaintances, but no friends that she could confide in, or ask for help. Nobody who would understand exactly why this day was so hard for her.

The time passed faster than she'd thought possible. Breakfast in a diner, and hours spent browsing in a bookshop were followed by an early dinner in the corner of a shabby bar in Soho. How she'd ended up there, she wasn't sure, but she felt more at home in this part of the island than anywhere else.

The last couple of hours had been spent drowning herself in a wine glass, and batting off advances of guys who thought she was easy game. Even in her inebriated state, the last thing she wanted to do was forget her mother with an easy lay.

And here she was, full circle, thinking about the last five years and how she'd royally fucked things up. She glanced at her watch, trying to work out – through the haze of alcohol – what the time would be in London. It was way too late to call up Claire or Ruby. They'd both be tucked up safe and warm in bed.

That left one other number. She dialled it before she'd even thought it through, like she'd left all common sense at the bottom of her empty wine bottle. It only rang twice before she was connected.

"Hanna?" His voice was soft and warm, with a hint of concern.

"Richard." She took another sip of wine. "I just wanted to call and say how sorry I am."

"Are you okay?"

She could hear a thrum of voices in the background. Hanna wondered if she had disturbed him, maybe taken him away from dinner with Meredith.

"The way I left you after mum died. I should never have walked out on you without explaining why. I've been thinking about it all day, and I—"

"Christ, I hadn't even realized the date. I'm so sorry." He sounded agitated. She could imagine him running his hand through his thick, coarse hair. He was probably the only other person thinking about the day her mum died five years ago.

She laughed harshly. "I really shouldn't have called. I know you're with Meredith now, and I'm so pleased you have found each other. You deserve happiness." Her words slurred off her tongue and into the mouthpiece.

"Have you been drinking?"

"A little. But I'll let you get back to your evening."

"Are you at home?" he asked.

"I'm in a bar."

"Alone?"

"Yep."

"Fuck," he swore softly. "I'll send Jack over to drive you home. Where are you?"

She looked around for evidence of the bar name, coming up short when she realized there was nothing on the inside of the room. Then she glanced down, noticed the beer mat and smiled.

"Murphy's. In Soho."

"Don't move." His words were a command, and she took him seriously. She didn't even want any more of the claret sitting in the bottle in front of her. All she really craved was the soft warmth of her duvet and the cleansing oblivion of sleep.

She sobered a little in the fifteen minutes she was waiting. The bartender brought over the tab, and a glass of water, and she swallowed it down, hoping to cleanse her system of alcohol. Then he was walking into the bar, carrying his black woollen coat over his arm.

"Richard!" Just seeing him there made her jump. "I thought you were sending Jack."

"I decided to come with him," he answered quietly, his eyes scanning her face in concern. "It was a good excuse to leave dinner early."

He looked tired. In the dim light of the bar she could see lines pulling at the corner of his eyes, dry and deep. She bit her lip, aware he was being kind.

"Is Meredith with you?" She swallowed hard. Knowing he was with another woman was one thing – seeing them together while she was at her lowest ebb was another.

189

"She's visiting her parents. It was just me and three hundred and fifty of New York's finest." He grimaced. "So believe me when I say you did me a favour." Standing up, he pulled her coat from the hook at the side of the booth. "Now let's get you home."

Hanna stood and turned, putting her arms into the sleeves as he held her jacket, allowing him to pull it over her shoulders. He held on for a moment too long.

$\mathcal{L}$ETTING OUT A small breath of air, Richard turned her around and helped her to fasten the large buttons on the front of her coat. This wasn't how he'd envisaged his night panning out. He'd planned a nice, civilized dinner, perhaps followed by a whisky or two, and then an early night. Instead here he was. His body felt electric, as if by seeing her he'd come alive. His nerve endings stabbed like a thousand tiny needles.

He hesitated for a moment before taking her hand in his. But then, he saw two of the guys at the bar turn around to stare at Hanna, a look of disappointment on their faces, and he felt the need to mark his territory. Even if it wasn't his to claim.

"You really don't need to do this," she mumbled, just before she tripped over her own shoe. He tried to restrain a laugh, but it came out strangled, causing her to stare at him indignantly. "Do you find this funny?"

"A little," he admitted, putting his arm around her shoulder to lead her to the main door. She kept veering to the right, like a car whose steering was slightly off-kilter. "But I'll try to restrain myself."

"Good. Because I don't want to have to hit you."

"Which one of me will you hit?"

"Both," she muttered, trying to uncross her eyes.

She stumbled against him again, and he held her close, deciding not to point out the obvious. By the time they were in the car she felt sleepy, burying her head in the wool of his jacket, her voice languid as she continued to spout a mouthful of drivel.

"Do you remember when we first met?" she asked him. "You were all smart in your evening suit, and I was a hot ball of mess."

"That's not how I remember it." He was murmuring into her hair, breathing in the aroma of her shampoo. "You looked hot as hell in that waitress uniform." Memories of black hair and kohled eyes assaulted his senses. "I couldn't wait to show you my PlayStation."

She laughed, then hiccupped. "Is that a euphemism?"

"I'm not sure," he admitted, looping his arm around her shoulder and rubbing her arm with his finger.

"I can remember being impressed by your... ardour."

Jack brought the car to a stop. Even at eleven o'clock on a Tuesday night, the streets were crammed with traffic. Richard wondered if Hanna would make the journey without falling asleep.

"I'll take that as a compliment."

"You should."

The car was filled with silence, and Richard let his head fall back, working out his next move. He wanted to make sure she got back to the apartment safely, knowing today of all days was difficult for her. If he could just put her to bed and watch her sleep, he'd feel better about the whole thing. He tried to suppress the anger he felt with himself, and her friends, for letting her go through this alone.

Twenty minutes later, Jack pulled up outside the apartment on the Upper East Side. Hanna was so quiet that he wondered if she really had fallen asleep. But as soon as the car came to a stop, she lifted her head up and stared at him.

"Thank you for the lift."

He was confused for a moment, before realizing she intended to go into the apartment without him. For some reason, that wouldn't do.

"I'll see you in, make sure you're safe."

She laughed. "I think all the druggies and murderers have gone home for the evening. The scariest thing in there will be Mrs Van Kemp staring at my shoes with disdain, and telling me I'm lowering the tone again."

"Humour me."

She nodded rapidly, then started to jab her hand, trying to release her seatbelt. He bit back a chuckle before leaning across to unfasten it for her.

"Stop laughing at me." She gently slapped at his arm. "It isn't funny."

He'd spent enough time at his father's apartment to know the doorman, nodding at him as he half-carried Hanna to the elevator. Through the thickness of her winter coat she felt small and vulnerable, and he wondered if his need to protect her was just a natural reaction to her size. Perhaps, as with Ruby, he wanted to shelter her from the world and keep her safe.

The thought cheered him as he grabbed the door key from her bag and slid it into the lock. Flicking the light switch on with one hand, he supported Hanna with the other, his arm curving around her waist. She kicked off her shoes, and they landed on the tiled floor with a clunk.

"Do you want to do a scan of the apartment, make sure Ted Bundy isn't hiding in the washer-dryer?" A flash of amusement lit her eyes.

He offered her a small grin before taking her coat and hanging it neatly in the hall closet. "The scariest thing you need to worry about is the hangover you'll have tomorrow morning."

Walking to the kitchen, Richard pulled a tall glass from the cupboard. Filling it with water, he carried it to the guest room, placing it on the bedside table.

"Where do you keep your painkillers?" he asked, trying not to watch as Hanna unpinned her hair. It cascaded down her shoulders. "I'll grab you a couple, and then I'll be gone."

She blinked in the mirror, her eyes meeting his. "In the vanity cabinet above the sink."

Richard walked into the bathroom, surprised at the lack of cosmetics and products littering the sides. Grabbing the blister packet of Panadol, he brought it back to her bed.

Hanna sat on top of the coverlet, her head resting against the headboard, and he popped two pills out, placing them gently in her mouth. Lifting the glass to her lips he encouraged her to drink, unable to stop himself from running his hand through her hair as she swallowed.

"That feels good." Her eyes were closed as his hand caressed her. "Can you stay for a while?"

"You need to get into bed." He reached around to her back and pulled down her zipper. The movement felt too intimate, and he had to try to suppress his reaction to her proximity. "You'll feel better after a good sleep."

"You're so nice." Her voice was just a murmur, and she shuffled closer to him, her head nuzzling into the crease between his shoulder and neck. "And you smell great. You always smelled great, even in the mornings. It's one of the things I miss most about us."

"You miss the way I smell?" He tried to turn it into a joke, but she started to peel her dress away from her body.

193

He was instantly hard.

"Close your eyes, I just need to change." Her command was pretty weak, and more than a moment too late. He did as instructed, anyway, digging his fingernails into his palms, trying to stop himself from touching her. If he saw the soft, pale arc of her breast, he'd be done for.

The bed undulated as she struggled with her clothing. He stayed as still as he could, battling with the incredible urge to open his eyes. Did she look the same as he remembered, all soft skin and gentle curves? Or had the last five years changed her on the outside as well as within?

He'd never thought of himself as the type to cheat. He was engaged to a woman who trusted him implicitly, and he wanted to deserve that trust. The thoughts whirling around in his mind were completely indefensible. He felt like shit.

"I'm decent." Hanna lay back on the bed, her hair fanning out across the white cotton pillowcase. "Thank you for everything."

"You're welcome." Even as he spoke, he could see her starting to flag, her eyelids fluttering as her face took on a peaceful expression. He reached out and smoothed the hair away from her eyes, feeling her smooth skin dimple against the hard pads of his fingers. She sighed gently, and he felt his erection harden further, as he stared at her flushed, swollen lips.

Just a taste.

He leaned forward and brushed his lips against hers, and her soft breath bathed his skin. Her eyes flew open and she stared at him. She threw her arms around his neck, and pulled him against her, crashing her mouth to his. Every inch of him was dazzlingly awake, pleasure shooting from his balls to the tip of his toes.

Moving his hand down her body, brushing his fingers against her breast until she started to moan, he allowed himself to feel the most frightening emotion of all.

Hope.

IT WAS LIKE everything in the room exploded into brilliant Technicolour, sobering her faster than a bucket of ice water. The moment his lips brushed hers, she knew she'd reached the point of no return. He was the sun and she was in orbit – circling, attracted to him. Everything about him made her burn.

The mattress dipped as he rested above her, hips scraping against hers, and she couldn't help but gyrate, feeling his hardness grind against her stomach. His fingertips brushed down her side in light, feathery strokes, making her nipples hard and her thighs damp.

"Hanna." He exhaled against her cheek. She closed her eyes and tried to stop herself from responding. She tried to distract him by grinding again.

It seemed to work.

"Let me—" He didn't wait for permission. He pushed her tank up to her neck, baring her breasts, and as he stared down at them, his tongue snaking across his lips, Hanna could feel his dick twitch against her once more. His fingers teased, making her nipples pebble, and the pleasure shoot down to her groin.

Her inner monologue started to distract her. The fear they were really going to do this was swiftly replaced by the agony they might not. Somewhere, deep inside, she knew doing this was wrong, but she repressed the thought, burying it under the intense need shooting through her nerves.

It was hard to look him in the eye. Hanna wasn't sure what would be there, wasn't even certain what it was she wanted to see. Desperation, perhaps, or maybe a need reflecting hers? What she feared was regret, sadness, or a hint of pity, and she knew if she saw any of that, she would curl up and weep.

She didn't want to cry. She felt too good for tears or for regret. She'd waited far too long to feel his mouth pulling at her nipples, bathing them gently before scraping his teeth on her flesh.

She needed to get her mind to shut the hell up.

Sensing her fears, Richard cupped her chin with his hand, lifting her face until she couldn't avoid meeting his stare. When her chocolate eyes met hunter green, she knew she was completely wrong.

They flashed fiercely, narrowed and dark, and the way he stared made her feel breathless.

"I need—" Like Richard, she couldn't finish her sentence to let him know what she wanted. She didn't have to. His hands cupped her ass, fingers pulling at her shorts until they were softly dragging against her thighs, leaving her exposed and desperate. Cool air met damp skin, making her buck a little, trying to create friction from a vacuum. Her thighs were sensitive and clammy as he dug his fingers in, gently prising her apart.

That felt so good.

His fingers dipped, caressing the damp skin in the crease of her thigh. He pulled her apart, until she was more exposed than ever, gliding against her, then pushing until her body released, inviting him in. This time she moaned – a low, pleading half-breath, flexing her hips until his fingers were inside her.

Richard moved down her body, his lips finding her core, tongue pointed and strong, dragging against her and making her buck in time to his rhythmic movements. The dizziness in her head had nothing to do with the wine she had consumed, and everything to do with the sensations he was creating. Her hands ached to touch, and she let them flutter toward him, sliding them into his hair, tugging until she could feel him groan against her.

Hanna's eyes opened wide, her mouth wider, and she let out a noise somewhere between a scream and a cry. Richard pushed a third finger inside as she began to clench against him, intensifying the pleasurable sensation until her knees began to quake.

She was so close.

As soon as he withdrew his hand she felt empty. His leg slid inside hers, his knee brushing against her calf. She reached around fumbling at his buttons, her fingers slipping like an over-excited child opening a birthday present. Finding purchase, she pulled his fly apart, feeling his zipper unhook, tugging at his trousers until he got her message, wriggling his ass to help her pull them down.

Richard took over the task, pushing them down past his calves, and she followed him with her hands. She caressed his flesh, feeling his hard thigh muscles stretched under taut skin.

"Take off your top." He knelt on the bed, pulling at his shirt. She dragged her tank over her head, flinging it across the floor in her desperation to be naked. His knees were on either side of her thighs, caging her in, making it hard not to stare at the outline of his hardness through his dark shorts.

Reaching out a finger, she traced a line down to his balls. He grew a little harder, the head of his erection emerging from his shorts, and she watched as a small bead of pre-come formed there. Leaning forward, she licked it off, and a strangled groan escaped from Richard's lips. She did it again, running the blunt end of her tongue against him, and then twirling it around, kissing and sucking him with her mouth, using her hands to push his shorts a little farther down his hips.

Richard reached his own hand around to cup the back of her head, encouraging her lips into a steady rhythm. Dragging her tongue down the underside, she pulled her mouth back up, licking, kissing, tasting.

"Stop." He steadied her head, and for the first time she looked up and caught his eyes. Her lips were still wrapped around him. His own mouth was swollen, still glistening, slightly parted to allow his short breaths to meet the air. "I want to be inside you."

His words hit her blood like a shot of heroin. Hanna moved her head back, watching his hardness spring against the defined muscles of his stomach, then grabbed at his shorts, desperate to pull them from his body.

"Lie down." He placed his palm flat against her shoulder, pushing her back onto the mattress, sheets soft and silky against her back. Kicking his shorts from his ankles, Richard moved over her, hands caging her head, until she was unable to turn, cornered like a hunted animal.

She was almost too wet. His hips pushed against her tender thighs as he lined himself up against her, pausing for a long, drawn out moment, before thrusting, pushing inside.

"Richard." Her words were little more than breath.

He kissed her again. She could taste herself on his lips. His hips flexed, and he withdrew, dragging himself against her like a bow against a violin. She squeezed her eyes shut, trying to keep her response under control.

"Open your eyes. I want to see you." Richard's movements were steady, but his words were not. He felt like heaven between her thighs, and she squeezed them tighter, hooking her heels around his back, dragging him in.

She was drowning. She wasn't sure if he was going to save her or push her under.

"Are you close?" Richard's breath was getting harsher, his movements erratic, and she knew he was nearing release. Hanna opened her mouth, but her words were drowned out by the sensation of his finger rubbing her, making small, delicious circles, drawing out her pleasure like an artist.

She cried out, burying her head in the dip of his neck, feeling his clamminess against her lips. His hips crashed against hers, her moans stifled by his flesh, her body clenching hard against him.

His groans amplified as he moaned against her ear, and even if she couldn't feel him pulsing inside her, she would have known he was coming from the change in his breathing. He whispered a soft oath as he peaked, and she felt herself spasm again, grinding against him, as they clung to the long moments like slaves to sensation.

Then it was over.

Her wet, sticky thighs cradled his hips, his skin heavy against her body. Their harsh pants became longer, thinner, like stretched-out breaths, as they both crashed down. Reality hit them like a wrecking ball.

Lying naked beneath the man who she was all kinds of fucked up about, still hard inside her, Hanna knew she must look like shit. Her brown hair was crazy against the light blue of the pillow, her make-up skewed from a day of crying and a night of over-consumption.

His hips lifted up as he withdrew, and Hanna let her head fall back onto the mattress, as she stared up at the silver and glass light fixture above the bed, letting the brightness of the bulbs burn into her retinas. Even with her eyes closed she could still see them, like a ghost of what could have been.

"Hanna, I..." He sounded as awkward as she felt, all stuttering consonants and drawn out vowels.

She blinked a couple of times, burned-in images turning from black to white, making her eyes sting. Richard rolled over beside her. She watched as he reached out, and then stopped himself, hand hovering in mid-air.

"Don't." Her voice was low and scratchy. She swallowed hard, feeling the dry woolliness of her throat. She wanted him to pull her into his arms.

"I'm sorry. I had no right to take advantage."

"You didn't, I wanted it, too." She bit down on the inside of her cheek. The pain felt good.

Richard rolled onto his back, flinging an arm over his face, covering his eyes. She allowed herself to look at his body, her gaze moving from his neck, down to the taut, flat skin of his abdomen. Only moments before, that body was pressed down on her own, creating a burning fire as flesh touched flesh.

Now, she was shivering.

"Come here." He pulled her against him, and her eyes fluttered shut. She wanted him to leave, but was desperate for him to stay. Knowing he was so close and yet so far away was achingly painful, numbed only by the sweet surrender of sleep.

Rather than think anymore, she submitted to its siren call, her need for oblivion stronger than ever.

WHEN SHE WOKE the next morning, Hanna tried to pretend it was a dirty, alcohol-induced dream. But the ache between her legs was too real, and she didn't have to reach down to feel the evidence of last night's activities. She only had to inhale Richard's scent to remember what happened in clear, vivid detail.

She lifted her hand up and ran her fingers through her hair, her progress hampered by the knots created by rampant sex and restless dreams. Daylight forced its way through the thick fabric of the curtains, slithering through the area above the rail.

"I didn't mean to wake you." His voice was soft, his touch sure, as he sat down on the bed beside her. He was dressed, wearing just his pants and white shirt from the night before.

"You're leaving?"

"I have a meeting at seven. I can't get out of this one." His words were laced with regret. Then he leaned and brushed his lips over her forehead, leaving a trail of ice across her skin.

"Oh." She frowned, trying to think of a suitable response. It was like her brain hadn't caught on to the fact she was awake yet.

"Can we meet this evening?" His mouth feathered her skin. "We need to talk."

She gnawed at her lower lip, the reality of the situation hitting her like a curveball. There was so much to talk about. She didn't know where to begin.

"I've got interviews all day. I'll be free at six."

"Interviews?" His forehead wrinkled. She reached out a finger to smooth them. Even the sensation of his skin against hers was enough to light her flame.

"For my replacement... bad timing right?"

The story of their lives...

"I'll pick you up at six. Don't make any rash decisions."

"Why not?" The unspoken words were like a scab. She wanted to pick at it, make it bleed.

"Because I want you here with me."

"I'm not a cheater, Richard, and neither are you." Except they were. They both were.

The muscles in his cheek twitched as he looked down at her. In the half-light of the morning his skin looked warm and tan. She wanted to kiss it all over.

"When Meredith comes back next week, I'm going to tell her it's over."

Just like that, her heart felt like it had grown wings and flown out of her chest. Though welcomed his words were like a bolt out of the blue. In the course of a day she had gone from having nothing, to possibly having it all.

They were so close.

"Okay." Her words came out as a whisper, and she sat up, the sheets falling from her body to reveal her naked chest. The twitch in Richard's cheek got stronger, and she rapidly grabbed the sheets and pulled them up to her shoulders.

"I want to touch you so badly," he confessed, his hands balled into fists as if he were restraining himself. "But I've fucked everything up so far."

"Richard—"

"No, hear me out. You know I love you, I've always loved you, and you don't deserve to be anything but first in my life. I shouldn't have slept with you while I was still with her."

"You were drunk. We both were."

"It doesn't excuse anything." He was agitated now, long fingers raking through his hair. "Let me try to fix this; let me do this right. Can we try to just be friends until next week?"

Hanna sighed, relief flooding her chest. "That sounds good to me."

*I*T TOOK ALL day, but she finally found the right man for the job. Like Hanna, Paul Spence came from a music-journalism background, and his knowledge of the New York scene rivalled her own in its encyclopedic nature. She felt a little sad she wasn't going to be working alongside him in New York. They'd hit it off from the start, and she'd spent half the interview asking him questions about the gigs he'd been to recently, arguing good-naturedly with him about the merits of various groups.

"It's been a pleasure meeting you, Paul," she said, as the elevator car arrived. "You'll be hearing from us very soon."

As soon as he walked into the elevator, she turned and made her way back to her office. She grabbed her coat, shrugging it on, excited that she only had half an hour before she would see Richard again.

How had she stood being apart from him for all this time? Like a sculptor, he had taken the dull-grey clay of her life and made it into something beautiful. She felt so alive.

It was five past six when her cell rang, and she tried not to smile when she heard the jarring chords of 'Last Night' by The Strokes blaring out of her purse. Richard had been busy reprogramming her cell while she was asleep. She liked these flashes of humour, amongst the seriousness of their situation.

"Hello?"

"Hanna?" He sounded breathless. Beneath the timbre of his voice she could hear the familiar sounds of the city: humming motors, beeping horns and the perpetual drone of police sirens.

"Are you outside?" She didn't bother to disguise her enthusiasm. She was just so damned happy.

"Sweetheart, there's been a change of plan."

"Oh?" The excitement poured out of her like sand spilling from a broken timer. "Are you still coming to pick me up?"

"Meredith's been in an accident." His voice was monotone. Hanna frowned for a moment, trying to think of something to say – a reassuring word, a peaceful sentence. But the only thing in her mind was pure, blind panic.

"I'm on my way upstate now. It sounds bad." His voice cracked and she ached to touch him. Her hands curled around the thin air of her disappointment, a poor substitute for his body.

"I don't know what to say, I'm so sorry."

"I'll call you when I know more. Give me some time, okay?"

She took a deep breath, letting the oxygen fill her lungs, holding it inside until the burning need to exhale took over her mind. Letting it out with a whoosh, she eventually calmed herself enough to reply.

"Concentrate on Meredith. Let me know how she is."

"I love you." His words were desperate. Hanna tried to hold on to them, like a child catching a bubble as it danced through the air. When she opened her hands she feared it would be gone.

"I love you, too." There was nothing else to say. Her mind was bursting with the things she wanted to tell him, but they would have to wait. Now, she had to let him go. He still belonged to Meredith. Until he severed the tie, Hanna was the one on the outside looking in.

The guilt that she'd suppressed all day was growing like Topsy in her mind, and she wondered if it was a judgement from above or just plain bad luck.

She began to suspect it was a little of both.

THE FOLLOWING WEEK, Hanna was leaving the office, pulling her coat tight to block out the wind. It was already getting dark; the evening sky was a cloudy grey, and though the weather was dry the air tasted of snow. She was going to miss the extreme highs and lows of living here – the stifling heat of summer, the bright oranges of the fall. London was a beautiful city – and the one closest to her heart – but Manhattan had been such a wicked love affair.

The wind was whipping up Second Avenue, and she turned up the collar of her coat, regretful she'd left her scarf in the office. A black sedan idled at the curb, grey vapour clouding from the exhaust, and she watched with interest as the back door opened.

"Hanna."

Richard climbed out of the car, putting his feet on the sidewalk, and she found herself moving toward him. He looked so drawn; his skin was pale, his hair messed, and she wanted to throw her arms around him and pull him tightly to her.

"I thought you'd still be with Meredith."

In the week since Hanna had last seen him, they'd only managed to speak on the phone a handful of times. Most of Richard's day had been made up of sitting with his fiancée, sorting out her insurance, and arranging her transfer to New York. Perhaps that was why he was here.

"I've been interviewing nurses." His voice was the same monotone she'd been hearing all week. It was like he was trying not to feel anything. "Meredith's being helicoptered back tomorrow."

"How is she?" It was a stupid question. They were both standing here, restraining themselves from touching each other. The only thing stopping them was Meredith's health.

"Still not able to move very well. The doctors say we have to give it some time. They say with intense therapy there's hope she'll be on her feet soon."

"That's good news." The wind lashed against her cheek, making her pink up. A solitary flake of snow fell in front of her eyes. The thick clump danced in the air, in no hurry to reach the ground.

"I hope so." He looked as awkward as she felt. Snow began to fall heavily. He cleared his throat, glancing up at the roof of her building, and she remembered he owned it. It was so strange, the way everything in her life led back to him.

"I'm leaving next week." The agony of being unable to touch him was pulling at her soul. "But I don't want to go."

He was agitated, and she could see his eyes flash as he tried to calculate something in his mind. "Why don't you get the hell over here?"

She was in his arms before he'd finished the sentence. It didn't seem enough to just hold him tight, she wanted to climb inside him until they were one person.

"This is all so fucked up." She looked up at him. His eyes were glistening, too.

"I have to help Meredith get back on her feet. She can't live alone yet; she needs constant supervision." He twisted his fingers in Hanna's hair. "But once she's up and healed, I'm going to tell her everything. Then I'll be on the next flight to London."

She dipped her head and nuzzled into his chest. His coat was slightly damp from the snow, and she could see the little beads of moisture clinging to the wool fibres. Those words were more than she had hoped for; it was almost a promise for a future that could be theirs. But the thought of enduring months of pain, of wondering, was too much to bear.

"I love you." She ran her fingertips along the cold skin of his cheek. She paused for a moment, trying to think of the right words. "But we can't carry on an emotional affair while you're engaged to somebody else. I've been on the other side of that and it would kill me to hurt somebody else in the same way."

His hold on her loosened. "I know. I'm such a shit."

She tried to smile. "You aren't. Circumstances could be better. At least we won't be tempted to see each other."

"They invented these little things called airplanes—"

"You know what I mean. While you're still with Meredith we need to stop this thing. Come find me when things are better for you. I'll still have the same address, and I know you have my cell number."

"It could be months."

"I'll be there."

He stood right in front of her, tipping her chin with his finger, lowering his own until his forehead was touching hers.

"You promise?" He was so close. She was losing herself in the green of his eyes. It took every ounce of willpower she had not to kiss him.

"I promise."

Twenty

15th June 2010

*I*T WAS EMBARRASSING, and more than a little worrisome, that Hanna hadn't even realized anything was wrong until two days ago. She'd been sitting in Tom's garden, watching him lose his wrestling match with his shiny gas barbecue, and trying not to giggle, when she first noticed the tiny kick. It felt a little like indigestion, though she hadn't eaten anything, despite her overwhelming hunger. Her friend Natalie had taken one look at the way Hanna clasped her stomach with over-protective hands, before pronouncing, "You're pregnant."

A long discussion about the ability to have periods whilst being pregnant ensued, followed by a mad dash to find a pharmacy that was open on a Sunday. Natalie had eventually returned with three tests – all different brands, a bag loaded with prenatal vitamins, and a bumper box of tissues for the tears she knew would ensue.

Now they were in Tom's car, heading for the prestigious Portland Hospital, where he'd arranged for an ultrasound. Despite Hanna's protests, he'd argued she deserved the best care, and he'd pay for the initial consultation.

"Have you told him yet?" Tom asked, as the car swept past Regent's Park. The grass was littered with half-clothed bodies, desperate to take advantage of the mini heatwave in London. Hanna wondered idly if the weather in New York was as warm.

"I've been putting it off," she admitted, fanning her face with her hand. Despite the noisy whir of the air conditioning, the interior was stifling, and she couldn't seem to cool down at all. "I want to see the evidence for myself before I call him."

She was dreading it. Hanna had a vision of Richard jumping on the first plane out, and sweeping her off her feet in a protestation of love. What if that didn't happen? It was four months since she'd seen him last, and made him promise not to contact her until he was ready. She felt like she was cheating, forcing things.

She hadn't heard anything from him – not a word – and she'd been avoiding the Larsens for fear he was staying with Meredith for good. Waiting was hard enough; rejection would be a hundred times more painful.

"Were three pregnancy tests not enough proof?" Tom asked. Hanna watched his dimple twitch above the curve of his jaw. "You should have told him already."

"What if he doesn't want it?" She voiced her worst fear. It didn't make her feel any better.

"It's not his choice to make," he replied. Taking her hand, he rubbed his thumb across her palm. "Even if he doesn't want it, you know I'll always be here for you."

Her heart clenched. Tom was too good to her sometimes – this was definitely one of those occasions.

The car turned into the hospital's private parking lot. Outside the front entrance, a few photographers leaned on the walls, waiting for the next big celebrity to emerge.

"Are you sure you want to come in with me? What if somebody sees you?"

If the paparazzi spotted him, they'd both end up as headline fodder. The Portland Hospital was a hotbed of celebrity births, and photographers routinely hovered outside, hoping to catch an exclusive.

"Nobody's going to see me. I've arranged for a space next to the back door, and we'll run in and out." He pulled something from his pocket. "Anyway, I've brought my beanie with me."

Hanna laughed as he pulled the black, woolen cap over his blond curls. He always knew how to diffuse the tension, whether it be asking her to marry him when she found out she was pregnant – to which her answer was *no* – to putting a winter hat on in the middle of the hottest day in fifty years. She was so thankful to have him around.

Tom's money talked, and it had a lot to say. Their parking space was the best in the lot, and as soon as they walked through the back door, she was ushered straight into an examination room. There was no hanging around in the waiting room or form filling required. A couple of signatures, and she was lying on the bed, top up and jeans down, cool gel being poured on her stomach.

"You must both be so excited," the radiographer said. Hanna felt herself blushing at the inference and glanced over at Tom. He didn't seem perturbed at all.

"We are." He winked at Hanna. She tried to smile back.

"Well, I'm going to take a look, make sure everything is okay, and I'll turn the monitor around and show you what there is to see." The radiographer's voice was calm and reassuring, but the butterflies still flew around Hanna's stomach. "You think you are around four months, is that right?"

"I think so."

"Well, there won't be too much to see, but I'll try to point out some of the good stuff."

Hanna looked down at her stomach, all shiny from the gel, and wondered how she hadn't suspected a thing. The slight protrusion seemed obvious now, her stomach rounding up from her pelvis in a small arc.

Tom leaned forward and took her hand in his. He looked more nervous than Hanna as the radiographer silently moved the wand across her skin. Hanna squeezed him back, flashing him a reassuring smile to try to calm him down.

The radiographer turned around and smiled at them both. "Okay, it all looks good."

God, those words were perfect. Hanna hadn't known the baby even existed until two days ago, but suddenly her world revolved around a tiny being no larger than an avocado.

Then she saw the monitor.

Her mouth fell open at the green and black image. Tears stung at her eyes, as she looked at the screen, seeing the tiny outline of a baby. She'd expected to see little more than a blob, but she could make out a head, legs, and little arms flailing around as the radiographer pushed the wand on her belly.

"Jesus," Tom whispered. Hanna turned to see tears pouring down his face. Her throat felt tickly and dry, and though she opened her mouth, she couldn't speak.

It was a baby. *Her* baby – hers and Richard's, and it was everything she wanted. Nothing in the world mattered more than the tiny thing growing inside her.

"The baby looks perfectly healthy, and measures around four and a half inches. I've put your expected date of confinement down as 3rd November, but because you don't know the date of your last period, it's not precise."

"You're going to have a baby before Christmas." Tom's excitement was infectious, and Hanna grinned madly. She was already picturing a tiny infant, all bundled up in a Santa outfit, cute and cuddly, and surrounded by love.

"I'm going to take a few photographs for you now." The radiographer held the wand still and pressed a button on the keyboard, lips curling down in concentration. "The baby doesn't seem to want to pose. He or she is a feisty little thing."

A flash of pride warmed Hanna's heart, and she wanted to hug herself with glee. She was pregnant with a healthy, feisty, gorgeous baby, and in around five months' time she was going to be a mother.

A mother.

"He's so beautiful." Tom leaned in closer so his head was right next to Hanna's and they both stared intently at the monitor. The baby moved its arm again, like it was waving.

"*She* is," she corrected, unable to tear her eyes away. Five months seemed so far away. Her mind started to make a list of things to do: move house, build nursery, and buy shit loads of useless equipment even though she'd never use any of it.

"Okay, I'll put your referral through. The obstetrician will want to see you next week, and I'll be doing some more tests at week twenty." She cleaned her stomach off. As Hanna sat up and adjusted her clothing, the radiographer handed the photographs to Tom, who took them greedily.

"There you go, Daddy. The first ones for your collection."

Tom laughed and didn't bother to correct her, making Hanna wonder if he was already feeling a little proprietorial about her child. She was unsure if it was a good thing or not – she didn't want to complicate things with Richard more than she already had.

But then she thought about it, and if Richard refused to help her, perhaps it was a good thing to have Tom by her side. She didn't want to go through this alone, and he seemed over the moon about her pregnant state. It wasn't as if there was anything romantic between them; they were just good friends.

"Tom, you can't tell Ruby about this, not until I've spoken with Richard, okay?" The last thing she needed was for the Larsens to find out before she'd told the father.

"My lips are sealed. But you know I'm gonna get a mini Fatal Limits T-shirt made for your kid."

She laughed. "This baby is going to be the coolest on the block with you for a godfather."

"Seriously? I'm gonna be a dad?"

His enthusiasm made her breath stop. Those were the right words, but from the wrong mouth. "A god dad," she corrected, but her words didn't seem to dent his ardour at all. "You get to spoil the kid rotten and take him or her out for its first drink."

"Can I do it soon?"

"Only if it's for a bottle of milk." Hanna let him take her hand as they left the room. "In the meantime, I'll accept foot rubs and home-cooked meals."

"It's a deal." He winked, and she let herself feel a tiny spark of hope. If Tom was this excited, perhaps Richard, too, would be over the moon.

ANNA DIDN'T GO back to the office after the appointment. She wanted to centre herself, consider the implications, and prepare herself to make the telephone call. She planned to do it in the evening, when it would be lunchtime in New York, and she stood a chance of catching Richard undisturbed.

She paced her flat, unable to concentrate on anything, or sit still long enough to let the fear take hold. In the kitchen, she cleaned the hob even though it was already sparkling, then she moved to her bedroom and rearranged her T-shirts into colour order.

Anything to avoid the need to think.

Five o'clock came and went. She was prevaricating, telling herself that ringing him on the dot of five was a little too keen, and he'd probably still be in a meeting. By the time the hand on her kitchen clock was showing ten past, she swallowed hard, and wished she'd asked Tom to stay with her. This was the hardest thing she'd ever had to do.

At quarter-past five she felt a tiny flutter in her stomach. Even the baby was getting tired of her procrastination, and Hanna rubbed her skin, unsure whether she was trying to reassure herself, or her unborn child. She owed it to him or her to tell their daddy. And she owed it to Richard to tell him the truth.

She unlocked her phone and opened up her contacts. Pressing her finger on Richard's name, she pushed it down on the green phone symbol and watched the call connect before putting her cell to her ear.

One ring, two, and then three. Each moment stretched beyond time, and the nausea in her stomach rose up until her throat tightened.

"Hello?" A female voice. Not what she was expecting.

She took a deep breath. "May I speak with Richard, please?"

"Who's calling?"

"Hanna Vincent."

There was a long pause. She was about to repeat herself when the voice on the other end of the phone replied. "Hanna, this is Richard's mother, I'm not sure if you remember me."

"Yes, I remember you, Mrs Maxwell." How could she forget?

"He's not available right now. He's with his fiancée."

"I really need to speak with him, it's quite important." Hanna surprised herself with her vehemence.

"I don't think anything is as important as Meredith's health," Caroline replied tersely. "She's been told she will be in a wheelchair for the rest of her life. The girl is crippled, Hanna. Whatever you want to say, please don't bother, you can only cause them hurt." She paused momentarily as if to allow her words to sink in, before adding, "Don't call him again."

Hanna froze. For a moment she couldn't breathe, couldn't hear her own heartbeat. Reality fell like a ton of bricks, her previous certainty deserting her. It couldn't be true, could it? When she last saw Richard, he was hopeful that Meredith would be able to walk again. How he must have suffered, knowing that she was unable to walk, and he would need to stay by her side.

She wanted to see the news in black and white, so she opened her laptop and typed Meredith's name into the search box. The details of the accident flashed on to her screen. There was no news beyond the initial report back in February. Hanna felt her heart break as she remembered the vibrant, vivacious blonde, and tried to imagine her confined to a wheelchair for the rest of her life.

How could she ever tell Richard she was having his baby when he was needed so much? If she told him now, would he desert his fiancée and come to help her? Could she ever look him in the eye and respect him if he did? Was she able to put him in that position, where he had to choose between his fiancée's health and being with his child?

She knew she couldn't.

He would grow to hate her – and maybe their baby – for making him choose. He was a good man, almost too kind, and she knew his instincts would be telling him to stay with Meredith. All she had to do was remember how he had given up his dreams to take over Maxwell Enterprises after Leon died.

She hung up without saying a word, putting her hand over her heart, and feeling it clatter against her palm. Her whole body shook as she pressed more buttons on her phone and lifted it again, immediately calming upon hearing Tom's voice.

"I need to leave London until the baby is born."

This time she wasn't running. She was stepping down, putting others before herself. Though it broke her heart to know she would have to cut herself off from her surrogate family, she knew she wouldn't be able to see the Larsens. If they were to tell Richard the truth about the baby, she knew his heart would be torn in two.

Twenty-one

25th April 2012

"*PAT-A-CAKE, PAT-A-CAKE, BAKER'S man.*" Hanna touched Matty's tiny palm to hers, the slapping sound of skin on skin making his little eyes light up with delight. She repeated the song, and he squealed happily, nodding his head to encourage her to do it again.

He'd been awake for ten minutes, after a long afternoon nap, and it looked like he was going to make it through until Tom arrived. He'd made Hanna promise to keep his godson up until he got to his Villa in Nice, desperate to see how Matthew had changed in the few months since he'd last seen him.

"Row." Matty's vocabulary still consisted of single-word sentences, but each day he understood more. His face became so animated when Hanna asked him to find his shoes and he toddled back with them in his hand, standing proudly on his chubby legs.

Hanna took his hands in hers and began to sing 'Row your Boat'. As always, he held his breath until she got to the bit about crocodiles, and then he would let out an almighty shriek, doubling over with giggles when she put her hands over her ears in an exaggerated fashion, pretending he had deafened her.

Christ, how she loved him. From the moment he was born and placed in her arms, it was like the sun had come out after hiding behind clouds for months. The adoration she felt for him bubbled up inside her, squeezing her heart until it physically hurt. She would move mountains for this boy, slay dragons, battle through the mines of Moria if she had to. Nothing was too good for him.

Hanna had given birth in a hospital just outside Nice. An easy, uncomplicated birth, it was like a herald, welcoming the easiest, happiest child she'd ever had the luck to come across. Not that he didn't cry – she was used to waking up in the night, finding his pacifier, offering him an extra feed. But even then, she was so conditioned to his needs, that it didn't seem like a drag to have to pull herself out of bed. She counted herself way too lucky for that.

She'd tried to push the memory of Richard out of her mind, but he was never far away, always floating on the edge of her thoughts. She'd done the right thing; she really believed that. While Meredith was paralyzed and consigned to a wheel-chair, at least Hanna had a beautiful future planned out with her little man, even if he'd never be able to know his father.

Now Matty was nearly eighteen months, no longer a baby. Matthew Richard Vincent was her little man, light brown hair curling over his head, big brown eyes following her whenever she walked around the room. Hanna counted herself lucky that she'd spent nearly every day of the past year and a half with him, working from Tom's villa, writing Fatal Limits' biography, as well as writing for *The Buzz*.

She'd adapted Tom's orangery into an office. Her laptop rested on a vintage, white wooden desk. In the corner – piled high in a garish, plastic cornucopia – stood Matty's toys. Every half-hour or so, she would take a break, sit with him and build bricks until he pushed them back down. She loved to hear his gurgling guffaws.

"Do you remember Uncle Tom, Matty?" She lifted him onto her lap, burying her face in his soft, downy hair. "He likes to sing to you."

Matty babbled something unintelligible, and Hanna played their usual game. She pretended to understand what he was saying, talking back to him as if he was just another adult.

"That's right; he recorded that song for you."

'Dear Matty', released in February 2011, had gone platinum. Everybody thought it was a love song dedicated to a new girlfriend. Only the group and Hanna knew that it was really declaring Tom's love for his newborn godson. Every time she heard it, the song sent chills down Hanna's spine.

Matty climbed onto Hanna's lap, pushing himself up to standing, lacing his fleshy arms around her neck. His wrists still had little rolls that looked like somebody had put elastic bands over his skin. Every day he was getting stronger, slimmer, more like a child. Only the delight of getting to know him better was enough to quell the sadness that her baby was growing up.

A loud three-tone beep from her phone alerted her to an incoming text. Lifting Matty from her lap, she balanced him on her knee, walking over to the corner of the glass room. Her iPhone was still lit up, and she picked it up, scraping her finger across the screen.

Landed in Monte Carlo. Should be there in a couple of hours.

The final leg of Fatal Limits' world tour had been in Australia, and Tom had taken a couple of weeks off to relax and do some surfing. He'd flown home to London a week earlier, and was planning to join Hanna in Nice for a while.

They needed to go through the final proofs of the biography, and hoped to spend some time together since Tom had been away so much after Matty was born.

Hanna had only been back to London a couple of times herself. She still kept her flat there, knowing one day she might want to move home. But at the moment, she was settled in France. Matty loved the gardens of Tom's villa, and going to the beach. It was an altogether more peaceful way of life.

Plus, she didn't have to worry about bumping into the Larsens.

Will put the champagne on ice. Fish fingers for tea.

She smiled as she sent him the text. One of his favourite parts of being a godfather was trying Matty's food. During his whirlwind visits to France between tour dates, he'd enthusiastically feed Matty the frozen, pureed food that Hanna had made. Often he'd eat more than half himself, in his 'one for Matty, one for Tom', routine.

Best make an extra portion. I'm bringing someone with me.

Now, that was intriguing. To the best of her knowledge, Tom was single, although Hanna suspected he had his regular hook-ups in some of the towns he toured. Her hope that he would get together with Ruby seemed to go nowhere, and part of her suspected it was Hanna's fault. In the carefully drawn lines between herself and the Larsens, Tom had placed himself firmly in Hanna's camp.

Not that she expected him to choose. She still kept in touch with Ruby and Claire, almost surprised that they accepted her lame-ass excuse for not being able to see them. She'd invented an agreement between herself and the 'reclusive singer' she was writing about, saying she couldn't reveal her whereabouts to family and friends. Perhaps it was Claire's experience with New York eccentrics that led her to believe anything was possible, or Ruby's preoccupation with her PhD in Molecular Physics. Either way, it had been embarrassingly easy to cover up Matty's existence.

$\mathcal{T}$HE FRONT DOOR banged, and Matty started babbling, splashing his hands in the bathwater.

"You here?" Tom called out at her from the hallway.

"In the bathroom," Hanna shouted back, her face covered with a grin. "It's a bit of a disaster in here."

Within moments, the bathroom door had flung open and Tom was standing in front of her, an absurd smile moulding his lips.

"Matty boy!" He leaned over the bath and squeezed Matthew, who smashed his fists in the water in protest. Tom's expensive black T-shirt was soaked.

Hanna drew her lips together tightly in an attempt to quell her laughter. Matty looked a little perturbed, both by the break in routine and Tom's over-enthusiastic hug. He was getting weird about people he didn't see very often. Hanna hoped it was a phase.

She stood and hugged Tom, feeling the wetness of his T-shirt soak through to her blouse. "How was your flight?"

"Long. I spent most of it asleep." He rubbed at his eyes with the heel of his palm, as if to confirm his exhaustion.

"I bet your friend loved that."

"My friend?"

"Whoever it is you brought with you? The one I've prepared dinner for."

"You mean Ruby." Tom laughed, and the words made Hanna's blood run cold.

"Ruby, as in Larsen?" Her voice dropped to a whisper. "You've brought Ruby here?"

221

Tom put out a hand and rubbed the top of her arm. "It's a long story; there are a few things you need to talk about."

"I'd say there are."

Hanna looked up to see Ruby standing in the doorway.

"You said you'd wait until I'd spoken to her." Tom walked over to Ruby and curled his arm around her waist. "This isn't going to be any easier if you're at each other's necks."

Hanna felt her throat constrict. Panic made it hard to breathe. She felt betrayed by Tom and afraid that now the dam had been opened, the cozy little life she had built for Matty and herself was being threatened by those she missed the most.

"Ruby, I'm so—"

Matty splashed the water again, this time enough to get water on Ruby's top. Hanna watched as a smile broke out over Ruby's face, her features softening as she looked at Matty.

"He's beautiful."

Hanna just nodded, unsure what to say.

"I can't believe you didn't tell me about him, Hanna. I can't understand why you didn't trust me. We're supposed to be friends, Jesus, you're my best friend, and all this time you've been emailing me with stories of reclusive artists and hard-to-write stories."

"I am kind of reclusive," Tom pointed out, earning a slap on the arm from Ruby.

"Don't think I'm done with you, either." Ruby shook her head at him.

"It's not Tom's fault. I asked him not to tell anybody."

"He told the fucking world, Hanna. He wrote a song about your son, for God's sake." Ruby's face fell again. "Yours and Richard's son."

Hanna didn't bother to deny it. The resemblance was growing along with Matty. His newborn dark hair had fallen out, to be replaced by Richard's light brown tones. Only his eyes resembled Hanna's.

"Can I just get Matty ready for bed?" Hanna pulled her wet, wriggling son out of the bath, wrapping him snugly in a white, fluffy towel. "We can talk when he's asleep."

Ruby's gaze remained on her nephew, her eyes gentle as she watched him chew at the towel. "Sure. I'm going to go unpack. You've got half an hour."

MATTY WAS ALMOST asleep when she sat with him on the chair, finishing the cup of warm milk she had given him. His whole body was relaxed against her, and she could feel his breathing slow until it reached the cadence of sleep. Only then did she lift him up and place him in his cot, switching on the nightlight and monitor, before padding out of the nursery and gently pulling the door closed behind her.

She was dreading this. Part of her was so angry with Tom for putting her in this position without any warning. Mostly, she was furious with herself. The situation she'd put Tom in was untenable, particularly if he'd been reconnecting with Ruby. To ask him to lie was completely unfair.

Hanna walked into the open-plan living room. The evening sun was orange, slowly creeping toward the horizon. It lit the room with an amber glow, reflecting from Tom and Ruby's skin until they looked almost otherworldly. She watched them for a moment, as they sat close together, heads bent toward each other as they talked. How long had this been going on? They looked way too close for two people who had hooked up in the past few days in London.

"Would you like a glass of wine?" Tom stood up and approached her, wearing a conciliatory smile. She attempted a wan smile back, trying to convey that they were okay.

"I'd love a glass of Sancerre." She'd actually love the bottle, but she wasn't going to win any mum of the year awards with that attitude.

Tom left the room and Ruby stood up, her face youthful in the dull evening light. Hanna felt the pull before Ruby even moved, and within moments they were in each other's arms, a mess of tears and recriminations, hugs and anger.

They were sisters. The underlying love pinned them together no matter what.

"I'm so mad at you." Ruby sobbed into Hanna's shoulder. "I need you to tell me why." Hanna lifted Ruby's face, kissing her cheek, feeling their tears intermingle. The lump in her throat grew so big she was finding it hard to speak.

"I—" Hanna stopped herself, trying to think how to explain her actions. "When I found out I was pregnant, I called Richard to tell him. Caroline picked up his phone and told me about Meredith."

"About Meredith?" Ruby clarified.

"About her not being able to walk, after the accident." They were both breathing a little easier, and Hanna took Ruby's hand and led her to the sofa. They sat down, knees touching, and continued to talk.

"Meredith can walk." Ruby was perplexed. "She couldn't at first, after the accident, but she was soon up and okay."

Hanna shook her head. "No, Caroline told me she was confined to a wheelchair for life. That's why I didn't tell Richard, because I couldn't bear for him to leave her for me."

Ruby was as still as a statue. "That's not true."

"I did!" Hanna protested. "I called and I was going to tell him."

"I mean the part about Meredith. That was a lie. Caroline lied to you."

It was like Hanna's heart stopped beating. Just about died in her chest cavity. Why the hell would Caroline lie to her about Meredith's ability to walk? It didn't make sense, unless she was trying to keep Hanna and Richard apart. Which would mean everything was a big, fat lie. The thought sickened her to the pit of her stomach. All those months of being alone, raising a child without a father was for nothing.

Nothing.

What the hell was she going to do? She'd lied to Richard by omission, thinking it was for the best, but really she'd stolen his son away from him. There was no way he'd ever forgive her for that. And there was no chance Hanna would ever forgive Caroline. She wanted to scratch her eyes out, scream at what her careless words had done. The bitch had stolen all of their futures.

Hanna shook her head, the tears flooding from her eyes. "No."

"Yes. Meredith's perfectly able to walk. She walked right out of Richard's life."

"No!" Hanna screamed. "I didn't tell him about Matty so he could spend his life with her. Taking care of her."

"Hanna, he finished things with Meredith nearly two years ago. He came to London and found you were gone. He was so angry; I can't even tell you what it was like. I was scared he was going to break something, or himself. I didn't dare tell him that we were still in touch by email."

Hanna wasn't sure if she was going to vomit, or if she really needed that drink. Where the hell was Tom with her wine? She hoped he brought the bottle. If only she'd tried to call him again, or spoken to Ruby and let her know. She could be with Richard now, watching him play with his son, maybe rolling

225

him a baseball or teaching him to kick a football. God, she was so desperate to go back and change everything.

"He's not with Meredith anymore?" Hanna felt the need to clarify. She wasn't sure what she wanted the answer to be.

"No. He's not with anyone that I know of. Not that he talks to me about that sort of thing. I've been staying with him while I'm at Columbia."

"That's nice, that you two reconnected." Hanna's response was automatic. The thinking part of her brain was still firmly stuck in Manhattan, in a penthouse apartment. She could almost see Matty running along the expensive wooden floor, his face lit up as Daddy came home after a day's work. Another sob escaped Hanna's throat as she realized this was a scene she would never get to see.

"It's been amazing." Ruby's eyes flashed with happy memories. Tom walked in carrying a bottle of wine and three glasses.

"Is it safe to come in yet?" he asked, putting the glasses on the wooden coffee table, pouring the cold, pale wine into them.

"We haven't scratched each other's eyes out, if that's what you're asking." Ruby grabbed Hanna's hand and squeezed tightly. "Now we just need to talk about how you're going to explain this to Richard."

Hanna was still numb, unable to mould her thoughts into anything resembling sense. She let Ruby take the lead, submitting to her friend's suggestions.

"I'm not sure if he'll even talk to you," Ruby confessed. "On the rare occasion your name is mentioned, he usually leaves the room."

Hanna's heart dropped. Of course he must hate her. Her last words to him, when they saw each other in New York, were a promise she would wait for him in London. No wonder he was so angry when he got there and she was gone.

Again.

Would he hate Matty, too? Her heart clenched at the thought of anybody despising her child, but if Richard was angry with Hanna, he could well reject his son. Matthew was the perfect combination of them both, in looks as well as temperament, and Richard would clearly be able to see Hanna's half shining through.

Either way, she couldn't put it off any longer. It wasn't her choice to make. She wanted to call him right now, spill the truth over the phone as soon as possible to make up for lost time. But it wasn't the sort of news you gave when you were thousands of miles away.

"I can't tell him over the phone. I'll have to fly to New York." She pulled at a fingernail with her teeth. "I'm not sure how Matty will take to that, though." Hanna could picture her son running up and down the aisle, screaming at the other passengers. The vision made her shudder.

"Leave him here, with us," Ruby suggested. "I'm desperate to get to know my nephew, and I know from his song that Tom's already in love."

"He's going through a clingy stage." Hanna wavered. She could see the sense in Ruby's suggestion. She just wasn't sure she could bear to be without him.

"Give us a couple of weeks to bond with him. If you think we're up to the job, then you can fly to New York, tell Richard and fly right back here. I promise we'll treat him like a king." Ruby's voice betrayed her excitement. Hanna softened as she saw Tom staring at her, his eyes burning brightly.

"Will Richard even agree to see me?" Hanna wondered, knowing her words were tantamount to an agreement. Ruby leaned forward and hugged her tightly, her loud squeal making Hanna wince.

"Probably not," Ruby replied. "But I'll call and make an appointment with him in my name. You can go and tell him at work. At least if he's surrounded by people he can't go completely crazy."

It seemed like Ruby had everything planned in her mind. In a couple of weeks, Hanna would be catching a plane to New York. Fear fought with excitement in her stomach, mixing with the alcohol she was knocking back. The thought of seeing Richard again made her legs shake.

She would do it because he deserved to know about his son. She would do it because Matty deserved to have a father. Most of all, she would do it because she loved him so much, she thought her heart might burst.

Twenty-Two

12th May 2012

*I*T WAS EARLY afternoon when the plane touched down at JFK. The landing was bumpy enough to make her already-queasy stomach lurch hard. For the first time in all her transatlantic trips, she was distinctly aware of her own mortality. Fears of what would happen to Matty if she died played havoc with her thought patterns.

All the more reason to tell Richard, the snarky part of her brain informed her. Hanna quashed the thought.

Even her own psyche was against her.

She hadn't bothered checking in any baggage. Her return flight was booked for the following day, and carry-on luggage would be enough for one night. Toiletries, make-up, and a change of clothes were all she needed until she could step foot in France again.

The queue at immigration moved fast. Each step toward the glass booth was a step closer to telling Richard the most shocking news of his life, and Hanna felt the need to dawdle, to prevaricate. She fiddled with her dark-blue passport, wondering if she would have been better off using her European one. The queue was so much longer on that side of the room.

Closing her eyes, she remembered the way Ruby had hugged her before she left the villa in Nice. Her words of encouragement, whispered in Hanna's ear, were enough to plant a seed of hope that eventually Richard might forgive her for running yet again. She hadn't had time to nurture the seed yet – to let it bloom into any kind of plant. She hoped she wouldn't kill it.

"You've been out of the country for a while ma'am?" The immigration officer was tapping into his computer with his right hand, staring at Hanna's passport, held open by his left.

"I have joint nationality. I've been living in Europe."

"Are you planning to stay for a while?" He glanced up at her, his eyes enquiring.

"Just until tomorrow. I'm meeting with a friend."

The officer closed her passport and handed it back to her. "I hope you have a nice stay, ma'am." His eyes were already on the next passenger. Hanna picked up her bag and moved forward, through the barrier. She could feel time counting down like a ticker clock on New Year's Eve. The thought made her excited and fearful.

She bypassed the luggage carousel, making her way to the door that led into the main terminal. The air conditioning made her skin pucker with goosebumps, but from the look of the sun shining through the glass wall of the terminal, it was a beautiful, spring day.

Standing in the line for a taxi, she practiced their conversation in her mind. *Tell him as soon as possible*, she reminded herself, *if you beat around the bush he's either going to throw you out or kill you*. The news that he had a son was like a Band-Aid, and for Richard's own sake, she needed to rip it off fast. She could deal with the wound later. To tear it away inch by inch wouldn't save them any misery in the long run.

Whatever she did, it was going to hurt.

Getting to the front of the line, Hanna climbed into the yellow taxi, pulling her bag in behind her. The black vinyl seat was cold against her skin, and her eyes automatically met the driver's in his rear-view mirror.

"Where to?"

"Financial district. Corner of Pine and Nassau."

"Maxwell Enterprises?" the driver clarified.

"Yes, that's correct." Hanna prayed that Ruby had managed to sort out her security pass as promised. If she had to call up to Lisa to get it sorted out, Hanna had the feeling she might bolt.

The journey was mercifully long. The streets were a tangle of cars and trucks, fumes angrily pumping out as vehicles remained stationary. Hanna sat back and listened to the music coming out of the cab's stereo system, allowing the regular rhythm to calm her heart. In the years since she'd been here last, it looked like the taxis had been upgraded. There was a screen showing their exact location, occasionally interrupted by advertisements for local companies. Their slow progress was clear to see as she followed the flashing red dot along the streets.

It was 3:00 p.m. local time when the cab pulled up on Pine. Hanna handed the driver sixty dollars, telling him to keep the change, and then opened the door, stepping out onto the street. The sounds didn't seem as jarring as they used to – perhaps her year of living here had inured her to the cacophony. The familiar smell of exhaust fumes and food carts assaulted her nose in a delicious way.

Her confidence seemed to have returned. In her skinny jeans and black T-shirt she was out of place amongst the grey suits, but rather than feeling inferior, she smiled a little, remembering that her own work seemed so much more fulfilling, and allowed her to stay at home with her son. In comparison the workers seemed like prisoners; their uniforms may have been classier and made-to-measure, but they were just as caged as a murderer in San Quentin.

Security was surprisingly easy. Her name was on the list, and a pass had already been printed for her. She clipped it to the waistband of her jeans and headed for the bathroom, needing to give herself one final glance-over before she went up to his office.

When she emerged – make-up touched up and hair calmed – Hanna made her way toward the bank of elevators at the corner of the lobby. She'd been here a few times before: when she was dating Richard before her mum died, and then later, when she was living in Manhattan. This time felt different. The walls seemed closer together, the elevator more ominous. Maybe it was she who had changed, rather than the building.

Pausing outside the door to the outer office, she took a deep breath to bolster her resolve. Squaring her shoulders, she reached her hand out to push the handle down, rearranging her features into a neutral, unreadable expression.

Then she walked in.

"Hanna?" Lisa's face indicated her confusion. The other two administrators in the room glanced up, their keyboard-tapping momentarily paused as their faces betrayed their interest. They must have been new; Hanna didn't recognize them.

"Hello, Lisa. How are you?" She'd always liked Richard's assistant.

"I'm good, thank you. And you?"

Hanna tried to smile. "Fine. Is Richard available?"

"He's in meetings all afternoon. I don't think he was expecting you." Lisa's response was polite as always. Her expression indicated her regret.

"I'm his three-thirty. Ruby booked the appointment for me."

"Oh, that will explain it. I'll let him know you're here."

Hanna wanted to back right out of the room and hotfoot it back to JFK. Was she ready for this? She hadn't seen him for so long. Everything about the situation made her nerves tingle. The light feeling of nausea that swirled around her stomach intensified. If she wasn't careful, she was going to be sick.

You are in control, she reminded herself. Tell him the news, give him a chance to digest it, and get out.

She wasn't going to panic; she wasn't going to lose control. Hanna kept her breathing steady, even as her heart began to race. The last thing she needed was to collapse in his outer office.

"You can go in." Lisa's voice brought her back to the present.

"Can I leave my bag here?" Hanna indicated her small carry-on bag. Lisa took it with a smile, and gestured toward Richard's door.

This was it.

Was she ready? Would she ever be? The only thing she knew for sure was that she owed it to Richard, and to Matty, to tell him the truth. She'd just have to deal with the fallout. One foot in front of the other, she crossed the room until she reached his door, her eyes caressing the familiar dark oak, fingers reaching out to let herself in.

Hanna pushed the door open, the hinges creaking lightly under the pressure. The room had been redecorated at some point in the past year or two, the cream walls repainted a paler white, the furniture replaced with sleeker, modern lines. It made her sad to realize that life had gone on without her. How would Richard react when he discovered just how life had continued without him?

"What are you doing here?"

Richard was leaning on his desk, ankles crossed, his arms folded firmly in front of his chest. His suit jacket hung on a stand behind him. Though she tried not to look, she couldn't help but follow the lines of his clothes all the way down his body.

He had filled out nicely since she had last seen him. The thin cotton of his shirt clung to his biceps, skimming his taut abdomen as it tucked into his dress trousers. His hips were still lean and tight, and she closed her eyes as she tried not to remember how they had felt between her thighs, as he had moved inside her, breathing softly in her ear, as she had moaned and whimpered and—

She shook her head. She wasn't standing in his large, oak-panelled office just to take a trip down memory lane, as pleasant as that might be. She had flown here, over three thousand miles, to tell him what he deserved to know.

Inappropriate laughter bubbled up in her throat as she considered the ridiculous melodrama of the situation. Her seventeen-year-old self would be rolling her eyes, wondering how this twenty-nine-year-old woman had managed to turn a seemingly promising life into a soap opera.

She glanced up at his face, looking at his lips, which had turned down into a deep scowl. His eyes had narrowed beneath his brows, and his straight, patrician nose was slightly crinkled in response to her presence.

The contempt he felt toward her was radiating from him.

Hanna tried to keep her breathing steady, reminding herself that although she was in *his* office, on the penthouse floor of *his* building, this was *her* show.

She was in control.

If he viewed her with contempt now, God only knew how he would feel once he'd heard what she had to say. He had been an integral part of her life for so long – as a friend, a confidant, even a lover – but never before did he have the power to break her.

"As nice as it is to see you," he drawled, the tone of his voice making it patently clear that her being in his office was anything but nice, "I have a meeting in five minutes. Exactly what is it that you want?"

He had no idea, but this was it. Time to open her mouth and tell him what he needed to hear. Her arms suddenly felt heavy, and her fingers trembled, a physical manifestation of her nervousness. Her laughter was replaced by something more unsettling as she tried to take in a deep breath and form the words that she had travelled all this way to say.

Her tongue darted out to moisten her lips. She watched his gaze move down to her mouth. He stared at her with dark eyes, watching as her teeth drew in her bottom lip.

"Richard." Her voice was surprisingly strong. She could do this. She could tell him the truth, and then get the hell out of here.

Back on a plane.

Back home.

Back to *him*.

"Richard, we have a baby."

The silence that followed was palpable. Hanna could almost taste Richard's confusion as she watched expressions flitting across his face. She had done what she came here to do – had told him the truth – and now she was preparing herself for the fallout.

Richard remained frozen. She wondered if she should repeat herself. Her feet shuffled beneath her, wanting to move toward him, to get her close enough to touch him.

That kind of thought was dangerous.

"We have a baby?" he repeated.

"Well he's a toddler now, but he was a baby. Once." Damn it, she was babbling now, her nerves shining through. It took every ounce of effort she had to meet his eyes. Her body recoiled when she saw the anger and confusion radiating from them.

"What the hell is going on?" He frowned, the deep creases in his forehead emerging as he tried to absorb her news. "I don't understand what you're saying."

She realized she needed to show him proof, rather than try to explain. Her hands were shaking again, but she managed to control herself enough to pull her cell from her pocket, trying to steady her fingers as she pulled up her photos.

"When I left New York in 2010, I was pregnant. I didn't realize it then, in fact I didn't find out for a few months, but the last time we were together, we made a baby." Her voice lingered over the final words. She still found the fact amazing.

"Are you certain he's mine?"

His question was legitimate, but it still cut her to the quick. "Absolutely."

The momentary silence was like a wall between the two of them. Hanna wondered if she would ever be able to breach it. She decided to continue, to give him all the information and then get the hell out of there. She wished she could hold Matty in her arms right now. She needed his presence to ground her.

"His name is Matthew, he was born on November twelfth. He's eighteen months old." She moved forward to show Richard a photograph on her iPhone, picking one she took a couple of days before. Matty was standing up in Tom's living room, holding a ball as he attempted to throw it to Ruby. His joy at playing with his aunt was written all over his face; and he was biting his lip in concentration.

"That's him?" Richard's voice was dead. "That's my son?"

Hanna nodded, the lump in her throat preventing her from speaking. She'd dreamed of this moment so many times, and his lack of emotion was killing her. Then a moment later, as she saw Richard's face twist with anger, she longed for his previous, calm demeanour.

"I need to get out of this room. Stay here," he spat, not giving her an option. He stalked over to the door that led to the outer office and wrenched it open. When he slammed it behind him, she heard a lock turn.

He'd locked her in.

He trusted her so little. He was so sure she'd run, that he felt he had to lock her in.

Or perhaps he was trying to protect her. The next moment, she heard something being thrown across the outer office, and the loud vibration of his voice as he shouted, followed by Lisa's gentler tone, murmuring to him.

Hanna walked to the dark-brown leather sofa by the large, picture window and sat down, fingers tapping on the iPhone she still held in her hand.

I've told him. She sent the text to Ruby.

Within moments, Ruby had sent a reply. *How did he take it? He's locked me in his office.*

Are you okay? Is he okay? Bless Ruby. She always supported them both.

He's left the room. I'm fine. I think he's throwing furniture around.

A few minutes later, Hanna heard the door unlock, and then saw Lisa's face appear as she pushed it open.

"How are you doing, Hanna?"

Hanna tried not to smile. Everybody was asking her the question they should ask Richard. She was fine. A little shaken, very worried, but fine.

"Is Richard all right?"

"He's a little angry. It's none of my business, but I think I got the gist. I told him to get some fresh air and come back when he's calmed down." Behind Lisa, Hanna could see the debris all over the floor where Richard had thrown pen pots and other office equipment. "Can I get you a drink while you wait for him?"

"I'd love a glass of water, thank you." She hadn't realized how dry her mouth was until Lisa had offered. The confrontation had sucked all the moisture from her.

It took more than twenty minutes for Richard to come back. While she waited, Hanna texted Ruby a few times, learning that Richard had been speaking with his sister on the phone, and seemed calmer than before. Hanna braced herself anyway when the door opened, afraid of what side of Richard she might see.

"I'm sorry I locked you in." His first words calmed her. "I needed to get out before I caused any damage."

"I'm the one who should be apologizing."

Richard ignored her expression of regret. "I've asked Lisa to book us on the first flight to France. There's a plane leaving tonight."

"I've got a flight booked for tomorrow—" She began to protest, but Richard waved her off.

"It's done. While I wait for my luggage to be dropped off you can give me a few answers." He moved toward her, sitting down on the leather chair opposite her. In the glare of the afternoon sun, his features seemed sharper. She felt the strangest urge to trace the line of his jaw with her finger.

"I'd be happy to."

Richard leaned back, running his hands through his hair. "Why didn't you tell me? Was it in retaliation for me staying with Meredith while she got better? Because that's pretty fucking low." His words tumbled together, and Hanna could feel each one pierce her heart.

She shook her head rapidly. "I wanted to tell you. I didn't find out until I was four months pregnant. As soon as I had the scan I called you." She picked up the glass of water and knocked it back. "Your mother answered. She told me that Meredith was consigned to a wheelchair for life, and that you were looking after her."

Richard's hand was still in his hair, now tugging rather than smoothing. She resisted the urge to pull his arm down.

"My mother said *what*?" His voice was pure ice.

"She said Meredith was never going to walk again, that she would be stuck in a wheelchair forever."

The silence that followed was thick. It took Richard a while to cut through it. "Why would she say that?"

Hanna's heart felt like it was being squeezed by a vice. She was so scared he'd believe Caroline over her. Why wouldn't he?

"I don't know." She shook her head. "But I believed her." Hanna wanted to go back in time, relive that telephone conversation and ask Caroline more pointed questions. But she'd been so emotional, reeling from the discovery that she was pregnant, desperate to talk to Richard and tell him the news. Caroline had taken advantage and cut her off before she'd even begun.

"You don't know." His voice had taken on that dead tone again. She was finding it so hard to read him. His face was like a mask, and she wanted to reach out and grab him, shake some feeling into him. "So why didn't you call me again?"

Hanna licked her dry lips. "Because if I told you I was pregnant, you would have left Meredith. I couldn't do that to her, I couldn't do that to you. I thought she was paralyzed

239

and she needed you. I knew it would tear you in two to decide between us."

"It was all a lie." His previous stoic face was overrun by emotion. "My mother lied."

"She didn't know I was pregnant." Hanna's voice wavered, and she could feel the tears pricking at her eyes. "I should have told you."

He pushed himself out of his seat, pacing the dark wooden floor. "I can't even tell you how fucked up I am right now. I'm so angry at my mother, and at you. I'm even furious Ruby got to meet my son before I did. If you weren't the mother of my child, I'd probably want to kill you."

Hanna could feel herself shaking again. His frame of mind was swinging all over the place, and she could understand why. If she'd just found out about a child, eighteen months after the fact, she'd be angry, too. Not to mention confused and frightened.

She looked at him. "You said you had questions, as in plural?"

"What's his full name?"

This was going to hurt, she thought. "Matthew Richard Vincent."

"You named him after me?"

"I couldn't give him your surname, so I gave him your first name. Matthew means *Gift from God*." She allowed a small sigh to escape her lips. "He truly is a gift, Richard."

"Is he healthy? Is he happy?" His words shot out like bullets.

Her heart clenched. Even in the most emotional turmoil of his life, he was asking about the well-being of others. She tried to quench the love for him that was threatening to spill out of her.

"He's perfectly healthy. He's had all his immunizations. There have been a few falls and bruises, but nothing major." She attempted to smile at him through her tears. "He's the happiest kid you could ever meet. He's always smiling, loves playing games. When I walk into the house after I've been out, the sweetest, most beautiful grin seems to split his face in two." She was waxing lyrical now, on a roll. "And he's so clever. He already knows so many words, and he was walking before he was a year. You'll love him."

The rapt expression on Richard's face told her he already did.

"I need to see him." His voice cracked. "I can't believe this is happening."

Hanna wanted to reach out and touch him. The maelstrom of emotions was taking its toll on Richard. She was desperate to help him. "I'm so sorry. I wish you could have been there when he was born."

"Was it an easy birth?" He stopped pacing and moved back to sit with her. This time he was beside her, and it gave her a spark of hope.

"It felt like he was ripping me in two, but he was worth all the pain. The moment they put him in my arms I realized I'd do it all again in a heartbeat."

"Have you got any pictures of when he was a baby?"

"All the newborn ones are in an album at home. In France. I've got a few of when he was crawling." She scrolled through her phone and showed the photos to Richard. He looked at them all, his eyes lit up as he regarded his son.

"He's beautiful," he whispered.

"I can't wait for you to meet him."

"Ruby let me listen to him on the phone. He said your name."

Hanna swallowed, her smile eclipsed by the tears as she thought about Matty. She missed him so much it hurt. Her arms ached from his absence. She reached up and wiped her damp cheeks.

"He's such a clever boy."

The door opened and Lisa put her head around the space. "Jack's here with your luggage. Do you want to go straight down?"

"Yes." Richard's reply was crisp. He walked over to his desk and booted down his computer, packing up his laptop along with some files. As he zipped up the bag, he turned to Hanna. "Have you got Wi-Fi at your place in France?"

Hanna nodded, wondering just how long Richard was intending to stay. Then she started to worry about his intentions. He couldn't remain in France forever. Was he going to try to take Matty away from her? He had every right to request joint custody, and no matter how much it would break her heart, she wouldn't be able to refuse him.

She'd thought she'd be able to tell him the news, and then go back to France. She'd assumed her life would remain the same, only enhanced by the fact that Matty would get to know his dad. If her life was complicated before, it was nothing compared to what the future would bring.

Richard walked into the outer office and picked up her bag, hoisting it over his shoulder. Hanna trailed after him, her heart still racing as she thought about the future. Part of her was so excited she'd see Matty in less than a day's time. The other half was so afraid she was finding it hard to breathe.

It remained to be seen, whether the hardest part was over yet.

Twenty-Three

13th May 2012

WHILE LEANING BACK in the leather seat, Richard glanced over at the small, round window, noticing they were finally over land. The patchwork of fields far below was enough for him to know they were flying over Europe; even from the sky it was so very different from the US. Smaller, prettier, it somehow suited the temperament of its inhabitants.

One of which was his son.

His son.

He could repeat the words over and again in his mind, but they weren't sinking in. For the first time ever, he had taken a pill before getting on the plane – enough to calm his edgy nerves, and to stop him from wanting to alternately kiss and kill Hanna Vincent. She was asleep next to him, her long, mahogany hair splayed out over the headrest of the seat. Two transatlantic flights in less than twenty-four hours had knocked it out of her. The exhaustion was written across her beautiful face.

He glanced back down at his open laptop, scanning his eyes over the emails he had downloaded before getting on the plane. When he'd asked Lisa to book them on this flight, she'd automatically cancelled and rearranged all of his meetings, though it looked like he'd have to do some via video conference. He hoped to hell Hanna's Wi-Fi was up to the challenge.

Another surge of rational anger swept through him. His face contorted as he tried to control the fury, as his hands balled into desperate fists. He couldn't look at her, couldn't think about what she had done without wanting to cause her pain. It was killing him.

A stifled sob brought him out of the red cloud, and he turned his head to see Hanna had woken up. She was staring at him, her hand covering her mouth, cheeks shiny with tears. His anger abated, replaced by concern, and he cursed his alternating moods.

He wasn't going to reach out and wipe away her tears. Not this time. Not even if his hand was already hovering, desperate to touch her cheek.

"I'm sorry." Her voice was little more than a whisper. "You look so angry."

Richard took a deep breath. This was no place to have this conversation, no matter how desperate Hanna was to be absolved. The overhead lights were dimmed, but the constant movements of the stewardesses, and the numerous travellers who were walking down the aisle to the bathroom, made their cocoon anything but private. The recriminations would have to wait until they'd landed in France, until they were alone in the villa.

Until he met his son.

The seatbelt light illuminated over their heads, followed by an announcement from the head steward that they were beginning their descent. Richard stared out of the window again, amazed at the beauty of the land below. The bright white light of the morning sun pierced his eyes. New York already seemed so far behind, like a city of dreams.

"I've arranged for a car to pick us up from the airport." He tried to keep his voice conversational. Being in close proximity to her was such a bad idea. Every emotion it was possible to suffer seemed to pass through him whenever he looked at her. He tried his hardest not to.

"Thank you."

"Ruby and Tom are going to meet us at the villa. After that they're travelling to Monaco for a few days. It will give us a chance to sort things out."

He could feel Hanna tense up. Her arm was millimetres away from his, and he watched as her fingers tapped nervously on the leather rest. Clutching his thigh hard, he damped down the urge to curl his hand around hers, to rub his thumb along her knuckles until she calmed.

"They're leaving?" she asked, her voice tremulous. "I was hoping to spend a little time with Ruby."

Richard shook his head, still staring at her hand. "I want some time with my son, away from everybody else."

Another barely contained sob. He didn't need to look at her to know she was biting her lip. He knew everything about this girl: the way she laughed, the way she cried.

The way she lied.

The plane was descending fast, and he could feel his ears numb up as they tried to adjust to the altitude. Hanna reached forward and grabbed a bottle of water from the cup holder and started to gulp rapidly. He'd forgotten how sensitive her ear canals were, but now he could remember in stark resolution those few flights they took together from New York to London, and how he'd stroke her hair as she swallowed desperately, trying to equalize the pressure in her head.

He licked his dry lips. He wasn't going to look at her.

Her hand lifted away from the armrest, and he assumed she was grabbing at her ear. His gaze followed the wake of her movement until he was looking at her thick, wavy hair. It glowed almost red in the reflection of the bright light streaming through the porthole of the plane. Her fingers curled around her ear, and when he moved his eyes to look at her face, he could see it contorted with pain.

"Come here." He pulled her head against his, threading his fingers through her hair. He massaged her scalp in a long-forgotten rhythm, feeling her relax against him as he continued to caress.

She was still crying. Her tears were falling onto his shirt, moistening it where her cheeks touched him. The heel of his palm touched her other cheek, wiping it dry as he moved his hand against her.

"Thank you." Her voice was muffled by his chest. He wasn't sure what she was grateful for – the human decency of trying to quell her pain, the fact he'd finally touched her, or maybe the hope they could find a way through this mess and come out on the other side with a level of amicability.

Once off the plane, they separated at passport control – Hanna having to go through the European side, while he remained with the herd of people trying to make their way through 'rest of the world'. She waited for him by baggage reclaim; she'd even picked his bags up from the carousel and placed them on a waiting trolley. Their interactions reverted to being excruciatingly polite.

The journey to the villa took under an hour. It was a bright spring day; the fields were full of greenery and the roads were full of small, noisy cars, barely obeying the rules of driving. Every now and then a tiny car, usually a Renault or Citroën, would swerve around their taxi and Hanna would flinch.

When they pulled up to Tom's house, Richard felt his mouth drop open. When Hanna had called it a 'villa', he had imagined a quaint country cottage, maybe two or three bedrooms complete with peeling white paint and rotting wooden shutters. Instead it was more of a palace. Even for someone like Richard, who was used to wealth and property, it was large. It kicked him in the stomach to know his son was growing up within these walls.

The driver climbed out and unloaded Richard's suitcases from the trunk, passing Hanna her small carry-on with a wry smile. Richard lifted all three bags and they walked together toward the front door, both silent, drowning under the weight of their own thoughts. It wasn't until they reached the entrance that Hanna broke the silence.

"How do you want to do this?" She sounded more confident again, as if being on home turf was giving her the advantage. "Shall I introduce you as a friend? Not that Matty will understand, he's only little, but I don't want to do anything to make you uncomfortable."

"I'm his father, Hanna," Richard replied, the anger returning. "Perhaps we can start as we mean to go on?"

Hanna swallowed and nodded. "Okay. But he doesn't always warm up to strangers immediately. You need to give him a bit of time. Don't get upset if he doesn't come to you right away."

Before he had a chance to respond, the door was pulled open in front of them. Richard looked up to see Tom standing there, a huge grin on his face and a small child in his arms, wriggling with desperate excitement.

"He couldn't wait any longer, Hanna. He was running for the door."

Richard tried to bite back the jealousy as Matty reached his arms out for his mother, babbling wildly. Hanna grabbed him and held him tight, burying her face in his hair, telling him how much she missed him.

She missed him?

How the hell did she think Richard felt?

As if she could hear his thoughts, Hanna lifted her head up and looked at Richard, her lips curling into a smile. She turned slightly, so he could see Matty's face, and every ounce of anger brewing in his body disappeared.

His son was beautiful.

His dark brown eyes were deep and expressive. He stared at Richard with interest, lifting his hand up and sucking on his thumb as he appraised him. Light brown hair flopped over his forehead – a colour Richard had seen in enough photographs of his own childhood to know it would eventually darken into a deeper brown, making Matty resemble his father.

Matty's scant eyebrows pulled down into a frown, not in sadness so much as concentration. He pulled his hand away from his mouth – his thumb still glistening from being sucked – and pointed at Richard.

"That?"

Hanna caught Richard's eye again, her features reassuring. "That's Daddy, darling."

Matty shrugged, unperturbed by the news, the words meaning nothing to him. Richard wasn't sure if he was relieved he was being accepted so easily, or angry he was robbed of a tearful reunion.

His heart rate sped when he saw his son staring up at him. He was so beautiful. It was like the best parts of both of them had been moulded into something perfect and new. Richard tried to regulate his breathing, to calm his reaction so he didn't frighten his child. Matty reached out and touched

Richard's face, the tiny frown lines between his brows disappearing as his lips curled into a delighted smile.

"Dat."

The touch of his son's soft hand on his own face was indescribable. He wanted to close his eyes and suck in the emotions, grab his hand and hold him closer. He wanted to snatch Matty from Hanna's arms and swing him around, show him how happy he was to see him.

His son.

His.

"Hi, Matthew." The corners of his lips threatened to reach his ears, his grin was so wide. "How are you doing?"

Matty nodded, as if he understood, and reached out to Richard, squirming in Hanna's arms until she lifted him across. It took Richard a moment to realize what was happening, his body reacting before his mind. Before he knew it, he was holding his son in his arms, their faces so close he could feel Matthew's rapid breaths bathing his skin.

"Hmm." Matthew poked Richard's cheek with his finger and laughed. His infectious giggle caused Richard to chuckle back. He tightened his arms under Matthew, delighting in the sensation of holding his son, amazed at how light he felt – yet how perfectly he fit in his arms.

"He's beautiful." Richard stared at Hanna with new eyes. How could he hate somebody who had made something so perfect?

"He likes you. He doesn't usually throw himself at people." Her voice was steady but he could see her eyes glisten. She tucked a lock of hair behind her ear and glanced away. "Has everything been okay, Tom?"

Richard had forgotten it wasn't only the three of them and glanced up at Tom with surprise. "Hi, Tom." He reached out a hand, adjusting Matty so he was holding him firmly with his other arm.

"Richard, it's good to see you." Tom's grin was as huge as Richard's. "It's been a long time coming." He raised his eyebrows at Hanna. She had the good grace to look ashamed.

"Where's Ruby?" Hanna pushed herself on to her tiptoes so she could glance over Tom's shoulder and into the villa. "I thought she'd be the first out to see us."

"She overslept," Tom replied with a mock whisper. "I've been up with Matty since five."

Matty nodded rapidly, as if he was joining in the conversation. "Up."

"That's right, Matty. Up and awake. Makes me really happy." Tom's voice was deadpan. "It's all over to you now, Richard. Enjoy."

"I intend to." Richard's face seemed moulded into a permagrin. "I can't see the early mornings being a problem." Not even mixed with jet lag. He didn't intend to miss a moment more with his son.

"Hi, Richard!" Ruby's voice carried through the tiled entranceway and out of the door. The loud clattering of her running down the stairs was followed by a vision of green, hurtling herself across the hall and barely coming to a halt in front of her brother. "I can't believe I missed the big reunion. I've been planning it for days." She turned around and punched Tom on the arm. "I told you not to bring him out here."

"Lay off the violence," Tom chided good-humouredly. From the way his eyes lit up as soon as Ruby arrived, Richard could tell there was something more than friendship going on. He shook his head slightly, trying to get the thought out of his mind. The older brother act would have to wait; he had bigger fish to fry.

"Don't you love him, Richard? Isn't he gorgeous?" Ruby had already forgotten Tom's infraction, and started to make faces at Matty, who giggled in response. "You look so natural holding him. Have you ever held a baby before? Do you know what you're meant to be doing?" She looked almost disappointed to have to stop and take a breath.

"I held you for hours when you were a baby. All clingy and whiny, not to mention constantly needing your diaper changed." Richard raised his eyebrows at Ruby, and her cheeks flushed as she glanced across to see if Tom had heard. "So I think I'll do fine."

The day passed in a blur of diapers, food, and bright plastic toys. In between naps and play, Richard marvelled at how what must seem like a normal Wednesday to anybody else was like a day of miracles to him. His attention was constantly on his son, watching his chubby legs wobble as he ran from room to room, the constant need to rush seeming to be his main motivation in life. He was energetic right up until the moment tiredness hit, and suddenly, like an electronic toy whose battery had run out, he flagged and curled up in Hanna's arms, sucking at his thumb and pointing at a book.

Hanna showed Richard how to run the bath to hit the right temperature, how to change Matty's nappy so his constant wriggling didn't cause a bigger mess. Everything she did seemed accompanied by a soundtrack of advice and experience, and part of him wanted to push her away and tell her to leave him alone. He was an intelligent guy, he was pretty sure he could handle an eighteen-month-old child.

Bedtime was perfect. Matty's room had been decorated before Hanna gave birth, though she'd refused to find out the sex of the baby. It felt warm, and calm – like an island oasis after a storm. The two of them walked him into the nursery together, Hanna holding Matty tightly against her chest, and he lifted his head up and struggled until she lowered him down, letting his tiny feet touch the warm wooden floor.

He toddled over to the pale blue bookshelf, pulling out a well-worn dog-eared book and holding it out in front of him. Walking toward Richard, he offered it to him with an expression on his face that was hard to read.

"Story." Like he knew Richard was a novice, Matty held out his hand, curling it around Richard's, and together they walked over to the blue-and-cream plaid rocking chair next to his cot. Richard sat down, helping Matty as he clambered onto his knees, curling up on Richard's lap with his thumb in his mouth.

He held Matty's head against his chest, luxuriating in the warmth flowing through his veins. It was almost impossible to believe only two days earlier he hadn't even known of Matthew's existence. Now Matthew *was* Richard's existence.

"Read," his son commanded, and Richard suppressed a grin. He unfolded the cardboard book, being careful not to pull the paper away from the edges any more than they already had been, and began to read in a soft, deep tone.

"Once upon a time, in a land far away..."

He turned the pages, reading the words and sharing the pictures with Matty, watching as his son's eyelids began to droop, his thick, pale lashes sweeping his face. Richard reached a hand out and gently cupped Matty's cheek, feeling the softness of his skin and the plumpness of his tired smile. His heart clenched with the thought he'd always have him, always be able to hold him in his arms. Matty was his now, as much as he was Hanna's, and he was determined never to let him go again.

Out of everything that had happened in the past twelve years, from the way they first met, to the way she had run away from him yet again, he couldn't regret a single moment. Not if it had led to the birth of this child. No matter what he felt toward Hanna – or how he regarded her actions to date – he couldn't bring himself to hate a woman who had nurtured Matthew in the way she had.

All day he'd watched the love spill over from her eyes as she watched their son, played with him, picked him up when he was crying and chastised him when he did something wrong. Every movement she made, every word she spoke, was with Matthew in mind.

He was clearly first in both their lives.

When Matthew was asleep, Richard kissed his soft, light brown hair before lifting him gently into his cot. Pulling the blanket over him until his body was covered, he lingered a moment longer, burning the image of his peaceful son into his mind so he could think about him all night.

Richard turned to leave, seeing Hanna standing by the door, tears pouring down her face. She was wringing her hands as she stared at the two of them. Part of him wanted to touch her, to pull her into his arms, but he didn't want to give her false hope that all was well between them.

All was far from well.

"Can we talk?" she asked.

"Not tonight." He was firm. "I'm exhausted, I'm going to bed."

"When then?" Hanna was persistent and his cool facade disappeared.

"On my schedule Hanna, not yours." He was angry, and she shrunk away. "It's been a hell of a day and I've got a lot to think about. Good night."

"Good night." Her words were faint and tremulous. It took everything he had to walk away.

But he did it, and he knew why. This wasn't about them anymore. It wasn't about a girl and a boy who were foolish enough to let love slip through their hands. It was about their son, a beautiful child who only deserved to know a life full of happiness and joy.

Matty was Richard's life now, and nothing else was going to get in the way.

Twenty-Four

18th May 2012

THE RAIN WAS beating down on the tiled roof, drumming like the hooves of a thousand horses. Hanna sighed loudly, watching as Matty ran from room to room, desperate in his need to expend some energy. The summer storm had started suddenly. The yellow-blue of the morning sky was quickly painted over by grey, the heaviness increasing until the clouds could no longer contain the rain. There was no gentle patter of raindrops against the window; the storm started as it meant to go on: hard and harsh.

Matty wasn't an indoor child. He needed fresh air and grass and sand. He loved to explore, picking flowers and running after scurrying animals, squealing with frustration when they eluded his grasp. Being stuck inside was mere containment. The pressure of his unexpended energy seemed to grow until Hanna felt it could burst the roof off the house.

He was banging on the door to the orangery. Richard was inside, working on his laptop. He had muttered something about a video conference during another of their strained exchanges. Hanna pulled at Matty's arm, hushing him as she tried to drag him away.

"No!" Matty's face compressed with anger. Hanna swallowed hard and mustered up her mother-courage.

"Come away from the door, Matty." Her voice was firm. It was something she had learned; firmness meant you were listened to.

"Not." Matty shook his head and turned away again, hammering his fist against the wood. Hanna sighed and scooped him up, lifting him away from the door. For a moment Matty stared at her, his mouth agape as if he was surprised she had actually defied him. His lips trembled and his eyes shut tightly, a wail escaping his throat.

She tried to walk away as fast as she could, but Matty had surprisingly strong lungs. Only a moment later, Richard opened the door, walking out into the hall and gazing at her and Matty with a questioning look.

"Is he okay?" His voice was soft as he stared at his son.

"I'm so sorry, we didn't mean to disturb you. He's going stir crazy."

It was killing her in small, measured stages. A glance here, a tightly polite word there. Every interaction with Richard was torture, from the mornings at the kitchen table feeding Matty, to the evenings when he brushed past her and went straight to his room.

Hanna was desperate to talk. She was dying to listen. She didn't care if he wanted to vent, to tell her how much he hated her – he could shout and scream all he wanted to. She could take it, far better than she could take his intense, innate politeness.

He had been there for five days. Five days of walking on eggshells and tiptoeing around their future. It was like he knew this would be greater torture than shouting at her and berating her.

It was.

Matty started to struggle in her arms, wanting to be put down, and desperate to run over to his father. Richard advanced toward them, a smile tugging at his lips, and when he was only a few feet away Matty reached his chubby arms out, wriggling harder in Hanna's grasp.

"Dad." He was almost shouting. "Daddy."

Hanna froze.

Her chest swelled, pressuring her ribs until she thought she was going to explode. She looked at Richard, noticing his watery eyes. She wanted to wipe the tears away before they formed.

"He said my name."

Hanna nodded, her own tears escaping. Richard lifted Matty from her arms, pulling him tightly against his chest, cradling his son's head in his large palm.

"Can you say it again, Matty?" He whispered. "Say 'daddy'."

Matty looked up at his father, his eyes sparkling as he realized it was another game. He was good at these.

"Daddy." His words were rewarded with a squeal from Hanna and a kiss from Richard. They looked at each other again, and Hanna noticed a softness she hadn't seen before. She wanted to wrap it around her body and snuggle within it.

"Such a clever boy." She reached out her hand and stroked his head, his soft strands caressing her palm.

Richard continued to stare at her, and she could feel a blush creeping across her face. Like a magnet, she was drawn in, her own eyes stuck on his. Emotion bubbled within her like a just-opened bottle of champagne. He hadn't forgiven her – she knew that much, and what was worse she could understand it – but she couldn't quash the hope that one day he might.

"I need to finish my conference." Richard's voice was thick with emotion. There was a tick in his jaw, and she wanted to cup her hand around his chiselled features and smooth out the tension.

"I'll take him," she offered, reaching out her arms. Matty struggled and held tightly on to Richard. It made them both smile.

"He can come in with me, if that's okay. It should only be a few minutes." They were back to being polite.

Baby steps, she reminded herself.

"That's fine. I'll be in the kitchen if you need me." *Ask me to join you. Please invite me in.*

"We'll be fine." He turned around and walked back to the orangery, pulling the door open so he and Matty could walk inside. Hanna rolled her bottom lip between her teeth as she watched Richard's retreating back, recalling the text message she'd received from Ruby that morning.

Give him time. He's worth it.

WHEN EVENING CAME, Hanna's body ached from polite smiles and walking on tiptoes. Over the past few days, they had fallen into a routine of eating dinner with Matty, followed by his bath and bedtime. Richard participated eagerly, his face glowing as he played with his son, running around the house and avoiding the elephant they both knew was there in the room.

"He's asleep," Richard whispered as he walked out of the nursery.

Hanna smiled and walked past him, knowing he would be heading right for his bedroom. She stopped at Matty's cot, leaning over to stroke his peaceful face, her fingers lingering on the plump skin of his cheeks.

"Goodnight, sweet prince." She kissed her middle and index fingers before pressing them to his forehead. Bedtimes were always bittersweet; part of her was relieved, knowing at the end of a long day of running after him she would have an evening of rest. The other half missed his smiles and giggles, and the sensation of his warm arms curling around her in love.

She walked quietly out of the room, pulling the door closed behind her. She was so caught up in her thoughts it took her a moment to realize Richard was still standing there, leaning against the wall. His hands were shoved in his pockets, the tendons of his arms tense and defined.

"Do you want to talk?"

Her stomach lurched. It was the moment she'd been waiting for all week, but now it was here she was trembling with fear.

She nodded, unable to speak for a moment. Richard pushed himself off the wall and headed for the living room. She trailed in his wake, her mind a myriad of thoughts and worries.

There was an open bottle of red wine on the coffee table next to two half-filled glasses. Hanna wondered if it was a good idea to drink alcohol with Richard near. He already filled her senses until she thought she would burst. How much worse would it be to face him with the false bravado that wine would give her?

"I thought this might help." He lifted a glass and offered it to her. Hanna grasped the stem, feeling the fragility of the crystal. She wondered if it would snap if she got any tenser.

"Thank you," she murmured, sitting opposite him. The coffee table was between them, a welcome barrier. Lifting the glass to her lips, she took a sip, letting the warm, soothing fluid dance around her taste buds before swallowing.

Richard cleared his throat. "Our son is beautiful."

She nodded again, the lump in her throat growing. "He is."

"I'm still so fucked up over everything that's happened, but we need to concentrate on Matty." He was running his finger around the rim of his glass. "His happiness is the most important thing."

"It's all I care about," she agreed with a small voice.

"You're a wonderful mother, Hanna. I don't want to take him away from you."

She felt like she could breathe for the first time in forever.

"But I need to be with him, too," he added, before whispering. "Now I've gotten to know him, I don't want to let him go."

"I know." Her heart filled with love. "I want you to be with him. You're his father, and he loves you." It was clear to her, from the way Matty stared up at Richard adoringly. "I've never seen him accept anybody so fast."

Richard drained his glass, before setting it down on the table. "But the fact remains, we live in different countries. Hell, we're on different continents for Christ's sake."

There it was again: the barrier which had haunted them for twelve years, only now with added complications.

"We can make this work," Hanna argued, unsure of who she was trying to convince. "If we're both willing to try."

Richard leaned forward, and for a moment she wished the coffee table would disappear.

"I'm willing to try."

Her mouth was too dry to swallow, and she could feel her heartbeat start to race as his stare remained on her face. His eyes were dark in the ambient glow of the lamplight, but the green halo surrounding them kept her gaze captured.

"We'll move to New York, Matty and I." Her mouth

opened before her brain engaged, but she couldn't bring herself to feel sorry. "I'll find an apartment and we can share custody there."

His eyebrows rose with surprise. "You'd do that?"

Hanna was almost as shocked as him. She slowly nodded. "Yes, I'd do that. Matty deserves to see you, not only for holidays, but in the evenings, and on weekends. I can't think of another way."

"I don't know what to say."

She gave him a small smile. "There's no need to say anything. I'm doing this for me as much as for you two." She leaned forward and put her glass down on the table. At the same moment, Richard reached out and captured her hand in his. She gasped at the contact, the warmth of his hand, and the roughness of his skin. It was the first time they had really touched in two years. Memories flooded her soul, until they were a constant ache in her chest.

She stared at the way his hand curled around hers, the warm hue of his skin contrasting with her own, paler flesh. Drawing in a ragged breath, she willed herself to lift up her eyes, wanting to see what emotion was behind his move.

When she finally looked at his face, she saw him staring back. His expression was tender. She knew he was grateful for her offer, and nothing more, but it didn't stop her heart from racing as she took in his gentle smile and the shallow lines around his eyes. The years hadn't diminished his beauty; he seemed to have grown into his looks, and the way the emotions were spilling out of her gut she knew one undeniable fact.

She was still in love with Richard Larsen.

*

ANNA TRIED NOT to grimace as they walked across the tarmac, but it was a losing battle when she saw the white jet waiting for them. It was lower to the ground than she was used to, six galvanized metal steps away, and the five portholes facing her were gleaming and bright.

She turned to look at Matty, who was clinging to Richard's neck with one arm, his other pointing at the plane.

"That?" he asked, and Hanna allowed herself to smile.

"It's a plane. It's going to take us up into the sky." She reached out and touched his cheek.

"All the way to London," Richard added.

And the frown was back again.

"You okay?" he asked, noticing the way she withdrew.

Hanna nodded her head. She would be, once they got the trip to London over with. She was afraid to see Claire and Steven, and was thinking of staying in the hotel when Richard took Matty to meet them. She knew she was a coward, but there was only one way this meeting could possibly end.

In tears.

"I'm afraid this thing is only taking us to London." Richard tapped his hand on the jet, making a clanging, metallic sound. "We need to fly scheduled to New York."

"How dreadful." Hanna allowed herself to crack a smile. "I hate slumming it."

Richard's lips twitched. "It wasn't you I was feeling sorry for. It was all the other passengers once we let our boy loose on the plane."

Hanna closed her eyes and tried to picture Matty running up the aisle of first class, knocking over drinks and disturbing angry businessmen. Maybe a three-day layover in London wasn't such a bad thing after all.

They climbed up the steps. She took Matty from Richard's arms as he stopped to chat with the pilot, discussing the flight plan and arrival times. Walking into the main cabin, she felt herself gasp; it was so very different to the standard class she usually frequented. The bright colours of the airline had been replaced by muted cream leather and dark walnut veneer. It had a calming effect, and as she sat down in her seat, with Matty in her lap, she allowed herself to relax.

"We'll be leaving in ten minutes, they're doing the final check," Richard explained, as he walked into the cabin. Matty's head turned automatically at his father's voice, his eyes seeking him out as he walked over to them. "Hey little guy, are you looking forward to the flight?" He looked up at Hanna. "Did you bring a bottle for his ears?"

"It's right here." She pointed to the table in front of them. "I've filled it with water."

They were both afraid he'd inherited Hanna's ear problems. She had trouble every time she flew, and the thought of her son going through the same sort of pain was too much to bear. They'd brought bottles and pacifiers in the hope he would be able to suck and alleviate any pressure in his canals.

"If your ears hurt, I can take him," Richard promised, helping Hanna fit the seat belt extension around Matty's waist. He was too young to sit alone in a seat.

"I'm hoping they'll be okay since it's a shorter flight. It's the one on Friday I need to worry about."

Richard rubbed the top of her arm, and she felt herself stiffen. She didn't want to let him know how much his kindness affected her.

"We'll see. I'll be there to help."

It took Richard longer to get through passport control, again. Hanna used the time to change Matty's diaper and freshen herself up, trying not to look too closely at her drawn face in the mirror as she applied a stroke of lip gloss. When they emerged, Richard was waiting for them, his eyes as tired as Hanna's.

"If it makes you feel any better, it will be my turn for the interrogation in New York." She stopped herself from reaching out a hand to cup his cheek.

"You have an American passport," he pointed out.

"I do, but Matty doesn't. Not yet."

Richard lifted his son from her arms, placing him on the handle of the trolley he was pushing. "What's on his birth certificate?" His voice was light, but she could sense the tension behind his question.

"Just my name." She had registered him at the Consulate in France.

"We'll need to change that, too." Richard frowned, looking down at Matty. "He needs to have my name there. I'll speak to my lawyers."

Hanna glanced up, taking in the concern on his face. This was clearly important to him. "Of course. We'll need to sort out some sort of visa for him if we're going to stay in New York."

"Lisa's already on to it. Everything should be ready for Thursday."

Richard set up Matty's buggy, and Hanna lifted him in gently, pulling the straps across him, tickling his legs enough to make him giggle. She hadn't asked Richard where they were staying, or how they were getting there, but she was suddenly desperate to know.

This was London. It was her city, her playground. She was delighted to be home, if only for a few days.

"Where are we staying?" She manoeuvred Matty's buggy across the polished tile floor. Richard matched her pace, pushing the luggage trolley. It was piled high with suitcases full of clothes and toys and the usual baby paraphernalia.

"I've booked us a suite at the Dorchester," Richard said. "There are two bedrooms. I've asked for a cot to be put in your room."

Hanna smiled. She didn't like the thought of their son in his own room in a strange place. It was much better to have him with her. "Thank you for arranging it."

He stared for a moment, allowing a grin to pull at his lips. Her heart stopped beating for a moment.

"I should thank you. You're the one uprooting everything and moving thousands of miles."

"It's the right thing to do," Hanna said simply. Richard reached out and squeezed her hand, where it gripped the handle of the buggy. Her breath hitched at the unexpected gesture.

"Thank you, anyway," he whispered. She lifted her hand and squeezed back.

They were nearly at the end of the walkway when Richard's face dropped, his mouth falling open. He stopped walking, glancing at Hanna with concern, and she felt her heart start to race.

Something was wrong.

"I asked them not to do this." He held her hand tightly, as if he was afraid she'd run. "I'm sorry, Hanna, I promise I'll be with you."

She followed his line of sight. Standing at the edge of the crowd, staring at the two of them with open mouths, were Steven and Claire. Neither looked particularly happy – or pleased to see them – but she noticed with relief their expressions softened as soon as they saw Matty. He was wriggling in his buggy, singing to himself.

All hopes of avoiding confrontation seemed futile. She allowed Richard to pull them both toward his parents, his grip on her hand never wavering. She inhaled deeply, trying to keep her breaths steady, rearranging her expression to try to hide her fear.

"Richard!" Claire ran across the last few feet, flinging her arms around him. Hanna watched as he hugged her back, before turning to Steven and shaking his hand. They all leaned down to talk to Matty.

Matty's face crumpled, and his mouth opened to emit a loud wail. Claire and Steven jumped at the sound, stepping backwards to give him some space. Richard could feel Hanna tensed beside him, and when he looked at her face, he saw concern and agitation etched across it. He knew her well enough to understand that she wanted to comfort her son, but was afraid to upset his parents by pushing through and lifting Matty out of his pram. He squeezed her hand and leaned down, unstrapping the buckles across his son's waist and lifting him out, murmuring comforting words as he cradled his head.

"Shhhh, it's okay, it's okay."

Matty pulled his thumb between his lips, slurping on the tip. Soundless sobs made his chest hitch rhythmically, his eyes wet as he scrunched them tight. "Mama..."

Richard turned to Hanna, who reached out and cupped Matthew's cheek, her hand reassuring as she stroked his soft skin.

Claire stood up. "Hanna."

"Claire. How are you?" Matty grabbed Hanna's hand and she squeezed him back.

"I don't know. I really don't know." Claire shook her head, her curls bouncing on her shoulders. "I can't even tell you how I'm feeling right now."

266

"I can. I'm pretty pissed, Hanna." Steven interjected, causing Claire to place her hand on his shoulder. He stood up straight, his startling blue eyes cold as he stared at Hanna, shaking his head slowly. "What the hell were you thinking?"

"Wait a minute..." Richard stepped forward, handing Matty to Hanna. She lifted him by his padded bottom. He wrapped his hands around her neck, chest still wracked with sobs. "Whatever happened here is between Hanna and me. I don't need you to fight my battles."

Claire stepped between them, her face unreadable. "There's no fighting going on here, Richard. We just want some answers. I think we're entitled to that."

Behind her, Steven had the countenance of a man on the edge. He held himself too still, his face too calm. For the first time in his life, Richard could feel himself having to front up to his father. Hanna remained silent, and from the corner of his eye he could see her trembling. He wanted to reach out and pull her toward him, crush her in his arms.

"This isn't really the time or place, Claire. I said we'd meet you at the house so we could avoid just this sort of spectacle." Richard gestured at the crowded airport. They were being jostled every few moments by passengers trying to get past.

"I just want to speak to Hanna, okay? Not as the mother of your child, or the girl who left you, but like the daughter I used to know." Claire wiped a stray tear from her eye. "Can we go and get a coffee or something?"

He turned to look at Hanna, who nodded quickly. Matty was staring at them all, his thumb still attached to his mouth. The tears had dried to a shiny trail on his cheeks, reflecting in the harsh glare of the airport lights.

"Claire, Steven, this is Matty." Hanna inhaled deeply before stepping forward. "Matty, this is—" She frowned and looked at Claire. "What shall I call you?"

"I'm not sure. I've never had to think about it." Claire stood for a moment, lips pulled down as she thought things through. "I guess my mom was a Grandma, so I'll be the same." She turned to look at Steven. He was staring at Matthew, his eyes scanning his hair and his face.

"There's no doubt about it, he's the spit of you, Richard." He reached out a finger and tickled Matty's chin, making him hiccup a watery giggle. "I suppose 'Pops' will do."

"Matty, can you say hello to Grandma and Pops?" Hanna asked him, bouncing him in her arms.

Matty pulled his thumb from his mouth with a pop before pursing his lips. "Hi." He waved his hand.

"Clever boy." Richard smiled, reaching out to caress his curls. Matty grinned and clapped his hands, not afraid to blow his own trumpet.

"He's beautiful." Claire pulled Richard toward her, hugging him tightly. "I'm so proud of you, darling." Richard stepped back, face flushing with embarrassment. He wasn't sure what to say in response.

"He *is* beautiful," Steven agreed. "Hanna, I apologize for my anger. You need to give me a bit of time to get over this."

"You shouldn't have to apologize." Her face fell. She was clasping Matty against her body like a talisman. "I know this is all my fault and I can't tell you how hard I'm going to try to make up for it." She looked over at Richard, her eyes catching his.

"It isn't all your fault," he interjected. He collapsed the buggy and put it on top of the cases, before turning to squeeze Hanna's shoulder. "We all fucked up somewhere along the way. I should have called you, and my mother should have told me *you* called…"

"Caroline knew about this?" Steven's voice was icy. He lifted his hand and dragged it through his thick blond hair. "What the hell?"

"She told Hanna that Meredith was in a wheelchair and I'd never leave her," Richard told his father. Despite the bustle of the airport, it was as though the five of them were suspended in a bubble. People were giving them a wide berth as they walked around them. Richard wasn't sure if it was because of the latent anger in the air, or the way they were all holding themselves so upright it looked unnatural.

"I'd called to tell Richard about the pregnancy," Hanna added. "She didn't know, though, that I was pregnant, I mean."

"It doesn't really matter whether she knew or not. She's an interfering—" Steven managed to catch himself in time. From the corner of his eye, Richard noticed Claire trying to bite down a smile. "Have you spoken to her about it, Richard?"

"I'm not ready to speak to her at all. When I do – if I do – then I'll be sure to give her your regards."

Matty squirmed in Hanna's arms until he was facing Claire. He reached out his hand and touched her hair, making Claire laugh when he tugged. For the first time, Steven's face softened, a half smile whispering across his lips. Richard's breath escaped in a gust.

They walked over to a café near the exit, trying to avoid the milling passengers. Hanna and Claire walked ahead, Claire holding Matty's outstretched hand, a smile plastered over her face. They all knew the ordeal wasn't over yet, that the divides hadn't been bridged, but Richard could feel himself hope that one day they would be.

If he squinted his eyes and looked into the future, there was nothing he wanted more than to be surrounded by all the people he loved.

CRASHING SOUND COMING from another room woke him up. His eyes were bleary and glued by sleep, the room dark and unfamiliar. He rubbed them a little, trying to orient himself, the strange green light of the bedside clock not helping him to work out his location.

His mouth was parched, and he reached out to the table next to his bed, his hand groping for a glass of water. He came up empty.

It took Matty's wail to echo through the wall before he realized exactly where he was.

In London.

In a hotel.

In the middle of the night.

He sat straight up in his bed, reaching behind him to flick the light switch on the wooden headboard. The bedside lamp glowed warm and yellow, enough to illuminate but not startle. Everything in this room had been planned to pamper and coddle.

There was another cry, followed by a lower voice. Hanna was murmuring to him, maybe trying to relax him back to sleep. From the sound of his angry riposte, Matty was having none of it.

Pulling back the covers, Richard swung his legs out of bed, glancing down to check he was covered enough to be seen. His plaid pyjama bottoms hung from his hips, his chest bare and glowing under the glare of the lamp.

He walked across the expensive carpet and out into the main room, pushing the door open quietly in case Matty had already dropped back to sleep. Hanna was pacing the wooden floor in her bare feet. The polish on her nails was almost black in the half-light. Matty struggled in her arms, his hands beating her back as she made a doomed attempt to placate him.

"Everything okay?" Richard's voice was soft as he approached her, but she jumped, nevertheless. Hanna looked up at him, her eyes wide, giving him an apologetic smile.

"I'm so sorry, we didn't mean to wake you up. He escaped from the cot. It must be shallower than the one we have at home." One of the straps of her camisole had slipped down her shoulder revealing smooth, alabaster skin. It looked like porcelain in the dark room.

"Is he okay?" Richard's brow furrowed. "It must have been a long way down."

Hanna smiled. "He's fine. He made it into this room before I was even aware what was happening. I swear he has a bright future ahead of him as an escape artist."

As if he realized they were talking about him, Matty wailed again, his tone taking on a desperate edge. He looked up at Richard with red-rimmed eyes, his face screwed up in anger.

"Do you want me to take him?" Richard's voice was still low. He was distracted by her skin. He could remember the way it tasted.

"I think he's frightened; he doesn't recognize where he is. I feel a bit disoriented myself." Their eyes caught and locked, and for a moment they were silent, feeling the blanket of energy pushing down on them all. Then Matty opened his mouth again and screamed.

Richard reached forward and ran his hand across Matty's cheek. It surprised him enough to quiet him momentarily while he took in the change. "Hey, Matty, it's sleep time," Richard murmured, his hand gentle but firm.

"Daddy." Matty reached out to him, his voice a plaintive wail. Richard scooped him up, relieving Hanna of the burden, holding his son tightly against his chest in an attempt to make him feel safe. It seemed to work; his breathing became slower, more regular, and his hand moved up to his mouth, thumb extended. Richard rubbed his back, swaying gently in time to a silent rhythm, his head buried in his son's hair.

He smelled so good.

"Shall I try to put him down?" Richard asked, looking up at Hanna. She was standing by the dining table, fiddling with the kettle.

"Yes, please. I think I'll put him in the bed with me. I don't want to risk him falling out of his cot again, it could have been so much worse."

Richard walked into her room, the fragrance both familiar and enticing. It reminded him of lazy days in London, and frantic nights in New York. Matty yawned, thumb firmly stuck in his mouth, and let Richard lay him on the undented pillow, his eyes fluttering under the weight of his fatigue.

"Try to sleep." He leaned forward and kissed Matty's cheek, the plump skin smooth against his lips. Matty sighed, twisting his body until he was lying on his side, legs curled under his diapered rump. He stayed for a moment, watching his son as his lips worked themselves against his thumb, the occasional slurp breaking the silence of the night.

"Sweet dreams," he murmured, walking out of the bedroom and pulling the door closed behind him. He glanced around, spotting Hanna sitting on the plush upholstered sofa, her legs curled beneath her, hands wrapped around a mug of tea.

"I made you one, in case you're thirsty." She pointed over at the table. Richard walked over and retrieved the cup. The steam rose up as he lifted the mug to his lips, hot sweet liquid spilling over the rim into his mouth. He swallowed it like a dying man.

"Thank you."

"You're welcome." Hanna's reply was rigidly polite. Richard wondered what would crack the barrier, bring it falling down until all that was left were raw wounds and honesty.

"I never got to apologize for the ambush at the airport." He smiled nervously, trying not to look at her too closely. Even though the pyjamas she had on were fairly conservative – a tank and long, black trousers – they were strangely erotic to look at, knowing she was bare underneath. He knew all too well what she looked like when naked.

His conflicting emotions were hard enough to handle in the daylight, let alone the dark gloom of night.

"It wasn't your fault. I knew I had to see them at some point." She took another sip, soft lips touching china. He watched as she swallowed, eyes closing momentarily to savour the tea.

"I thought it went surprisingly well, considering." Richard sat down on the sofa beside her, his legs inches from her feet. He wanted to lift them up, put them on his lap and rub them.

He didn't.

"They're always gracious. I know it must have been hard, being civil to me after all that's happened." Hanna reached forward and put her cup on the coffee table. "They seemed to like Matty, though. That's all that matters."

"It will get easier, you know, every time we tell people." He watched her breath hitch when he said the word *we*. "Things can only get better."

She smiled, lighting up the dark room. Despite her tiredness, and the tension of the day, she was still heartbreakingly beautiful, like a work of art. Since becoming a mother, her breasts were rounder, her cheekbones more defined. But it was the inner change that affected him the most, watching her interact with their son. He could so easily fall in love with the way she adored Matty.

Hanna cleared her throat. "I haven't told my dad yet. I was going to visit him after telling you while I was in New York. I guess I'll catch up with him after we arrive." Her brow crumpled.

"If it makes you feel any better, I'll be having a talk with my mother when we get back, too," he replied.

Hanna raised her eyebrows. "It never ends, does it? Just when you think the hardest part is over, something else comes up to take its place."

Richard reached his hand out, then pulled it back, running his finger over the pattern of the sofa. Lifting his head, he looked at her, his expression serious. "You know, when I came to London to find you gone, I thought I'd never be happy again." Her face stilled at his words. "I thought it would be so easy; I'd come to your flat, sweep you off your feet and carry you back to Manhattan."

Hanna leaned toward him, eyes glistening. She looked like she wanted to say something, but her lips remained still, her teeth worrying the bottom one.

He took another breath, not sure where he was going with this. He wanted to tell her – needed her to know – just what he'd been through. But to hurt her was to hurt himself.

"I feel like I've just existed for two years, like I put things on hold. And to know that I could have spent those two years with Matty and with you..." His voice broke before he could finish his sentence.

"I'm so sorry." Hanna scrambled to her knees, grabbing his hand and pulling it against her face. "I know I fucked everything up. If I could go back and change it I would." Her tears moistened his fingers, and he moved his thumb against her cheek, wiping them away. "I hate that you missed out, and I hate that I believed you were still with Meredith. Even worse than that, I had a piece of you with me, and you had nothing."

Richard twisted his hips, turning to face her. Her skin was smooth under his rough fingers, pulled taut against her cheekbones. Just a few inches and he could caress her neck, tangle his fingers into her hair. Pull her against him until their lips...

He shook his head, trying to empty it of conflicting emotions. He wanted to pull her onto him, kiss the holy shit out of her, and grind his aching body against hers until she was begging him for more. But there was a deeper, angrier part of him that wanted to shake her until her teeth rattled, scream at her until she was begging him for mercy.

He needed to go to bed, alone. He didn't trust himself not to hurt her. He couldn't depend on her not to hurt him. The web just kept getting stickier.

THE FLIGHT TO New York was as fraught as they'd expected. At first, Matty had been distracted by the movies on the screen in front of him: Hanna pointing out his favourite characters as she tried to stop him from taking the earphones off his head. Then he'd gone through a manic twenty minutes halfway through the flight, trying to escape from them and run down the aisle, not understanding that he needed to sit still. Richard had held him, walking him around the cabin until his head nodded heavy with sleep, before laying him across their laps, hands stroking as he dreamed peacefully.

They didn't speak of the previous night. Hanna's tears, and his own embarrassing response were buried at the bottom of their bigger troubles. Matty was their shield and their glue, binding them together while allowing them to ignore everything else that went on between them.

"I've asked the staff to prepare rooms for you and Matty," Richard said, his hand stroking his son's hair. "I've arranged for a bed instead of a cot, in case of any more Houdini escapes."

Hanna tried to crack a smile. "He'll have to stick to safe-cracking and base jumping instead, I guess." She met his gaze. "Thanks for letting us stay while I look for something more permanent."

It was early evening when they arrived at his apartment. Matty was surprisingly subdued, as if he'd worn off all his energy on the plane. His head lolled against Hanna's arm as he stared out of the car window, his teeth scraping rhythmically against his thumb. Occasionally, something would take his interest and he'd point, using single words to ask what it was. Hanna would patiently say the word, explaining more about it, and Richard tried not to watch the way her lips moved as she spoke.

He was going crazy having them so close to him, but it would be so much worse when they moved out. He wanted to find a way to keep them near, so he could watch over them, and make sure they were safe. It wasn't enough just to have them in the same city, he wanted them under his roof.

Jack brought their luggage up, putting Hanna's cases in her room, unsure of what belonged to her or Matty. She'd packed a smaller bag with their overnight things, and quickly bathed him before putting him in a snug onesie covered with pictures of cars. Richard lingered in the room, watching his son play with the plastic toys he'd asked Lisa to order for him, smiling as he crawled from the plastic garage to the kitchen, his eyes wide with delight.

"It looks like Toys 'R' Us just threw up in your apartment," Hanna observed, watching Matty bang a plastic saucepan against his head. "It seems so incongruous."

Richard scratched his chin. The apartment clearly hadn't been decorated with children in mind; a glance at the white walls and raw silk upholstery was enough to give that little snippet away. But somehow, having his son here, being surrounded by childhood paraphernalia, attracted him to the apartment more than any thousand-dollar designer could.

"I just ordered the basics. We'll have to work out what else we need." He caught her eye. Her chocolate brown irises were huge, and she stared right back, her lips slightly parted. Then she looked down, eyelashes grazing her cheeks, her fingers trembling as she reached for their son.

"I'm going to put him to bed. We've a long day ahead of us tomorrow."

THE FOLLOWING AFTERNOON he was waiting in Central Park, standing at the duck pond and watching the children throwing bread. Hanna and Matty were due to meet him at 1:00 p.m., but it was already quarter past. He was starting to worry.

Somebody threw something heavy in the pond, and the large splash startled the birds, causing them to flap their wings and skim the water in their haste to escape. Richard craned his head, spotting a group of teenagers standing across the water from him, laughing uproariously at their own foolish actions.

"I'm so sorry we're late." Her voice was thick, her eyes rimmed with red. Matty ran toward him and grabbed his suited legs, sticky fingers pulling at the worsted fabric.

"How did it go?" He didn't need to ask. Her expression said it all.

"My dad was difficult. Told me I was just like my no-good mother. Then he called Olivia who shouted down the phone, and I could hear her say Matty would be better off if we had him adopted." She was staring at the ground, her fingers twisting at her bracelet. He wanted to reach out and calm her movements.

"I should have gone with you. I wanted to." He was going to do it; he needed to – for her sake as well as his. Stepping forward, he squared his shoulders, one hand reaching out to touch her arm. She glanced up at him, eyes shiny, opening her mouth to say words that came out silent.

The next moment she was in his arms, her slim frame enveloped by his. Richard hesitated momentarily, trying to work out where best to put his hands, before placing them in the middle of her back, rubbing her through the thin material of her dress.

"I'm so sorry she said that," he murmured. "You know she's wrong, though. Matty's been the best thing that happened to both of us in a long time."

"He said he didn't know me." She sobbed into his shirt. "That he didn't *want* to know me. I know I lied to him by omission, but he was so cruel." She lifted a hand from his arm and wiped her face, dark smudges of mascara smearing across her finger. "He reacted so much worse than you did, and you had so much more to blame me for."

"I've got so much more to thank you for, too." Richard scooped Matty up in his arms, and the three of them held each other like a real family. He wanted to close his eyes and inhale the aroma of happiness. "We still have a way to go before we sort everything out, but at least we're both willing to try."

They walked over to a bench, and he watched the way the muscles in her calves flexed with her movement. In the week since they'd been back in New York, she had caught the sun from spending her days with Matty in the park, showing him the animals and letting him run free across the grass.

In the evenings, he'd come home to his apartment with a heart so full it was almost painful. To see Hanna standing in the kitchen, preparing Matty's tea, cut him to the core. It was such a pleasant burn. He had to question himself; was he still attracted to her for who she was, or was he just wanting the perfect family unit? The way his body stirred whenever she bent over or leaned down so that the smallest swell of breast was showing told him it was the former.

She was busy pulling Matty's lunch from her oversized bag, scrabbling around for her baby wipes and a bib. Matty leaned back on the bench, swinging his legs back and forth, and singing to himself using made-up words.

"Did your dad even look at Matty?" Richard knew he was pulling at scabs, but found it hard to believe Philip would reject his own flesh and blood. It reminded him of a harsher, more painful confrontation he needed to have with his own mother. One he was putting off.

"Just a glance when Matty pulled some papers off his desk. Then he huffed and picked them up, telling me the office was no place for a child." She ripped the foil from the yoghurt pot, dipping the spoon in before raising it to Matty's mouth.

"Maybe you need to give him time. He's had a lot to take in." He suppressed a smile, aware his words referred to himself as much as Philip Vincent.

"I'll let him call me when he's ready – *if* he's ever ready." Hanna plucked a wipe and smeared it across Matty's face. He scrunched up his nose in protest, twisting his head to evade the cloth. She tickled him under the chin, enough to make him giggle, and then lunged forward, catching the yoghurt before it dribbled from his mouth. Her expression of victory was enough to make Richard grin, and she turned to catch his eye, her own smile brightening her features.

"What?" she asked.

"You were looking so pleased with yourself," he replied. "Like catching a bit of yoghurt was tantamount to winning a Pulitzer or something."

"If you had to do as much laundry as I have, every dollop on a baby wipe is a major win." She leaned forward and rubbed the wipe on Richard's face, the sweet aroma of the cloth invading his senses.

"Hey! I haven't eaten any yoghurt today." He grinned, leaning forward to pick out another wipe. "If anybody needs cleaning up, it's you." She tried to scoot away, wriggling her behind along the bench. Richard mirrored her every move, following her like a stalking lion. He was inches away from her face, and he watched her expression change as she looked up at him, her breath hitching at his proximity.

Her tongue darted out, moistening her lips, and a high colour appeared on the apples of her cheeks. From the corner of his eye he could see Matty still swinging his legs, slowly eating a banana while he stared at the birds swooping down from the trees.

Richard leaned forward, dragging the wipe against Hanna's skin, cleaning away the mascara smudges that had gathered from crying over her father. Their gazes locked, blocking out the rest of the world. Their laughter faded beneath the intensity of their connection, lips loosening and dropping until it was replaced by need.

"Your skin is perfect," he whispered, his fingers dragging along her cheekbones, his attempts at cleaning her face abandoned. "I'd forgotten how soft it was."

Hanna swallowed as he continued to caress. She reached out and put her hand under his jacket, sliding it against his waist. His thin cotton shirt did nothing to dull the sensation of her touch. He wanted to pull it out from his waistband and push her hand inside, encourage it up until her palm rubbed against his bare chest. It wasn't enough just to look at her anymore. He needed to feel.

"Will you have dinner with me tonight?" The words escaped his lips in a rush. Hanna's brows dipped in confusion, her hand gently squeezing his waist.

"What about Matty? I can't leave him with a babysitter, not yet."

She hadn't said no. It made him smile.

"We'll have it at home. We can put Matty to bed, and I'll order in. Just the two of us. It will give us a chance to talk."

Her face lit up with a smile. "Yes, please. I'd love to have dinner with you."

Richard didn't care what it took; he was determined to do this right. He wanted to woo the hell out of this girl, to sweep her off her feet until she could never run again. They'd been careless before, letting love pour through their fingers like sand through an hourglass. Neither of them was innocent in the clusterfuck they'd found themselves in. They'd both given up before they should have.

This time... he was determined this time he wouldn't let her get away.

Twenty-Five

1st June 2012

"TRY TO KEEP still," Hanna urged Matty, making a futile attempt to fasten his diaper before putting him in his pyjamas. Matty laughed, kicking his legs in a bicycle-movement, trying to twist his body from the mat. She tapped his rump playfully, leaning in to blow a raspberry on his stomach, his soft skin vibrating loudly under her lips.

"No!" He wriggled again. "No that."

Hanna stopped tickling him and looked up. "No that?" She tried to hide her excitement; she couldn't remember him ever stringing two words together before. Until now his communication had been limited to single-word sentences.

"No." Matty was firm.

"Let's get you ready for bed, then." She lifted him up to standing, rolling up the legs of his pyjama pants and helping him to step into them. "You need to get some sleep, little man."

"No sleep." He was on a roll, and made her laugh. She couldn't wait to tell Richard about this new development.

"That's right, Matty. No sleep yet, not until Daddy gets home." She pulled his top over his head, tugging it down. "But then, definitely sleep."

As soon as she finished dressing him, Matty escaped from her grasp, running across the pale wooden floor of his bedroom, to the floor-length window on the far side. The evening sun warmed his face, lending him a golden hue, and he jumped up and down, pointing at the cars on the street below.

A crashing noise from the hallway made Hanna turn away from the windows, her brow creasing in consternation. A moment later she could hear Richard's voice.

"Hanna? Matty?" He sounded almost frantic. She'd barely stood up before he rushed through the door to Matty's bedroom, panting for breath, his chest rising and falling rapidly. He walked straight over, pulling her toward him, crushing her tight frame with his strong arms.

"Thank fuck." He tucked her head beneath his chin. "I had this horrible feeling you'd be gone."

This wasn't good. She put her arms around him, hands hesitantly rubbing his back. "Where would I go?"

Matty ran to them, squealing. Richard bent down and scooped him into his right arm, pulling Hanna back to him with his left. He leaned forward until their foreheads touched, his eyes a blink away from hers. She could feel his warm breath washing over her face.

"Richard, what's happened?"

Matty grabbed Richard's face and pulled it away from Hanna's, leaning down to push his own against it. "Da." He cupped his father's cheeks with his plump hands, laughing when Richard butterfly-kissed him with his eyelashes.

Richard inhaled deeply, managing to gain control of his breathing. He kissed Matty one more time before putting him on the floor, turning to face Hanna once more, a look of fear moulding his features.

"I called my lawyer today, asked him if I could put some sort of restraining order on you to stop you leaving the country." He looked as though he was admitting to a mortal sin. Hanna stepped backwards, trying to work out why her heart beat a little faster.

"What did he say?"

"He said I needed to talk to a shrink." Richard's laugh was dry and cold. "So I did. I talked to somebody."

"Oh." Her heart was racing. Hanna wondered whether it was from fear or attraction.

"Hanna, we've really fucked things up." His voice was gritty and deep. He reached his hand up and dragged it through his hair, causing the ends to stand up. "We have no trust."

"I trust you." Her voice was small.

"You don't. If you trusted me, you'd never have left – either time." He reached out a tentative hand, brushing her cheek with his fingertips. "You never once trusted in my love for you."

"And you don't trust that I'll stay." Hanna started to pick at the skin around her nails. She felt despondent. He was right; their lack of trust was like a huge mountain between them. "What did the shrink say?"

Richard smiled. "That I need intense, expensive therapy."

Hanna laughed in spite of herself.

"But seriously, I know no matter how much I want to, I can't handcuff you to the copper pipework, or file a lawsuit against you." He paused for a moment before carrying on. "If you don't want to stay, nothing I can do will change that."

"Richard, I—"

He held his hand up. "Please let me finish. When I was talking to the therapist, I realized something about myself. I may have told you I loved you, but I never really convinced you that you were worth loving. When you left, it's because you thought I wanted – or deserved – something more. And both times you were wrong."

Matty grew bored of the conversation and ran over to his toy box, pulling out his favourite stuffed toy.

"You do deserve more."

Richard shook his head. "You don't get to decide what I want, or what I need. I have to make something very clear to you before we even start to talk about the future." He rocked on his heels. "I've loved you since the day we met. I've always loved you, even when you've been far away and I haven't been able to see you." He stepped toward her, his hand caressing her neck. "If you ever want to leave, don't do it because you doubt my love for you. Do it because you don't want me, or because you want something better for yourself. I love you, Hanna Vincent. I'll always love you and there's nothing I want more than to have you in my life."

Hanna could feel her lip tremble as his fingers tangled into her hair. She was going to cry, she knew it, but before she collapsed into his arms, she needed to tell him something, too.

"Richard..." Her voice cracked, and the tears started to fall before she was ready. "I'm not going anywhere." She glanced across to Matty, noticing he was completely absorbed – playing a strange game with his teddy bear that involved lifting him onto his head before nodding, and watching him fall to the floor. Hanna covered Richard's hand with her own, feeling the warmth of his fingers on her skin. "I've made so many mistakes, but I'm not going to subject Matty to any of that. He deserves to know you and to be with you. I could never take him away."

She looked at him through thick lashes, watching the way his mouth remained downturned. "And more than that, I don't want to go. I want to be with you, I want us to be a family." She glanced down at the floor, trying to find the right words. "I love you, too. So much it makes me cry." She laughed through the tears, feeling them drip onto her chin. "I'll only leave if you tell me to."

"I'm never going to tell you to go," he whispered, brushing the wetness from her cheeks.

"Then you can take the handcuffs back to the shop." She glanced down again, feeling a blush steal across her cheeks as she thought of other uses for them. Richard laughed, as if he knew exactly what she was thinking.

He brushed her neck with his thumb one last time before pulling away, smiling wryly at her. "I was supposed to say this all at dinner. I guess I jumped the gun."

"It needed to be said." She felt her heart lift up in her chest. "I'm glad you did."

A small smile played at his lips. "Well, I'm going to run you a bath, and I'll put Matty to bed and get dinner ready. Don't come out of your room until I tell you, okay?"

She looked at him through narrowed eyes. "What have you got planned, Mr Larsen?"

Richard tapped his nose and winked. "Patience is a virtue, Miss Vincent."

*T*HE BATH WAS warm and fragrant, and she could barely bring herself to climb out. Her eyes were heavy with relaxation; her limbs loose, like somebody had removed the bones from them. She leaned across and blew out the lit candles, finally sitting up. The water sloshed around her waist, drying in rivulets across her body. Hanna stepped out onto the fluffy mat, pulling a soft, cream towel around her chest.

She chose a plain, black dress – short enough to show her still-youthful legs to their best advantage, long enough not to embarrass Matty, were he ever to notice. She dried her hair quickly, growing bored of preening, and twisted it into a bun before applying some scant, natural make-up.

A knock at the bedroom door made her stand up from the velvet stool and walk across the soft carpet of her bedroom. She glanced in the full-length mirror hanging on the wall next to her bed, noticing how dark the shadows under her eyes were, she wondered if it was from exhaustion, or a sign of age.

When she pulled open the heavy, oak door, Richard was standing behind it, dressed in a pale blue shirt and dark grey trousers. His shirt was unbuttoned at the neck, and she felt her eyes scanning the dip of skin where his throat met his chest, following the sparse hair which led downward.

She swallowed. Hard.

"Are you ready?" The left corner of his mouth curled into a lopsided grin. "Or did you want to invite me in for coffee?"

Hanna burst out laughing. "Is it going to be that kind of date?"

"I sincerely hope so." He reached out and took her hand. "But I should feed you first."

He pulled her into the hall, her bare feet padding on the pale wooden floor. Richard raised his hands and placed them on her shoulders, his eyes scanning her body. "You look beautiful."

She smiled. "Thank you. You're not so bad yourself." She chided herself for making the understatement of the year. His cotton shirt moulded to his body, revealing muscles in all the right places. His trousers fell from his hips in the most delicious way.

"Thank you." He looked like he wanted to say more, but instead turned and walked her down to the dining room, his arm loosely slung around her shoulders. Hanna leaned into him, his body warming hers through the thin fabric of their clothes.

The table was set with a heavy white cloth. The cutlery was laid precisely, two wine glasses at each setting. In the middle, a silver candelabra held three tapered candles, glowing from the flames flickering above. Richard pulled her chair out and she sat down, letting him push her back in.

"This looks amazing." Hanna looked around the room, her eyes wide with excitement. "You didn't have to go to all this trouble."

"I wanted to." His voice was thick. He walked over to the sideboard, pulling their plates from the warmer. "I told you I want to do this properly."

As he sat down opposite her, he reached for the bottle of Merlot, pouring them each an over-full glass. Hanna wondered who he was trying to get drunk: her or himself.

"Did Matty go down all right?" she asked, lifting her cutlery and spearing a piece of carrot with her fork.

"Fine. He was asleep before I even got to the second page of his book. He must have worn himself out at the park."

Or maybe he knew his parents needed a little alone time.

"You're so good with him." She glanced up. "Thank you."

Richard shrugged. "I'm his father."

"I know, I remember the conception." Suddenly her cheeks burned. She wanted to whack herself around the head for her inappropriate comments. Reaching out, she picked up her wine glass, tipping her head back to take a large mouthful.

"So do I," Richard replied softly.

She couldn't look at him; she couldn't. Yet her eyes drew up as if pulled by magnets.

"I'm so embarrassed," she admitted, making Richard laugh.

"Don't be. You always were honest. It's one of the things I love about you."

Love. She swooned again, wanting to pour the whole wine bottle down her throat. Her body was tense with anticipation.

"You know, I was thinking today, in between talking to my lawyer and the shrink, that we're essentially an old married couple." He lifted the bottle of Merlot and topped up both their glasses. "We live together, have a child together, and we spend the evenings talking deep into the night about things which concern us most." He glanced up at her through thick, dark lashes. "All that's missing is the sex."

Hanna spluttered, coughing out her mouthful of wine. She lifted the napkin from her lap and used it to dab at her mouth, wishing she could hide herself behind it.

"And the ring," Richard continued. "We're missing that, too."

"Don't forget the fabulous wedding album. We can look at it and reminisce all about the way our families fought and hated us, and ended up throwing plates at each other." She grinned at him. "No old married couples are complete without that."

Richard raised his eyebrows at her. "I'm not kidding. I know we have a lot to work through, but eventually I intend to marry you. I want you and Matty to be Larsens."

Hanna wanted it, too. She wanted it so much she could barely bring herself to imagine it. She thought she might die if it were taken away from her now. She could picture it so vividly: the ring on her finger, the kisses before he left for work, his arrival home, scooping Matty up into his arms, walking over to her and kissing the hell out of her.

The babies.

She needed to calm down. She was getting ahead of herself. They needed to take this slowly – for Matty's sake as well as theirs. Neither of them should run into the fire without preparing themselves for the burn.

"I'd like us to be yours." It was an evening for truths. She wasn't going to hide behind her insecurities any more. Life had taught her that road only led to trouble and misery.

Richard's smile was brilliant, his eyes as watery as hers when she glanced up at him. He reached out to touch her hand, running his finger from her knuckles to her wrist. Her skin erupted into goosebumps, tiny hairs standing up on her flesh as she closed her eyes, feeling the intensity of their connection.

They finished their meal, taking the plates and cutlery to the kitchen, and loading up the dishwasher together. Every now and then Richard would take something from her, his hand lingering on hers, long enough to let her know exactly how he felt.

It was electrifying.

When the room was clear, Richard picked up their glasses and the half-empty wine bottle, carrying them over to the sofa. He put them down on the coffee table, patting the seat next to him. His eyes were dark and intense as he watched Hanna walk over, her expression betraying her trepidation.

"What are you thinking?" he murmured, twisting his body until he was facing her.

"I'm scared." She was almost impressed by her own honesty.

"If it makes you feel any better, I don't put out on first dates." He winked and picked up her glass, passing it to her.

"I do." She took a large sip. Richard's laughter was drowned by the blanket of attraction covering them both. "I'm not sure we've ever really made it to a first date, have we?"

He screwed up his face in thought. "Not that I remember."

"Although you did take me to a restaurant in New York

for a date about ten years ago," Hanna smiled. "I think you introduced me to one of your exes."

He laughed. "That wasn't a date."

"It was!" she protested. "Well, I thought it was. I took you to a concert, you took me out to dinner. It felt like a date to me."

"If I took you out for a date, I certainly wouldn't introduce you to my ex," he replied pointedly. "I like to think I have more class than that."

It was Hanna's turn to laugh. "You're unbelievable. Your memory is so selective I'm scared you're losing your mind." She leaned forward and put her glass down before hitting him on the arm. He grabbed her wrist, his eyes staring down at her hand. He looked at her pointedly, pulling her toward him until their faces were inches away. She blinked twice, her stomach contracting at the intensity of his gaze.

"I remember every single moment with you, Hanna. I remember how young and surprised you looked the first time I saw you, when you were standing next to that god-awful Christmas tree in my father's house. I remember how your eyes lit up when I saw you in the pub in the Cotswolds, watching some shit band desperate to become world famous." His lips curled into a smile, only inches away from her own. She was desperate to breach the distance. "I remember the way you looked underneath me, the first time we made love. Your eyes were so bright and wide, and your lips trembled when I moved inside you." He closed the distance, his breath washing over her skin. "I remember every single, fucking minute, Hanna. That's what makes me lose my mind."

Richard crashed his mouth against hers, his hand cupping the back of her head, tipping it back until she was looking up at him. She reached out and placed her hand on his neck, feeling his soft, short hair as it graduated into his neckline.

His tongue danced along her bottom lip. She touched it with her own, feeling it brush against her, then plunge into her mouth. She moaned against him, her eyes shut tight, wanting to feel every part of his body on hers. He pulled her closer until their chests were touching, but it still wasn't enough, her body demanded more. She clambered over him, straddling his legs, and he cupped her ass, dragging her body against him. Their chests touched, and she arched her back, her nipples singing in response to his proximity.

"Jesus." He pulled away, eyes gleaming. "I've missed you so much." He moved in again, kissing her hard until they were both breathless. She didn't want it to end.

"I want you to take me to bed." She was so desperate to feel him naked against her, on top of her, inside her. It was like her body was awake for the first time in years. She needed to know he felt the same way.

"Hanna..." He kept her close against him, his fingers tangled in her hair. "I want it, too. But we need to take this slowly."

She leaned forward and kissed him again, this time taking control, easing her tongue into his mouth, grinding herself down on him until she could feel his excitement growing beneath her. He grabbed her behind, standing up and wrapping her legs around his waist, and she threw her arms around his neck, never once breaking their kiss.

"You've persuaded me." He moved his lips against hers. "Fuck taking it slowly." Striding across the living room, he headed for the door, breaking their kiss so he could look up and find the handle. As he was about to push it down, the telephone in the hall rang, the tone indicating it was the concierge calling.

"Give me a minute." He placed her gently down, and walked over to the telephone, lifting up the handset. Hanna watched as the intense excitement melted from his features, her body already feeling the absence of his warm embrace.

"Okay, thank you." He put the receiver back on the cradle with a clatter, running a hand through his messed-up hair as he stared at her apologetically.

"That was the front desk... my mother's on her way up."

Twenty-Six

1st June 2012

ICHARD WALKED FORWARD and unlatched the lock, the muscles in his back tensing as he pulled the heavy door ajar. The light from the hallway spilled across the wooden floor, and he stepped back to let his mother through.

Caroline Maxwell entered the room wearing a pink chiffon cocktail dress, with a matching wrap draped across her shoulders. She had pulled her blonde hair back from her face with a barrette, revealing smooth features that belied her age. Though Richard had never asked, he assumed some of her yearly vacations involved interactions with scalpels and over-expensive surgeons. She certainly had enough money for it.

Whoever they were, they'd done a good job.

"What is she doing here?" Caroline gestured at Hanna with a manicured hand. Her plump lips pulled back into a scowl, though any accompanying lines were noticeably absent. "Actually, don't bother to explain; I've heard it all from Olivia Vincent. She seemed delighted to tell the whole gala about my new grandson." She glanced over at Hanna, her nose wrinkled with disdain. "I can't believe you're letting Hanna fool you with her white trash lies."

Richard could feel the anger bubbling beneath his skin, and his face heating up as he stared at her angrily. She held her thin frame tall as if she was the wronged party in all of this, making him want to wring her scrawny neck and scream at her. She needed to know what he'd lost because of her lies. Her calmness only served to irritate him.

"I don't think you want to start taking the high ground here." He was unable to hide his bitterness. "Because you're going to fall."

Caroline laughed. It was a thin, fragile chuckle, which made him wince. "I have never been so embarrassed in my life." She pulled at the diamond pendant hanging from her neck. "'Oh, I hear you're a grandmamma, Caroline. Didn't you know Richard and Hanna have a child together? How awful, they've kept it a secret.'" Her sarcasm cut through the room like a knife through butter.

Richard reached for Hanna's hand, not wanting her to be hidden. He wanted her next to him – needed her beside him – to show her he wasn't ashamed of their relationship. He was proud she wanted to be his.

"Well, that's just perfect," Caroline sneered, staring at him as he pulled Hanna into his arms. "What the hell does she do to make you run back every time? Is she good in bed, is that what it is? Because there are people you can pay for sex..."

Hanna pulled her body from Richard, stepping forward with her hand outstretched. He watched as her open palm made contact with his mother's face. The impact was hard enough to cause Caroline to stagger backward.

"Don't you dare compare me to a whore," Hanna said. Richard had to clench his hands together to stop himself from applauding. "I'd be grateful if you could keep your voice down, there's a sleeping child in this house."

A livid red line formed across his mother's cheekbone. She stared at Hanna with sparks beneath her eyes, her face twisted with anger. "Are you going to let her talk to me like that?" Caroline demanded of him. "She assaulted me."

"I don't *let* Hanna do anything. She's her own woman, and she's welcome to do whatever she wants in our home." He could feel his heartbeat elevating as it clattered against his chest. He wanted to pull Hanna against him and give her some reassurance. "But if you ever compare her to a whore again, I'll throw you out in the street."

Caroline shrank noticeably, her eyes starting to water. "Why are you so angry at me? I'm not the one who lied to you about a child, or suddenly walked in years later pretending it was yours." She patted down an errant strand of hair. "Have you even had a DNA test?"

Richard glowered. "Matty is mine; I don't need a DNA test to tell me the truth." He glanced along the corridor, his eyes resting on the closed door to Matty's bedroom. "I'm angry at you because the only reason Hanna didn't tell me she was pregnant was because of your goddamned lies." He was getting louder. He needed to get his anger under control.

"I don't know what you're talking about." Caroline's voice was dismissive. She rubbed her cheek. "I've never lied to Hanna."

"You did!" Hanna replied. She was trembling like a frightened animal beneath his embrace. "I called Richard's cell phone and you picked up. You told me Meredith was never going to be able to walk again."

"I think I'd remember something like that. When did you call?"

"When I found out I was pregnant. In June 2010," Hanna replied. She wrapped her hand around Richard's waist, looking for something to cling to.

Caroline shook her head, the tiniest of lines forming between her eyebrows. She blinked a couple of times before looking at Richard, her expression accusatory. "June 2010, wasn't that when you told Meredith you didn't want to marry her?"

Richard thought for a moment, letting Hanna's hand on his waist calm him. It was hard to remember the events of two years ago, though certain dates were etched in his mind. Like the time he told Meredith he didn't want to be with her, or when he flew to London to find Hanna had disappeared again.

His stomach turned over as a memory flashed through his mind. He could remember his mother calling him at work, telling him he had left his cell phone at home. She had been at his apartment with Meredith, helping her to pack her things. Caroline had offered to have his cell couriered into the office.

"When you spoke to Hanna, were Meredith and I already separated?" He curled his fingers into a fist, feeling the need to hit out. Every single moment of the past two years were for nothing. They'd been so close to their forever, to having everything they'd ever wanted. A few words from his mother had been enough to bring it all tumbling down. "You told her Meredith was crippled when we'd already split up?"

"I thought you'd change your mind about the separation…" Caroline whispered, her voice trailing off.

Beside him Hanna had her hand clasped firmly over her mouth, the horror of the situation making the tears run down her face. Richard wondered if she had the urge to lash out and hit something – anything – the way he did. The anger was too much; he didn't know how to control it without exploding.

"You remember telling her Meredith was crippled?"

Caroline nodded, her body cowering away from him. He was aware he was acting like a madman – his body coiled like a snake ready to pounce. Only Hanna's hold on him was enough to anchor him to the ground, to stop him from doing something he might later regret.

"Why the hell would you do that? Do you realize Hanna was calling to tell me she was pregnant? I lost eighteen months of my son's life because of you."

His mother put her hand up to her chest, clutching with her aged fingers. "I didn't know—"

"You knew enough to send Hanna packing. You knew enough to not even tell me I'd had a call on my cell. Don't play the innocent in this, you're guilty as hell." His body was so tense he wanted to scream, to lash out… to do anything to let the tension go. Every moment standing in front of his mother was a reminder of what he'd so very nearly lost.

What he *had* lost.

"Did Meredith know about the call?" His voice dripped with acid.

Caroline shook her head, her face distraught as she stepped forward, reaching out her hand. "Richard, you don't have to do this. We can speak to the lawyers, arrange for you to have custody. You don't need to have Hanna living here."

It took a moment for her words to sink into his consciousness. She wanted him to leave Hanna, and take Matty away from her. The callousness of her suggestion was the nail in the coffin of their relationship. He wanted to get her far away from his family, so she was unable to poison them the same way she'd tried with him.

He hugged Hanna tighter, burying his face in her hair for a moment, kissing the silky strands.

"We'd like you to leave now." His voice was muffled by Hanna's hair. He couldn't look at his mother, or bring himself to show her out. Nausea swelled in his stomach as he recalled her final words to Hanna on the day of the terrible phone call. He felt bitterly ironic as he addressed his mother, "Don't come back again."

"Ever?" Caroline's voice raised an octave. Hanna stepped back from Richard and placed a reassuring palm on his chest. She shook her head lightly, as if to tell him to hold fire. Deep down he knew she was right; he shouldn't make snap decisions in the burning heat of his anger, but it took all the strength he had not to manhandle his mother out of the door.

"Not here. I don't want you anywhere near my family." Hanna gasped as he said the words. "I know I can't avoid you at Maxwell Enterprises, but I don't intend to let you anywhere near my private life."

"But I'm your mother." Caroline pulled herself up to her full height. "I deserve your respect. I can't believe you're choosing her over me. Stop this nonsense."

Richard gestured at the door, shooing his hand like he was dismissing a dog. "I'm just grateful I get to choose. I've found choice a very scarce option in the past few years."

Caroline gave him a final, angry glance, her thin lips pursed as she shook her head and reached for the door. As he watched her retreating back he felt nothing but relief. It was like the final block to his future had been smashed to smithereens. He allowed a small smile to tug at his mouth.

After Caroline left, Hanna seemed muted, like somebody had painted her over with a grey-wash. He wanted to steal back the moments to when he had her in his arms, her legs wrapped around his waist. Things had seemed so joyful and easy; he didn't know how to recapture that feeling.

"I think I'm going to bed. It's been a long day." Hanna gave him a wan smile. "Hopefully things will seem less bleak in the morning."

He knew she was right. The moment had passed, for now, and they needed to give themselves time to let the wounds heal over. It didn't make him feel any less disappointed, though.

"If it makes you feel any better, the worst is really over. Our parents know, and none of their reactions were unexpected." He tried to reassure her.

"Even Steven and Claire are angry with me."

Richard shook his head. "They're not. They were shocked, and surprised, but I spoke with Claire today and they're planning on visiting soon. They're so excited to have you and Matty in their lives."

He reached forward and cupped her cheek with his palm. Her skin was soft and damp with tears. Richard ran his thumb across her high cheekbone and pushed his fingers into her hair, pulling her toward him until her face was buried in his chest.

"I forgot to tell you, Ruby called today. She's coming back to New York next week." Hanna's voice was muffled by his shirt. "She wanted to know how you felt about Tom coming with her."

Richard laughed, his chest vibrating against her face. "Does she really want to know?"

Hanna pulled back, lifting her head to his, her eyes crinkled with amusement. "Not really. I told her to call you directly." She ran a finger along his stubbled jaw. "You're not going to give her a hard time are you? I think the two of them are meant for each other."

He winced at the thought of his sister being meant for anybody. "I suppose it would give me a chance to have a frank talk with Tom," he replied, his tone teasing.

"Poor Tom. I suppose it's a good thing I don't have a big brother to come and hunt you down."

His face grew serious. "I wish you did have someone who

would have hunted me down. I know Tom was on your side, and eventually he told Ruby, but an angry guy with a shotgun could have prevented so much misery."

"By burying you underground before you even met Matty?"

Richard shook his head. "No, by looking after you and making sure I lived up to my responsibilities."

Her hand still lingered on his face. He turned his head to kiss her fingertips, his body reacting as she stroked them along his lip. He watched through heavy lids as her mouth opened, and she pulled her full bottom lip between her teeth, worrying it in a way that sent heat straight to his groin. She plunged her thumb into his mouth, her expression leaving him in no doubt about her feelings toward him.

"You should get some sleep." His voice was thick with need. He wanted to follow Hanna into her bedroom and drag the clothes from her body. He wanted to comfort her with every inch of his own. But he told himself to take things slowly, regardless of how desperate he was to be inside her. They had the rest of their lives to be together, he wanted to do this right.

Hanna nodded. "It's been a long day." She smiled wanly, her hand reaching out to stroke his handsome face. "You should get some sleep, too."

"I need to finish up some work before I go to bed." He knew he wouldn't be able to sleep, regardless of the fatigue weighing him down. The knowledge she was only a room away was certain to keep him awake.

Richard leaned forward, brushing his lips across her soft cheek. "Sweet dreams, Hanna." Digging his fingernails into his palms to stop himself from carrying her to his bed, he turned around and walked to the office, aware of her eyes burning a hole in his back.

He hated taking this slowly.

HANNA SLEPT FITFULLY – the covers weighing down on her body making her feel sensitive and overheated. She almost woke herself up, thrashing in the bed, perspiration beading on her chest as a rivulet ran down into her cleavage.

In her dream she could see Matty and Richard. She was standing on dry, arid ground, her feet glued to the earth as her boys ran away from her, until they were just tiny figures in the distance. She screamed at them to wait, but they didn't hear her. She tried to run, feeling the earth crumbling beneath her bare feet, making no progress. Perpetually moving yet staying in the same place.

"No..." She started to cry, wanting to catch up with them, watching through a curtain of tears as they walked farther into the red horizon. Her legs gave way, her body crumpling into the hot, dusty ground, and she hammered her fists against it, tears dropping onto the parched earth.

"Hanna." She heard Richard's voice, and in her dream she saw him turn, his movements halting when he noticed her crumpled form. "Hanna, can you hear me?"

"Come back." She was vaguely aware of her dream-like state being invaded by reality, the image of Richard and Matty fading into the fog of her consciousness.

"It's just a bad dream, baby. Wake up." She could feel Richard's cool palm stroking her face and she blinked, trying to open her heavy eyelids.

"Am I awake now?" She couldn't tell reality from imagination, but she reached out to touch his hand, stilling it as he tried to calm her.

"Yes you are," he replied. There was amusement in his voice. "Would you like some water?"

She sat up, her eyes adjusting to the half-light. Her heart was hammering against her chest. "Yes, please." She glanced at the alarm clock; the hazy red glow of numbers telling her it was one in the morning.

"Here, take a sip." His voice was low as he lifted the glass to her lips, his eyes dark as she swallowed the cool liquid. Hanna let the water moisten her mouth, feeling it cool her as it slipped down her throat.

"I'm sorry I woke you."

"I haven't been to sleep yet," Richard admitted. "I was trying to finish up some work."

A glance at his attire told her he was speaking the truth. His cotton shirt was unbuttoned at the collar, rolled up to reveal strong forearms peppered with hair. His shirt had come untucked from his trousers, hanging loosely to his hips, wrinkled from a long evening of work.

"I just went to check on Matty when I heard you call my name. I thought you must be having a good dream." There was a smile in his voice. "Imagine my surprise when your dream turned out to be a nightmare."

Hanna closed her eyes, trying to erase the image of her boys so far away in the distance. "You kept running away from me." She swallowed, still tasting the arid dirt in her mouth. Richard, sensing her need, lifted the glass to her lips once again.

"I'll never run away from you." His voice was heavy with emotion. "That should have been enough to tell you it was a dream."

Tears stung at Hanna's eyes, pooling on the rims, making her vision blur. Richard reached out to stroke her hair, his fingers gentle as he caressed her neck, moving his fingers down to her bare shoulders.

"You're driving me crazy," he confessed, tracing tiny circles on her skin. "Every part of you."

Her breath hitched. Memories from earlier in the evening played on her mind – vivid reminders of how close they had come to consummating their burgeoning relationship. As he sat on the bed, his strong body dwarfing hers, she found herself wanting to submit to his possession.

He drew a line up her spine with his hand, resting on her neck for a moment before he dragged it around, spreading his fingers across her throat.

"Just here," he whispered, "I can feel your pulse jumping beneath your skin, and the way your breath catches in your throat."

Hanna said nothing, watching his green eyes heat up, his tongue snaking out to moisten his lips.

He moved his hand to her chest, to the dip between her breasts, his fingers strong against her damp skin. "And here, I can feel how fast your heart is beating." He splayed his fingers out, moving his palm until it brushed across her nipple, his rough skin causing her sensitive peak to harden. She gasped as a pleasurable sensation shot straight between her legs.

He rolled her nipple between his thumb and forefinger, the pleasure becoming a steady pulse between her thighs. She looked at him beneath half-closed lids, his face dark as it revealed an expression of raw emotion.

"Please kiss me." She arched her body against him, her lips trembling as he leaned down to capture them. His soft breath fanned against her face, warming and exciting her. He took his time, his kiss slow and soft, making her want so much more. He dragged his lips from hers, snaking a trail down her neck.

"Richard..." She closed her eyes and felt the sensation of his lips sucking at her skin. It made her nipples pebble, the heat between her thighs becoming damp and needy.

He tugged at her camisole, pulling it from her body, and pushing her shorts down until she was a naked, quivering mess.

"You're so beautiful." His stare was heated, and she felt her body reflect the warmth of it. "Every single inch of you is perfect." He reached out to touch her neck with the pad of his finger, drawing a line from it to her breasts, teasing her nipple before trailing down to her stomach. She felt herself flinch with embarrassment as he traced the faded silver lines of her stretch marks

"They're really ugly." Hanna reached out to take his hand, trying to move it from her stomach.

"They're not ugly, they're amazing." Richard shook his head, leaning down to kiss them with an open mouth. "They're a reminder of what we made, of what you carried. They're you." He followed them with his lips, leading to the base of her hips, his breath hot as he stared at her body. His hands were soft yet firm on her thighs as he gently urged them apart. She could feel him blow against her fevered centre, his lips worshipping her body, as his words did her soul. He pushed his tongue inside, steadying her flailing thighs with his strong hands. She moaned loudly, bucking against him, hands curling into his coarse hair as he dragged her to a peak.

Hanna closed her eyes, surrendering herself to the sensation, her body tensing beneath his touch. She could hear herself gasping as he increased the pressure, pushing her to the edge, her hands gripping the sheets as he tipped her over, her insides clenching with pleasure as she moaned his name over and again. She arched her back, her orgasm suffusing her body until she was only half conscious of reality.

She was vaguely aware of him shedding his clothes as she came back down from her high. He drew himself up, his body heavy on hers. His hardness dug into her hip, its heavy weight as reassuring as its rigidity. She reached down and curled her hands around him, running her thumb around the tip, spreading the moisture beading there.

"Do I need a condom?" His voice was urgent, and she felt him pump against her hand. She squeezed tighter, drawing a moan from his lips.

"I'm covered."

And she was, every inch of her was dominated by his body above her. She closed her eyes, trying not to cry out as she felt him line up against her, his tip stretching her as he tried to still his hips. He was everything she remembered, everything she wanted and hoped he would be. She was drowning beneath his touch.

"Open your eyes." His voice was rough in her ear. Her lids fluttered open, tears spilling out as she returned his heated gaze, her heart stuttering as she saw the intense emotion behind his stare. His lips were dry above his tense jaw, and she reached out a finger and ran the tip across his mouth.

"Please, Richard…" She pushed against his hips. He reached down to still her movement, his heated gaze locked on her. Her heart pounded against her rib cage.

"Give me a moment."

She stopped moving and gazed back at him. They breathed heavily in unison, and she waited for him to move, and strip away the last fragment of sanity remaining in her grasp.

"Now." He flexed his hips, sliding inside until she was so

full it made her sigh. The sensation was overwhelming, and she could feel hot tears slide down her cheeks, her emotions too raw to contain.

"I love you…" Her words were breath. They danced through the air like an invisible thread, drawing them together.

"Love you…" A gasp, a promise. He said it again, just to hear the words.

His lips crashed against hers, their tongues tangling as her salty tears mixed with their kiss. She reached up, her hand cupping his jaw, her eyes gleaming with every emotion he wrung from her body.

"Love…"

WHEN HANNA FINALLY woke up the next morning, Richard was already dressed and Matty was in bed with her, his chubby arms wrapped around her neck.

"He's been awake for a while," Richard admitted, the dark circles beneath his eyes a testament to his broken sleep. "I brought him in to bed with us just before six."

"He's such a monkey." She buried her head in Matty's soft curls, inhaling the powdery aroma of his baby shampoo. "Are you leaving already?"

"I've an eight o'clock meeting." Richard was knotting his tie. She wanted to reach out and drag him back into bed with it. After last night's revelations she felt exhausted, like she could sleep for a thousand years. If she was going to hibernate, she wanted him there as well.

"I meant to ask you something last night." Matty sat up and crawled across the bed, launching himself at Richard's suit-clad legs. Richard caught him just in time, making him laugh as he swung him up in the air. "That therapist you spoke to yesterday, does he give discounts for referrals?"

Richard caught her eye, his expression soft as he smiled at her. "I'm an expert negotiator."

"I want us to make a fresh start. Maybe we can talk things through with him as a couple?"

She knew their history couldn't be erased in a few moments of bliss. Richard's frantic arrival yesterday told her they had issues they needed to resolve. For the first time, she felt confident they could work through them together.

"I'll call him today," he promised, leaning down to capture her lips with his own. He dropped Matty onto the mattress next to her. He bounced on the springs, liking it so much that he scrambled to his feet and jumped up again.

"Meet me for lunch," Richard suggested, shrugging his jacket on. She stared at him, trying not to lick her lips as she took in his gorgeous body, perfectly attired in a Gucci suit.

"You really want to let this one loose in your office?" Matty was still bouncing, and Hanna pulled him toward her, grabbing him around the waist as she tickled his belly.

"I'll get Lisa to order some toys in. I can't go a whole day without seeing you." His brows knitted into a frown. "Maybe we need to talk to the shrink about co-dependency as well."

Hanna laughed. "We may as well get our money's worth. We'll be able to throw in parental abandonment, too."

Richard leaned across the bed and kissed her again. "Are you sure you're okay after yesterday?"

"I feel surprisingly fine. It wasn't as if we didn't expect your mum to go ape-shit. As for my dad, we'll just have to see where things go." She let Matty curl his arms around her neck, his face buried in her shoulder. "The two most important people in my world are in this room. I don't care about anything else."

"I'm going to miss you this morning." He ruffled Matty's hair, causing him to squeal in protest. "Both of you."

"If you don't leave soon you're going to miss your meeting." Pulling the bedcovers around her, she leaned forward to push him away from the bed. Richard caught her wrists in his hands, pulling her toward him until her face was buried in his chest. Matty was sandwiched between them, wriggling with amusement.

"I'd prefer to stay here," he murmured, burying his head in her hair.

"Go!" She laughed.

He released her, pressing a final kiss on each of them. "I'll see you at twelve," he reminded her as he left. She picked up a rolled up pair of socks and threw it after him, missing by a mile.

Pulling Matty into a hug, she watched Richard's retreating back, a warm fire of contentment burning in her body. She couldn't stop the smile from creeping across her face as she realized that finally, after so much time, they'd both got exactly what they wanted.

Each other.

Twenty-Seven

31st December 2012

THE CATERERS HAD arrived at the crack of dawn to prepare the house for the annual New Year's Eve gathering. Hanna watched them in the kitchen creating tray after tray of canapés and desserts. Her heart clenched as she remembered the way her mum would direct proceedings, her radio in one hand and a cell phone in the other, shouting down both mouthpieces at the same time.

"Are you okay?" Claire reached out a hand and stroked her cheek. "I'm so happy you agreed to come."

"We wouldn't be anywhere else."

The three of them had flown into London on Christmas Eve, planning to spend the festivities with Steven and Claire. The entire family had delighted in sharing their first Christmas with Matty. Hanna fell in love with the family all over again, their adoration for her son evident in everything they did.

"It must bring back memories, though. Sometimes I find it so hard to believe your mother isn't with us anymore."

Tears formed in the corners of Hanna's eyes. She reached up to wipe them away, determined not to spoil the day with sad memories. She was ready to make good ones – for

Matty and the rest of the family – though it was hard to forget the past.

"I'm so sad she never got to meet Matty. She would have loved to watch him run around the house like it's a giant playground." Hanna closed her eyes for a moment. She could almost picture Diana's delighted smile.

"You know, if she could see you now, she'd be as proud of you as I am." Claire pulled her into an embrace, and Hanna wrapped her arms around her, closing her eyes as she allowed herself to be loved.

"Do you really think so? I'm pretty sure if she was here now, she'd be hitting me around the head with a wooden spoon."

Claire didn't reply, and after a moment Hanna pulled back to look at her. Claire's face had frozen, and Hanna was fearful enough to reach out and give her arm a little shake.

"Oh my goodness, I forgot about the recordings." Claire put a hand against her chest, looking crestfallen. "All those messages she left for you. They're in a box in the study."

"Recordings?" Hanna asked, confused. "What recordings?"

"Don't you remember our project, the one in the nursing home? Diana recorded messages for you. I was supposed to give them to you at specific times: your wedding, your first child. I can't believe I forgot. I should have given you the first one when I learned about Matty."

"Can I listen to it now?" Hanna could feel the excitement course through her body. In the years since Diana's death, memories of her mother had become thinner, like a piece of elastic pulled too tight. Sometimes she couldn't remember exactly how she sounded. And now, to know there was a recording – and those words were meant for her – was almost too much to bear.

311

"Of course you can." Claire grabbed her hand and pulled her out of the kitchen, and they made their way down to the basement. In the corner, behind a large oak door, was Steven's office.

"What did you use to record her?" Hanna was all too aware of the deterioration qualities of certain media.

"I used a Dictaphone, and had them put on to a CD. Diana was very specific."

Inside the office, Claire pulled a CD from the shelf. The blank, plastic cover reflected the light streaming through the window. She passed it to Hanna who held it for a moment, turning the plastic sleeve over in her hands. Her mind went back to those dark days of 2005, when Diana's death had caused her to lose so much more than just a mother.

"I don't know if you want to listen to them all, or just the one about your first child. After all you've been through, I don't think Diana would be angry if you wanted more."

"I think I want to hear them all, if I can." She hugged the CD to her chest. "Will I have time, before the boys are back?"

Steven and Richard had taken Matty to the park, hoping to wear him out enough for him to sleep through the party. Hanna suspected it might be Steven and Richard who turned out to be exhausted when they got back.

"We didn't get to record too much. She was very weak; she couldn't talk for too long." Claire bit her lip, looking down at the floor. "If they get back before you finish, I'll stall them."

"Will you stay for the first one?" Hanna wasn't sure if she could listen alone. She already felt jittery, like the merest touch could send her on a crying jag.

"I'll stay as long as you want, sweetheart."

Hanna pulled the CD player toward them, lifting the lid to place the first shiny disc inside. She started to press play, but

Claire shook her head, reaching out to press the forward button. "Why don't you listen to the one about your first child? It seems the appropriate place to start."

"Okay." Hanna nodded, sitting down on Steven's expensive black chair. There was a small crackle from the speakers before a slight hum started, signalling the recording was working.

"Hanna..." Diana's voice was thin, like a leaf on the wind. Hearing it transported her back to a time when she was a daughter, not a mother. "I'm not sure how this works anymore. I've recorded a message for your wedding, but so many people have children before they get married. Either way, I want to tell you how proud I am of you." There was a pause, followed by soft murmuring. She could imagine Claire helping Diana to drink some water. "Congratulations, my beautiful girl, on having a child of your own. I know you'll make a great mother, like you were the best daughter. I'm only sorry I can't be there to hold my grandchild in my arms, and to reassure you whenever you start second guessing yourself." There was another pause, and this time Hanna could feel the tears start to pour down her face. She didn't bother to wipe them away; there were too many, and she needed to let them out. "If I had to give you one piece of advice as one mother to another, it would be to savour everything. Being a mother isn't easy, but every moment is a gift, and it's been my privilege to watch you grow up into the amazing girl you are today. Make sure you take the time to enjoy being a mother. Play, sing, and dance with your child. Don't let time steal these precious moments away from you." Hanna was openly sobbing, her body wrapped in Claire's arms. "I love you so much, Hanna – you and my grandchild. I'll always be here, in your memories and your heart."

The white noise of the recording faded away to nothing, and Hanna reached out her hand, wanting to stop the CD before it progressed to the next section. She was going to listen to them all – she needed to – but first she had to take some time to assimilate the miracle of hearing her dead mother's voice.

"Thank you," she whispered into Claire's shoulders as the older woman held her tightly. "I'm so grateful you gave this to me."

Claire said nothing, reaching out a hand to wipe the tears from Hanna's cheeks. Her light blue eyes were soft and kind, and Hanna could see the love spilling out of them. She was so lucky to have had a loving mother, and now a caring surrogate. She was determined to look after Matty the way they'd both taken care of her.

RICHARD RETURNED LATER that afternoon, carrying a tired Matty in his arms. Steven trailed behind them, his whole demeanour wracked with exhaustion. Hanna had cleaned up her face, having listened to the recordings twice before putting the CD back in its box. She planned to take them back home when they flew back to New York.

Laying Matty down on the sofa, Richard pulled his tiny shoes from his feet and unzipped his bulky jacket. Hanna reached out to cup her son's cheeks, cold and rosy from the London wind. Matty giggled at her touch, as he tried to fight against the fatigue claiming his body.

"Did Daddy wear you out?" she asked. Richard laughed, as he pulled her into an embrace.

"Matty wore *us* out, that's for sure," he said, running his lips across her neck. She reacted automatically, her body firing up in response to his touch. "But I'm hoping he'll sleep well tonight."

She didn't fail to catch the unspoken hint behind his words. It made her smile.

They fed him early, bathing him and putting him in a clean set of pyjamas. Steven and Claire had created a nursery on the second floor, and it was filled with toys they had given Matty for Christmas. The three of them sat on the soft carpet, building towers with large plastic bricks. Hanna and Richard raced to see who could build the tallest, and when they fell down Matty clapped with pleasure. By seven, he was all but keeling over, his eyelids heavy with the sleep he was trying to fight.

Hanna read *The Grinch*, making Matty laugh with her silly voices and funny expressions. When she reached the final lines, Richard joined in, his timbre deep and playful. She wanted to run into his arms and kiss the hell out of him.

"He's almost asleep," she whispered. Matty was curled up into his usual ball, his thumb firmly latched between his lips. "He looks so peaceful when he's dozing."

"He's perfect," Richard agreed. "We should definitely make some more of those."

Her heart beat faster. They'd talked about their future at couples therapy, and discussed trying for more children at some point. Knowing she was already thirty, and Richard thirty-three, made her feel a little more concerned. If they wanted a big family – and they both agreed they did – eventually they'd need to make some decisions.

"We definitely should."

He pulled her back against him, until her spine was moulded into his chest. Curling his arms around her waist he dipped his head until his lips brushed against her neck, sucking gently against her skin.

"How about we practice tonight?"

"Mmmm," Hanna agreed, her eyes squeezed tightly shut as he continued to caress her. "We've been practicing a lot, haven't we?"

"You think we're ready for the match?" She could feel him smile against her neck.

"I'm ready."

"I want to make you a permanent signing to my team first." Richard loosened his hold on her waist, spinning her around to face him. He reached out and cupped her jaw, his fingers caressing the skin behind her ear. "After that we can talk about adding to the offense."

Hanna laughed. "You're confusing me with all these analogies here. Are we talking about our family or a football team?"

Richard inclined his head toward hers, capturing her lips between his own. Wrapping his hand around the back of her neck, he pulled her closer, his tongue snaking a hot trail of fire across her mouth.

"I'm not talking about football, Hanna," he murmured, moving a hand down to cup her behind, his fingers digging into her skin. "I'm talking about us."

"Us?" She ran her lips along the firm line of his jaw, capturing his earlobe between her teeth, sucking it enough to make him moan.

"I want you to marry me." He could hardly get the words out between his sighs. "I want you to be Mrs Richard Larsen, and for Matty to have a whole team of brothers and sisters."

It was Hanna's turn to smile, and she pulled back to catch his eye. "You forgot the getting on one knee bit. Not to mention the ring."

"I have a ring." Richard's protest was fast. "I was saving it for the right moment."

She glanced around Matty's nursery, noticing he was fast

asleep. He was oblivious to the changes taking place between his parents. "Is this the right moment?"

Richard laughed. "I was going to ask you beside the Christmas tree in the hall, at the stroke of midnight. But somehow this seems to be the perfect time and place; just us and our boy."

"It does," she agreed. A flash of lightning exploded inside her body. To know he wanted her – not only as the mother of his child, but as his wife – made her want to fling open the windows and shout it out for everybody to hear. In their years of separation she had never thought it could be as good as this. Everything she'd dreamed of was finally within her grasp. It was almost too much to take in.

"So will you?" His voice was more urgent now, causing her to look at him in confusion.

"What?"

He was getting agitated, and she reached out a hand to calm him. Before she could touch his face, he dropped onto one knee, grasping her left hand between his fingers.

"Hanna Vincent, you are the love of my life. You've given me the most beautiful child who is the centre of my universe. I'd be the luckiest guy in the world if you'd give me yourself."

Hanna dropped to her knees, too, grasping his face between her hands, kissing him over and over again until they were both laughing. "Yes, yes, of course I will. I thought you knew that already."

His face turned serious again as he took her hand and kissed it, his lips lingering on her palm. "I wanted to make sure. But thank you for saying yes."

"Thank you for asking." Her eyes twinkled as she leaned forward until their foreheads touched. "I thought you never would."

*

_T_OM AND RUBY arrived at 8:00 p.m., their faces bright and happy as Hanna and Richard shared their news. An hour later, the party was in full swing, and Hanna was chatting to virtual strangers, accepting their congratulations and discussing everything from the state of the economy to how wonderful the London Olympics had been. Though she'd watched it from two thousand miles away, on a flat screen, she'd still felt proud to be British.

She was getting another glass of champagne when Ruby ran over, her dark hair flying as she called Hanna's name.

"I feel like we haven't had a chance to talk all night. Let's go hide away and talk about boys."

Hanna laughed, grabbing a second glass for Ruby. "It feels weird when those boys are Richard and Tom. I'm pretty sure you don't want to hear any gory details about your brother, and I sure as hell don't want to hear them about Tom."

Ruby grinned. "Not even the way he uses his—" Hanna clamped a hand across Ruby's mouth, shouting at her to be quiet. Ruby giggled before nipping at her palm. "Seriously, Hanna, I want you to know how excited I am about your engagement."

"Me too." Hanna couldn't resist glancing at her ring. It was a large, pear-cut solitaire, set on a platinum band. Richard had chosen an elegantly simple design. It proved how well he knew her. "I can't wait to be your sister."

"It's going to be so great. Especially now I have my own place in New York and won't have to be around you newly weds. You were gross enough when you were dating."

Hanna blushed as she remembered how often Ruby would walk into the apartment to find her and Richard kissing, their hands hastily snatched back from whatever part of each other's bodies they were exploring. It only took Ruby a month of living with them to decide she needed to get her own apartment while studying at Columbia. Steven had helped fund the investment.

"You and Tom aren't much better," Hanna pointed out.

Since the two of them had gotten together in April, Ruby and Tom had been inseparable. He had moved to New York, staying in Ruby's apartment while he decided what to do with the band. Richard hadn't liked the new development one bit.

"When are you two going to do the deed, anyway?"

Hanna wrinkled her nose. "I don't want a big wedding. I'm hoping he'll whisk me off to Vegas and we can get married in front of a really bad Elvis impersonator."

Ruby laughed. "I don't think that's really Richard's style, do you?"

"Regretfully not." Hanna tried to think what his style *would* be. She wanted to commit herself to him in front of their closest family. Anything else would be superfluous.

"Whatever happens, I know you two are perfect for each other," Ruby said, her champagne glass clinking against Hanna's. "I've known it for years. It's a shame it took you both so long to work it out."

"Tell me about it." Hanna smiled wryly. A moment later her heart leapt as she felt two strong arms encircle her waist.

"Am I interrupting anything?" Richard asked, brushing Hanna's cheek with his lips. "I want to dance with the future Mrs Larsen."

Hanna blushed at his words. There was something about the way he claimed her which made her melt inside. He held her close as he moved her around the room, his hand cupping the swell of her bottom as it dipped beneath her dress. His other hand held hers, his strong palm encompassing her own. She felt delicate beneath his dominant form.

"You look beautiful tonight," he said. "In fact, you look damn sexy in this dress."

"Thank you." Her smile was coy. She wanted to flirt with this man, show him exactly what he was letting himself in for. "You look rather gorgeous yourself, Mr Larsen."

She moved her hand beneath his jacket, placing her palm against his back.

"Are you trying to seduce me?" His voice was rough as she continued to move her hand. She could feel him start to harden against her hip.

"Why would you say that? I'm practically a married woman."

"I'd hate to upset your 'almost' husband." He leaned forward and brushed his lips against hers. "But I really want to see what you're wearing under this dress."

"What makes you think I'm wearing anything?" She batted her eyelashes at him.

He swallowed hard. "I think I'm ready to leave."

"We're sleeping here. We can't leave the party before midnight." Hanna laughed.

"Watch us."

He stopped dancing when they were near the staircase, his hand still firmly holding hers. As he practically dragged her up the stairs, she found herself giggling, having to stop every few seconds to catch her breath.

"Come on, we've got a lot of practicing to do," Richard urged, pulling at her hand. When they reached the top of the staircase, he bent down, scooping her up into his arms and stalking to their bedroom.

"I'm pretty sure the whole carrying over the threshold thing isn't meant to happen until after the wedding," Hanna pointed out, hiccupping in a fit of giggles.

"This isn't a threshold carry. This is an 'I want to get you into bed as quickly as possible' carry." He pushed their door open and threw her on top of the covers.

"I thought it was an 'I can't wait to see what's under your dress' carry." Hanna reached up to grab his hand and pull him on top of her. His solid body knocked the wind out of her, making her breathless.

"I *can't* wait to see what's under your dress." He snaked his hand up her leg. Shrugging his jacket off, he unknotted his tie before pulling her sparkling silver sandals off, throwing them to the floor.

"There's really nothing to see." She knelt up, helping him to unfasten the buttons on his shirt. "I'd hate to disappoint you."

"If there's nothing under that dress, I can promise you I won't be disappointed." His shirt was next to come off, revealing his firm chest. Hanna reached out to touch it, tracing her fingers over the ridges of his muscles. Her hand moved down, unfastening his belt and pushing his trousers over his hips, and as he stood to push them farther, Hanna could see his black boxers tenting under the pressure of his hardness.

"I can see you're ready for some practice," she murmured, running a finger over his tip. She felt him twitch.

Richard leaned forward and kissed her, his tongue brushing against hers as they opened their mouths, her hands roaming across his naked torso. She felt him pull the zipper of her dress down, easing the fabric from her shoulders until it pooled around her waist, leaving her breasts exposed.

He dipped his head to capture a nipple between his lips. Sucking it into his warm, wet mouth, he dragged his tongue against her until her vision turned to stars. His hand reached out to caress her other breast, his thumb peaking her nipple and making her back arch.

"Does it feel like I need to practice?" he murmured against her breast. She shook her head madly though she knew he couldn't see.

He pulled her dress off the rest of the way, throwing it to join the rest of their clothes in a heap on the floor.

She lay naked on the bed, looking up at his dark, desirous eyes, her body clenching at the strength of his need. He ran his fingers up her legs, pausing at her inner thighs to tease, his thumbs digging in to the soft skin.

"Every time I saw you tonight I wanted to drag you to bed." He moved until his head was between her legs, his lips and tongue caressing her inner thighs. She reached down to run her fingers through his thick hair, her hands encouraging his lips to where she needed them the most.

"Richard, please." She opened her legs wider. He smiled against her thigh as he heard her desperation.

"Please what?" He kissed a line up her thigh, stopping at the apex, his breath heated against her core.

"Kiss me."

"Where?" She could hear the laughter in his voice. She was torn between hitting him and pushing his face closer.

"There."

She ran a finger down her damp flesh. Richard captured it with his hand, pulling it away until she was a ball of frustration.

"This is mine." He kissed her right there, and her legs buckled, her eyes squeezing shut at the intensity of the pleasure.

"I know," she breathed, submitting herself to his touch, to his tongue and his lips and the way he liked to adore her. "All of it, all of me. It's yours."

*

AFTERWARD, HE HELD her tight, his naked body spooning hers. His erection was only half gone as he rocked gently against her ass. He curled one arm around her waist, the other across her chest, his hand caressing her breast as they tried to capture their breath.

"I'm pretty sure we're as practiced as we're going to get." Hanna smiled as she leaned her head back against his chest.

"They say practice makes perfect," he agreed. He moved his leg between her own, the hard warmth of his thigh a welcome distraction.

"We definitely make perfect babies." She could feel the heaviness of sleep starting to weigh down upon her. She wasn't ready for this day to end.

"That we do."

Hanna reached her arm back to curl her fingers into his hair, making her breasts push harder against his palm. "Thank you for making this such a great holiday. I've loved every minute of it."

"So have I. I don't want to go back."

She was glad he felt the same way, and their time in London meant as much to him as it did to her. It wasn't only the chance to reconnect with his family, although that had been wonderful, it was the fact they had spent their first holiday season together with their son, knowing there were so many more to come.

"We can come back to visit soon," she suggested. "Maybe at Easter."

"I'd like us to buy a place over here. I've got a plan." His voice was full of smiles. She twisted her head to look at him.

"You're full of surprises tonight, Mr Larsen. Care to share your plan with your future wife?"

He moved his hand to her hip, pulling her bottom against his hardness, grinding himself against her. "I'm looking into taking Maxwell Enterprises public. I'm hoping within five years I'll be able to retire from the company."

Hanna turned until she was facing him, reaching her hand out to cup his jaw. "You really want to leave Maxwell Enterprises?"

Richard smiled, his jaw moving beneath her hand. "When the time is right, I definitely want to leave. I think it will take a few years to work out the IPO and get the right team in place."

"What are you going to do after that? You're a little too young to spend your life on the golf course."

"I want to do more charity work, maybe expand the Maxwell Foundation to include overseas aid. I thought it might be something we could do together."

She could feel her eyes start to water. "It sounds amazing. I can't think of anything I'd rather do than work with you."

"In between making babies, of course," he said playfully as he winked at her.

"And the practicing," she reminded him.

He pulled her against him until their bodies were aligned, his erection hard against her thigh. His mouth brushed against her neck as his hand squeezed her ass, making her gasp out loud.

"Ah yes, the practicing," he agreed, rolling his hips until his tip was nudging her entrance. "I'd never forget about the practicing."

"That's good," she murmured, as he pushed inside her. Her intake of breath was sharp as he filled her completely.

"It is." He kissed her again. "It's very good."

Twenty-Eight

31st December 2014

"IS SHE ASLEEP?"

Richard looked up from the chair beside the crib. It was dark in the room, though a small nightlight shone from the corner – like everything else in there it was pink. Hanna had teased him mercilessly about his decorating choices, telling him newborn babies could hardly see, let alone distinguish colour, but he'd had free rein over the nursery and had taken advantage of it.

"Not quite." He flashed a smile at his wife. Lily let out a soft cry, and began to snuffle. Her tiny eyes were squeezed shut, her hands grasping a velvet elephant chosen by her Aunt Ruby. At four months old, Lily had only a smattering of hair across her pale head, as delicate as spun gold. Richard reached down to stroke it, marvelling at its soft silkiness. Like everything else about his daughter, it was mesmerizing.

Hanna walked into the room, and headed toward him, fixing the clasp on her white-gold bracelet. "One down, one to go." She smiled. "Matty's out like a light."

"I'll look in on him before we leave," Richard promised. "The car's booked for eight. We have plenty of time." Glancing up, he took a good look at his wife, taking in her elegant red dress and the way her hair was swept up into a low chignon. "You look beautiful."

Hanna blushed, and there was something almost magical there. Causing her cheeks to pink up was one of Richard's favourite hobbies. He'd managed to find a variety of ways to make it happen, some of them not for public consumption.

"Why, thank you, sir." Hanna gave a mock-curtsey then backed out of the room. "I'll see you downstairs in ten. Now work your magic, Daddy."

Daddy. That had to be one of his favourite words. For years it was a title he never thought he would have. Even when he'd discovered that Matty was his son, it felt like a label he had to earn, not one easily given. But now, with two children, the word defined him. Along with *husband*, it made him whole.

It gave him peace and happiness in equal measure.

Lily let out another cry, surprisingly loud for such a scrunched up little thing. He scooped the baby into his arms, pulling her against the thick wool of his suit lapel. She nuzzled, her mouth rooting for food that definitely wasn't there.

"Hey Lily," he crooned. "It's time for sleep."

She blinked at him with big blue eyes, and yet again he was entranced. From the moment Hanna had told him of her pregnancy he'd felt a pull to this tiny human. It was his first chance to witness a baby develop inside the woman he loved. His first opportunity to feel a kick, to see an ultrasound – to watch his child growing and moving and becoming a real, live person. At night he'd sleep curled around Hanna, his hand covering her swollen stomach like a shield. He'd protected his wife as though she was carrying some kind of precious cargo – which in his estimation she was.

Of course, Hanna had found the whole thing highly amusing. Having been through a pregnancy before, she wasn't as spellbound by the changes, or desperate to buy everything the childcare books recommended.

"All you need is a couple of babygros and a blanket," she'd told him when he suggested they should start ordering in equipment. "Honestly, we'll be holding her most of the time."

Not that he'd paid any attention. As far as Richard was concerned, his baby deserved everything his Black Amex could buy. He'd had plenty of fun testing its limits.

One thing it couldn't buy, however, was a pain-free birth. As excited as he'd been, watching Hanna go through the pain of labour and childbirth had been excruciating. But the moment his Lily had come into the world, squealing loudly at the indignity of her birth, they both knew the agony was worth it.

It was love at first sight.

Lily's breaths evened out, her eyes closing again, and Richard laid her back in the crib. She'd left a trail of baby-drool on his jacket, a dark patch of blue that he wore with pride. Although she was fast asleep, he lingered for a while, staring at the way she breathed out, her tiny bow-lips pursed, as if she was trying to snuff out some candles. She didn't fight sleep like Matty, with his tight fists and restless squirms.

Before going downstairs, Richard checked on his son. At three-and-a-half Matty was in a big-boy bed, the duvet covered with bright yellow minions. As always, the covers were twisted around his legs, leaving his torso uncovered. When he got up in the morning, Matty's bed often looked like a disaster zone.

Pressing a kiss to his son's forehead, Richard walked quietly out of his room and made his way down the stairs. Hanna was waiting for him in the hallway of their apartment, scrolling through her cell phone. When he stepped closer, she gave him a brilliant smile.

"The limo's here. We should probably go."

"You've given the babysitter our numbers?"

"Of course." Her voice was indulgent.

"And told her where we'll be?"

Hanna gave a mock sigh. "Richard, I've told her our star signs, our favourite foods and the last time we went to the doctor. The poor woman knows everything about us. Now shall we go?"

He frowned. "Why did you tell her about the doctor? Do you think one of the kids is getting ill? Should we stay home?"

She threw her hands up in the air. "For goodness sake, I was kidding. It's Emily; she's looked after Matty for years. She's qualified, and knows first aid. They'll be fine, darling."

Richard hesitated. "I don't know. Maybe we should stay home tonight. Wait for another night when Ruby or Claire can babysit."

"Oh no, buddy, you're not stopping me from going out. Not when I've been looking forward to this for ages. You may get to go to the office every day, but I've been stuck in with a newborn for months. And if we don't leave now I'm going to end up leaking everywhere." She looked down at her chest with disdain. "These things are already four sizes too big."

"They're perfect." One of the things he'd loved the most was how pregnancy had affected his wife's body. It had made her softer, fuller. As if to prove it, he reached out and pulled her against his chest.

"You would say that," she grumbled. "You're not a walking milk factory."

He smiled. "If I could do it, I would. You know that."

Her eyes widened. "Oh no, that would be a step too far. Even for the father of the year."

Fifteen minutes later they were sat in the back of the limo as it made its way through the crowded New Year's Eve streets. Despite avoiding the roads around Times Square they were still moving at a crawling pace. Richard glanced out of the window to see pedestrians overtaking them.

"So I said we'd pop in to see the Parkers before ten, and then to your parents before midnight. Plus your dad said something about an after-party dinner." Hanna raised her brows. "I did mention that Claire might like to go to sleep at some point, but Stephen was having none of it."

Richard's lips twitched, though he tried to bite down the laugh that lingered. "Would you want an early night on New Year's Eve?"

"No, but I'm hardcore. Poor Claire's been running herself ragged all month."

The mention of running made Richard glance at Hanna's dress. Cut just above the knee it exposed her pretty legs, one of the first things he'd noticed about her all those years ago. Though she had changed and matured – they both had – her thighs were still as enticing as ever.

He was so engrossed with staring at his wife, Richard hadn't noticed the limo taking a turn until he looked up, and realized they were making their way downtown. Both his parents and the Parkers lived on the Upper East Side, miles away from their current location.

"Where are we going?" he asked, his face a mask of confusion.

Her expression of happiness was dazzling. "It's a secret."

He tipped his head to the side, trying to work out her plans. "Come on, you can tell me."

329

"No way. That wouldn't be any fun. So just be quiet, drink your champagne and look pretty, okay?" Hanna said, pointing at his glass.

It was his turn to grin. Taking a sip of his champagne, he tipped the glass at her. "Yes, ma'am."

The limo pulled up to a sidewalk in downtown Manhattan. Richard looked out of the window again, this time sitting up straight when he recognized where they were.

"The Mercury Lounge?" he asked, running a hand down his dark-blue jacket. "I'm not sure I'm dressed for the occasion."

Hanna took his glass, grabbing his other hand with hers. "You never were dressed for the occasion. From what I remember, you stood out like a sore thumb last time."

"Hey, if I could remember what the hell I was wearing I'd protest. But I'm never knowingly under-dressed."

She leaned closer still, pressing her lips to his. "I wanted to take you back to where it all began. Well almost. Since we can't fly back to London, this was second best."

They climbed out of the limo and made their way along the sidewalk, staring up at the familiar grey cutout letters of the club. Beneath the sign, rustic wood-framed windows stood proud, reflecting Richard and Hanna in the dirty glass.

"Are we going in?" he asked.

"Oh no." Hanna shook her head. "Not dressed like that. Anyway, the life-changing part wasn't being inside the Mercury Lounge, it was what happened outside that counted."

They came to a stop beside a roughed-up wall. Graffiti was scribbled across it in varying states of legibility.

"Outside?" Richard clarified. "I don't recall much happening outside."

"Do you remember the snow?" Hanna was enjoying this

330

far too much. She'd always had a better memory than him. It came in useful for birthdays.

"Of course I do." He gave a fake laugh, as though he couldn't believe she was asking. "And I remember the band and the way we danced. I haven't forgotten a thing."

She stepped forward until she was invading his personal space. Not that it felt like an invasion. More of a welcome visit.

Rolling on to the balls of her feet, she raised her lips to his. They were only inches apart. "What about our first kiss?" she murmured.

He could have screwed his face up and pretended that he couldn't remember, but he was too entranced by her nearness to even do that. "What kiss?"

She pressed her lips against his. While they were still touching, she asked, "Have you forgotten?"

Richard couldn't help himself. Cupping the back of her head with his hand, he leaned into the kiss, sliding his tongue slowly against hers. When they parted, he was breathless. "I'd never forget our first kiss, and it definitely wasn't here."

"Oh yes it was. You tried to shove snow down the front of my shirt and then you kissed me."

"I didn't."

"Are you calling me a liar?"

Richard grinned. "Babe, I'm calling you a romantic. That would have been a perfect first kiss, if it were true. And I agree that I thought of kissing you. God knows I fantasized about that from the moment we met. But our first kiss didn't happen outside the Mercury Lounge. It happened a few years later at my apartment."

"No way."

He wanted to laugh. How could she forget such a thing? Hanna, the girl with the memory of an elephant, had actually

331

forgotten their first kiss. Maybe he should be upset or angry that she couldn't remember such a significant thing. But then again, he *had* wanted to kiss her outside the Mercury Lounge. It was all he'd thought about for weeks after that night out. Was there really any shame in her memories being different from his?

"How disappointing." Hanna's face fell, and she picked at a stray thread on her coat. "I swear I've believed that for years. It was as though we were star-crossed lovers, destined to be together from the start."

He captured her by the waist. "Sweetheart, we *were* destined to be together from the beginning. From the instant I met you, almost fifteen years ago to the minute, I knew I had to have you."

She rolled her lip between her teeth, instantly arousing him. "I remember," she said throatily. "The PlayStation. Your reaction."

"I'm having the same reaction right now." He pulled her closer, as if to prove it was true. "I can't seem to control myself around you."

"Well, you may have spoiled my surprise, but at least you're making up for it." She pressed herself into him. "Happy almost-kiss anniversary." Hanna pressed her lips to his again, this time running her hands through his hair.

"We didn't come here on New Year's Eve," he muttered.

"All right. But it was December, so bear with me."

"Crazy girl."

"I know."

"But I love you anyway."

"You'd better."

This time he took control of their embrace, angling her head with his hands so he could kiss her soundly. Hanna's eyes were closed, her lips were swollen, but her voice was as clear as a bell when she said the words.

"Baby, I love you too."

"YOU'RE LATE, IT'S almost midnight." Steven pulled open the door of his and Claire's uptown terrace, where Richard and Hanna were standing on the stoop. The frozen night followed them inside, the icy wind mingling with the hot air and noise within.

"We've only just left the Parkers'." Hanna was breathless. "I hope we didn't cause any problems."

Richard patted her behind, though Steven couldn't see. "That's right. Lots of old acquaintances to meet. Plus the limo was really slow."

"Very slow," Hanna added.

"Almost stationary, you might say."

She couldn't even look in her husband's eye. The things he did to her in the privacy of that limo were still making her blush. Who knew a strong, upstanding man like Richard Larsen had a deviant side?

They'd only been at the Parkers' cocktail party for half an hour before they had to leave, knowing that Steven and Claire would be waiting for them to arrive at their party. Since their move back to New York earlier in the year, Richard's parents had been talking about holding a New Year's Eve get-together in their brownstone.

Well, at least they'd finally made it. Even if Hanna's hair wasn't looking quite as flawless as it had when they'd got into the limo. Not that Steven seemed to notice, he was too intent on herding them into his house.

"Well, grab a drink and come and join us. We're in the living room."

They followed him into the huge space, filled with couples dressed smartly, hair coiffed and voices over-loud. It was like stepping back in time – all the way to 1999 – when Richard was a student and Hanna had been his waitress.

They'd come a long way since then. Loved and lost and then found each other again. Had two babies and settled in a city that Hanna never thought she'd be happy to call home. But she did. Or maybe happiness had found her.

Either way, she was more content than she'd ever been.

Claire spotted them just after they'd reached the centre of the room. Leaving her guests, she ran over, throwing her arms around each of them in turn. "Where have you been? We're about to watch the Times Square Ball drop."

Richard brushed her cheek with his lips. "Sorry we're late. We had an emergency."

Claire picked a hair from his jacket. Long, brown, and distinctly feminine. "So I can see," she said drily. "Still, you're here now. Let me get you some champagne."

The next few minutes were consumed in small talk, updating Claire on what Matty and Lily had done in the two days since she'd last seen them. They gossiped about Tom's latest world tour, and how Ruby had managed to finish most of her thesis while sitting on the band's bus. Nathan and Lucy were still in England, celebrating the festivities with her family, leaving Richard as the only Larsen child at the party.

No wonder they'd been so conspicuous by their absence.

Just before midnight, Richard topped their flutes with champagne and led Hanna through the glass doors that opened on to the back yard. The walled courtyard was lined with hundreds of twinkling lights, like a fairy grotto in the middle of Manhattan. He took her hand, helping her down the old stone steps, until they reached the roses, bare and woody after a long, chilly fall.

"Come here," he whispered. "It's cold."

"Is it? I hadn't noticed." Though she smiled, she didn't protest when he circled her in his arms. Her own were exposed to the cool night air, and he rubbed the tops of them to keep her warm.

"Will they realize we're gone?" she asked him.

"They're too busy watching the ball drop. Anyway, New Year's Eve was always ours. Even the first time we met, we managed to escape from everybody."

Her eyes twinkled in time with the lights. "As I remember you dragged me to your bedroom."

"I have something similar planned tonight."

She couldn't help but laugh. "Except this time we'll be joined by a four-month-old milk monster and a three-and-a-half-year-old demon."

Her final words were drowned out by the noise of fireworks, as New York hailed the dawning year. Still holding his champagne glass, Richard leaned in, placing a soft kiss on her lips. The sounds of celebrations escaped from the house. People were singing and wishing each other a Happy New Year, but still Richard and Hanna stayed outside, just the two of them, savouring the moment of joy.

When he kissed her again, another explosion crashed overhead. It lit up the sky with trails of white fire, cutting a pattern through the blackness.

"Happy New Year, sweetheart," Hanna whispered.

He cupped her face with his hands, enjoying the feel of her cool skin on his palms. Running his lips along her jaw, he murmured against her. "Let's make this year the best one yet."

Epilogue

27th August 2021

"MUM!" A SCREAM came from the wooded area to the left of the stage. Hanna whipped her head round and searched for the source of the cry. She saw Lily run out from the shade of the trees, her seven-year-old face screwed up with righteous indignation. "Matty says girls can't climb trees."

Hanna watched as Lily stalked up to her, hands on hips, hair looking like she'd been dragged backward through a hedge. Her clothes were covered with the dusty-red evidence of the ground.

"Did he now?" Hanna's voice was low, but she could see Matt lingering in the shadows. Like Hanna, he would be chewing his lip, afraid of the consequences of his actions.

Lily was trying to hold back her tears. Hanna could tell they came from anger, rather than sadness, and it warmed her. "And everybody knows I can climb higher than any of them." Lily waved her hand dismissively, referring to Matty and her cousin Nathan Junior.

"Try to ignore them, sweetheart." Hanna pulled Lily toward her, wrapping her arms around Lily's scant frame. "They're jealous, and maybe a little worried for your safety."

"I wasn't climbing that high, Momma," Lily scoffed. "I wanted to check inside the bird's nest."

Hanna squeezed her eyes shut trying not to think of the danger her daughter was placing herself in. She wanted her children to grow up with a healthy dose of the great outdoors, knowing the world was theirs to explore. But it was so hard to create boundaries, and to stop them from pushing things too far.

Lily hugged her mum back before pulling away and running back into the woods where, no doubt, she would hound her cousins until they admitted she was the best climber. Hanna watched as Matty sidled toward her, his face pulled back into a scowl as he approached.

"Have you heard from Dad?" He glanced down, but Hanna could tell he was chewing his lip again.

"Not yet, sweetheart." She reached out and squeezed his shoulder. Matty was the most sensitive of her children, and the one who was closest to Richard. They were the two boys among a host of girls, and they clung to each other. When Richard was away, Matty was like a lost soul, counting the hours until his dad returned.

"Will he get here in time?" Matty looked up at her, and she could see the trepidation in his eyes. Her heart clenched for him.

"Sweetheart, if your dad says he'll be somewhere, he'll be there. Unless there's a major catastrophe or something is physically stopping him, he never breaks a promise."

He looked up at her, his face shining with hope. "I really want him to be here."

Hanna pulled him close. "I know you do, darling. And he wants to be here, too. He couldn't talk of anything else when he called yesterday." She gave him a small smile. "But regardless, you really need to stop teasing your sister. You're driving her crazy."

"She drives *me* crazy," he complained. "She's always tagging after me and NJ." Nathan Junior and Matty were as thick as thieves, despite there being two years between the cousins. It warmed her heart to see her children surrounded by family, like fish swimming in a sea of love.

"I need you to be my big man today, Matt." She knew he hated his nickname, although he'd always be Matty to her. "Without Daddy here, I need all the help I can muster to get this show on the road."

She looked around the camp, amazed at how much they'd achieved over the years. From an idea in Richard's head, the Leon Maxwell Memorial Summer Camp had grown not only to encompass those children affected by 9/11, but now reached out to neglected and poverty-stricken children throughout the US. Hanna had been working all week with the 150 children to put on a show, and the performance was due to start in less than three hours.

The field was already full of spectators, sitting on blankets and picnicking, waiting for the show to begin.

"I'll help, Momma." Matty buried his head in her shoulder, and she was reminded of how much he'd grown recently. Like his father, he was tall, looking much older than his ten years.

"Thank you," she whispered in his hair.

"Do you really think Dad will be back in time to hear me play?" he asked again. Richard had been away for two weeks, working with the Maxwell Foundation to provide aid to poverty-stricken children in West Africa. He had planned to arrive home the previous day, but emergency talks with the local chiefs had delayed his departure.

"He'll be here." Hanna didn't need to think twice. In the past eight years of their marriage, he hadn't let her down once. He sure as hell wouldn't let down his own children.

"Okay then." Matty was slightly mollified. She watched him lope over to the stage area where Tom was working with a group of roadies, trying to set up the PA system to his own exacting standards. Tom leaned down and whispered something in Matty's ear, and Hanna put her hand to her chest, watching as the two of them started to plug in leads. Tom showed his godson where each one should go.

"It all looks like it's coming together." A warm voice to her left made Hanna whip around. Claire was standing right behind her, holding a sleeping Molly in her arms. Molly's thumb was stuck in her mouth as she sucked it voraciously. Hanna reached out to touch her soft, downy hair. At two, she was the baby of the family, and doted on by all of them.

"I'll be glad when it begins," Hanna admitted. "The kids are all so jittery."

"It means a lot to them, having people come and listen. Most of them have never had the chance to perform before."

Hanna nodded, trying to swallow her tears as she thought about how neglected some of these children were. One week out of fifty-two wasn't enough to make a difference, and it made her angry. She glanced across to the lake where Sean Flynn, the camp director, had organized a series of games for the afternoon to take the kids' minds off the impending performance.

"You and Richard have done wonderful things since you ramped up the Maxwell Foundation." Claire reached out her spare hand and rubbed Hanna's arm. "I'm so proud of you both."

"Thank you." Hanna felt herself choke up. "We couldn't have done it without you."

It was true. Claire had worked as hard as the rest of them to raise funds: organizing galas and charity dinners in New York. All things Hanna naturally shied away from.

"I'll put Molly down for her nap." Claire pointed toward the hut that served as an office, where Hanna had erected a travel cot at the start of the summer. Hanna nodded and mouthed a 'thank you' as Claire walked toward it.

Claire and Steven had moved back to the States a few years earlier. They'd proved to be such a support for Richard and Hanna as well as their little family. Nathan and Lucy had settled down in Connecticut, and though Tom was still touring a lot, he and Ruby had made their base in New York.

The city Hanna had grown up hating, had suddenly felt like home.

She still loved London of course, and they took the children there often, staying in the beautiful house they'd bought in Putney. But she no longer felt the yearning, the desperation to get away from New York. Even though they lived in Connecticut now, she often travelled into Manhattan for meetings or to do some shopping.

"Mum, Mum, look who's here!" Lily came running out of the trees again, pointing her finger in the direction of the car park. "It's Uncle Shake!"

"Lily Larsen!" Hanna scolded. "I've told you not to call him that."

With his strange tics, and inability to keep his hands still, the children chose the nickname for Daniel Maxwell. It didn't make Hanna happy about it, though.

"He said he likes it," Lily retorted, her red hair flying everywhere as she changed direction and ran toward her uncle, throwing herself into his unsteady arms.

Daniel put his arm around Lily and they walked toward Hanna, a grin splitting his face as she hugged them both.

"We missed you." Since they bought their house in Connecticut in 2013, Daniel had been a regular visitor, stay-

340

ing for months at a time, living in the small cottage set back in the grounds so he could have some privacy. She'd grown used to having him around, and when he went away – which he did at least four or five times a year – she hated to see the empty cottage where he used to be. He was still a wanderer at heart, and she suspected that the spectre of his addictions hadn't quite been conquered. But he was still a dear part of their family and loved by them all.

"I missed you, too." He squeezed her waist. "Any news from Richard?"

"He should be here soon," she replied. "His plane was due to land by three. Matty's beside himself with worry."

"Is he ready for his big day?" Daniel asked, his eyebrows knitting into a frown. Matty had been playing the drums since he was six years old, and Tom had offered for him to be the drummer for Fatal Limits' opening number. His nerves had been growing by the day.

"He's scared to bits," Hanna confessed. "If Richard isn't here soon, I don't know what he'll do."

"I'll go talk to him." Danny was already walking across the grass, his right leg dragging as he strode. He cut a strange figure – looking like a young boy even though he was nearly forty. She was thankful he was here, along with Tom, to lend Matty some support.

Checking her watch, she decided to join them at the stage. She was ready to start the soundcheck, needing to know everything was going to plan. Backstage was a hive of activity as everybody tried to ensure that all the last minute preparations were complete. From the electricity, to the sound, to the lighting, everything had been planned to go off without a hitch.

"Hanna," Tom whispered, wrapping his hand around her upper arm. "Can we have a quick chat?"

She looked down at her clothes. She had about half an hour to get showered and changed into the dress she had hanging up in the office. The ratty cut-off shorts and band T-shirt she was wearing really weren't suitable for greeting donors.

"Sure." She allowed herself to be dragged to the side of the stage.

"Matty's refusing to play. He's suffering from a severe case of stage fright." Tom's face was coloured with sympathy.

Hanna felt her heart clench. She knew how important today was for her boy, how excited he'd been to play alongside his hero. To know the jitters were stopping him from fulfilling his dream broke her heart.

"I'll speak with him."

Tom brushed his hand across her cheek. They both shared the privilege of being married to Larsens, and their familiar friendship had been maintained over the years. He and Ruby were named in her will as guardians for her children should something happen to Richard and her.

Hanna found Matty sitting under a maple tree, his arms wrapped around his knees as he rocked in time to a silent beat. She guessed he was hearing music in his head; he was constantly singing or tapping out rhythms. Even at the age of ten, music was his life.

He was like his mum in that respect.

She flopped down beside him, mirroring his posture. He glanced at her, his eyes bright with tears.

"Hey baby." She nudged her elbow against him. She didn't want to ask him what was wrong. She knew from experience it was best to let him volunteer.

Matty grunted and dipped his head between his knees. His rocking continued, and she reached out a hand and wrapped her arm around his shoulders, wriggling on the ground until they were closer.

They sat silently, and she closed her eyes, wishing she could absorb all his fears and take them away from him. She hated this part of being a parent – watching her child go through pain and fear and not being able to make it disappear.

"I don't want to play." His voice was low when he finally spoke.

"You don't?" she asked.

"I'm scared." He said it like he'd committed a crime.

"What are you scared of, sweetheart?"

Matty played with a lock of her hair. He rubbed it between his fingers, letting it drop back to her shoulder.

"I'm scared I'll look stupid. What if I can't match the beat to the song? What if everybody laughs at me and thinks I'm a douche?"

Now wasn't the time to reprimand him for his language.

"You've practiced that song until it's almost second nature," she reminded him. "I don't think you'll forget the beat."

Matty huffed. "I don't want to let you or Dad down."

She closed her eyes, lowering her head until her face was buried in his hair. She inhaled deeply. He still smelled soft and sweet, like her little boy.

"Matthew, I can promise, you won't let us down. I'm so proud you're even going to try sitting up there on the stage. Even if you dropped every beat, I'd still be the one at the front with a huge grin across my face." She tipped his face up until he was looking at her. "You're my son. I'm so proud of everything you do."

A lock of brown hair fell over his forehead, and Hanna had to restrain herself from pushing it away from his face.

"Do you think Dad will really get here in time?" His lip wobbled.

"I really do." She squeezed his shoulder, understanding what his fear really was. Not that he might mess up, but that Richard wouldn't get there in time to see him. "If he was running late, he'd get a message to us somehow."

The smallest hint of a smile played on Matty's lips. "Okay. I'll do it." He pushed himself up, kicking at the dust as he walked away. She watched him go, wishing he didn't have to grow up so quickly.

The final minutes passed quickly. She helped the roadies get the instruments ready and supervised the grips as they finished setting up the electrical equipment. As she was finally ready to go and get herself dressed for the evening ahead, she noticed a plug hanging loose halfway up the screen.

Hanna looked around, trying to see if there were any electricians still around, but they'd all left to get a drink. She knew if she waited for them to come back it would be too late. She grabbed the worn metal stepladder and climbed it, reaching up to reconnect the hanging plugs.

"Christ, you look sexy in those shorts."

She looked down to see Richard standing at the bottom of the steps. He was wearing a crisp white shirt tucked into navy pants, his eyes shielded by dark Ray-Bans. His smooth attire made her feel like a mess.

"Richard!" She scrambled down the steps, jumping off the final few into his open arms. He held her under her butt, his hands digging into the cut-off denim as she wrapped her legs around his waist. He turned and pushed her back against the screen, his hips grinding into her thighs as he moved his mouth to hers.

"I missed you, baby." His breath was warm against her skin.

Hanna moved her lips along with his, feeling his tongue push inside her mouth. He brushed it against her own, the softness contrasting with the hard grasp of his hands. She gasped at the way he made her respond.

"I missed you, too," she breathed when he pulled away. "So much."

He released her, letting her feet fall back on to the ground.

"How was Namibia?" she asked

"We managed to get the agreement to build the school." His expression told her how relieved he was. "They should break ground next week."

"That's amazing." She stepped forward and kissed him hard. "I can't believe you talked them round."

He ran a hand through his hair. "It took a lot of negotiation. It was good to have Dad there with me. They seemed to think his white hair meant he was in charge."

Hanna didn't want to let Richard go. He'd been away for two weeks, and she'd missed having him in her bed, and in her arms. But she knew their children were as desperate to see him as she was.

"Have you spoken with Matty yet? He was so afraid you might not make it in time."

"Yes, I saw him with Tom. He seemed cool as a cucumber."

It made Hanna smile. Matty was so desperate to please his father that he tried to show no weakness. Luckily, she was there to put Richard right.

"He was having a major attack of stage fright, but I think he'll be okay now."

"And how are my girls?" He slung his arm around Hanna's shoulders. She leaned into his touch.

"Lily is with Nathan and his boys, railing at the injustices of the world, and Molly is having a nap." Hanna checked her watch. "Speaking of which, it's time to wake her up and for me to change into something more appropriate."

Richard scanned her body with hungry eyes. "What's wrong with what you're wearing?"

She laughed. "A threadbare T-shirt and shorts showing half my ass probably won't go down too well with some of our donors." They were nearly at the collection of huts forming the administrative centre.

"Fuck the donors," Richard whispered in her ear. His hand dropped down to cup her behind, his fingers pushing beneath the denim and caressing her bare skin.

Before they walked into the office where Claire was sitting, patiently watching over her granddaughter, Hanna took the opportunity to kiss the hell out of her husband.

He kissed her right back.

AFTER SHE HAD dressed, Hanna carried Molly out into the field. Her two-year-old was alert and content, her ringlets bouncing against her soft cheeks as they walked. Hanna loved these moments with her youngest. She'd been a much-anticipated baby, born after two miscarriages and a labour which seemed to last forever. After the roller coaster of emotions they'd put the whole family through, Hanna and Richard had agreed she would be their final baby.

That didn't stop Hanna from longing for more.

She found Lily and Richard standing with a group of donors. They were all staring with rapt expressions as her seven-year-old extolled the virtues of the school the Maxwell Foundation was building in Namibia. Hanna wondered how long it would be before Lily demanded to go and see the building for herself.

Steven and Claire were sitting on some garden chairs, and Lucy laid out a blanket next to them. She was feeding her

346

brood with sandwiches, though Nathan seemed to eat more than the rest of the family combined.

Ruby was behind the stage, watching Tom and the band as they kidded around with Matty, trying to make him forget his nerves. Hanna walked over to greet her, and Molly reached out for her aunt, who swung her into her arms, blowing raspberries on her chubby face.

"Hey Molly-Moo. Did you have a good nap?" Ruby glanced up at Hanna. "Christ, she looks more like Richard every day."

"Lucky girl," Hanna murmured. "And how are you feeling?"

Ruby had entered her second trimester, though her stomach still hid the evidence of her pregnancy. She hitched Molly onto her hip and smiled, as her other hand reached out to rub her belly.

"So much better. Tom says he's glad I can stay awake after six. He was beginning to think I had some sort of sleeping disease."

Hanna reached out and stroked Ruby's arm. She still felt maternal toward her, despite Ruby being nearly thirty. She'd always be her little sister, the girl who was afraid of going to school. She'd been so excited when Ruby and Tom had finally decided to try for a baby, and slightly amused when Ruby fell pregnant in the first month. Tom was already driving all of them crazy with discussions of names, and whether a crib or a Moses basket would be a better option.

"Make sure you still get lots of rest. Think of it as saving for the future," Hanna said wryly. She couldn't remember the last time she'd managed to have an unbroken night. If it wasn't Molly waking up crying, it was Lily having nightmares or Matty unable to sleep. Not that she regretted a single moment of it, but she couldn't help but daydream of a freshly made bed and eight uninterrupted hours.

"I will." Ruby grinned, passing a struggling Molly back to Hanna. "It looks like the boys are ready to go." She gestured over at the band who were in a huddle, arms around each other. Matty looked incongruous within their circle, his tiny arms next to their big, brawny ones.

"Richard's saved us a spot at the front." Hanna and Ruby walked around the stage, pushing through the crowds of people gathered for the concert. Richard and Lily were standing with Nathan, while the rest of the Larsen clan had decamped to the bleachers. His eyes lit up when he saw Hanna, and he reached a hand out, pulling her and Molly into his arms.

"What song are they starting with?" He had to speak loudly to be heard over the hum of the crowd.

"He didn't say," Hanna replied. "He's keeping it a secret."

Richard leaned over to whisper something to Ruby, brushing his lips against her cheek. Her face lit up, reminding Hanna how much Ruby adored her big brother. Before she could say anything else, Fatal Limits walked onto the stage. Tom led them out and slapped Matty on the back as he climbed up into the drummer's seat. She watched as he twirled his drumsticks, throwing them in the air and catching them, causing Molly to squeal with delight as she watched her brother horsing about.

Tom walked up to the microphone. "Hello, everybody." The crowd cheered wildly. "I'd like to thank you all for coming tonight to see these talented kids put on a fantastic show." He paused while the applause continued. "We're going to start the evening off with a couple of songs. We haven't played together for a while, so forgive us if we miss a few notes."

Hanna smiled at this. Fatal Limits had split up over five years ago, but had agreed to come together to play this charity event. Just one more thing to be grateful to Tom for.

"And for our first song, I'd like to introduce you to a friend of mine. This is Matt Larsen, our drummer, and my favourite godson." He winked at Matty who smiled back shyly. Hanna and Richard clapped loudly, causing Molly to put her hands over her ears.

"Can you beat us in, Matt?" He called out. Matty lifted his drumsticks, his face frozen in concentration as he silently counted his beat. He started a slow rhythm, his sticks cueing in Robert on guitar, and everybody started to scream as they realized the song they were starting with.

Hanna felt tears come to her eyes as she watched her son play in time to the song Tom had written for him. 'Dear Matty' had been a number one hit for Fatal Limits the year after Matty was born, long before she had told Richard about his son. It was bittersweet to watch their son accompany Tom's band as they played it.

She couldn't take her eyes off him. Richard squeezed her hand before lifting Molly from her arms. Salt stung at her eyes as a sense of pride overwhelmed her. Matty looked like a professional, never missing a beat, always leading the song. She bit her lip in an attempt to stem the flow of tears.

"He's fantastic," Richard whispered in her ear, and she could only nod. Her ability to speak seemed to have been swallowed up by the emotions sparking through her body. To be standing there with Richard and their girls, as they watched their son in his first performance seemed absolutely perfect. She couldn't have asked for anything more.

THE CONCERT LASTED for two hours, and Hanna found herself crying more than once as she watched all the campers put their hearts and souls into their performances. Many of them came from deprived backgrounds and had never been to a theatre or to see a concert, yet they came across as consummate professionals. Even those with stage fright managed to swallow it down and take fearful steps across the stage.

By the time it was over and all the donors had been thanked, Molly had fallen asleep in Richard's arms. Her tiny head lolled against his shoulders as they walked toward the camp, her mouth moving softly as she breathed. It hurt Hanna's heart to see her husband holding their last baby, and it made her want to make more with him. He was such an amazing father to them all.

"Claire said she'd take the children tonight," Richard whispered. "She thinks you deserve a break."

Hanna looked at him quizzically. "Are you planning something?"

"Only a bit of quality time with my wife." He winked, walking into the large family cabin they'd built a few summers ago. "Maybe you can put those shorts back on."

She laughed. "They're the most horrific things I've ever worn. I think I cut them down myself a few years ago."

"They're the sexiest thing you've ever worn." He put Molly down in her cot, lifting the blanket over her sleeping body. "I can't stop thinking about the way you looked in them."

"My ass was half hanging out."

"My point exactly." He pulled her toward him and brushed his lips across her forehead. "It's how I like you best, all dressed down, with a band tee on, your hair flying in the wind as you watch the music play. It reminds me of when I first met you."

His fingers lingered on her bare arms. Her body tingled to his touch.

"Maybe you should always wear a tuxedo. That's how I remember you."

"The hotel staff would think we're crazy." He pushed his fingers into her hair. "You in cut-offs and me in a dinner suit. I'll look like your sugar daddy."

Hanna grinned. "It sounds delicious. You pay for dinner and I'll pay you in kind." She stood on her tiptoes to push her lips onto his. She could feel him harden against her stomach. Her own body clenched with need.

"I like the way you negotiate," he murmured before kissing her hard. His tongue plunged into her mouth, lashing against her own. For long moments they continued to move against each other, their hands wandering as they reconnected. Hanna felt him grab her ass to pull her against him, his hardness pulsing against her.

"Get a room," Nathan complained as he walked into the cabin. "Jesus, anybody would think you were newlyweds."

"Give me a break. I haven't seen my wife in two weeks." Richard laughed into her hair. "And I have got a room, so thanks for the suggestion."

Nathan stopped mid-walk. "Are you guys going to a hotel?"

"Don't even think about it. I asked Claire first," Richard warned.

"It wouldn't be too hard for them to look after all the kids. Lucy and I could join you there."

Hanna started to shake with laughter as she felt Richard bristle. Their romantic night was fast turning into a family reunion. She let her husband stew for a moment before stepping in.

"Nathan, if you let us go alone, I'll look after the kids for you next weekend. That way you can plan something nice for you and Lucy."

Nathan looked at her, cupping his bristled chin with his hand. His eyes narrowed as he considered his options.

"You'll look after them for two nights? Friday and Saturday?" he questioned.

Hanna nodded. "You don't even have to hurry home on Sunday."

"It's a deal." His face split into a grin. "I can't wait to tell Luce. I can't remember the last time we were alone."

"Nor can I," Richard replied dryly, before turning to Hanna. "Shall we go say goodbye to Matt and Lily, sweetheart?"

IT WAS GONE midnight by the time they got to the hotel, and the restaurant had already closed. They ordered room service, sitting in the complimentary robes as they devoured burgers and fries, Hanna's bare feet resting in Richard's lap as they talked.

"I promised the children we'd be back in time for breakfast," Richard admitted, setting an alarm on his phone. "We have six hours and twenty-seven minutes left of alone time."

"I'm glad you planned it to a 'T'," Hanna replied. "I'd hate to miss out on those twenty-seven minutes."

"You can do a lot in twenty-seven minutes," Richard protested, his fingers rubbing gentle circles on her feet.

"*You* can!" She started to laugh. He moved his hands up her legs, stopping to caress her calves, his fingers delighting in the sensation of her soft skin. He'd missed this – being alone with her, making each other laugh. Making each other do other things.

"Lily says she's sick and tired of this world being run by men. She's planning to run for president when she's eighteen." Richard looked up at Hanna as he spoke. "Apparently there should be laws against boys teasing girls."

"She was fed up because NJ and Matty said she couldn't climb the tree."

Richard pulled her toward him, lifting her hips until she was straddling him. Her knees rested on either side of his thigh. "She reminds me of you. I remember how feisty you were when we first met. I got hard looking at you."

Hanna leaned forward to wrap her arms around his neck, wriggling on his lap. "You got hard when you pulled my ass against you."

"I always get hard when I pull your ass against me, sweetheart."

He pushed up so she could feel the evidence of his arousal between her thighs. He was enjoying this: their gentle banter, the touching and kissing. When they were apart he was constantly thinking about her. Being together gave him peace.

"Are you going to do something about it?" she asked archly. The smirk on her face belied her amusement.

"I'm not sure. I feel like we skipped a whole stage in our relationship. Maybe we should try dry humping." He flexed his ass and brushed against her again, causing a groan to escape her lips. There was nothing between them except their underwear, their robes hanging open from frantic touching.

"You go ahead and dry hump." Hanna licked a trail from his ear to his neck. "It's a bit too late for me. I'm wet already."

Richard laughed. His head tipped back as she ran her lips down his neck. "I think we can work with that."

"I love the way you're so adaptable." She ground herself down on him. Richard reached out to grab her hips, steadying her against him. He wasn't joking about the dry humping. He was already reaching the edge.

"I find negotiation leads to a result which satisfies all parties." He winked before tipping her chin up, capturing her mouth with his own. Her hands pushed inside his robe, the terry cloth falling from his shoulders until his chest was exposed. She dipped her head to lick his nipple, the sensation shooting straight to his dick.

"Can we finish the talk right here?" he asked.

"You're the one who's over forty, darling. If you think your back is up to sex on the couch, far be it from me to say no." She shrugged off her own robe, naked apart from her boy shorts. His mouth watered as he scanned her body, taking in her soft skin, full breasts and sweet, undulating hips. He didn't know which part of her to attack first.

He chose her breasts. He ran his hands over them before pushing her down to the couch, her hair cascading across the dark fabric. He rolled her until she was lying on her robe, figuring the soft cloth would be preferable to hard leather.

"You know, it's less than a year until you hit the big four-oh." He ran his lips down her throat. "You won't be able to make fun of me then."

"I'll always be able to make fun of... oh!"

He wrapped his mouth around her nipple and sucked, effectively silencing her. She arched her back, pushing herself into him, and he placed a hand under her spine to support her.

Christ, he loved this woman. They'd known each other for more than twenty years, been married for eight, and had three beautiful children they both adored. Yet he could never get enough of her, regardless of where they were. He wanted every part of her. The feisty girl who wouldn't take shit from anybody. The loving mother who worshipped the ground their children walked on. The beautiful wife who delighted in teasing him, and always gave as good as she got.

"Next time we do this, you're going to wear those shorts," he growled, finally sliding his tongue against her.

"Yes, god yes," she agreed.

"I'll push them to one side, and plunge my fingers inside you, feeling you clench against me as I suck you hard." Oh, he was pulsing now. He felt the urge to take her hard, to make her head hit the arm of the sofa every time he thrust.

"I'll cut off every pair of jeans I've got," she warned.

"You do that, sweetheart."

He laid his body on hers, feeling their flesh coming together until they moved like one, an overwhelming sense of peace engulfing him. After two weeks without his family, without the woman he adored, he was finally home.

He loved every moment of it.